Pride Publishing books by Brian Lancaster

Single Books
Companion Required
Any Day

I0598136

ANY DAY

BRIAN LANCASTER

Any Day
ISBN # 978-1-83943-747-2
©Copyright Brian Lancaster 2021
Cover Art by Erin Dameron-Hill ©Copyright October 2021
Interior text design by Claire Siemaszkiewicz
Pride Publishing

ANY DAY

Dedication

A huge thank you to all the readers who reached out to me after reading Companion Required. At the end of each book there is a note saying the author would love to hear from you, but honestly, this author dearly would. So thanks for reaching out Mark DQ, Jenny K, J Denise, Karen R, Mary G, Bill, Leo and Guy —
to name but a few.

Thank you also to my LGBTQ+ friends from around the world (Timothy M, Marion M, Chris J, Kenji N, Micelle L, Liang T, Carmen R, Shane W, Tony T, Joj Dii, Michael R) who supported me in reading and reviewing, and even, in one instance, added my novel to their book club.

Thanks again to the wonderful team at TEG for helping me shape the story and for your professionalism, support, helpful assistance and friendliness.

And last, but not least, to my husband Christopher, who seems to love me despite my many faults. Thank you for being there when I sleep and when I wake, for being patient with me whenever I need time to write, and especially for keeping the fridge stocked with cheese.

Chapter One

Sunday

Sunday morning, Leonard Day lowered himself into the plush black leather chair at his sixteenth-floor office desk. Still wearing his warm grey tracksuit and saffron Bluetooth headphones, he sank back into the soft padding, pressed a button to boot up his laptop, then placed his phone and car keys alongside the mouse mat designed to resemble a Persian rug.

Issuing a bark of laughter only he could hear, he ripped off the two fluorescent-pink Post-it notes, one stuck in the middle of each of his monitors. Both carried warnings in vivid purple felt-penmanship — one to 'Go Home!' and the other to 'Get @ Life!' Shaking his head but still grinning at being caught out again, he dropped the notes into his wire wastebasket as his gaze trailed to the day outside the room.

Framed by the tinted office windows, a beautiful spring morning had woken to life. Sunlight glistened off the rain-slick roofs of regimented rows of South London terraced houses. From a music app playlist on his smartphone, the opening strains of Vaughan

Williams' *Symphony No. 5 in D major* provided the perfect soundtrack to the tranquil morn.

Naive perhaps, but he used to think none of his staff knew about his habit of slipping into the office on Sunday mornings. He went there not so much to check figures and plan the week, but to avoid being at home on what had once been his favourite day of the week. The easiest way to change a habit is to create a new and better one, his late Qigong teacher had once advised. So after performing a regular morning routine of gentle moves and stretching exercises in the back garden and after locking up the house, Leonard escaped to his office, the perfect distraction and a familiar sanctuary in his otherwise solitary world. And his team were none the wiser.

Until the day Kieran had rumbled him.

His young, energetic marketing manager, who had impeccable attention to detail, had caught Leonard out a few months ago. Kieran—dropped off at the office each weekday morning before anyone else arrived—had noticed reports on Leonard's desk on Monday morning, ones that hadn't been there the previous Friday because Leonard had been travelling. Confronted, Leonard had confessed but had tried to fob off the action as a one-off urgent business need. Kieran hadn't bought the excuse, and, like the Post-it warnings this morning, he often booby-trapped Leonard's desk. *'If you insist on everyone having a work–life balance,'* Kieran had stated aloud at a staff meeting, *'then you should set an example and live by your words.'*

Had Leonard listened to the office designer's recommendations, he would now have a lockable corner office. But ever since taking the floor space, Leonard had insisted on open-plan for everyone, the only enclosed spaces being a fish tank — glass conference room — at either end of the office. Leonard's desk sat in the middle of the open space, the same size as everyone else's, surrounded by a team he considered his surrogate family. And he loved being in the thick of things. None of his team just *worked* for him. They contributed, not one of them complaining about extra effort when business ramped up, not one having anything but positive things to say about their working environment. Leonard preached work–life balance — even if he didn't exactly live by his own ethos — and made sure nobody stayed beyond five-thirty every day unless absolutely necessary. And every Friday, to show his gratitude, he either prearranged snacks and drinks in the office from four-thirty if he happened to be away or took them to a local wine bar. In the office, at least, Leonard found smiling effortless.

But Kieran didn't miss a trick. On his day off, he'd brought his Cockapoo canine rescue called Ed into the office — a fiery red bundle of havoc — and had tried to persuade an amused Leonard to get a pet dog himself. Leonard blamed his schedule, which meant him being regularly away from home, travelling to various parts of the country for a week or more, assessing listed buildings or attending antique shows or car auctions. Kieran hadn't bought the excuse.

'*Sorry, Len,*' he'd said one Friday evening as the whole team had gathered around a wine bar table for drinks. '*But I'm calling bullshit for three very distinct reasons. First off, you can employ a dog sitter for when you're travelling. I can even provide names. Second, did you or did you not employ Izzy here as your assistant director for the sole purpose of reducing your workload?*'

Only Kieran dared challenge him publicly this way, always in a light-hearted, tongue-in-cheek manner. He'd wanted intelligent, creative, personable Kieran as his number two. But when Kieran and his husband Kennedy had added twin boys to their family unit, many of their priorities had changed.

'You already know the answer to that.'

'Then let her. She's more than capable of hunting out grubby antiques around the country, or looking over run-down, borderline derelict properties.'

Isabelle had sat smiling down at her glass of Merlot and said nothing.

'Remind Kieran again what they're called, will you please, Isabelle?'

'Listed buildings,' Isabelle had said, laughing along with the rest of the team.

'We call them listed buildings, Kieran. But thank you for your advice. Your point has been made and will be taken into consideration.'

'Then I rest my case,' said Kieran, folding his arms and sitting back.

'Hang on, you said three reasons.'

'Ah, yes. Thirdly – and most importantly – Ed needs a playmate.'

'Of course he does. Let me think about it.'

Leonard raised his gaze to Kieran's haphazard workspace and smirked. The monitor had been plastered randomly with an assortment of colourful Post-it reminders in his distinctive handwriting while trade magazines lay open across the keyboard. Pride of place on his desk sat a large, framed photo of him, his husband and their kids. Another showed their cheeky-faced mutt with what looked like a television remote control in his mouth. Thirty-two years old and Kieran had surrounded himself with so much love. The quiet young man Leonard had first encountered on a cruise ship had blossomed into a doting husband and father. Leonard turned forty-seven in May, and what did he have? A handful of successful businesses, but there it ended. At home? Not even a goldfish. Then again, perhaps he'd already had his time in the light.

The real reason Leonard had not followed through on the dog plan was because he didn't share Kieran's affinity for pets. During his childhood he'd broached the subject once only—he must have been seven or eight at the time—and both parents had stated their disgust at domestic animals, dismissing them as unruly and unhygienic. There the conversation had ended. Both accomplished scientists—microbiologists—they'd lived in a simple semi-detached a few miles away from the university campus. Work had been their lives. His father specialised in mycology, the study of mushrooms, toadstools and other fungi, and particularly how various species can kill or cure. At the same time, his mother, more interested in classification, had concentrated her efforts on microbial taxonomy—the naming and classification of micro-organisms. As couples went, they could not have been a more perfect match.

For a few seconds, he stared at his Cisco desk phone, toying with the idea of ringing them. Usually the call entailed dull generalities and awkward silences, neither party having much of any interest to share. Both parents had retired from university life. Heaven only knew what they talked about at home.

Being an only child, Leonard wondered if he had been an experiment rather than a child born of intimacy. Neither parent had demonstrated the kind of tactile warmth or fondness he had witnessed in other families. Not that his were uncaring or cruel in any way. Nutrition and learning had been equally valued in their house. As academics, they had encouraged his studies, praising him for good grades while trying hard to mask their disappointment when he failed at any subject related to the pure sciences. Their frustration had been mitigated when he'd excelled at mathematics, social sciences and, in particular, business studies.

After a quick check of message headings in his inbox, most of which he had already opened and drafted replies to — he never sent his team emails over the weekend — he returned to the one containing attachments sent by his finance officer. Spreadsheets often proved too long and detailed to open on his home laptop but displayed adequately on his two monitors. End-of-month figures popped up on his screens, much as Leonard had expected except for the incredible numbers on their latest venture, the online auction. Between the two of them, Isabelle and Kieran had come up with the idea as an extension of their antiques and artisans site. Traffic had increased tenfold, but more importantly, sales in both had skyrocketed. He folded his arms, sat back in his chair and allowed himself a private moment to gloat.

Fortunately for him, a single-minded determination to focus in the field of business management had allowed him to study for his undergraduate degree in Bournemouth, far enough away that his parents only deemed the occasional visit home necessary. When the time had come to leave at the age of nineteen, he had been able to fend for himself, had learnt to appreciate his own company. A more challenging lesson had been in realising he had developed a singular attractiveness in his late teens. One female college student had referred to him as the sexy lone wolf, but despite getting plenty of offers from girls, his heart hungered only for other boys.

After scanning other columns of figures, and satisfied all of them headed in the right direction, he checked the time on his phone — ten o'clock. An hour before he needed to set off for the hotel in York to spend two days in business meetings and viewing potential properties around the area. Far enough from home he might even try for a random hook-up using the app he had recently discovered and downloaded. Kieran had been right about one thing. At some point, he needed to get himself a life.

Although made in jest, a quip about him by a male friend on a cruise holiday still stung. Thinking Leonard to be out of earshot, someone had asked this friend why he'd nicknamed Leonard 'Any Day'. He had replied, *'Because any day is better than Lenny Day. The man is a walking misery.'* Overhearing this, he had been shocked to the core. When had he changed from being a sexy lone wolf to a *'walking misery'*? Naturally Kennedy had stepped in to defend him even though, in fairness, the friend had less-than-respectful names for all of their acquaintances. The main problem? Leonard had sensed the truth behind the quip. Maybe he needed to make more of an effort to be cheerful outside of his day-to-day.

As he closed down programs on his laptop and pulled off his earphones, he raised his head and froze, his attention drawn to a distant sound.

Barely audible beyond the building's thick glazing, somewhere out there in the suburbs, cutting through the constant hum of traffic, came the peal of church bells. For as long as comfortably possible, he held his breath, squeezing his eyes shut and absorbing the simple melody.

Church bells, like Sunday mornings at home, reminded him of Kris. And without warning or witness, he was overcome by the kind of immobilising grief that he had hoped would have receded after the death of his lover ten years ago. He rarely allowed himself to wallow in thoughts of their time together, but the memory blindsided him and filled him with such warmth and love and togetherness. And when those tender recollections inevitably melted away they would leave him emotionally desolate, standing alone in the stark coldness of reality. But for now he would allow himself to listen to the bells, and wallow and remember…

Until the shrill ring of his desk phone drowned out everything.

For a moment, he sat there, appalled at the intrusion, glaring at the device, deciding whether or not to answer. Eventually, after several rings, he relented.

"Days-Gone-By Enterprises," he answered gruffly, ripping a tissue from a box on his desk and dabbing at his eyes.

"Leonard," came his mother's stern voice. Although no explanation had been forthcoming, she no longer called his mobile phone. "I tried you at your house but you weren't answering. You need to come home. Your father passed this morning, and I need your help arranging things. When can you be here?"

"What?" said Leonard, caught off guard. "Oh, God, Mum. Dad died? I'm so sorry. What happened?"

"Not now. When can you be home?"

"I — I can come now." He had a case in his car for the business trip. By some stroke of fate he had even

14

packed his black Hugo Boss suit for meetings. With a few clicks of his phone he could cancel the York trip. "I suppose I could be there around three or four. Traffic willing."

"I'll get your room ready."

"Mum, what—?"

Before he had a chance to probe any further, she ended the call.

Annoyance bubbled in him. Most of the time he accepted his mother's natural candour, and admired her ability to view and deal with the world dispassionately. Right now, he wished he had a parent who could be sensitive to the emotions a son might be feeling at the passing of the only father he would ever have. Perhaps she knew without asking that he considered grief an old friend.

As he left the office, he did something he hated and called Isabelle on her day off to hand over the reins for the week ahead. At home, his own house, everything would be fine.

Striding across the empty car park, Kieran's words came back to him and cemented inside. He needed to find a life. At the moment, he seemed to be surrounded by too much death.

* * * *

Torrential rain met him halfway down the motorway. The automatic windscreen wipers of his SUV hissed furiously to clear the runoff blurring his vision. Cars slowed to a crawl. Leonard finally signalled off the Norwich Southern Bypass. Through the wall of rainfall, landmarks began to bring back memories.

On his left, the building-block medical centre soon gave way to thick woodland or fallow fields of long grass lining the road on Longwater Lane. Farther on, he passed through the familiar village of Costessey and the King's Head pub where he'd had his first-ever pint of beer at the illegal age of fourteen. The Red Lion would have been closer to home, but everyone knew everyone in Drayton.

Once he crossed the River Wensum, dense overhanging branches plunged his SUV into gloom along the narrow lane leading into the heart of his old town. Initially he had reasoned that setting off before midday would avoid him having to navigate tight and often single-width roads at night. But the rain had brought early darkness, which meant moving slowly, headlights on full beam. As he crawled around another curve in a lane crowded on both sides by trees, hoping not to meet another driver in the opposite direction, the phone in his dashboard display beeped with an incoming call.

Kieran.

"Hi, Kieran. What's up?"

Instead of Kieran, the voice of his partner Kennedy came through the car speakers.

"Isabelle phoned Kieran. Said you'd had a family emergency that's taken you way out east. He wants to know if you're okay, and if there's anything we can do to help?"

In the background Leonard could hear a baby screaming. Two kids to look after, both men with full-time jobs, but he knew them well enough to recognise the genuine offer of help. Leonard breathed out an inaudible sigh. At some point, he needed to remind himself to thank the world for what he had, and stop mourning what he didn't.

"Not really, Kennedy, but thanks for asking. Dad passed away, that's all I know right now. Mum hasn't told me much. He was seventy-five, not old really. But he had a heart condition, although I understood he had that under control. I suppose you never really know. So there'll be arrangements to make. Registering the death, booking the funeral, contacting family members, checking if he had a will and other nonsense. Mum will need my help with that. But you could remind that husband of yours to keep an eye on Isabelle in case she needs assistance. She's going to be stepping into my shoes while I'm away."

"That's a given," came Kieran's voice in the background. "And don't worry. We promise to water your plants, feed your fish and walk your dog—"

"Slap your husband for me, Kennedy, will you?"

"And Izzy and I can take care of the Cheltenham manor project, as well as the meeting with your accountant on Wednesday."

"Shit, I'd completely forgotten. I can always dial in—"

"Let me and Izzie take care of it, Len. It's what you pay us for. Go do what you need to do. Izzy's got a degree in finance. And I think between the two of us we can translate what he's telling us into layman's terms and work out what needs to happen next."

"Okay, point taken. Thanks, Kieran."

"Sorry, he can't come to the phone," came Kennedy's voice again. "Little Clint's having a meltdown and refuses to let anyone but Kieran touch him. Take good care of yourself, Len. Let us know when you're back and we'll drag you over for drinks and dinner—"

"And nappy changing," came a distant voice.

"Thanks, guys. Appreciate the call. Love you both. And the kids and the pooch."

The call succeeded in making him feel lighter, but as he drove out of the darkened lane into the outskirts of his old town thoughts returned to his plight. Drayton dragged up mixed emotions. Having lived for most of his adult life in the hustle and bustle of South London, he remembered the towns around Norwich from childhood as being frustratingly sedate, full of people living out their twilight years in bungalows with well-tended gardens.

When he finally turned the car into his old road, a shiver ran through him. Memories returned, of traipsing along the street alone in the early hours to get his bus, a lone and lonely wolf.

He sat behind the wheel for a full five minutes, before finally taking a steadying breath, grabbing his suitcase from the passenger seat and opening the car door. He dashed the short distance through the rain to the front door. Nothing about the house appeared to have changed. The same frosted glass on the single-pane front door, surrounded by racing green woodwork, matching white net curtains at every window. The front yard had been concreted over, leaving only two ceramic pots containing small fir trees on either side of the front bay window, a testament to the inhabitants who cared nothing for gardening.

Almost immediately, his mother answered the door and ushered him inside. Once the door closed, she turned her face to allow him to kiss her left cheek. Never one to show emotion, his mother had always been hard to read, and he had never been able to understand her mood. If anything, she looked older but not distraught as some wives might be on losing their husband. She had even been to the hairdressers, probably in readiness for the funeral they had yet to arrange. The dress she wore — a simple plain pale green affair — she'd had for years. As always, her reading glasses hung from a silver chain around her neck.

"Take your bag up to your room. Your house keys are on the nightstand. And take those boxes of books with you. Been sitting there for weeks waiting for your father to take them up. I'll put the kettle on. Then you can work out what needs to be done."

She gave no formal greeting, no words of sympathy. In her typical impassive way, she got straight down to business and as usual, he did as asked. Once he had dropped everything on the floor in his old bedroom, he sat on the edge of the mattress and looked around. Nothing had changed. Single bed, small oak wardrobe, desk and chair with a table lamp. Whenever he'd come home from university for the holidays, he would spend as little time as possible in the room or in the house, both of which he'd always found oppressive. Unlike other boys' bedrooms, he'd had no posters, stickers or toys on display, nothing to let a person know this room belonged to a boy. At twenty-two, when he'd met Kris and they'd moved in together, although he still came home from time to time, he'd rarely stayed over.

Minutes later, he was back in the kitchen.

"What happened, Mum?" he said as he joined her for tea at the kitchen table.

"He died in his sleep. Last night we went to bed together. When I woke in the morning his body was cold. Doctor Nguyen came this morning to do a preliminary check and then they took him away. Said he needed to report the death to a coroner because the cause of death was sudden and unknown. So they'll do a post-mortem, but he suspects heart failure. We'll know more tomorrow morning."

"Can we organise the funeral yet?"

"As soon as the body's released. Which, as I say, is likely to be tomorrow. After that we'll get a medical certificate. In the meantime, you'll need to go through his things—insurance policies, university pension procedures. Fill out any necessary forms. I've got everything else organised, but you're better at that kind of thing. I'll bring the box files down."

Over the next two hours, she brought paperwork for Leonard to wade through. She instructed him to make a list of things he needed to do and people he needed to contact. Thankfully something that had changed since his last visit was the laptop computer his father had invested in, which was, fortunately, not password protected. Leaving him to finish up, his mother excused herself to prepare dinner. They sat in silence through a meal of pork chop, carrots and green beans—his mother cooked as simply as she lived. Afterwards, as Leonard stood at the sink washing dishes, the doorbell rang. Twisting his wrist, he checked his watch, wondering who could be calling on his mother. Seven-thirty. Maybe a neighbour.

"See who that is," said his mother, sitting at the table with a cup of tea in front of her, and without even looking up from her magazine.

Something irritating registered then, a memory coming back to him about her reliance on other people to get what she wanted—subliminal bullying. She'd been good at it too, still was if after one phone call her son came trotting home. Usually, she'd had his father or her assistants at the college to run around for her. Was she expecting him to return home for good to take care of her? If so, they would need to sit down and have a cold, hard conversation. He wiped his hands on the dishcloth and headed towards the oversized silhouette behind the mottled glass of the front door.

"I knew that had to be your monster wagon. Little Lenny Day. Sorry to hear about Uncle Colin."

"Eric? How are you?" asked Leonard with disbelief, opening the door wide and noting the rain had stopped. Cousin Eric, son of his mother's brother, had lived along the same road throughout their childhood. Funnily enough, they'd never really connected as kids, mainly because boys considered two years' age difference cavernous. Touching fifty now, he'd lost most of his hair and had a large potbelly protruding from his brown corduroy jacket. But his pronounced Norfolk accent was unmistakable. "Come on in."

"Actually, I wondered if you fancied a pint. Down the Lion. It being Sunday night and all."

"Who is it?" came his mother's voice from the kitchen.

"Cousin Eric," called Leonard, then more quietly added, "I'd love a pint. If only to get out of this bloody mausoleum for five minutes."

"Tell him I'll pop over to see Marcie first thing tomorrow morning," called his mother.

"I'll let her know, Auntie Gerry," Eric called back. "I'm just going to drag cousin Len out for a pint. Hope you don't mind?"

As he spoke, Len heard a movement from behind.

"He's only just got here," came his mother's voice.

"I'm fine," said Leonard, plucking his jacket from the coat rack. "And I won't be long."

"But you haven't finished the washing up."

Leonard put his foot down.

"I'm going for a pint, Mum. I'll be back later."

Ten minutes' walk and they entered the bright interior of the Red Lion. Despite a healthy crowd of Sunday imbibers, Eric found them a spare booth while Leonard went to the bar.

"Do you still live in Drayton?" asked Leonard as he set down the two pints of Guinness and took a seat opposite Eric.

"No," said Eric, looking vaguely disgusted. "Not anymore. Just visiting Mum and Dad. They love seeing the kids. But we're only in Kettleston, half an hour's drive from here. The wife, Bev's, the designated driver today. The light of my life. Are you married yet?"

"No," said Leonard, not wanting to discuss his private life. "Too busy."

To deflect, he started telling Eric about the businesses he'd kicked off after university, which usually piqued people's interest, mainly talking about the trials of renovating listed buildings, valuable antiques he had stumbled upon, and the vintage car market. Eric seemed to relish Leonard's stories, having himself left school at sixteen and gone straight into retail. His life had been far humbler. As the manager of a small local supermarket, he made a good enough living, enough to support his family of four. Beverley, his wife, had been a checkout assistant in the store, which was how they had met. Proud of his family, Eric brought out his phone and showed Leonard snapshots of them on their recent family holiday to Turkey. Leonard let himself relax and enjoy Eric talking about the various excursions and adventures they'd enjoyed as a family. When a message popped up on the phone display, Leonard happily handed the device back.

"It's the boss telling me we're leaving at nine. This will have to be my last."

After the diversion he began involving Leonard in the conversation, discussing their childhood in Drayton, about their school and the people they both knew.

"Talking of which," said Eric, his eyes widening and with a sharp twitch of his head. "Did you see who's over there at the bar, perched on a stool?"

Leonard peered over Eric's shoulder to where a big man craned over his beer glass, his body squeezed against the wall at the far end of the bar. His broad back to them, he wore an untucked red and black plaid shirt and jeans, with short curly hair of dark red and naturally tan skin. With his back to them, Leonard could not make out the face.

"No idea."

"Yeah, you do. That's Adrian Lamperton. He went to the same high school as us."

Leonard's gaze darted back again. Adrian Lamperton. Sports prodigy. Mixed race. He was built like a bulldozer and insanely good-looking. How could he ever forget? Drayton didn't have a secondary school, at least hadn't when they were growing up, so Leonard had taken the bus each morning to attend school in Norwich. Cranmer Secondary School for Boys had been a horror from the moment he'd arrived. Older students like Adrian usually blanked the younger boys, so Leonard had been taken by surprise at being singled out by this fifth former, Lamperton, in his first week at the school. '*Gay Lenny*', he'd called him in front of his pack of sports morons, a hardly inventive nickname which had raised an instant cackle. During the first assembly of winter term a teacher had called the register for pupils using their surnames followed by their given name, hence 'Day, Leonard' became Gay Leonard then Gay Lenny. From that first encounter, the name had stuck with some kids, almost at the same time as Leonard's mind and body had begun to realise the truth in the name-calling. Never one to suffer fools, Leonard had initially ignored the taunt. Still, with handsome and sporty Lamperton soon becoming the most popular boy in the school, his entourage and followers had taken up the chant. Strangely enough, Lamperton had only ever used the name that one time. He'd seemed almost embarrassed when he'd passed Leonard in the corridor, thrusting his gaze to the floor and making every effort to avoid meeting Leonard's glare.

Even as a fourteen-year-old, Lamperton had been big — tall, large-boned, broad-shouldered and with not an ounce of fat. His shaggy mess of curly copper hair at odds with his milky coffee West Indian complexion meant he could always be spotted across the playground or in a crowd. Leonard had noticed more than he wanted to, even though he'd told himself he did so to avoid ever running into the older boy. At school, Lamperton dazzled on the rugby field, and despite his height and size, could move like an express train. Other players had rarely found courage enough to get in his way once he took off down the field. He'd appeared uncomfortable in his skin off the pitch, often hunching forwards, his head hung low, his eyes permanently lowered. Back then, like a lot of boys, Leonard had suffered from the blight of adolescent acne. For some reason, Leonard remembered that Lamperton had managed to avoid the condition, his tan skin remaining freckled but flawless and unblemished in the year before he left.

There had been popular rumours about him being singled out by a talent coach for a rugby league team and being offered a place in their youth scholarship scheme once he reached fifteen. After his examinations, Leonard had packed his bags for college and escaped from Drayton without a backwards glance. He'd assumed Lamperton had been one of the lucky few to chase his dreams, but the melancholy-looking figure hunched at the bar seemed to tell another story.

"Yeah, I remember him now."

"Used to play rugger. Pretty bloody good, too, if I remember right. You never played the sport, did you?"

"Not in high school. Unless I had to. But I got into tennis at college. Didn't Lamperton get an offer to play for one of the big clubs?"

"Leeds Rhinos? Never happened. Didn't finish school. Something to do with his father."

"Oh, yes?"

Eric leant forwards then, his shiny nose not far from Leonard's face, his voice lowered.

"Apparently, he's a poofter."

"His father?"

"No! His father's dead. Him. Adrian Lamperton."

"Oh."

Leonard raised an eyebrow and looked over again. Something they had in common.

"You wouldn't know to look at him, would you?"

Leonard threw himself back in his seat aghast and studied Eric to assess whether he truly meant the remark.

"Poofters have a look now, do they?"

"You know what I mean. He doesn't, you know, have any of those mannerisms. And, apparently, he's in the building trade."

"Seriously?" said Leonard, wondering if he'd stepped back in time. "Where the hell is Gareth Thomas when you need him? Is that still how you identify a gay man in this backwater? Jesus, Eric, I've worked beside lots of men who are interior designers, some with flamboyant mannerisms, but only a few were gay. Add to that the brickies or roofers I've employed, built the size of a Rolls-Royce jet engine, totally straight-acting but openly gay and proud, and you'd frankly give up trying to pigeonhole anyone. I thought those clichés died a death with the last century, but they're clearly still alive and well in Norwich."

"Okay, okay. Calm down, Mister Politically-bloody-correct," said Eric, laughing feebly. Leonard felt rattled but was not in the mood to lecture his cousin. Instead, he suggested they should drink up and go before excusing himself to use the pub's toilet.

When he returned along the corridor, the formidable figure of Lamperton came towards him, his gaze trained on the floor in front of him. As he approached, he raised his head and met Leonard's scrutiny. For a split second, something resembling recognition widened his eyes, but almost immediately the gaze fell back to the carpet. Without slowing his pace, he passed Leonard in silence.

Only Lamperton's eyes spoke of a troubled life, with shadowed bags beneath them and permanent worry lines carved between his eyebrows. But what Leonard remembered most of all was the colour, an incredible golden-brown hue which complemented his tan skin and dark-red hair.

So Lamperton had turned out gay, too, thought Leonard. *Isn't life full of little ironies?*

Chapter Two

Habit

Adrian Lamperton strolled the street towards his flat, a taupe and mandarin backpack dangling from his right shoulder, downcast eyes scouring the pavement. Lenny Day's face haunted his thoughts. Angry Lenny — the moody junior at Cranmer Secondary — back then already a good-looking boy, had indeed grown into a fine-looking man. He sported a full head of dark hair with a few grey wisps and a matching beard, both well-groomed, which made him even sexier. One of the untouchables, unfortunately. Even if there had been a remote possibility of Lenny being attracted to other men, he was well out of Adrian's league. Too good-looking, too smart, and more than likely successful bearing in mind how comfortable he seemed in his skin. No, Lenny Day was light-years from anything Adrian had to offer.

High school had been a long time ago. Lenny had been one of the few who hadn't hero-worshipped Adrian, had openly scowled at him during his early years there, every time they'd passed each other in the school corridor. To this day Adrian had no idea why, which is why he'd avoided his gaze earlier when they walked past each other. Not that Lenny would remember him. Adrian raised his head when the sign for Hope Street came into view and breathed out a chuckle. No hope, more like, he thought, then wondered what had brought Lenny back to town. People who managed to escape from Drayton rarely returned.

Caught on a rogue breeze, odours of fragrant fried food caught his stomach's attention and had his mouth watering. Turning a corner, he faltered to a stop outside one of Drayton's two Chinese takeaways, Hong Kong House, and peered inside, relieved to find the waiting area empty. As soon as the door pinged open, a cheeky young Asian face shot up from behind the counter.

"Lemme guess," said the son of the Malaysian Chinese owner who was far too young to be working there but enjoyed bantering with customers. "Sweet and sour chicken balls in batter, special fried rice and crispy spring rolls?"

Staring at the boy, Adrian wondered if he was becoming predictable, whether he should choose something different. Absently, he walked to the counter, picked up a copy of the laminated menu and scanned both sides. But he already knew he'd order his usual. Uncle Pat, who had taken him in and found him a job after the events he never wanted to remember had gone down, had once called him a '*creature of habit*'. At the time Adrian hadn't understood the expression, but now he could see how insightful his uncle had been. Putting the menu back down, he nodded to Bernard.

"Thought so. You're one of our reliables, Mr Ralph," said the boy, scrawling the order onto a notepad as if he could hear Adrian's thoughts. Since his first time to the takeaway, the boy had referred to him as Mr Ralph, and he'd never known or asked why. Until one of the young bar staff at the Red Lion had overheard him mentioning the fact and started laughing, told him he was being compared to the lead character in an arcade game called Wreck-It Ralph.

"Hey, why don't you download our app? If you order online, they remember your past orders, so you just press repeat each time. And we'll have everything ready for you to pick up. Or we can even deliver straight to your door, save you a trip."

Adrian rubbed a hand across his mouth to cover his grin. The way the world continuously sought out ways to streamline everything in life and, in doing so, avoid human contact, he'd never have to step outside his front door again. Oddly enough, that simple thought simultaneously warmed and terrified the hell out of him.

"Don't even know how to operate the camera on my phone." That wasn't strictly true, but he enjoyed seeing the look of shocked disgust on the boy's face. "If I had my way, I'd still be using my old Nokia 3310."

"They're back in production, did you know? Nokia's resurrected them. Sick retro styles in bright colours, but all fitted with modern apps and add-ons. Pretty damn cool, actually."

Adrian shook his head and breathed out a sigh of exasperation.

"Ha! I bet you still have one of them Sony cassette things—"

"Walkman."

"—and a crappy old black and white television the size of a packing crate?"

"Just put my order in, please," said Adrian firmly, while still unable to keep the smirk from his face. Although he didn't have a Walkman, he did have an old-style colour television. The old boxy type as the boy had correctly guessed, not a modern flatscreen.

"Hello, Mr Lamperton. Don't worry, love. I've already prepared your order," came the cheerful voice of the boy's mother, only her mouth and nose appearing in the small kitchen hatch before she issued a scary screech. "Bernard! I told you before. Stop annoying the blinking customers."

"Yes, Ma," called the boy, while sharing a conspiratorial grin with Adrian.

Adrian paid up the usual amount, and as he took a seat on one of the chairs dotted around the walls, his mobile phone rang.

"Lamp—"

"It's Pete," interrupted the familiar voice of his pal, Pete Ross.

"Hey, mate. What's up?"

"Job's off next week."

"Oh," said Adrian, unable to mask his disappointtment. "I see."

"Old man Mackerson pulled the plug. Says he doesn't have the funds right now."

Adrian cursed silently under his breath. He'd been relying on work at the Mackerson property mainly to keep him busy but also to help top up his depleted current account until May when better weather usually meant business ramping up. Work in the building trade had almost seized up since before Christmas. The Mackerson job—laying the foundations and building the extension at the back of the house—would've kept him busy and in credit for the next three months. Now he only had a couple of odd jobs to tide him over.

"Have you forked out for any gear?" Adrian asked.

"Partially. But nothing I can't reuse, if he pulls out entirely."

"Okay. Well, thanks for letting me know."

Pete stayed on the line, probably sensing Adrian's disappointment.

"Look, if anything else comes up in the meantime, I'll call you."

"Thanks."

"But you know what it's like this time of year."

"Of course I do."

With the call ended, he threw himself back in the chair. Somehow or another he needed another plan of action, not really because of the money but because too much time alone and being inactive might threaten to put Adrian back in a dark place. And he never wanted to go anywhere near there again.

"Were your ears burning last Friday?" asked the boy, Bernard, peering over the counter.

"My what?"

"Your ears. Mrs Sullivan at 26 Collywell Lane was in here nonstop talking about you. I think she fancies you."

Adrian dropped his gaze to the floor and grinned. Septuagenarian Eileen Sullivan had been widowed for two years. When his mother mentioned any of her church friends having problems about the house — Mrs Sullivan's being her broken central heating — Adrian took that as a cue for him to help. The poor woman had spent most of the winter in one room under a blanket, using an old electric heater to keep her warm. Adrian knew most heating systems and, by trial and error —

checking the thermostat, boiler pilot light and bleeding the radiators—had gotten her system back up and running. When helping his mother's friends, payment always came in terms of a large mug of tea. One of his builder buddies had told him he was too nice for his own good and would make a hopeless businessman.

When he looked up, a bag of food sat in a white plastic bag on the counter. Getting to his feet, he went to the counter and found Bernard playing an arcade game on his phone.

"This mine?" he called out.

"See anyone else in here?" said Bernard, without even looking up from the game.

Adrian huffed out a sigh, picked up the bag and headed out, but stopped to hold the door open as a young couple walked in, hand in hand. For a few seconds, he watched, envying their closeness, before flipping up the collar on his jacket and heading for home.

Barely a soul inhabited the high street on his way back. From time to time, cars hissed by on the damp tarmac, their wheels slick with the recent rain. As he turned the corner into the road where his apartment block lay, he stopped abruptly.

Parked on the road behind his truck sat a familiar white Ford Fiesta, the number plate instantly recognisable. The occupant had clearly spotted him because the driver's door began to open. Annoyance spiked in Adrian, even though he tried to tell himself to remain calm.

"What do you want, Nick?" he called out, remaining where he stood.

"Come on, Ade. Is that any way to greet a mate?"

"You're not my mate. Go home to Janice. She needs you."

"Like hell she does. She won't let me near her."

Nick leaned against his car, and even with a hand braced on the bonnet for support, he still swayed. He'd been drinking heavily.

"She must be about due, so of course she's irritable. Go home in case she needs you."

"Bollocks. She don't even want touch — want me to touch her. Told me to leave her alone —"

"How much have you drunk?"

"What do you care? Fuck all else to do these days."

Adrian let out a deep sigh. Six months ago, one Friday night, he'd made a classic mistake. Usually when the need to let off sexual steam took him, he would board the two-hour express train to London and book into one of the bulk standard hotels he knew so well for the weekend. Once there, he would trawl the abundant gay scene for a random and, most importantly, anonymous hook-up. Exorcise the demons, so to speak. Best of all, he could do so and disappear in the morning, knowing he'd never have to see or hear from the person again.

Why he'd wandered into the small gay bar in Norwich — Chappies — tucked away down one of the backstreets, he couldn't say. Rule number one in his book — never hook-up on your doorstep, because even as a city, Norwich was simply too small. But he had broken the rule and there at the bar he'd stumbled upon handsome Nick, who'd bought him a drink and chatted amiably then eagerly accepted the offer to come back to Adrian's apartment. A voracious bottom, Nick had pushed all the right buttons for the no-strings hook-up — no foreplay, kissing or intimate touching, just a pure sexual workout—then disappeared. With hindsight, he should never have agreed to swap numbers, or to subsequent casual sex.

Two months ago, they'd bumped into each other at midday on the pedestrian crossing on the high street in Norwich. Nick had been pushing a young boy in a pushchair and had accompanied a beautiful but heavily pregnant woman. A flustered Nick had quickly introduced Adrian as an old friend from school and presented his wife, Janice, and son, Todd. Since then, Nick had turned up twice to Adrian's flat and been told to go home in no uncertain terms. Adrian had taken only one of his calls, where Nick had repeatedly apologised until Adrian quietly accepted before telling him to have a good life. At first, he'd also blocked Nick's number, until the man had started ringing his shared site office, leaving messages with his workmates.

"Look, I just want a chat. Don't have anyone else. Five minutes. And looks like you got enough grub in the bag for two."

"Nick, you've got to stop this."

"I'll just stay for a minute, I promise."

"And you'll get a cab home, if I call one? You're not driving in that condition."

"I said I promise, didn't I?"

"Don't mess me around, Nick. I'm not in the mood. I'll make you some black coffee, give you a share of this food then call you a cab. That's it. You're not staying."

Adrian's flat, a former council block, sat in a tree-lined side road off Drayton high street. Nick staggered ahead of him over to the now-familiar double-glass front door and the entry system. Adrian joined him and punched in the number, and a few steps inside unlocked the front door to his apartment. Standing to one side, he let Nick in first and from the rancid breath, could tell Nick had drunk his fair share of beer and spirits that night.

Adrian closed the door behind them and followed with soft footfalls on the tiled floor. At the end of the corridor, Nick had opened another door into the compact flat with its single bedroom, separate bathroom and an open kitchen overlooking the small living area. Since moving in five years ago, Adrian had made a few improvements—replaced the windows at the front with double-glazing to cancel out the noise of traffic, added a modern kitchen and appliances to make the place more functional, even provided a lick of paint to freshen the home up. His only personal touch came in the form of black and white photographs lining the hall corridor of old houses he'd helped build or renovate. In his living room, a poster-sized picture of one of Kevin McCloud's Grand Designs projects, one of his most ambitious projects set on the borders of Wales and England, filled his living room wall.

"Sit down and I'll make you a coffee."

Familiar with the layout, Nick headed straight for the settee, but perched unsteadily on the arm and watched Adrian move around the kitchen.

"Got anything stronger?"

"Don't you think you've had enough?"

"Fuck's sake," said Nick, scowling at the carpet. "You sound like my missus."

Adrian stopped filling the kettle and stared at Nick. After a moment, he went to the fridge and pulled out a can of lager. For a second, he was about to toss the tin to Nick, but then thought better and brought it over.

"Thanks, mate."

Adrian said nothing, and once he'd watched Nick snap open the ring top, he returned to the kitchen to plate the food.

"How do you do it?" Adrian asked calmly.

"How do I do what?"

"Live with yourself. Sneaking around and getting fucked by men behind your wife's back?"

"You may find this hard to believe, but I love Jan. And I don't know what you're thinking, but sex between us is amazing. I have no complaints there. She just can't give me everything I need."

Nick took an emphatic gulp of the beer, swaying a little on the arm of the chair.

Having finished divvying up the food, and pulling out a couple of forks from the cutlery drawer, Adrian brought both plates into the living room and handed one to Nick.

"You've seriously never been with a woman?" asked Nick, putting his beer down and shovelling a forkful of fried rice into his mouth

"No."

"What? Not even in high school? Good-looking bloke like you?"

"Not even in high school."

"A boyfriend, then?"

"No boyfriend."

Adrian didn't want to talk about his situation. He had dealt with his fill of messy and complicated things at far too young an age and didn't need any more now.

"Bloody hell. That sounds lonely."

"I do okay. I get what I need, whenever I need it."

"Yeah, don't you just. That huge fucking cock of yours is addictive. Why do you think I keep coming back for more?"

Both men continued to eat in silence. When Nick put down his half-eaten food on the coffee table and picked up his beer, Adrian spoke.

"So you're bi, then?"

"Suppose so. Whatever that means."

"Aren't you worried she might find out? I mean, surely I'm not the only bloke you've fucked around with behind her back? Norwich isn't exactly huge."

"She won't find out," said Nick decisively, finishing his beer and crushing the can in his hand.

"Good luck with that. Do you go with other women, too?"

"Never. Why is that so difficult for people to understand? You know what my perfect scenario would be? To fuck Jan while someone like you fucks me from behind. Just the thought makes me hard. Don't suppose you'd be up for it if I—"

"No!"

Nick snorted and continued shovelling food into his mouth.

"Worth asking. What do you do for fun, then, Ade?"

"Work."

A silence fell between them. Nick dropped the empty beer can onto his plate.

"I need to piss," he said, standing unsteadily.

"You know where it is. I'll call the cab company."

"I can do that. I have a speed-dial number plugged into my phone. Let me pee first."

Without waiting for a response, Nick stumbled down the corridor to the bathroom. With Nick gone, Adrian boiled the kettle, pulled down the biggest mug he could find and added two heaped spoonfuls of instant coffee. Nick needed to sober up a notch before facing his wife. Once he'd finished clearing their plates, he filled the mug with hot water, stirred, and brought the drink over to the small coffee table. Nick had still not reappeared.

"Nick, are you okay?" he called out.

After five minutes without getting a response, Adrian headed to his bathroom to find the room empty, and pee over the toilet seat. In his bedroom next door, he found Nick lying face down diagonally across the double bed, snoring softly. Not only that, but he had managed to remove his trousers and lay there with them around his ankles, his underpants pulled down to his knees to reveal the beautiful smooth globes of his arse. Just then, the handphone on the bed next to him began ringing, with one word appearing on the display. JAN. Adrian put his hand on Nick's shoulder and shook him roughly.

"Nick! Wake up, you idiot."

Adrian's efforts produced only a couple of gulped snores from Nick, who remained asleep. After a moment's hesitation, Adrian picked up the persistently ringing phone and answered. Before he had a chance to speak, a shrill voice hurled expletives at him down the phone. Once she had calmed down, Adrian began to talk.

"Hi there, Janice. This is Adrian, Nick's — um — school friend. We met on the high street. No, no, don't panic, nothing bad has happened. Nick had a bit too much to drink and turned up at my flat, and now he's passed out, fast asleep. I've been trying to wake him and pour him into a cab, but I don't think that's going to happen. I can't even get him to wake up. Yes, I don't mind letting him sleep it off here, I suppose. His car's outside, so he can drive home in the morning. No, it's fine. I understand. You take good care."

After ending the call, Adrian stared down at the sleeping beauty. Had he been a less honourable man, he might have slipped on a condom and had his way with Nick, which was the reason Nick had come round that night. But that boat had well and truly sailed.

After pulling off Nick's shoes and jeans, and pulling up his underpants, Adrian arranged him more comfortably on the bed. Once finished, he grabbed a blanket from his bedroom closet and made himself as snug as possible on the settee.

With the light still burning from a standing lamp, his thoughts drifted back to the face of Lenny Day.

In another life, he thought, *I wonder if we might have been friends?*

Chapter Three

Funeral

On Friday morning—the day of his father's funeral—Leonard stood barefoot in the middle of his parents' overgrown back lawn still in his grey silk pyjamas. Beneath clear skies and mild sunshine, perspiration beaded his forehead from the range of movements he had performed. At first—for only a fleeting moment—he'd sensed the damp grass beneath his toes and wondered what his mother's neighbours might make of the strange man performing exotic routines in her back garden. But once he had begun, as soon as his mind switched off and his muscles stretched and burned, concentrating intently on performing the range of precise Qigong movements—The Eight Strands of Brocade—nothing had been able to penetrate his concentration.

Seated finally in a lotus position on his workout mat and surfacing from meditation, conscious once again of his surroundings, he surveyed the yard with a critical eye. Should the weather remain dry, he would attempt to tidy the small garden during his stay. On looking back towards the house, he noticed his mother moving around in the kitchen.

Neither of them spoke as they breakfasted on boiled eggs and buttered wholemeal toast with a glass of freshly-squeezed orange juice. With all the preparations for the funeral ceremony made—more easily than Leonard had anticipated—they had little left to discuss.

Much to his surprise, his mother had insisted on contacting people herself about the arrangements as well as sorting out the post-funeral gathering. A true professional, the local undertaker had taken care of almost everything else after getting a sense of their budget. Leonard had been left to sort out his father's correspondence—cancelling subscriptions and removing names from bills—as well as placing a small obituary in the local newspaper. Many of the tasks he remembered from when Kris died, although Kris' family had snatched those away from him after they'd stepped in and frozen him out of everything. At least today he would be there to bid goodbye to his father, a rite of passage Kris' family had denied him.

According to his mother, thirty-seven accepted the invitation to the chapel service, most of those medical professionals and other colleagues from the university. The former chancellor of the college agreed to provide a eulogy on behalf of other teaching fellows and the current executive team. Leonard would also speak, albeit briefly. His mother, who had never shown any desire to speak publicly, wanted to get the whole tiresome business over and done with as quickly as possible.

After he'd washed up and tidied away the breakfast things—they had settled into a comfortable routine of his mother preparing food while he tidied up—Leonard had a whole morning free, so he pulled out his laptop and caught up on work. Touching base with his team back in London had become a highlight in the otherwise monotony of staying with his mother.

"Hey, Leonard." Isabelle's cheerful face filled the screen. "How are things going?"

"Funeral today, followed by snacks and drinks at a local pub. Then all I have left is a meeting with my father's solicitor on Monday, to go over his will, which should be routine. So I'll stay the following week and be back in the office the week after, all going well. How are things your end?"

"Perfectly fine. Don't hurry back if you've got other things to deal with. The accountant meeting went well, as you heard. I've sent you a soft copy of the report and put the original on your desk. Murray Drummond and his crew let us down again—"

"What do you mean?"

"Reading between the lines, I think they've taken on more than they can cope with, so we're going to have to source someone else for the Cheltenham manor renovations."

"Again? That's four times he's done that."

"I know. I've tried GHB and a couple of other specialists, but they're all busy, too. Any suggestions?"

"Yes, delete Drummond from our preferred builders' list. Shit. I would have suggested GHB, but you've already tried them. Heritage. They're going to be expensive, but give Molly from Heritage a call, see if they're available. I'm getting a bit tired of us bouncing around trying to source decent builders. When business is good, we're the first they blow off, because they all want the easy, well-paid work. Of course, as soon as times are hard when the market slows down, they'll be on their knees begging us for work. Anything else while I'm on?"

She gave him a very brief update on their other sites. Everything seemed to be going fine. Only the building specialist for the listed building in Cheltenham had his temper frayed. He'd bought the property in the hopes of renovating and getting a buyer on board by May. But significant structural work would have to be undertaken, and approvals sought from the local buildings authority to ensure none of the listed building's original features would be affected.

"Kieran's out today in Sussex seeing a private owner of vintage Bentleys. Otherwise, I'd put him on. At least he isn't leaving rude Post-it notes on my screen."

"He's doing that to you now?"

"Yep. I think he's missing you."

Leonard laughed.

"Keep up the good work, Isabelle. In case I don't tell you enough, you're doing a fantastic job. See you soon."

Sweet girl that she was, she turned away to her right at that remark as though someone or something had caught her attention. But he spotted the telltale red tinges on the cheek caught on camera. She always blushed when anyone complimented her. *Funny little thing.* To save her embarrassment, he clicked off the program.

* * * *

Just after midday, dressed in a traditional black suit and tie combination—with an allowance of colour in the trademark handkerchief of light-grey and burgundy polka dot tucked into his breast pocket—Leonard held the front gate open for his mother. She'd chosen a simple long-sleeved black dress and carried a black handbag, but wore no hat or gloves. Across the street, a few neighbours he didn't know peeked through net curtains or stood outside their front porches to observe the black limousine filling the road. After his mother had called the funeral director's suggestion of a hearse '*morbidly garish*' and '*ridiculously expensive*', they'd agreed for the coffin to be taken directly to the crematorium. Leonard had put his foot down when she'd suggested he drive his own or his father's car, or that they ride the public bus.

"At some point, you need to take this contraption for a run," said his mother as they stepped off the kerb behind his father's navy-blue Astra, ready to climb into the back of the plush limousine. Leonard simply nodded, opening the limousine door for his mother and adding another chore to his already long list. The Astra had a thick film of grime on the bodywork, giving the machine a sheen of neglect. "And soon, too, before it turns into a lump of rust. The thing's been sitting there gathering dust for over a month."

"I thought you were going to learn to drive?" he asked before walking around the other side of the limousine and climbing into the soft leather seat next to her.

"Well, I didn't. Your father did all the driving. And it's too late now."

"Why is it too late?"

"My eyesight's getting worse. And I lack the confidence. Besides, I have my bus pass."

"Then you'll need to sell. No point having the car sitting outside the house doing nothing."

"Sell it then. The old rustbucket's no use to me."

"Can you not sort that out?"

"Don't you already sell motorcars? Besides, cars are a man's domain. You'll know what you're talking about when people come to view the beast."

And just like that, his mother had landed him with yet another task. Both sat in silence as the limousine moved painfully slowly down the road. Leonard focused his gaze out of the window, through the tinted glass, watching the real world go by. Once the funeral and other arrangements were completed, he would need to sit his mother down and have a serious talk about the future.

At the crematorium chapel two miles outside Drayton, the car park had already half-filled. His parents — both humanists — had specified cremation with non-religious ceremonies when their time came. Entering the small hall to Beethoven's Moonlight Sonata felt entirely fitting. Ending the service with his father's choice of song provided a glimpse into his rare sense of humour. He had chosen *My Way* by Frank Sinatra, which would undoubtedly raise eyebrows as well as causing a few stifled giggles.

Insisting on speaking first, Leonard struggled to come up with anything meaningful to say about his father and left the heavy lifting to the medical professionals his father, Professor Colin Day, had worked alongside, those who also had — very clearly — been good friends.

"My father and I were not what you would call close. But I believe we shared a mutual respect. One thing he taught me, something that has stayed with me throughout my life, was the importance of ambition, hard work and perseverance. My father personified those qualities and, although I didn't follow in his footsteps academically, they have served me well in business. I will miss you, Father, your patience, sound advice, and your wisdom. Wherever you are now, I hope you rest well."

With a quick nod to the celebrant, he returned to his seat alongside his mother. Fortunately, the former chancellor provided a long, polished and heartfelt eulogy, which compensated for Leonard's concise effort. When the curtains closed around the coffin and the Sinatra classic began, Leonard breathed out a sigh of relief. At a nod from the celebrant, he took his mother's arm and led them through a side door out to the chapel gardens.

For the next half hour, stood next to his mother, he listened to awkward, often repetitive condolences from people he had never met and thanked them for their kindness.

At one point a woman around the same age as his mother came up to introduce herself. Leonard recognised her as the woman who had planted herself in the pew behind them, and throughout the ceremony had muttered muted words to herself. At one point Leonard had turned around, ready to glare, thinking she might be talking on her mobile phone. Instead, he'd seen she had her eyes closed, hands clasped before her mouth, grasping a purple lace handkerchief to her lips and talking to herself.

Although Leonard could immediately see the resemblance to his father — the same grey eyes, straight nose and angular face — he had never met the woman before. Maybe her grey hair tied back severely in a bun accentuated the facial features. By her side a bald, heavily overweight man in dark glasses, around the same age as Leonard but with less family likeness, slouched untidily, giving off an air of boredom and indifference.

"Geraldine," the woman said to his mother, producing an overly sad smile before thrusting out a black-gloved hand. "My condolences on your loss. And my apologies we haven't been in touch more. I know you don't share our faith, but I hope you don't mind that I prayed for my brother's soul throughout the service. He is in the hands of Our Lord now."

Leonard's mother rarely displayed emotion but appeared to stiffen at the outstretched hand, before accepting the gesture. Once connected, and somewhat affectedly, the woman brought her other gloved hand to place on top of their clasped hands.

"Thank you, Millicent," said his mother, her awkwardness apparent, especially in the way she pulled her hand away.

"Leonard, this is your Aunt Millicent. Your father's sister. And this is your cousin, Matthew."

Taken aback by this new knowledge, Leonard nodded a welcome, before being pulled into a tight hug by the aunt. While holding him, she whispered in his ear.

"God bless you, Leonard. We'll speak later."

After another tight hug, she pecked a kiss on his cheek then let him go. The cousin, Matthew, stepped up, nodded and shook hands weakly, his fingers cold, damp and chubby. Leonard likened the handshake to clasping a pack of freshly opened sausages. Matthew also seemed incapable of making eye contact. Noticing other people waiting to pay their condolences, his aunt and cousin stepped away, before being swallowed up by the small crowd.

"My father has a sister? And I have an aunt and a cousin?" asked Leonard as an aside to his mother before the next well-wisher stepped up. "When were you going to tell me?"

"Millicent, the 'pious, pompous, poodle' your father used to call her. They live in Clifton, Bristol in the south. I had to invite her but didn't think she'd come, being as he stipulated a humanist ceremony. You know your father's views on any form of organised religion. Before you were born, he asserted his opinions at a family gathering — without me, thank goodness, because I was carrying you at the time — and harsh words were spoken. That weekend he came home and told me his sister no longer wanted anything to do with him or us. Not sure exactly what happened, but I know he felt a sense of relief, said he didn't want her kind of fanaticism infecting your childhood. So we cut all ties. We've only met them once since, at your grandfather's funeral. You'd have been mid-twenties then, living in London, busy working hard. And you have — had — three cousins. An older cousin, Luke, who passed away years ago, and Matthew and Mary, the twins. We still get a Christmas card from Millicent each year, something your father used to open, read aloud, and then, with a snort, cheerfully rip up and throw in the bin."

Although Leonard knew his father's views, he never imagined him to be a man who would let them come between family members. Whatever happened must have been severe, especially if he told his wife and son none of the particulars.

Once everyone who could come filled the Red Lion for the post-funeral gathering, Leonard felt grateful to have his cousin Eric attending, even though the conversation wasn't exactly riveting. Standing in one corner of the room, among other regulars, they could chat in virtual peace. Most of the twenty-something mourners who attended turned out to be college employees, current and former. A few came up to introduce themselves again, but most knew his mother well. The way she flitted from one small group to another, he guessed she enjoyed the attention. One minor consolation was him not having to stick by her side for the whole afternoon. Eventually she settled into a small booth chatting with Eric's mother, Aunt Marcie. Both sat red-cheeked nursing large glasses of red wine, a plate of sandwiches and sausage rolls between them.

When Eric excused himself to use the toilet and get more drinks, Leonard stood awhile on his own until someone tapped him gently on the shoulder. He turned around to see the solid frame and, frankly, handsome face of Adrian Lamperton standing before him. Adrian eyed Leonard's chest uncomfortably but stood his ground, eventually meeting Leonard's eyes. Absently, Leonard realised the man must have been marking his time to speak to him.

"You're Leonard Day?"

"I am."

With some uncertainty, Adrian held out his hand in greeting and Leonard was met with a firm handshake, his hand enveloped by Adrian's much larger, coarser one.

"Look, you probably don't remember me — "

"Lamperton. Adrian Lamperton," said Leonard, letting the hand go. "We both went to Cranmer High."

Where you labelled me Gay Lenny, he left unsaid.

Adrian smiled. Leonard did not reciprocate. Against his better judgment, he noticed Adrian had a nice smile, one that reached his eyes and made his whole face brighten. Up close, Leonard realised that on top of his light caramel, biracial colouring, he had cute orange freckles on his nose and cheeks. Something came back to Leonard then. Adrian's father had been a big West Indian man, popular in the community, while his mother had been a small, fiery Irishwoman. An unlikely combination, but unmissable in the small town. As for Adrian, he still had a full head of the dark-red hair Leonard remembered, but worn short now and showing signs of grey at the temples. A few years older than Leonard, he must have been touching fifty but looked in incredible shape.

"Or maybe you do," said Adrian. "Happy days, eh?"

"Yeah. Not so much."

Adrian's smile faltered then. Leonard didn't care. The guy had been an asshole to him at school.

"Look, I was in the other bar and noticed you all arrive. Maisie the barmaid told me the occasion and what had happened. I didn't know your father well, but heard he was respected around here, especially at the university. So I just wanted to pass on my condolences. And I'm not sure how long you're in town, but if there's anything I can do — you know — to help out in any way, just let me know."

"That's kind of you." Leonard's voice remained flat. "Sure."

Adrian's eyebrows flickered, and he appeared to want to say something else, or maybe expected Leonard to take up the conversation. Eventually the smile faded into silent awkwardness. Beating a retreat, he turned and moved away back to the other bar. Despite having tainted memories of the man, Leonard felt a tingle in his solar plexus watching the thick jeans-clad thighs, slim waist and solid shoulders of the man, not to mention the tight muscled backside moving off. *If only they belonged to somebody else.* With his gaze lingering, he barely noticed the slight figure approach him, but definitely caught the pungent odour of mothballs.

"Leonard?"

The woman, his Aunt Millicent, stood with a tall tumbler of what appeared to be sparkling water. His cousin, Matthew, stood slightly behind her in his charcoal suit and tie and dark glasses, like a personal minder. Never having met the family, he had no idea what his uncle looked like but guessed Matthew's father had similar looks. He had a bald pate surrounded by jet-black hair—a little too black to be natural—and a full face of chubby jowls and double chin.

"I'm sorry it's taken the death of my brother for us to finally meet. Your father and I didn't see eye to eye on many things. But in the end, he was still family, and as the Good Book teaches us, we need to love each other unconditionally despite our differences. Shame really, because you are about the same age as Matthew and Mary. Had we not been estranged, I'm sure you'd have been close."

Leonard wasn't so sure. Nothing about Matthew came across as congenial.

"Is Mary here?" he asked.

"Poor thing. Her husband has mobility issues. Otherwise, she would have been."

"Oh, I'm sorry. That must be difficult. Send her my best when you return."

"I will. So do you have faith, Leonard?"

Leonard had heard the question asked in different ways in the past, but knew innately what his aunt was asking. And the last thing he wanted was a sermon on the depths of his aunt's faith.

"If you're asking whether I follow any organised religion, then the answer is no. I'm on the fence. Agnostic."

"I see. And are you married?"

Leonard used to hate being asked the intrusive question, something that happened regularly in his line of work. But now he simply shrugged off the irritation and answered truthfully.

"I'm not."

"Ah, well. Marriage is not for everyone. Since his divorce, Matthew hasn't found anyone special, either. Have you, dear? Not for want of trying."

"Mother!" came Matthew's voice, a high, nasal sound. "Do you have to?"

Leonard tried hard not to smile.

"Don't worry, Matthew," he said, smirking over his aunt's shoulder. "It's a mother's duty to embarrass her offspring in public."

Leonard couldn't interpret the reaction behind the sunglasses, but Matthew's mouth remained unsmiling. Instead, he looked away while taking a sip from a pint glass of bubbly brown cola filled with ice cubes and lemon slices.

"Your father could be a difficult man, Leonard," said Aunt Millicent, her lips pursed.

Leonard's mood spiked at the comment, bearing in mind the occasion. Two hours ago, he'd had no idea who this woman was. Did she now feel familiar enough to justify judging his father in front of him?

"As I said at the chapel, my father had integrity. He was also principled and stood firmly by those principles, something he passed on to me. I have nothing but unconditional love and respect for him."

"Yes, yes. I'm sorry. I'm not trying to denigrate him in any way, especially for his transparently vital work in the field of science. I'm only talking about his closeness to the rest of the family. You probably don't know this, but he rarely saw any of us after he moved up here. Tragic really, because we were very close as children. I blame the university for brainwashing him with their godless ideology."

Leonard doubted anybody could have forced his father to believe anything without empirical proof, but felt best to leave well alone. He hoped his lack of a response might entice Aunt Millie to move away and looked around to see if Eric was on his way back. But Aunt Millicent had not finished.

"Will you be living back here with your mother?"

"Only until my father's estate is tied up. Then I'm back home."

"And where is that? Home?"

"South London. Balham."

"I see. Your mother said you've called the solicitor to run through your father's will on Monday, so Matthew and I will remain in town until that's finalised."

Leonard felt sure his father had no significant assets, apart from the house and his life policies. Everything would be signed over to his mother.

"You don't need to stay. I'm sure it'll all be pretty straightforward. If you prefer, you can leave my mother or me your contact details and we'll either email a summary or call you."

"Thank you. But I'd rather be here to find out in person."

* * * *

By late afternoon, only his mother and Aunt Marcie remained of the funeral guests. Even cousin Eric had decided to leave. Leonard went to join them. Both red-cheeked, they were giggling together like schoolgirls as he sat down at the end of the small booth.

"She's changed," said Leonard's mother when Leonard told her about his conversation with Aunt Millicent. "Not so prickly, and definitely not constantly thrusting her religious fanaticism down everyone's throats."

"But she doesn't drink," add Marcie, slurring a little. "So I wouldn't trust her no further 'n I could throw her."

"She told me her and Matthew are staying to attend the reading of Dad's will."

"Did she?" His mother frowned at that and stared at her drink. "Not sure why. He never mentioned leaving her anything. But I suppose she has a right to be there, being family. And the poor woman has had her fair share of misfortune."

"What do you mean?"

"Her husband, Michael, walked out on her and the kids some years back. So she's been on her own since then. Although it looks as though Matthew's living back home again."

Leonard sympathised but didn't consider a husband walking out tragic. Marcie voiced his thoughts before he had a chance to speak.

"Not sure I'd call that tragic. The poor sod probably had enough of her, if even half of what you told me is true."

"I remember the day Colin got a call from your grandfather to let him know. Said he thought trouble had been brewing between the pair for a long time. Ever since what happened to Luke."

"Who's Luke?" asked Marcie.

"Her oldest. Good-looking boy. Bright, too, by all accounts. Tragic."

"Why? What happened to him?" asked Leonard.

"I thought I'd told you. Luke took his own life. Still, let's not dwell on…"

Coldness filled Leonard.

His mother continued talking but he heard nothing more. For years he had raged and agonised about his helplessness when Kris succumbed to an incurable illness, and had eventually reconciled himself to his lover's death with the knowledge that he could have done nothing to change the outcome.

But the thought that someone could feel despair enough to consider taking their own life, to know a family member he had never been allowed to meet had done exactly that, filled him with a profound sense of sorrow mixed with injustice.

And a whole headful of useless 'what-ifs'.

Chapter Four

Breakdown

Stuttering across the windscreen, the worn wipers on Adrian's Toyota truck struggled to clear the sudden heavy downpour, failing to give him a good enough view of the road ahead. Mindful of the possibility of other cars heading his way down the small lane, he reduced speed, snapped his lights on full beam and craned forwards, squinting through the glass. Worst of all, the interior surface kept fogging up despite the heater being on full, blasting air onto the inside surface. When he turned into Burntwood Lane, with the tall hedgerow on one side and a wall of elm trees on the other providing a canopy of darkness across the road, he slowed to a crawl.

Just as well, because up ahead in a section partly open to the scant daylight, pulled into a lay-by, he spied the outline of a car. Silhouetted in the lights of Adrian's van, a distinctly male figure leant over the engine using a phone to shine light into the space beneath the bonnet. Worst of all, the poor guy had no hat or umbrella, only a jacket and jeans, and appeared drenched through. For a fleeting moment Adrian considered driving on, wondered if maybe the person had everything under control and might even be offended by his offer of assistance, however well-intentioned. Until a moment of self-reproach bearing his mother's voice hit him and he pulled the truck over.

He landed in a deep puddle as he jumped out and cursed momentarily before grabbing a couple of umbrellas from behind the seat. Using his back to close the cab door, he opened one of the umbrellas and headed towards the driver. Sensing his approach, the person straightened and stepped away from the car. Even in shadow he recognised the stance and build of the man. Lenny Day. Adrian's pace faltered a moment, until he took a breath and continued forward.

"Spot of trouble?"

Lenny's classy-looking cobalt-blue jacket had darkened with rain across the shoulders. Even the collar of his denim shirt had not escaped the shower, and the stylish blue handkerchief in his top pocket had all but wilted.

"Yes. But it's fine. I've got everything under control."

Adrian registered the sombre expression and heard the flat tone again, the one Lenny had used at the funeral gathering. This time Adrian was not going to be fobbed off. The man clearly had no idea what he was doing, standing and getting soaked in rain while trying to fix an engine with the light of a smartphone in one hand and nothing in the other.

"What seems to be the problem?"

"It's the engine."

Adrian resisted a smirk, resisted providing a quip about Lenny stating the obvious.

"Did it just cut out?"

This time Lenny's gaze bore into Adrian. Until something in his expression changed. As though a switch had been flicked, he seemed to visibly deflate, huffing out a breath and grimacing in defeat.

"Actually, I haven't got a clue what I'm doing, Adrian. This is my father's piece of shit Astra. My mother's been nagging me to take it for a spin so I thought today would be good while the weather stayed dry. Until the engine cut out almost at the same moment as the heavens opened. Some days you just can't win. To top it all, I can't even get a signal on my phone to call someone. Not that I'd know who to call around here. Do you think this is my father's idea of a parting joke?"

Adrian smirked and handed an umbrella to Lenny.

"Looks as though you're already soaked through, but try this anyway. I'm not a qualified mechanic, but I've had a fair bit of experience with engines. Want me to take a look?"

"Would you mind? I'll hold the umbrella over you."

After checking connections and getting Lenny to try the ignition a couple of times — with absolutely nothing happening — Adrian identified the culprit.

"Just before you pulled over, did you notice anything unusual?"

"Yes. The reporter on the local radio station promised sunshine all day."

Adrian looked away and smiled.

"About the car."

"Ah, so, the lights flickered a couple of times and there was an odd rumbling sound and a burning smell coming from the engine. And now the lights aren't working at all."

"Yeah, just as I thought. Faulty alternator, I'm afraid. And your battery doesn't look in particularly good shape either."

"Priceless. So what can I do?"

"Not a lot, I'm afraid. I can drop you at Ted's. He's the local mechanic. But he'll likely need to tow the car back to his garage. Suggest you grab anything you need, lock up, and I'll drop you there."

"Shit."

"Where were you headed? I can always drive you, if you want?"

"Home. As I say, I gave the car a run into Norwich. I was on my way back home for lunch when this happened."

Lenny seemed to hesitate then.

"Look Adrian. I don't want to put you out. I'm sure you've got more important things to do on a Saturday. Maybe you could call this guy, Ted, and I'll wait — "

"Not a chance. We can't get a signal for another half mile either way. Best I drop you there."

When Lenny peered around into the rain, considering the offer, Adrian almost relented. Nervousness had already settled in his stomach at the thought of having Lenny Day sat next to him in his truck. Until Lenny turned and produced a genuinely grateful smile.

"That's really kind of you."

While Lenny climbed into the passenger seat, Adrian folded up the umbrellas and shoved them beneath his seat before clambering in.

"I'd offer you a towel to dry yourself but it's covered in plaster dust."

"No problem." Lenny fixed his seatbelt in place, then dragged a clean handkerchief from his pocket and did his best to dry his hair and face. "Nice and warm in here."

Adrian started up the engine and after a quick check, put the truck into gear. Before long, they came out the other side of the tree covering and headed towards Drayton.

"Sorry," said Lenny. "Didn't really get a chance to chat the other day."

The way Adrian remembered things, Lenny hadn't wanted to talk. Not to Adrian anyway. He liked this chatty version of Lenny much better.

"You had a lot on your plate. Funeral, and all."

"So I didn't get to ask what you do?" Lenny turned to have a brief glance through the small back window of the truck. "For a living?"

"Building trade. Haven't gotten round to painting the name on the side of the truck. But I do plumbing, tiling, plastering, roofing. Pretty much the works. The only thing I'm not so hot on is electrical wiring. Can do the basics and make good on repairs, but I'm not qualified to rewire a house. Happily, I've been in the trade long enough to know some excellent people who can."

"Don't suppose you ever get involved in restoration work? Repairing heritage or listed buildings, that kind of thing?"

"Never been asked. But I'd imagine it's more specialised than what I do. Around Norwich it's mainly standard new builds, laying down patios, building extensions or renovating older properties, none of which you could call heritage."

Lenny nodded his understanding, and Adrian wondered what else had been behind the question.

"At school, people used to say you were going to be the next big thing, going on to play rugby for England one day. The field boundary was packed whenever you guys were playing at home. If my memory serves me well, you had quite the following."

Adrian kept his eyes on the road. Since school ended, he'd kept in touch with nobody, and whenever he bumped into anyone from those days, he always answered the question in exactly the same way.

"Didn't happen. Very competitive in the real world of professional sport. Don't think people truly realise what you're up against out there. Plus I liked playing for the fun of it, without the pressure, didn't want to turn it into a profession and lose the enjoyment. What I'm doing now is what I love, building things to last."

Even though the answer wasn't a lie, he would never tell the whole dreadful truth. But the answer seemed to stop people digging any further. Because nobody wanted to hear the real reason for him suddenly being yanked out of school and scraping a life on the streets of London.

"Have you always lived here? In Drayton?"

"No. Came back when my dad got sick. He passed away around ten years ago."

"I'm so very sorry. We have that in common. I know he was popular in the community. Wasn't he a church minister or something?"

Adrian did not want to talk about his father either. A mountain of a man, he had shone back then as one of the few prominent West Indian men in Drayton, a popular minister of the local Baptist church. People had come to him for everything, for guidance, support, advice and often for forgiveness, something he seemed to be able to dole out freely and generously to his congregation.

But not to his son.

"That's him. Minister of Drayton Baptist. I thought your folks were agnostic or something."

"Humanists. As scientists they preferred the human race to rely on critical thinking, together with rational and empirical evidence, rather than to follow organised religion, which they say is based on fairy stories and superstition. Even so, I still managed to get them to put up a Christmas tree each year. A small one, of course. My mother used to roll her eyes, but she could see how much the decorations meant to me."

"And the presents?"

"Especially the presents." Lenny had a nice laugh.

"How did you know about my dad, then?"

"At school in the lower sixth — you'd already left — our form head used to get people from different walks of life to come in and explain what they did. They invited your dad to give us a talk on the difference between Baptists and other branches of the Christian church. He was actually really good. Informative, but also funny."

"Yeah, that sounds like him."

"Did he make you and your mother go to his church, too?"

"My mother was a good Irish Catholic girl. Still is. But no, he didn't force us to go. I went a couple of times when I was little, but it wasn't for me."

"So you're not a believer?"

"I wouldn't — I wouldn't say that."

Lenny seemed intrigued but Adrian wasn't sure he wanted to go into his reasoning.

"Let's just say I've had a few special moments in my life when a prayer was answered. How about you? Are you an atheist, too? Like your parents?"

"Humanist."

"Humanists. Atheist. Same thing, isn't it?"

Somewhat dramatically, Lenny Day hissed in a breath before answering. Adrian took his eyes from the road for a second to witness the mix of shock and amusement on Lenny's face.

"You ought to have discussed that particular topic with my father while he was still alive. Over a pint or two at the Red Lion, preferably. You'd have been there for hours. He was more passionate about that particular question than he was about the indoctrination and controlling nature of organised religions. I unwittingly touched on the subject once and was rewarded with a diatribe about atheism being merely the absence of belief, while he viewed humanism as a positive attitude, a positive force and movement in the world, centred on human experience, thought and hopes. Personally, I'm still not sure where I stand, but in a sick world where people are finally waking up and trying to create sustainable ways to keep the planet alive and habitable, humanism seems to make more sense than passively offering the world a prayer. Do you notice how we're starting to hear people voice their irritation when government officials or politicians fall back on their standard 'our thoughts and prayers are with the families' monologue whenever natural disasters occur. I heard one woman on television saying, 'You can keep your thoughts and prayers. How about doing something?'"

"Amen to that," said Adrian.

"Or not, as the case may be."

When the two of them laughed together, Adrian found himself enjoying Lenny's company. Ahead of him in the road, he spotted the left fork which would take them to Ted's garage. As he steered into the road, he also slowed the speed of the wipers, the rain now reduced to a light drizzle.

"So what about you?" Adrian asked. "Back for good?"

"No. Only until I've got everything sorted out with my dad's estate and Mum's settled. Then I'll return to work."

"Which is?"

"I run a suite of online businesses. One of them being classic cars, of all things. So you'd think I would know my way around a motor car engine. But the types of cars we specialise in are vintage and often with unique designs, so I hire experienced mechanics to inspect the engine and other working parts."

"You're the boss?"

"I am, yes. I'm also involved in selling antiques, and restoring and selling old, and often listed, buildings."

"Which is why you asked me about the kind of building work I'm involved in."

"Busted. Always on the lookout for good workmen."

Adrian mulled the words over for a few moments.

"So you're successful?"

"Well, my accountant seems to think so. As do the talented team of people I have working for me."

"Yeah, I thought maybe you were."

"Thought maybe I was what?"

"Successful. You have that look about you."

Adrian sensed Lenny turn his way, eyeing him humorously.

"I do? And what kind of look is that?"

"You know. Smart. Intelligent. Confident. You always came across as being capable at school, independent, didn't need to be a part of a group to get noticed. I'm sure I'm not the only person who saw that in you."

When Adrian peered around, he saw Lenny now looking out the window, but in the reflection could see him smiling to himself. Had Adrian's comments amused him?

"What did I say?" he asked.

"No, it's nothing. Except I was anything but capable or independent back then. Lonely, maybe."

Adrian had no answer for Lenny's comment. He had always been a little in awe of young Lenny Day. To hear he had been lonely made Adrian feel sad, because had he known, he would have tried harder to connect with him.

Up ahead he spotted the familiar distinctive sign for Turnbull Motor Services, Ted's garage.

"Here we are. Let me come in with you. I know Ted well and can explain what the problem is."

Adrian pulled up on the forecourt, where a line of five cars had for sale stickers on them. Parking up, he jumped out of the truck as Lenny followed suit. A small glass office with a front door sat beside the double-fronted bays of the garage, almost every inch of each pane covered with adverts for different motor companies, components or brands of motor oil. In one of the bays, two young lads in navy-blue overalls leant over the bonnet of an old silver Mercedes which had definitely seen better days. Outside the second bay, one lad smoked a cigarette beneath a canopy.

"Hey, Pete," called Adrian, as Lenny stepped up and matched his stride, and they marched towards the office. He knew the lad well, often met him and Ted having a pint together in the Lion. "Is he around?"

"In the office." Pete nodded to the office door. "Doing sod all, as usual."

In his trademark orange overalls, Ted sat behind a cluttered desk in the small toasty-warm office and waiting area, running through invoices. After a bit of small talk, Ted acknowledging Lenny's father and his car, having provided an MOT each year, Adrian quickly cut to the chase. Ted listened intently until Adrian had finished.

"Ah, well, you caught us at a right good time." Ted's Norwich accent bordered on caricature. "Not exactly rushed off our feet right now, as you can see from those lazy bastards as are standing around out there. I'll get Pete to drive down after lunch, tow her back here. We'll do a service, too, if you want? If there's nothing too serious."

"No rush," said Lenny. "I'm only going to sell the thing, anyway."

"Are you now? And how much you asking?"

"To be honest, I'm not really sure."

Adrian knew Ted well enough to see the opportunity to make a fast buck, so he took the opportunity to intervene.

"Vauxhall Astra five-door Elite. Petrol, not diesel. One point six, probably low mileage, and in pretty good nick. As far as I could tell, the only things needing attention are the battery and the alternator. With a good service and a clean-up you could get well over three grand retail. Lenny will let you have her for two. Bargain."

Adrian was only vaguely aware of Lenny staring at him, because his full attention focused on Ted's unsmiling face and blank stare. Eventually Ted tilted his head back and laughed at the ceiling.

"You robbing bastard, Lamperton. Okay, let me look her over and if what you say is true, you've got yourself a deal. I've actually got a customer who wants a petrol Astra. Not interested in any of those diesel beauties on my forecourt."

After Lenny had handed over the car keys and shaken hands with Ted, they went back to Adrian's truck.

"So, Mr Day. Where to now?"

When he turned around, Lenny was staring at him and smiling.

"I can't believe you just did that."

"What?"

"I'd have been happy with a couple of hundred quid, just to get the bloody thing from cluttering up the kerb."

"And you call yourself a successful businessman? Shame on you."

This time Lenny roared with laughter and Adrian joined him, chuckling too.

"Don't suppose you fancy a pint and a spot of lunch at the Red Lion?" asked Lenny, surprising Adrian. "My treat not only for helping me out of a tight spot today, but also for getting my mother such a good bargain on the car."

Adrian smiled, but then turned to Lenny.

"You don't need to, Lenny. Call it my good deed of the day. I'm sure you'd do the same if you found someone in a similar situation."

"Lenny?" Leonard spat the word out and tried to look annoyed but his mouth grinning at the corner betrayed his humour.

"Oh, sorry. What do you prefer to be called?"

"No, Lenny sounds fine. The way you say it. And the truth is, I do want to have lunch with you, but I am also enjoying our conversation. So unless you have somewhere better to be, fancy joining me?"

Adrian started up the truck and grinned.

"I would be honoured."

Chapter Five

Will

Leonard's father had used the same solicitor for as long as Leonard could remember. Not that he had needed him that often in any official capacity. Once for conveyancing when they purchased their current home, another time for a dispute with a neighbour over a shared driveway, and, of course, for the writing of his last will and testament. Mr Dawson — neither Leonard nor his mother had any idea of his given name — used to be a sole practitioner, his office a single room above a newsagent on Norwich High Street, but had joined a larger legal firm some years back. Haven and Trollope, the new firm, stood in a modern characterless three-storey complex on the outskirts of town. One advantage to the location was the many parking spaces designated to the law firm clients. Leonard's mother insisted he drive around the car park three times until she pointed out a parking space that met her approval.

Best of all, the drive barely took half an hour, during which time his mother sat quietly, listening to the car radio which she insisted be tuned to BBC Radio 4, to a topical political debate. Leonard's mind had been elsewhere but he'd occasionally heard her tutting whenever she felt someone had made an inconclusive statement or had circumvented answering a simple question.

All day Sunday, while he had begun to tackle the back garden then cleared his business email, Leonard had mulled over his chance meeting with Adrian. By Sunday evening, he had almost called and invited him out for a drink. But he had no idea what Adrian did at the weekend, didn't know if he would be intruding, felt sure such a good-looking guy would have other plans which probably included a boyfriend.

Strange, really, but even though they had only just met — because they had never been friends — he felt really at ease in his company, as though they had known each other for years. After heading to the Red Lion, they'd enjoyed a couple of drinks, both opting for the same pub lunch of home-made shepherd's pie and fresh garden vegetables, and chatted about their old school.

Adrian had seemed purposely vague about his life after leaving the education system, deflecting with trite sayings such as *'oh, you know, here and there'* and *'a little bit of this and that'* which Leonard had taken to mean he didn't want to talk in detail about his young adult life. Sensing the guardedness, and knowing from Eric about Adrian being gay, Leonard had pointedly avoided probing into Adrian's romantic life and had noticed Adrian did the same with him.

What he had found out was that Adrian worked locally, although he had no jobs on right now. From stories of work he had carried out, Leonard could tell his popularity with the local community, including some regulars in the pub he had done work for at some time or another. As the afternoon wore on, Leonard had realised he liked Adrian and, before they'd parted ways, they'd swapped mobile phone numbers and agreed to meet up again after the weekend.

Inside the reception area of Haven and Trollope, after asking to see their identification, one of the two receptionists led them up a flight of stairs to a large glass conference room. Inside, Aunt Millicent and Matthew already sat there looking stiff and sullen and bored. After offering Adrian and his mother drinks which they both declined, the young girl left them. His aunt and cousin had already stood and after his mother had shaken hands with them, Leonard did the same. Once they took their seats, each pair on opposite sides of the table, the room fell back into an awkward silence.

To Leonard's relief, Mr Dawson entered not long after. In his mid-to-late sixties, he reminded Leonard of one of his old college professors, with his olive-green tweed suit, black and white polka-dot bow tie, steel-rimmed glasses with thick lenses and full head of pure white wavy hair held firmly in place with either too much Vaseline or hair gel.

He carried a thick manila folder that had a large label on the front. Leonard could easily make out the full name of his father in capital letters.

Without shaking hands, he lowered himself into the seat at the head of the table, immediately opened the folder and took out a single sheet of paper from the top.

"Good. Well. Thank you all for coming here today and being so punctual. Apologies for my tardiness, but I had a call from another client that went on longer than I had expected. I am Hubert Dawson of Haven and Trollope and the deceased, Colin Montgomery Day, appointed me as the sole executor of his will. This is a simple enough matter and should not take long. Rather than read all the legal speak in the formal last will and testament, I've had a one-sheet summary put together, but naturally, all those named as beneficiaries will receive a full copy of the legal document. Is everyone present comfortable with this?"

Although nobody spoke aloud, everyone around the table nodded their assent.

"Excellent. Well, in summary, the deceased left almost everything to his wife, Mrs Geraldine Olivia Day, which includes their unencumbered residential home, 14 Collier Drive, and all investments, shares and possessions in Mr Day's sole name, his pension and, of course, the proceeds from his life assurance policy."

That his father had left him nothing came as no surprise to Leonard. His father, being a pragmatic man, had spoken at length about the eventuality of his death, during which time Leonard had emphasised his own financial independence and his desire for his father to make sure Leonard's mother was taken care of by making her the principal beneficiary.

"There are two caveats to this under the General Provisions clause. The first is that he wishes to donate the sum of ten thousand pounds to the college research facility, and the second is that the family's country home, Bryn Bach in Wales, changes ownership to his son and only child, Leonard Frederick Day."

Leonard had never heard his father mention a holiday home before and began to turn to his mother for clarification. Before he could, Aunt Millicent let out a loud strangled gasp and sat forward in her chair, her hands grasping the arms of the chair. Only her son Matthew seemed unsurprised by her reaction.

"No! There must be some mistake. As the last surviving sibling in our family, I should be the one to inherit Bryn Bach. It's what our mother and father would have wanted, and something Colin promised should anything happen to him."

Mr Dawson sorted through the larger document, the full will, and flicked to a particular page marked by a yellow Post-it note.

"Mr Day's instructions are clear. Specific, straightforward and unambiguous, Mrs Darlington. And unless you have any legal documentation that supersedes the terms of this will, then there is no mistake. Leonard's father leaves in its entirety the farmhouse, Bryn Bach, in Disserth, Llandrindod Wells in Wales to his son, Leonard Frederick Day. He reviewed his will routinely at the end of each year, the last time being the December just gone. There is no mistake in—"

"He *promised* me. We spent our school holidays there as children, my brother, Colin, our parents and me. Until he went off to college on the other side of the country and thought himself too high and mighty to associate with us, especially when he met *her*." At that she glared pointedly at Leonard's mother. "And when my ex-husband started a new job in sales, when we had barely enough money to survive on, we still managed to provide summer holidays for our children because my father let us use Bryn Bach. We have many fond memories there. And in return we have decorated, maintained and cared for the place without asking for a penny in return. Since our father passed and left the cottage to my brother, he has not once been there. I know this for a fact. We still have friends in Newbridge. And my Matthew checks the cottage every year for broken pipes and defects, even though the place is deserted now. Falling to rack and ruin."

"This is all very well, Mrs Darlington. But legally the property now belongs — "

"What does he want with it, anyway? He's never even been there. None of them have."

Leonard peered sideways at his mother, noticed the disapproving assessment at her sister-in-law's outburst. She glared at her as she would a recalcitrant student. Poor Mr Dawson lifted his glasses and rubbed the bridge of his nose. If he was going to be completely honest, Leonard didn't care about a holiday home in Wales. He had enough old properties around the country on his books without adding one more to the portfolio. But his father had specifically left the place to him. Surely that meant something?

"What if we challenge the will?"

This time, Matthew spoke. Leonard felt a flash of anger ignite in him at the thought of a family member challenging his father's wishes. On his part, Mr Dawson appeared to agree because he sat up straight in his chair, his lips pinched together. With both hands pressed together beneath his chin as though in prayer, he leant forward, elbows on the table, and peered over the top of his glasses.

"I am not your solicitor, Mr Darlington, but had I been, I would have strongly advised you against doing so. Not only would you end up spending an unsightly amount of money in legal fees, but in my long experience, challenges of this nature are rarely successful. Possession truly is nine-tenths of the law in this country. Look, rather than go that route, why don't you begin by asking Mr Day junior if he would be prepared to sell you the property? Or come to some kind of arrangement with him?"

Aunt Millicent's eyes darted to Leonard, a glimmer of hope in them and a pinched smile replacing the previous unpleasant grimace.

"Would you, Leonard? Would you consider selling our lovely holiday home back to us? It holds such dear memories for me and my family."

"It's as good as derelict anyway," added Matthew, still unsmiling, but something lighting in his eyes. "We'd be doing you a favour taking the pile of worthless rubble off your hands."

Up until the frankly aggressive challenge from his relatives, Leonard had been even-tempered and might have considered coming to some arrangement, as Mr Dawson had put it. But now? He took a deep breath before replying.

"When I walked in here today, my only concern was to make sure my mother was taken care of financially, and it appears my father has done that. Until five minutes ago I had no idea he owned a farmhouse in Wales. But he clearly wanted me to have the place. So I'm not going to be hurried into making a decision right away. Before anything I'd like to drive down there and give the place a quick once-over. After that I'll make up my mind. But rest assured, Aunt Millicent, if I do decide to sell the property, I promise you will get first option to buy. My mother has your contact details. And Mr Dawson and my mother are witnesses to my promise."

"Excellent." Mr Dawson clearly wanted to move the matter along. No doubt, like Leonard, he hadn't anticipated anyone to challenge the will. "In which case—"

But Leonard's aunt hadn't finished.

"You're just like him, aren't you? Just like your father?"

Her caustic tone and scowl left nobody in any doubt about her true feelings, except this time Leonard had no hesitation in glaring back across the table.

"I hope so. And if that's what you see in me, then I am honoured." Leonard turned his attention back to the solicitor. "Sorry, Mr Dawson. You were saying?"

"Um, yes, so in order to finish matters off, I'll need you and your mother to sign the necessary paperwork, and then get copies made for our records. Shouldn't take more than another fifteen to twenty minutes. In the meantime, Mrs Darlington, if you and your son wish to leave, I can get someone — "

"Don't bother. We can find our own way out."

Without another word, they rose from their seats and left without bidding farewell.

After the door shut behind them, Mr Dawson waited a few moments before looking apologetically at Leonard and his mother, gently shaking his head but saying nothing.

"Did you know about this family house, Mum?"

"I didn't. Your father mentioned nothing to me. But you know him, he did nothing without thinking things through meticulously. In spite of what your aunt insists, if he wanted you to have the farmhouse rather than her, and made a point of specifying the fact in his will, then there is no mistake and you should trust his good judgement."

Before they left, Mr Dawson furnished Leonard and his mother with their copies of all the signed paperwork. Leonard thought they had finished, and began to rise until Mr Dawson handed him a bulky envelope.

"The deeds to the property will continue to be kept here, Mr Day, in our safekeeping, unless you wish them to be held elsewhere. But they will be transferred into your name. These are the keys to Bryn Bach. Somewhere on file we have a photograph of the place. I'll get my assistant to email a copy to you. And off the record, I agree with your mother. Your father clearly wanted you to have the place, and as such, he did so for a reason."

All well and good, thought Leonard as he and his mother strolled unspeaking down the plush corridor, but if that was the case, his father had taken the reason to the grave with him.

Chapter Six

Request

Adrian lay back into the corner of his sofa, bare feet up on the coffee table, drumming the fingers of one hand on the armrest, the remote in his other hand, flicking mindlessly from one television channel to the next. Nothing caught his imagination. Repeats of old shows aired on the major networks and sports he didn't really follow ran on the cable channels.

With no work on the horizon, and all the grocery shopping he needed already done, he had stayed indoors all day, trying to find things to keep him busy. After a morning run followed by an hour's workout with the multi-functional weight machine in his spare bedroom, he tackled his domestic chores. Right now, the apartment shone spotless, each room scrubbed clean, bedding changed, washing and ironing done, the open kitchen sparkling once again after a frozen microwave dinner of spaghetti carbonara and grilled garlic bread.

Being alone with his own thoughts made him cagey, threatened to unsettle and unnerve him, like an itch he couldn't quite pinpoint and scratch. He needed distractions. Exactly this kind of sullen mood had first led him to Chappies in town and to his chance meeting with Nick. And that would never happen again. Had it been any other day than Wednesday, he might have considered going to see his mother — however painful on the ear that might be. But on Wednesdays she had her church group meeting, which normally entailed a day trip out somewhere in their minibus. Honestly, his mother had a better social life than he had ever enjoyed.

During the good times, punishing manual work provided the perfect antidote. Arriving on-site early, working hard all day in the open air, pushing himself to get things finished even if that meant working late, then returning home exhausted when all he craved was fast food, a hot shower and sleep.

Most of his work on-site meant grafting alone. During tea breaks or after they had all clocked off for the day, he would often end up somewhere with their group of workers, most of them familiar, in a pub or café, grumbling about this or that, making one inappropriate joke after another about race, religion, gender, sex or sexuality. Nothing became taboo in this still largely male-dominated environment, where political correctness became cannon fodder for their funnies. Some knew about Adrian's sexuality. Nobody cared, treating him as they did everyone else. As communities went, he found the camaraderie comforting and supportive — and strangely liberating.

Today, all day long, his phone had remained silent. If only he felt more confident, he might have dialled any one of his builder buddies and dragged them out for a brew. But social connection had never been a strong point and he usually waited for one of them to call him. In a fit of irritation, he threw the remote down on the sofa just as the phone on the arm of the chair pinged with an incoming message.

With desperate expectation, he grabbed for the device.

Lenny Day.

Amazed at how reading a name could instantly put him in a better mood, he shifted his feet onto the floor and read the text.

Lenny: Fancy a pint at the Lion? I have a favour to ask.

Adrian grinned broadly as his thumbs flashed over the display keyboard with a response.

Adrian: Oh, yes? Should I be concerned?

Lenny: It's a job, actually. Only if you're interested. I'd rather explain in person than over the phone.

Lenny: Plus my mother's driving me up the wall and I need an excuse to get out of this house before I get put away for matricide.

Adrian laughed at the phone.

Adrian: Matricide? Is that something to do with beds?

Lenny: Funny man. So is that a yes?

Adrian: OK, you've got me intrigued. What time shall I meet you?

Lenny: It's 6:30pm. See you there in an hour?

Adrian: Done. And I'll have a pint of my usual as you're offering to buy.

Lenny: Did I mention anything about buying?

Adrian: I listen a lot better when someone else is paying.

Lenny: ;0) See you there.

His mood brightening, Adrian threw the phone on the couch before peering down at his clothes. Grimy grey tee, baggy sweats and flip-flops. He jumped to his feet and headed to his bathroom. With the Lion only ten minutes' walk away, he had time for a long shower and also to decide on something decent to wear. When he heard the voice in his head, he told himself to calm down. This was not a date, simply a new pal meeting up for a drink.

Still, no harm in looking good.

* * * *

Traditionally, except for diehard locals who had nothing else to do with their time, punters avoided the pub until later in the week. When he opened the door, he realised this particular evening was no exception. Adrian found Lenny sitting at the same table they had bagged on Saturday, facing the pub door with two pints of ale already sitting on the table. Lenny had clearly been anticipating him, because his gaze lifted from his phone towards the doorway and the smile that transformed his face had Adrian beaming instantly back, a tingle in his stomach.

"Evening, Adrian. You're looking sharp."

Adrian had picked out a pair of denims he filled out nicely, with a tight, long-sleeved burgundy tee — knowing the pub interior would be warm — and his wool-lined black hoodie hanging open. Lenny's reaction stalled him for a moment, the way his gaze travelled slowly up and down Adrian's body until their eyes met again. Only then did Lenny's smile falter and his eyes flutter to his drink, as though he had been caught openly checking him out.

Interesting.

Lenny recovered quickly, looking up and maintaining eye contact this time.

"Under Armour? The tee? I've got the same one in my wardrobe. Something else we have in common."

With a twinge of disappointment, Adrian looked down at his burgundy shirt, realising perhaps Lenny had not been checking him out after all.

"Oh, yeah. I like their designs. Got the same style in three different colours."

"Looks better on you. Anyway, thanks for coming. Pint of beer, as ordered. Sorry to drag your arse out on a Wednesday night. What have you been up to?"

After waving a greeting to the pub landlord, Adrian slumped down on the booth bench opposite. While sitting, he twisted out of his hoodie and once again found Lenny checking out his chest and biceps, or maybe the design of his tee. With a resigned sigh he wondered whether he was losing his touch. When he was younger, he used to be much better at interpreting the signs of attraction.

"Me? Not a lot. Stuck indoors all day. My flat has never been so spotless. I think I must have scrubbed the kitchen clean at least three times. My mum would be proud."

Lenny grinned and Adrian met his gaze, also smiling. Up close, he realised not only how nice his eyes were, a kind of slate grey, but how his greying beard betrayed dimples beneath whenever he smiled or laughed.

"Shame," said Lenny.

"What? Why?"

"Because I've been stuck inside the house, too. I should have called you. We could have had some fun together."

Adrian took a sip of beer and studied Lenny's face. This man bore no resemblance to the angry boy he'd known from high school. Not that they had ever really interacted. If they did get to know each other better, as he hoped they would, he vowed to find out why Lenny had been so antagonistic when they were younger.

"I thought you were sorting out your dad's estate or something. Doing all the legal stuff?"

"Done. We were in the solicitor's office for barely an hour. Pretty straightforward, actually. Well, most of it. Ted phoned me about the car this morning, by the way."

"And?"

"It's exactly what you said. New alternator and battery. But he says he'll also need to do some work on the brakes, steam clean the interior and patch up some of the bodywork, so he's offering me fifteen hundred cash."

"Bollocks. He's trying it on —"

"It's fine, Adrian. If it means the damn thing is no longer gathering dust outside the house, then everyone's happy. Mum doesn't want the car or need the money. Their mortgage is already paid off and the substantial money Dad left behind will take care of her even if she lives long enough to get a telegram from the Queen."

Adrian nodded, but felt irritated. Ted would most likely make over three thousand pounds on the second-hand Astra, probably nearer four. What rankled was the idea of a nice guy like Lenny being taken for a ride by an old crook like Ted. Oddly enough, Lenny sensed Adrian's annoyance.

"Let it go, Adrian. Remember I deal with the buying and selling of cars all the time. Not bulk standard ones, like the Astra. But don't you think I haggle when I get called out to visit the owners of old jalopies, usually left to rot in their garages? One guy wanted to sell off an old Daimler as spare parts and scrap metal. Honestly, we've made tens of thousands on some of the cars we've bought and renovated. And in my book, as long as you can settle on a good price that keeps both buyer and seller happy, then it's a win-win all round."

"Yeah, I suppose."

"Anyway, change of topic. Any work on the horizon?"

"Sod all. Not even a sniff."

Lenny stopped then, took a long gulp of beer and reclined against the back of the bench.

"Well, on that note, the reason I asked you down here tonight, apart from my mother annoying me to hell, is because I seem to have inherited a holiday home from my father. And before I decide what to do with it, I thought I'd go down there and see what kind of state the place is in. But I could really use a professional eye and a second opinion. So I wondered if you might be interested in being hired as my — not even sure what it's called — structural consultant?"

"Holiday home?"

"That's what they said. I've never been there, but my father's family used the place as a holiday home when they were kids. It's not a caravan, in case that's what you're thinking. It's a farmhouse in the Welsh countryside."

Adrian had worked on a number of cottage-style houses in and around the area, so had no reservations about whether he could be of any help.

"How many bedrooms?"

"No idea."

"Is it a one or two-storey structure?"

Lenny laughed and shook his head.

"Honestly, Adrian. It's all a mystery. Until the reading of the will, I had no idea the place even existed. All I know for sure is it's a holiday home, a farmhouse called Bryn Bach in a tiny Welsh village called Disserth. Although he promised to email a photograph to me, the solicitor gave me no blueprints or floor plan, which is why I want to go for a look-see. No idea what state it's in, so it might be just a pile of bricks. According to an online map application, the plot is in the Welsh countryside about forty minutes from the English border. My aunt mentioned the nearest main town being Newbridge. I thought I would book us into a local pub for a couple of nights — if you're onboard — and we can go and see exactly what kind of state the place is in."

"When?"

"So you're in?"

"Got bugger all else to do, have I?"

"When would be good for you?"

"How about after we finish these drinks?"

Lenny laughed, a sound Adrian had already begun to enjoy, as well as the way his eyes crinkled in the corners.

"I think we might both want to pack a bag first. So how does tomorrow sound?"

"Perfect. I assume we'll be driving there?"

"Yes, I'll take my SUV. I promised to drop my mother off in Norwich town centre at nine, but we could leave straight after. It's around five and a half hours cross country, depending on traffic. Let me confirm the booking."

Adrian warmed to the idea of a road trip, to the thought of getting out of Drayton for a couple of days. And the fact that a mystery surrounded the building made this break from the mundane even more of an adventure.

"So that means if we set off at ten with an hour's break for lunch, we should be there around five. Yeah, that would work. You know, if we took my truck, I could bring some ladders and equipment so we could do a proper check of the roof and guttering, assess the plumbing and check out any structural issues. But if we don't arrive until after five, it'll probably be too dark to do a full inspection until morning. Although I've got some floodlights we could use, ones I've employed on-site before. Does the place have utilities like electricity and running water — ?"

While Adrian talked, Lenny had been tapping something into his phone, but had started chuckling even before he looked up.

"Slow down a bit, Adrian. Loving the enthusiasm, but we're only going down to have a quick inspection of the interior and exterior. I wasn't planning on us going up ladders or knocking down walls. But maybe a small toolkit would be a good idea. As far as utilities are concerned, I have no idea. Sounds like it's been left empty for a number of years, so my guess is no. Also, you're right. By the time we get there, it'll already be getting dark, so I suggest we drive straight to the accommodation and head to the house first thing

Friday. I checked and found a pub hotel in Newbridge that provides accommodation, so I've just booked us rooms. Hope that's okay?"

"Brilliant."

Right at that moment, Adrian's phone buzzed repeatedly in his jeans pocket with an incoming call. When he squeezed the device out and saw the name on the display, he let out a soft, irritated sigh.

Nick.

If he didn't take the call, he knew Nick would leave messages and pester him with more calls all night. With a quick apologetic glance at Lenny, to pressed accept.

"Hey, Nick."

"Ade, how's it going?"

At least Nick sounded sober this time.

"Fine. What do you want?"

"I'm here at the hospital with Janice. She's most likely going to have a caesarean Friday morning, a planned one, something to do with the baby being turned the wrong way. It's usually straightforward enough, they say, but they want to keep an eye on her because her blood pressure's been a bit up and down."

"Sorry to hear that. What can I do to help?"

"So, what with me working, her mum and dad are looking after Todd until Janice gets back from the hospital, so I wondered if tomorrow night you might be free to—"

"Let me stop you right there, Nick. I'm going to be out of town until—" Adrian stopped and checked with Lenny, who mouthed the word 'Sunday'. For a change, he had a legitimate excuse to push Nick away. "Until Sunday. So I'm not going to be around. Sorry I can't help, but I hope everything turns out okay. Give my love to Janice."

"Yeah, thanks a fucking bunch, pal."

"Bye, Nick."

Adrian thumbed off the call and breathed out a sigh, slamming the phone down on the table.

"Problem?"

When Adrian met Lenny's eyes, he grimaced and shook his head.

"Nothing important. Someone pestering me for a favour I'm not in a position to give."

"Talking of which, how much do you charge?"

About to take a swig of beer, Adrian froze, Lenny's words confusing him, still irritated at the kind of favour Nick had been anticipating.

"How much do I charge for what?"

"For your professional consulting services?"

Finally, he caught on and, after a brief chuckle, put the glass down.

"Don't even think about it. I am not taking your money just to go and look at an old building that you said yourself might be just a pile of bricks."

"I can't ask you to give up your time and provide a professional assessment without—"

"Transport, food and accommodation. That's all I need. And a promise that if you do decide the place is worth keeping and you need a decent builder—that's me, by the way—then you'll give me first dibs at quoting for the job."

Instead of answering straight away, Lenny appeared puzzled, staring down at his drink, the smile still on his face but his head shaking gently from side to side. When his eyes finally lifted to meet Adrian's, he appeared ready to say something, but then hesitated.

Instead, what came out was a simple thank you.

* * * *

"Then who's going to pick me up? Look at this weather."

Leonard's mother sat unmoving in the front passenger seat after they had parked under shelter in the municipal parking block in Norwich town centre. Adrian heard Lenny breathe out a second soft sigh of irritation. Sat quietly in the back, pretending not to hear the exchange, Adrian stared out of the rain-spattered window, wishing he could be anywhere else.

"We talked about this last night, Mum. You have your umbrella. So get a bus. You keep telling me you don't use your bus pass enough. Or if you've got a lot of shopping, call a taxi."

"Taxis are expensive. I don't see why you can't wait until I've finished. Your father would have. I'm only going to be a couple of hours at the most."

"Mum, we have a five- or six-hour journey ahead of us. And we need to set off now if we're going to get there before dark. We'll be back Sunday afternoon."

"Sunday? I thought you were going to finish the back garden Saturday."

"Like I said, I'll do that next week if the weather improves."

"If? It's always if with you."

"I'm driving away now. So you either get out of the car this minute, or you'll be coming to Wales with us. Your choice."

Adrian noted a distinct change in Lenny's tone. To emphasise his point, Lenny pushed the button to start up the engine. After a moment, his mother yanked on the door handle, got out and made a point of slamming the door behind her. Without turning around, she headed for the carpark lift, which would take her directly to the mall. Adrian sat in the back saying nothing, observing poor Lenny's stiff posture as he watched his mother step through the elevator doors.

"Not a patch on my mother," said Adrian, quietly, after sitting there for a moment.

"Sorry?"

"Your mum's performance. Some of the wobblies my mum threw when I was a kid were worthy of an Academy Award. Your mum doesn't even swear."

Lenny laughed and turned in his seat.

"Come and sit up front. We need to get moving."

Once Adrian sat next to him, securing his seat belt in place, and once they had begun navigating their way out of the car park, Lenny let his frustrations out.

"Honestly, Ade. She drives me crazy. Do this, do that. I'm going to have to sit her down and have a serious chat about the future. I'm forty-bloody-seven and I've got a business to run. I can't be here permanently at her beck and call. Does your mother treat you the same way?"

"Are you kidding? She's busier than a barman on payday. I try to see her once a week, but she has so many friends. I usually have to book an appointment weeks in advance."

Lenny laughed aloud, and Adrian sensed some of the tension leave him. After a few moments of quiet, as they waited to join the mainstream traffic, he turned to Adrian.

"Thanks for agreeing to do this, Ade."

It hadn't escaped Adrian's notice, had warmed him, that Lenny already had a shortened name for him, even if it was the same one Nick used.

"No problem. Who doesn't love a road trip? Hey, do you want me to take a turn at driving at some point? I'm cool either way."

Lenny waited until the car had stopped at a set of traffic lights before answering.

"Let's see how I get on when we stop for a break. I enjoy driving long distances — do it all the time — so it shouldn't be a problem. But if you could be principal navigator, temperature controller and music selection director, then I'll be very happy."

"Now we're talking. But first things first. Stay on this road and follow signs for the A11. Secondly, how about some 80s music? Let's start with bands. Pop quiz. Which would you choose out of the following? Tears for Fears, Fine Young Cannibals, Fleetwood Mac or New Order. And let me just say, the answer to this question is vital if we are going to get along over the next couple of days."

A playful grin blossomed on Lenny's face. After taking one hand from the steering wheel and tapping his forefinger against his lips a couple of times, he nodded once.

"No competition. All of the above."

"Congratulations, Mr Day. That is the correct answer."

* * * *

Heavy downpours hampered their progress. Motorway traffic frequently came to a standstill due to the relentless deluge. Adrian noticed Lenny adhering strictly to speed limits and slowing when sudden heavy torrents hit, rendering his windscreen wipers almost useless.

To keep the mood light, he chose a channel with random songs from their youth and challenged Lenny to '*beat the intro*', by guessing the song title from the opening bars. Lenny seemed to enjoy the game, his competitive streak shining through. Occasionally he would also sing along to a song, not particularly in tune and often using unintelligible lyrics. A couple of times he caught Adrian smirking at his effort, and laughed good-naturedly. Lenny even told stories of his life at the time when one particularly memorable song climbed the music charts. Adrian had nothing to reciprocate. His few good memories of the early eighties were eclipsed by those towards the end.

Around one o'clock, rather than stopping at one of the generic motorway service stations, Lenny took them off a slip road and found a small café in Bedford, one he had frequented before. Once again Lenny made a great choice, ordering them both mugs of hot tea and the lunchtime special of steaming beef and ale pie with mashed potatoes and garden vegetables.

Before leaving the café and darting back through the rain to the car, Adrian offered to take a turn at driving, but Lenny wanted to keep going. Adrian understood, noticing him content behind the steering wheel, negotiating roads and bends and safely overtaking slower vehicles.

* * * *

Later than anticipated, Lenny brought the SUV to a smooth stop outside the brightly lit Manor Inn pub. Silvery shards of heavy rain continued to fill the headlight beams. Without a word, he killed the wipers followed by the engine and after a shared look, they grabbed their bags from the back seat and, holding them over their heads, made a dash for the front door.

With only one entrance to the pub, they stumbled straight into the heart of the toasty-warm bar. Carpeted throughout and with dark-oak-framed furniture and a blazing open fire, the place felt homely but also conspicuously empty.

"Looks like a setting from a family film," said Lenny.

"Or a horror movie," added Adrian.

Lenny snorted and moved further into the room, spotting a young girl behind the bar slowly cleaning a single beer glass. Adrian didn't hear what was said, but after a quick exchange of words, she called out to someone through an open doorway, before telling them to take a seat.

Minutes later, a woman with a large, black, bound ledger came out from a back room and waddled over to them. She wore pink-framed glasses on a gold chain and a long grey cardigan that had seen better days and which sat over a pale pink dress.

"Hello, my loves," she said, taking a seat at their table. "Megan Llewellyn, landlady. My husband, Roger, normally deals with bookings, but he's in Aberystwyth tonight at the national brewery convention, see? So you got me instead. Which of you's Mr Day?"

"That's me. I know the booking was last minute, but please tell me everything is okay? We don't relish the thought of driving back to Norwich in this weather."

"Know just what you mean. Raining knives and forks out there, it is. No, well, we got your booking okay. Only there is a slight problem."

Lenny looked to Adrian, who shrugged and waited for Mrs Llewellyn to continue.

"One of the rooms you booked, the Burton Room, named after Richard Burton — all our rooms are named after famous Welsh people, see? Anyway, this one has the king-size bed and is situated at the front of the pub, overlooking the village green. Best room in the place, my Roger says, usually the most popular during the summer months when we're at our busiest and — "

"Mam, get on with it, will you?"

The whiny voice came from the young girl behind the bar, who had put the towel over one shoulder and now leant on the counter behind the beer taps.

"You get on with cleaning them glasses," she called back, before meeting the eyes of Adrian and Lenny. "Honestly, kids today think they know it all. Now, where were I?"

"The Burton Room."

"Oh, yes. So. We had a down-pipe burst overnight right outside the bedroom window and rainwater came in through the frames and the ceiling. Weather's been like this all week, see? Whole room got flooded. Only found out when I went to get the room ready a couple of hours ago. Even the carpet will need replacing, which means the room's not habitable. I did try to contact you via the email you used — the telephone number gave me an unobtainable signal — but I imagine you were driving at the time. We have a single room in the attic, but we're in the middle of redecorating that one. So we only have the one available room, the Dylan Thomas, which has twin beds and an en suite bathroom. Now is that going to be okay for you? Obviously, I'll only charge for the one room."

"What telephone number did you use?"

"The one on the online booking form, love. Here."

When Lenny checked the form, he closed his eyes briefly and shook his head.

"I miskeyed the last digit. Should be a six, not a five. I'm really sorry, Ade. I messed up. Are you okay to share? Personally, I have no issue."

Adrian hesitated. He couldn't remember the last time he had shared a room with another man where sex had not been on the menu. Would sharing a room with Lenny be awkward? Even with separate beds, they would still be in close proximity. He felt Lenny's and Mrs Llewellyn's eyes on him.

"Look, my loves. Why don't I give you the key, and you can go and check the room first," said Mrs Llewellyn, probably sensing his hesitation, "see what you think?"

Adrian nodded slowly. Checking the room might give him time to think of something, if necessary an excuse for them to stay somewhere else.

"Sounds like a plan."

Chapter Seven

Wales

Located on the first floor, the Dylan Thomas room smelled faintly of fresh decoration and solvent from newly installed fitments. With grey carpeting and walls painted spearmint, the latter adorned with colourful abstract art in stark reds, greens and whites — the colours of the Welsh national flag — the space felt modern. Even the quality white duvet covers, sheets and pillowcases with the forest-green runners on the two double beds seemed more appropriate for a business class of hotel.

Leonard glanced at Adrian, who looked at the layout and furnishings with trepidation. Did he not like the room, or did he have a problem sharing? Had Leonard messed up? Undeterred, Leonard dropped his bag onto the bed nearest the window and went into the bathroom. Modern white and chrome appliances, new fixtures and fittings, with pristine white tiles on the walls and floor lent the space a clinical cleanliness. Not only did the room have a free-standing tub, but also a large shower cubicle. Leonard had stayed in a lot worse. He didn't notice Adrian's presence until a voice sounded from over his shoulder.

"How much did this lot set you back?"

"It's low season. The rooms are very reasonable. Besides, you don't need to worry. This is on my account, remember? But I reckon this will do nicely. Are you hungry?"

"I'm always hungry."

"Dump your bag and we'll go down and get something to eat before the kitchen closes."

After a slight hesitation, Adrian did as asked and headed straight out to the central stairway leading to the bar. Leonard stayed back to lock the door before stopping to check his phone for messages. He read a couple of updates from Isabelle but found nothing urgent, so hopefully no dramas. When he reached the saloon, Adrian already propped up the bar, his long legs crossed at the ankles, a pint in front of him. The landlady stood behind the counter, pulling one of the beer pumps to fill another glass, while also checking the glasses her daughter had cleaned and occasionally tutting. As soon as Leonard appeared, she smiled a welcome.

"Room to your liking?"

"Very much so, thank you."

"Lovely." She set the full pint of beer in front of him. Leonard smiled at Adrian, who had chosen which beer he would drink. "Let's have your credit card to check against the booking, and then you're all set to go. Breakfast's from seven until nine in the dining room around the corner of the bar. We get a selection of dailies in, too, if you like to read while you breakfast. Do you need dinner tonight?"

"We do, actually," said Leonard, handing over his business credit card. "Ade? Have you chosen?"

They ordered food, this time Adrian opting for local fish with chunky chips while Leonard went for the house special of lamb hotpot. Once they placed their order, Mrs Jones called out something in what sounded like Welsh down the corridor. Within seconds a big bear of a man wearing a white chef's apron appeared. Blind to Leonard, he gave Adrian a lingering once-over, smiled and nodded once. Leonard felt a pang of annoyance and drained a good third of his pint. Out of the corner of his eye, he saw the landlady pointing a finger between Leonard and Adrian before reciting something in Welsh which he assumed to be their order. After she made eye contact with him and nodded out into the saloon area, Leonard got the message and led them over to seats at a table near the open fire. Before sitting, Adrian put his drink on the table and quickly excused himself to use the restroom, a move which had Leonard feeling another stab of irritation. Was he going to chat up the chef? But he returned too swiftly. Leonard sensed a tension in Adrian but had no idea how to ask. Fortunately, the food arrived, generous portions that had Adrian's eyes widening. After silently swapping condiments and sauces, they both fell to enjoying their meal. Finally, Adrian spoke.

"Do you think we should have checked other options? Other hotels?"

Leonard stopped eating and gave him his full attention.

"Doubt there are any, Ade. Not this late in the day. Look, I know the one-room situation isn't perfect, but this place is otherwise ideal. We're about ten to fifteen miles from the location of the house. We won't find anywhere closer. Or do you have a problem sharing?"

"No, it's not that. I—I just don't want you to be uncomfortable. And if we're going to share a room, then there are a few things you ought to know about me." Adrian had stopped eating. His eyes fixed firmly onto his plate of food as he spoke.

"Go on."

"For starters, I snore."

"Yes, well. Join the club. Luckily, I have earplugs."

Kris had snored. At first, the sound had kept Leonard awake. Even with earplugs, he had still been able to hear the droning. Ironically, when Kris passed away, Leonard hadn't been able sleep due to the *absence* of snoring. A friend once likened the situation to people who complain about living near busy roads or motorways, who then find sleeping difficult when they stay in quiet places like the suburbs or the countryside.

"I—I'm also gay."

The comment caught Leonard unprepared, and he almost laughed but could see by Adrian's troubled face his difficulty at expressing the fact. Leonard answered softly.

"And?"

Adrian looked up at him.

"And I thought you ought to know. I don't normally tell people outright, although I don't hide the fact, either. But then I don't usually share hotel rooms with friends. Straight friends, I mean..."

Adrian appeared to be struggling over something Leonard already knew. But to tell him he knew might give the impression he listened to idle gossip. Instead, he leant forwards, placing his elbows on the table. To lighten the mood he reached over, snatched a chip from

Adrian's plate and popped the whole thing in his mouth.

"Seriously? That's what's worrying you?"

"Some guys can get funny when I tell them. And I didn't want to make things awkward between us."

"Do you take me for one of those narrow-minded idiots, Ade? It's cool. Look, unless you're about to confess to having a psychological condition that involves you sleepwalking and murdering roommates in their sleep, then we're good."

Adrian smiled with relief before narrowing his eyes at Leonard's hand.

"Fair warning, though. You pinch any more chips off my plate and you might want to consider sleeping with one eye open tonight. Just saying."

Leonard laughed aloud. Seeing the tension drain from Adrian's shoulders, he almost let on about his own orientation. Surely that would be for the best all round so they could loosen up around each other? Then again, maybe coming clean might make sharing the room even more uncomfortable. Adrian had, after all, called him a 'straight friend', so he had no idea about Leonard being gay. What also didn't help was the intense attraction he had developed for Adrian. Even if he hadn't shown anything knowingly, Adrian would surely guess by the little tells he couldn't help making, staring at Adrian's chest, or freckles, or his thick muscular arms and thighs. If he came clean all that might change and make this situation even more awkward, especially if he wasn't Adrian's type. More importantly, he had invited Adrian along in his professional capacity, to survey the farmhouse and give him an expert opinion, not to be his bedmate.

Besides, if anything between them were to happen, it would be doomed from the start. Adrian lived and worked in Drayton, Leonard in London. Maybe the physical distance didn't matter, but Leonard knew himself well enough to know he could never survive on a diet of daily telephone calls and text messages and the occasional weekend hook-up. Moreover, Leonard had never been a casual, one-night stand guy. Kris had been his first and only lover. If he decided to jump, he did so with both feet the whole way and expected a partner to do the same—no half measures.

"Are you okay, Lenny? I thought I'd lost you there for a moment. Having second thoughts?"

Leonard, who hadn't realised he'd zoned out, lost in thought, stared up into Adrian's eyes.

"No, but… Have I just been a complete knobhead? Did you want your own room because you're looking to get lucky over the next few days? I was, and still am, totally fine with sharing, but I didn't even consult you when I said yes, which is wrong of me. I hate to think I've just pissed on your—"

This time Adrian burst into laughter.

"What?" asked Leonard.

"You haven't pissed on anything. Genuinely, Lenny, my concern was for you. But if you're fine then let's leave it there. You can use your earplugs, and I promise I won't murder you as long as you don't touch any more of my chips. Are we okay?"

"We are. But remind me to consult you in future. I tend to travel on my own, so I usually jump in and make snap decisions. Okay, so back to business. Can I suggest an early start tomorrow? Are you okay to get up at seven-thirty?"

"Not a problem. And I'm happy to navigate again if you want. Do you have that picture of the place we're trying to find?"

From his jacket pocket, Leonard pulled the envelope given to him by Mr Dawson and pulled out the copy of the photograph handing it to Adrian.

"I have no idea how long ago that was taken."

"Have you checked whether the place exists on GPS? Or are we going to be playing this by ear?"

Right then, the landlady came to their table to collect their plates and Leonard used the opportunity to talk to her.

"Mrs Llewellyn. We're going to take the room. But can we have a quick word? Just need some information about the local area."

"Of course, dear. Be my pleasure. Not exactly rushed off our feet tonight. And you can call me Megan, if you prefer. Whenever I hear someone calling for Mrs Llewellyn, I expect to see the in-laws coming around the corner to scold me."

Leonard pulled out a chair for her to sit. First off all, she took the dirty plates away and dropped them off at the bar before returning.

"So a quick question," said Leonard as she took a seat. "How well do you know the area?"

"How well do I—?" she began, with a chuckle. "Better than most alive, I'd say. I've lived here in this pub with my folks all my life, at least up until I married. Twenty-five I was. Went to live with Roger's folks in Vancouver running his family's hotel until they sold up. Then we decided to come back and take over this place because my mum and dad wanted to retire. Been running the place ever since. So yes, I know the area very well, and most of the people who live here. What do you need to know?"

"I've inherited a house down this way." Leonard nodded to the photograph in Adrian's hands, and he placed the sheet on the table. "A farmhouse called Bryn Bach in—"

Leonard noticed the slight surprise in Mrs Llewellyn's eyes as she finished his sentence.

"Bryn Bach in Disserth? Yes, I know the place well. The owners—previous owners now, I suppose—used to come up from Bristol every summer. Sometimes at Easter, too. Mike and Millicent Darlington. Had three young-uns, one older boy and a twin boy and girl. They relatives of yours?"

"Mrs Darlington is my aunt, my late father's sister. After my grandfather died—he was the rightful owner—he left the house to my father, and Dad left it to me. We're going to look the place over tomorrow, so if you can help point us in the right direction, that would be really helpful."

Mrs Llewellyn got up, waddled to the bar and brought back a small tourist map.

"Good job you asked. The place is a nuisance to find unless you know what you're looking for."

"We've got GPS," said Adrian, holding up his phone. Mrs Llewellyn glanced at the phone and snorted.

"Good luck with that, dear. You'll be lucky to get a phone signal down that way, let alone directions. Look, I'll write you out the route with landmarks. That should get you close enough. It's the only house on the lane so once you find that, you're there."

As she wrote on the map and marked a few prominent spots along the way, she also talked about the Darlingtons.

"Loved this part of the world, they did. If not for the husband's sales job back in Bristol — they often came here without him because he was so busy — I think they might have thought about settling here. Every Sunday, they'd go to church and end up in here in the pub afterwards for a roast lunch. Her eldest came here a couple of times on his own. Loved the place, he did. Such a shame what happened to him."

"What did happen?"

"You don't know? Maybe it's not my place — "

"My mother said he took his own life, but she didn't know any details. Mainly because my father and his sister — my aunt — didn't get along. So I know very little about any of my cousins. I only met her and my cousin Matthew for the first time at the funeral for my father."

"Did you know your grandfather?"

"Grandpa George? Yes, I met him when we were kids. Not often, because we lived so far away. I think Dad felt guilty after Grandma passed away. So we'd go see him at least a couple of times a year."

"George and Rene Day. Yes, they used to own the house in Disserth. My mum used to talk about them. So your dad would have been Colin?"

"That's right."

Leonard realised Mrs Llewellyn, rather than being curious, was testing him, to make sure she had the right person.

"Your cousin, Luke, hanged himself. His father and brother Matthew found him. Terrible business. Twenty something years old, bright as a new star and everything to live for. Came as a huge shock to all of them, as you can imagine. Not much happens around here, so the incident touched everyone."

The same oddly detached grief he had experienced when his mother first told him rippled through Leonard again. Luke, his own flesh and blood, would probably have been less than ten years older than him. And something had driven him to take his own life. As a child he had always believed he came from an unremarkable family. Yet something terrible had happened to his cousin to make him end his life. While he grappled with the notion, he barely heard Adrian ask a question.

"Did he leave a note or anything?"

"Of sorts, according to his father. A piece of paper with a few words written in Luke's hand. Taken from the Bible, we think." She recited them slowly and solemnly. "Funny the things we remember, isn't it?"

Leonard felt a deep sadness. Clearly, the words had meant something to Luke.

"Those words are not from the Bible," said Adrian, surprising Leonard. "Although I can understand how you might think so. The line was penned by Wilfred Owen, one of the war poets. It's from a poem called 'At a Calvary Near the Ancre,' in which he likens the battlefields of the Great War to the crucifixion of Christ. The last verse has those lines which, I believe, are about the soldiers in the Great War who selflessly laid down their lives."

"You're a religious man?" asked Mrs Llewellyn, an eyebrow raised at Adrian.

"Not so much. But my father was a minister, and I had an old friend I used to read to because of his failing eyesight. He loved the war poets. And even though I wouldn't call myself a religious person, there are certain passages from the Bible that resonate — "

"But why?" Leonard heard himself say. "Why did he do it?"

Mrs Llewellyn's attention returned to Leonard and she appeared genuinely moved.

"Nobody knew, dear. To this day the whole thing's a mystery. Last time I saw them all together was the year before I got married and moved abroad, and everyone seemed in good spirits, especially Luke, who would have been around fifteen. Of them all, he was the most friendly and charming. And a handsome lad, too. Whenever they came into town, many a young girl in the village only had eyes for him."

"Did he have friends here? Or did he mainly stick with the family?"

"He had a couple of really close friends. Gang of Four, they called themselves. Good kids, too. Freya and Howie Williams, both older, and Pippa White, the youngest of the group. I got the impression Luke enjoyed time away from his family. Don't get me wrong. His sister was fine — quiet, but polite — but the twin brother was an odd sort. Harmless enough, but...odd. Looking back, I think he probably suffered from an undiagnosed form of autism. And his mother could be overbearing if you know what I mean? The younger son stuck to her apron strings like a leech. Not sure I ever saw him smile."

To Leonard, that sounded exactly like the Matthew he had met.

"After the ordeal," continued Mrs Llewellyn, "they rarely came back to the house. Understandable really. Why would they want to stay in a house where their eldest had hanged himself from a bedroom light fitting."

"He killed himself in Bryn Bach?" asked Leonard, aghast. That part of the story had not registered.

"Yes, dear. Didn't I say? They hadn't heard from him for two or three weeks, contacted everyone he knew locally and searched the places he used to visit out in Clifton. Eventually, the father and brother came down here and found him in one of the bedrooms. Had to deal with the whole aftermath with the police and emergency services. Millicent drove down later, to be with him and help out. As for the father — Mum said she'd never seen a man so utterly lost and defeated in her whole life. After that, we never saw them. Well, sometimes the brother would come, but only to check the place over, as I heard it."

Leonard began to understand why his aunt might want to keep the place, rather than have strangers living in the house where her first-born had killed himself. How on earth did a mother manage to console herself after such a dreadful tragedy?

"I'd better start clearing up," said Mrs Llewellyn, standing up from the table. "What time do think you'll have breakfast in the morning?"

"We're planning an early start," said Leonard. "How does eight sound?"

"Perfect," said Mrs Llewellyn. "And as you're our only guests, I'll cook breakfast to order tomorrow."

"Thanks for your help, Mrs Llewell — Megan," said Leonard. "I know it's early, but I'm ready to turn in after that long drive. How about you, Ade?"

"Yeah, me too. But you go on up while I finish my drink and then sign for our food and drinks."

"Don't let him pay for anything, Megan," said Leonard, to an amused Mrs Llewellyn. "Put everything on the room bill. Remember you're doing me a favour here, Ade, so I'm paying all your expenses. And I don't want any arguments."

"Whatever you say. Just make sure you leave the room door unlocked for me."

Leonard felt sure Adrian was being a gentleman, wanting to give him time to change and get into bed without worrying about Adrian being in the room. At some point he needed to clear the air with his new friend.

After the long drive and with a couple of pints of ale inside him, he already felt exhausted. He used the bathroom without showering, just a quick face wash before climbing into bed and checking his phone.

He had no idea when he fell asleep or what time Adrian returned, but woke the next morning with the mobile phone still sitting next to his pillow and Adrian in the bed across from him, his broad back on view.

Chapter Eight

Cottage

Adrian woke refreshed but disorientated to the sound of running water. Once his brain made sense of the unfamiliar surroundings, he looked to the bedside table, where the LED lights of the digital clock read seven-twenty. At first, he assumed the noise came from the drone of persistent rainy weather outside the darkened window. After a few moments, he heard variations in the resonance of the falling water, along with a familiar tuneless humming, and only then noticed the empty bed across from his.

Lenny had hit the shower already. Almost by unspoken agreement, they'd chosen to move carefully around each other. The previous night Adrian had purposely stayed behind for another drink, and chatted more to the landlady about the local area. Tiredness had not really been an issue for him, having spent all day in the passenger seat, but he wanted to give Lenny time to get ready for bed before he came into the room and locked up.

Still wearing his tee and sweatpants, he pulled himself into a sitting position at the side of the bed and scrubbed a hand through his short hair. Despite the pervasive smell of paint and the acrid odour of an industrial adhesive caulk odour he had used professionally when fitting bathrooms, he had still managed to sleep like a log.

The night before, he had spotted a small kettle sitting on top of the free-standing fridge. In preparation for the morning, he had filled the device with water and placed two empty mugs to one side. With Lenny still in the bathroom, and unsure whether to make him tea or coffee, Adrian opened a single coffee sachet and poured in the grains. Checking the fridge, he smiled when he saw the hotel had provided a half-pint carton of fresh milk. Coffee mug nursed in his hands, Adrian returned to sitting with his feet up on the bed and flicked through channels on the room television until he landed on a news station.

"Smells good."

As Adrian finished the last of his coffee, Lenny appeared in the doorway to the bathroom. Wearing a white bath robe, he rubbed his hair dry with a small towel. Even in the towelling gown that reached his knees he looked good, the dark hair of his chest enticingly visible. Adrian couldn't help giving him a full appraisal.

"Didn't know if you took tea or coffee."

"Nothing for me. Why don't you go and shower? Then we should head down and have a huge breakfast with a decent brand of tea before we get going. Not sure we'll eat again until tonight."

"Actually, after you came up last night, I stayed and asked Mrs Llewellyn to arrange flasks of coffee and tea and packed lunches. To take with us. Wasn't sure there would be any shops or other places to eat."

"See? I knew there was a reason for bringing you along. Now go and do your business while I get dressed."

"Will do," said Adrian, standing up from the bed and stretching. "And we're going to need a lot of waterproofs today, by the sound of the weather outside the window."

* * * *

Lenny had been spot on about the distance. With Mrs Llewellyn's directions and helpful landmarks that took them down a series of narrow winding lanes, they found the track leading to the farmhouse in about half an hour. Finding the property was another challenge altogether. Even with the GPS running, they drove past the entrance to Bryn Bach three times.

Patchy satellite coverage in that part of the world only made matters worse. Even with the SUV stationary, the blue dot representing their car moved around erratically like a flying insect trying to decide where to land. The lane itself—more of a dirt track bordered by overgrown shrubs and trees—was only wide enough to take one car and provided no signposting. Coming to a dead end, Lenny displayed skilful driving with smooth three-point turn, avoiding dropping the car into ditches on either side of the track.

Adrian had to put the light on in the car to study the picture Lenny had printed off. Nothing appeared familiar. The photograph of the cottage had been taken many years ago on a beautiful summer's day. Hedgerows and trees seemed to be well-tended in the picture. Today, even without being disadvantaged by the dreadful weather and the dull light, greenery crept into the lane, wild and unkempt.

When a streak of lightning flooded the road like a flashbulb going off, Adrian spotted their first clue. A bush had covered most of the white signpost to the farmhouse, but the sudden incandescence illuminated the wooden entrance to a driveway. Three long vertical slats of wood had a saltire diagonal cross, holding them together, while a small waist-high garden gate for those on foot sat fixed on the right side. At any other time Adrian would have shrugged off the structure as an old gate to a farmer's field. Putting a hand on Lenny's forearm, he told him to stop the car.

Clad in his well-used yellow waterproof jacket and trousers, Adrian jumped out into the downpour. After pulling back branches of the bush to show Lenny the sign, lit now by the car's headlights, he went over, unhooked the rusty latch and opened wide the long gate.

As Lenny pulled the SUV alongside, he lowered the window and leant out.

"Well spotted, Ade. We may as well leave the gate open. Nobody's going to find themselves down this way unless the poor sods are lost. And if that happens, I'll be only too pleased to help. We can close up on our way out."

Adrian nodded and got back into the car, even though he had an innate discomfort at leaving the gate open. Closing farm gates had been drummed into him as a young kid by his parents and teachers whenever they visited farms around Drayton.

The short gravel driveway sloped gently down. Untamed bushes and small trees on either side hid the house. Behind a sharp bend, the structure came into view. Due to the endless rain and gloom, the farmhouse appeared like something out of a horror movie, with its slick grey walls and darkened windows. Weeds overflowed from square planter boxes either side of the front door, flaky remnants of white paint barely visible.

They parked up right outside the front porch because of the rain, which hissed loudly on the gravel as Adrian pushed the door open. Both of them jumped down at the same moment. Leonard dashed for cover while Adrian took time to survey the house. Even with the reduced visibility, the building seemed sound.

"Come on, then," came Leonard's voice. "First impressions. Tell me what you think?"

"Nice." Adrian strolled to the far end of the house, following the line where the slate roof met the guttering. Large sash windows each composed of twelve square panes sat either side of the front door, while three smaller versions ran above, along the upper floor. "Very nice indeed."

"So not some pile of old rubble, as my cousin Matthew said?"

"Absolutely not. At a rough guess, Lenny, I reckon this place would have been built around the mid-eighteen-hundreds. No earlier. Something I can tell you beyond doubt right now is that Bryn Bach was never designed to be a farmhouse. Apart from there being no outhouses anywhere nearby and no direct access to fields, the place was carefully designed, either as a permanent home or a holiday hideaway for someone with money."

"Interesting. How can you tell?"

Adrian turned around and looked back at Lenny in his bright blue cagoule with the hood covering his upper face. Even without seeing his eyes, Adrian noticed Lenny's handsomely smirking mouth. Was he testing him? Surely Lenny knew more about historic properties than anyone. Adrian knew buildings instinctively, and, without a doubt, Bryn Bach had been designed by the hand of an architect.

"I know my expertise lends itself more to modern construction, but having worked in and around Norwich, you can't help picking up a few things about old buildings. Traditional farmhouses, for example, were built to be functional. Most were single storey and built by the farmer and anyone he could rope in to help. Old dwellings — called longhouses — provided shelter for both the family and their livestock, all living under the same roof. Can you imagine the smell? I can probably point a few out to you on the drive home. Those ones had solid walls of natural materials like stone, earth and wood and used lime for mortars and renders. Earlier ones had thatched roofs, but later on they used the more efficient slate, like this house. These days they're easy to recognise because they look as though they're ready to fall over.

"The same can't be said of this house," continued Adrian, taking a step back and, despite the rain, staring up at the house and pointing out features. "This building has pedigree. I know the façade appears older — flinty stone in the wall construction — but that's by careful design rather than necessity. Not just that, but this was built into a slope by engineers, which is not something your average farmer would have dared consider. At least not unless he had no choice and didn't mind running the risk of the whole thing sliding down the hill in the middle of the night. Especially in this kind of weather, which seems pretty common in this part of the country."

"I see what you mean," said Lenny. "This house does seem pretty solid, doesn't it? Someone spent money on getting the design right. I wonder who originally had it built."

"Look at those beautiful brick chimney stacks at either end. Definitely Victorian. Designed and integrated, not tacked onto the structure. Features have been carefully planned and incorporated. At a guess, I'd say the slate roof and stonework are sympathetic design features, locally sourced materials to make the structure blend into the countryside. Even the front door is larger than most you would see on local cottages. The classic portico over the door is typical of the era and complements the other house materials. There's nothing shoddy or simply functional about this workmanship. The sash windows, cast iron guttering and downpipes could have been installed later, but I'd bet money they're original. I'll also be interested to see the interior layout."

"Come on, then. I suppose we'd better go inside."

"Any chance we can take a look around the back first?"

Adrian had noticed an overgrown path of rough stone blocks leading to the back of the building and indicated the direction with his hand.

"Lead the way," said Lenny.

At the back of the house, tall French doors opened onto a sizeable patio area, moss-covered concrete slabs with grass and weeds rising in the gaps, all bordered by a shallow brick wall. Half a dozen wide stone steps in the middle with an ornate stone handrail led down into an overgrown back garden. Towards the back, the top of a rusted iron frame of a child's swing rose above the undergrowth. Beyond that, the beautiful Welsh countryside provided a stunning panorama. Adrian reaffirmed his original assumption that the house had never been a working farmhouse.

"Well, for a start, this garden's going to need levelling," he said, before turning and appraising the back of the house. "Windows appear sound on first inspection, but I'd be concerned about the guttering, which looks to be blocked with leaves and overflowing with moss in places. Hopefully that hasn't affected the interior walls with damp."

"My cousin mentioned coming down here every year to check the place over. Not sure what he did, exactly."

"I can see how the family would have loved the garden," said Adrian, looking out to the view again. "Not only the remote location, but the garden alone is a beautiful, safe space for kids."

"Yes, you're right. If I'd holidayed here, I'm sure I would have fond memories, too. Maybe my aunt has a point. Let's go and have look inside."

Adrian trailed behind Lenny on their way back down the path. Entering behind him through the front door, Adrian had to stop for a moment while Lenny picked up a pile of mail from the floor. Adrian looked down the corridor into the gloom, wishing he had brought a torch with him.

"At least the postman knows where to find the place," said Adrian.

In front of him, Lenny laughed softly. He used the light from his phone to check through a couple of the items. Stopping at one of them, he tore open the envelope.

"Will you look at this," he said, waving a sheet of paper at Adrian. "It's a bill from the electricity company in my dad's name. Looks as though he pays all the bills automatically through my parents' joint account. Can you try the light?"

Adrian reached over and tried the switch, which came on instantly, flooding the hallway with light.

"That's going to make checking the place over a little easier," said Adrian. "I was going to ask if you had a torch in the car. But we ought to make sure the electricity is switched off when we leave. This house would make a perfect home for squatters."

As they moved forwards, the scents of dust and neglect hit Adrian. A narrow staircase with a thin worn carpet led upstairs, while doors led off either side at the front and one down a narrow corridor to the back of the house. Leonard took the first door on the right and flicked on a light to reveal a spacious room that ran the length of the building, with a large fireplace in the centre.

Without furniture, the huge space appeared abandoned and soulless. Apart from the linoleum flooring — the only touch of colour in faded green and grey — the walls and ceiling had been painted in powdery matte white paint, shadowy cobwebs filling the corners.

"Bloody hell. Looks as inviting as a doctor's surgery," said Lenny, somewhat unkindly.

"Don't look at what it is, look at what it could be, Lenny. That fireplace, for example. With that old three-bar electric fire it looks like something my great-grandmother would have considered hi-tech. And why paint everything white? Beneath a couple of coats of paint, I'll bet there's an old black-iron fireplace, and those painted-over tiles are probably originals. I doubt you'd be able to have a real fire now — chimney flues will be blocked off for sure — but there are plenty of gas fires produced these days that resemble coal or log fires. Odd, though. Usually there'd be alcoves either side of the chimney stack, not flat, flush walls."

Adrian went over, tapped his knuckle on the wall on the right side of the fireplace and produced a hollow clunking sound.

"Plywood. Maybe the previous owner did that to make things easier when they wanted to wallpaper or repaint. Shame though. Little features like alcoves with armchairs or places to showcase an antique chest of drawers are focal points. Looks as though they wanted this place as low maintenance as possible, which makes sense if it was a holiday home. Even with all that, the main thing that strikes me straight away is the light. I know it's a bloody awful day, but look how much daylight comes into the place from the front and back. Amazing. Can you imagine this place on a summer's day?"

For the first time since they had entered the room, Adrian turned to look at Lenny. Arms folded, his glare followed the line of old linoleum, which had begun to crack and peel away from the skirting board.

"Hey, Lenny," said Adrian, catching Lenny's attention. "Stop nitpicking and see the bigger picture."

"Have you noticed what's missing?"

Adrian looked at the wide-open space, up at the ceiling with beautiful coving and picture rail. Even decorative plaster moulded roses around the light fittings.

"I'm not following."

"Why is there no furniture? Did my aunt not approve of leaving fixtures in the house?"

"Is there supposed to be furniture? Maybe check with your solicitor, in case there's an inventory," said Adrian. "Perhaps it's in storage. She may have worried about burglars breaking in and stealing things."

"Yeah, I guess so."

"Come on, Lenny. Let's see what state the kitchen's in."

Adrian's suggestion had been meant to get Lenny away from the main room and possibly brighten his mood, but entering the rounded archway into the kitchen left Adrian speechless. Probably last remodelled in the eighties — maybe before that even — the long room had teal-painted units and kitchen backsplash tiles in orange and brown that might have been tasteful once, but Adrian seriously doubted it. Nevertheless, a couple of things stood out for Adrian. An original fixture, the square sink of thick white porcelain appeared original and, on a quick inspection, flawless. If Lenny did decide to keep the house, the basin had to stay, Adrian would make sure of that.

All of the countertops had updated electrical sockets. Some houses he had worked on in Drayton had old round pin- plug sockets. On the plus side, this meant Lenny might not need to rewire the whole house.

Also, the ancient refrigerator was almost as tall as Leonard, and the four-ring gas stove and oven, although old and, in all honesty in need of replacement, looked in working order.

Adrian walked over and opened the fridge door, an action he instantly regretted and he slammed the thing shut. By then the acrid smell of staleness had filled the air.

"We're going to have to give that a thorough clean before we switch the thing on to see if it works. If you want to keep it, that is."

"It'll do for now. But put cleaning equipment down on your mental list."

"Done. How about we take a look upstairs."

Upstairs turned out to be pretty standard with minimal decoration. Two larger bedrooms and a smaller one, together with a family bathroom. Each of the rooms had similar metal bed frames with stain-mottled mattresses that had seen better days.

"These are king-sized frames. Nothing special, cast iron, robust enough," said Adrian. After surveying the room, he lifted the corner of a mattress to check the state of the base, a criss-cross of metal links. He had seen similar designs in some of the houses he had renovated, sturdy and well made. When he turned to Lenny to speak, he noticed him on the far side of the bed and hesitated. Lenny scanned the light fitting before moving towards the window at the view beyond.

"Amazing sight, isn't it?" said Adrian. "Even with those storm clouds."

Lenny didn't answer but kept his gaze on the panoramic scene in the distance. Eventually, when he spoke, his voice sounded strange, soft but troubled.

"Do you think this is where he did it? Luke?"

Adrian hadn't thought about the cousin, had been so caught up with the features and condition of the building he had forgotten about the story told them the previous evening. Lenny continued standing there, his arms folded around his stomach, staring out of the window. Adrian couldn't help the compassion that hit him. Without thinking, he moved over and put his hand on Lenny's right shoulder and squeezed gently.

"I wonder," Lenny continued. "If we'd had the chance to know each other, would we have been friends? Would I have been someone he could have talked to?"

"Were you around the same age?"

"He was older. There would have been about eight years between us."

"No disrespect, mate, but I can't imagine sixteen-year-olds of any generation confiding in an eight-year-old."

"Yeah, you probably have a point. I can't help wondering what might have happened if I'd —"

"You can't think like that, Lenny. What happened, happened. It's in the past and all the 'what-ifs' in the world will never change a thing."

Lenny's head fell forward then, and Adrian felt like pulling him into a hug but instead left his hand on his shoulder.

"I just hate to think of him being so miserable, so lonely and desperate that the only solution left to him was to take his life."

"Didn't the landlady say he had friends locally?"

"She did. You're right. I wonder if any of them are still around?"

"Ask her later. Come on, buddy," said Adrian, squeezing Lenny's shoulder again before letting go. "No point dwelling on the past. He's no longer in pain. Hey, let's go and see what kind of state the bathroom's in."

Fortunately, the bathroom provided no nasty surprises, apart from being dusty and dated like the rest of the rooms. Someone had chosen a hard plastic bathtub — a full-length tub in light pink surrounded by a pine frame — next to a small matching hand basin and matching toilet. Adrian quickly located and turned on the water main. From the remains left in the cistern, the toilet flushed easily, and the sink water drained away instantly. Once again linoleum had been used to cover the floors, this time a deep forest green, cracked and splintered in places. Everything would need updating should anyone want to buy the home. Adrian watched amused at the disgust on Leonard's face when Adrian turned on the sink tap, and heard a choking gurgle as light brown water coughed and spat a couple of times before running clean and clear.

"Why in the name of good taste would someone choose a matching pink bathroom suite?" asked Lenny. "Do you think they were colour-blind?"

"You have an issue with the colour pink?"

Lenny grinned then.

"Not in the slightest. Just not something I would have in my bathroom."

"But orange and brown tiles in the kitchen are fine? Honestly, Lenny, I'm beginning to think your family had taste issues. I hope it's not hereditary."

Lenny laughed aloud.

"Come on, Ade, you must admit. Plastic tubs alone are bad enough. Plastic tubs in pink should be made illegal."

"What can I say? Maybe they had a special offer on bathroom suites back in the day. Or maybe it was all the rage in Wales back in the seventies or eighties. Who knows? I told you. Look at what it *could* be. First off, this bathroom space is huge. You could either turn this into two smaller bathrooms and make one an en suite or create one amazing single bathroom. Although, if you're going to do route, I'd suggest putting a shower in here too and maybe a half bathroom downstairs."

Leonard always listened intently to Adrian's suggestions, this time with his hands on his hips while nodding and screwing his nose up at the bathroom furniture.

"Best of all, it's your house, so you get to have the first whack with a sledgehammer if you do decide to keep the place. Get rid of some of that mother tension."

"Never thought of that. Maybe you should have been a psychiatrist."

"Of course, the other alternative is to leave everything as it is and let your aunt, or whoever the new owners are, decide what they want to do."

"You know," said Lenny, stopping a moment and looking around, "in spite of the dreadful décor, I kind of love the vibe of the house. Even in this shitty weather. So I can only imagine how much better this would be in the sunshine and after a fresh coat of paint."

"You're going to keep her then?"

"What do you think?"

"Your choice, Lenny. But if you're asking my opinion, then I'd say you've got yourself a nice piece of real estate here. I bet you could have everything looking amazing if you're prepared to spend a bit of money."

"I know what you mean. And that's not the issue. It's whether I have the time to take on a new project."

Adrian watched as Lenny went over to the bathtub and turned on a tap, then checked the connection to the shower over the tub. Satisfied, he sat down on the edge and critically surveyed the whole room. Right at that moment, the ringtone of the song Master and Servant by Depeche Mode sounded on Lenny's phone. Even before he pulled out his phone from his jeans pocket, his eyes went to Adrian and briefly rose to the ceiling.

"Mother."

Adrian carried on looking around the room while Lenny took the call. He ran a hand over the pipes from the ceiling to the lavatory. Whoever had initially plumbed in the bathroom had not been professionals. Pipes ran outside the walls and along the floor, roughly painted over, with nothing concealed. While checking the work, Adrian couldn't help listening in to the call. After a while, he got the gist of the conversation. The aunt had been on the phone, pestering his mother about the farmhouse that was not a farmhouse.

"For heaven's sake, Mum. I've only just got here. Today is the first opportunity we've had to check the house over."

Adrian opened the wall cupboard in the corner which probably housed towels and other toiletries. A layer of dust covered all the shelves. They would need plenty of cleaning materials if Lenny decided to renovate.

"Well, if I'm going to be honest, I'm leaning more towards keeping rather than selling. Not only is it beautiful, but I know Dad used to come here for holidays as a kid. A lot of work is going to be needed, but I think it could turn out to be a good little investment."

Adrian smiled his agreement. Even the windows — lead-framed and cracked in places — could probably do with updating, but the potential was without doubt. The electrics would also need a thorough inspection, not something Adrian could do, but there was bound to be someone locally they could employ. Or better still, he could bring one of his reliable contacts from Norwich down for the week once they had gutted the place. Adrian could hear Lenny getting agitated by something his mother was saying.

"She said *what*?"

A moment passed before Lenny spoke again.

"Listen. If she keeps pestering you, stop answering her calls or give her my number. I'll be more than happy to speak to her if it means avoiding solicitors getting involved."

Adrian sat on the lid of the toilet and made no pretence about listening to the conversation.

"Fine. In which case I have my own solicitor. One I've been using for years."

Once again a short silence ensued, during which Lenny caught Adrian's eyes and mouthed a quick 'sorry'.

"Then you can tell her from me that the place is mine to do with what I want. If that means putting it up for sale or donating it to charity, then that's what I'll do. And if she really wants to start legal action, then please tell her to go right ahead. But she'd better bring her best game and get herself top representation. Because believe me, Mum, I *will*. As Dawson quite correctly stated, she's going to have a rough time if she goes down that route. Okay. Got to go. Bye, Mum."

After a few moments of thought, he turned to Adrian and thrust his phone away into his pocket. A fierce determination had replaced the usual calm expression, a look Adrian had never seen on Lenny's face before.

"Would you come down here and help me? I mean, would you be prepared to give me a quote on what needs to be done and work alongside me to do the renovations? Maybe provide me with some of your ideas and suggestions about how I could improve the place?"

"I'd be honoured. And I've already got some ideas of things you could do to modernise this place without losing its uniqueness. I'll make a few sketches when I get back. But right now, I'm going to fetch my notepad from the truck. Then we can continue making a list of what needs to be replaced and where any structural changes need to be made."

"Good idea," said Lenny, levelling his gaze at Adrian. "You'd think finding family you never knew you had would be a good thing. But it turns out my father was a better judge of character than I ever appreciated. And fuck it, not only for him, but for me, too. I've just this second made up my mind. I'm keeping Bryn Bach."

Chapter Nine

Confession

During their assessment of each room, and with a new resolve, Leonard felt a growing connection to the house. Adrian's continued enthusiasm and ideas for improvement helped. But knowing Leonard's father had holidayed there during his childhood, had probably spent happy, innocent days playing in the garden and going for local hikes, he felt an affinity with the place. Even the knowledge that a cousin had taken his life in one of the bedrooms did not deter him – it only made him more curious about a relative he had never known. According to Mrs Llewellyn, Luke had been at his happiest in Wales, in this house. And even though Leonard mentioned nothing to Adrian, the suicide note had left something of a mystery, one he wanted to try to solve.

Back downstairs, Adrian stood inside the arched door to the kitchen, his big hands on the hips of his blue overalls, surveying the walls and décor. Leonard admired his solid frame and quiet strength, the way he had effortlessly ripped up part of the linoleum before gently smoothing the palm of his bare hand along the surface to check the state of the floorboards, how he quickly and single-handedly hefted the king-sized mattress from the bed in the back bedroom before carefully positioning the stained mess against the wall. Strength and grace, traits Leonard found incredibly attractive.

"Let me just say right now that if for some batshit-crazy reason you decide to keep this kitchen as is, in another decade or two the design might—just *might*—become fashionable again."

Leonard snorted quietly and watched as Adrian went over and gently tugged open one of the lower cupboard doors, which instantly came away in his hand, the hinges rusted and broken.

"Or maybe not."

"Careful, cowboy. That's my kitchen you're destroying."

"And here's me thinking you had taste. It's only the top hinge. I can soon fix that back in place."

Adrian's humour kept him grounded. Admittedly, the kitchen had probably been left untouched for decades. Dull teal units with their stubborn doors, grease-speckled orange and brown kitchen tiles and sticky linoleum flooring of lemon and lime diamonds might have been tasteful for somebody once—but not anymore, and not for Leonard. He swore he felt a migraine coming on every time they stepped into the room.

"No, leave the door. And jot this down on your list. The whole kitchen needs ripping out. I'm thinking maybe we even take this wall down and open up the kitchen into the main living area. Lose the corridor altogether and put in a countertop island. What do you think?"

"I'd need to see the original floor plans to check if we're affecting any load-bearing walls," said Adrian. "But I don't think that would be a problem. And then you could put four-panel full-height sliding doors where the French doors are right now, open up the whole back of the house onto the patio, make the most of the view. You could brick up the back door in the kitchen leading into the garden then, use the space for kitchen units. There will be plenty more light coming into the house."

"Exactly what I'm thinking."

Strange really, but Adrian came up with ideas almost the instant a similar thought entered Leonard's head. They were most definitely on the same page.

"And promise me you're going to remove this plywood panelling either side of the fireplace," said Adrian. "Get the place back to its original setting. Every time I look, the eyesore makes me cringe. I'll bet money the chimney breast is either red brick or local flint that's been plastered over."

Adrian pointed out a spot by the fireplace, beside the picture rail, where panelling had split from the wall.

"And it looks as though the plywood is coming away already up there. Want me to yank that off now?"

"Steady on, Wreck-It Ralph. Let's wait until we have the right tools." When he peered over, Adrian had turned to look at him curiously. "I imagine when we come back next time there'll be plenty of mess to clear away. Let's not make any just yet. Hey, listen. In case I didn't make it clear, I want us to work on this project together on my spare weekends. I'd love to be able to clear a few weeks straight so we could just plough on, but I've been away from the business far too long already. And I'm going to need your guidance on what I can and can't do structurally. Other than that, we work alongside each other. Of course, I'll pay you, but I wanted to check you're okay with that?"

"Don't you want me to come down and keep things going during the week?"

"Not unless there are skilled jobs that I can't do. I want to be here to see the place transform with my own eyes, and know I've been a part of the renovation. Does that make sense?"

"As I said before, you're the boss, so you call the shots. I'm going to need professional help with some areas, such as taking down the wall between the living room and the kitchen and checking over the electrical wiring. Maybe I could do that on a weekday?"

"Absolutely. Just give me a heads-up. I'll get you a spare set of keys cut. And I need to come back to Drayton to tie up a few things with my mother next weekend, so maybe we can meet up again and drive here together. Now what about the staircase? Does that need repairing or replacing?"

"Are you kidding? That staircase is a work of art. Let's go check it out again."

On the way back to the stairs to the upper floor, Adrian pointed out the low rise and how stable the staircase was, no noticeable creaks or wobbly bannisters. Adrian had called it right. The essential structure of the place, at least, had been built by artisans, built to last.

"Beautiful piece of craftsmanship," said Adrian, once again verbalising Leonard's thoughts. "All we need is to sand off the paint, take everything back to the original wood and either treat the surface or maybe use a light varnish. And definitely get rid of that threadbare stair carpet."

Upstairs, at the back of the house, the bedroom overlooking the overgrown garden had a fantastic view of the countryside. Even on that bleak and stormy day, the scene through the large sash window took Leonard's breath away. Like the rest of the house, the room needed redecorating and furnishing, with only a simple mat on the floor and cast-iron double bed frame.

"I can't believe there's no other bedroom furniture. Do you really think your relatives put things into storage?"

"As I said, I have no idea. I might phone my mother, get her to ask my aunt. The way things are at the moment I don't want to talk to her unless I really need to. But I'm guessing they either didn't have any furniture — they only ever came here for short holidays — or gave what they had away if nobody was using the place. Based on the state of the kitchen and bathroom, I'm not sure I'd have wanted to keep anything they had anyway."

At some point, Leonard would need to buy furniture — or maybe choose from his online antique store — and perhaps arrange to have some sympathetic built-in storage included in the renovation. The same story applied to the two other bedrooms, the large one at the front and the small box room.

"Can I suggest that when we come back next weekend we stay here in the house?" said Adrian, out of the blue. "Get a feel for the place. If you're coming to Drayton anyway, maybe you could purchase a couple of new mattresses online from the big department store in Norwich. If I bring my truck next time, we can chuck them in the back for the drive down, then we can sleep in the house. I know it's not exactly five-star, but the bathroom works fine, the electricity's running — although we'll need to bring a couple of bulbs to replace those not working in the bathroom and the hallway. We'll also need some sheets and bedding. Downstairs is going to be a mess if we start down there — which would be my recommendation — so I suggest we bring the bare minimum. What do you think?"

"Sounds like you've got it all under control."

Adrian insisted they drag all three old mattresses downstairs near the front door, ready to put them in his truck for when they returned. They could dump them wherever local folk were allowed to dispose of unwanted items. Mrs Llewellyn at the pub would know.

While Leonard tested the water pressure in the bathroom and kitchen, Adrian managed to find a wooden stepladder in the old shed in the back garden and insisted on climbing into the loft space to examine the condition of the joists and rafters and check for leaks in the roof. Happily reporting back with good news, the loft only housing more dust and cobwebs, they continued the exploration of the house until the afternoon sun began to wane.

"Right," said Leonard, finding Adrian on his back on the floor of the kitchen, inspecting the water pipes. The man loved to get his hands dirty. "We're done here. I suggest we head back to the hotel and shower. And then I'm going to treat you to dinner at a steakhouse in town, one I found on my phone, a short walk from the hotel. My way of saying thank you."

Adrian seemed almost disappointed at having to stop working. Leonard noticed how animated and immersed he became when engaged in one task or another — a man in his element.

* * * *

The Italian steakhouse — a recently opened bistro with young inexperienced waiting staff, but a top-class chef — provided the perfect end to a long day. Leonard treated them to dinner and even ordered a nice bottle of Italian red. Adrian started with his usual pint of local beer but seemed to enjoy the wine, especially when Leonard held the bottle before him and began to inform him about the wine region. Abruzzo sat on the east coast of Italy, the red being a bottle of Montepulciano d'Abruzzo. He explained how the distinctive combination of blackberries and earthiness was believed to perfectly complement pasta and red meats. After only a few minutes, Adrian tumbled Leonard when he noticed him reading from the back label of the bottle.

During the meal, Adrian continued to enthuse about the house, the improvements Lenny should make to the property, and frankly, Leonard enjoyed listening to him.

"Honestly, Lenny, I'm with you all the way. Open up the kitchen into the main living area by taking out the corridor and make the whole place more communal. And that bathroom is huge. You've got enough space to install a decent-sized bath *and* a separate shower. I can visualise it already."

By the time they had finished the wine and Leonard had been brought a plain coffee — Adrian preferring another bottle of beer — and their cheesecakes arrived,

Leonard felt nicely relaxed. He noticed Adrian leaning back in his chair, sated, curiously eyeing Leonard.

"So come on. What's your story, Lenny? Married? Kids?"

Leonard stopped attacking the dessert and placed his fork down next to his plate to give Adrian his full attention.

"Do you know, you're the only person in the world who calls me Lenny."

Adrian's good-natured grin dissolved when no humour showed in Leonard's face.

"You don't like it? Why didn't you say?"

"It's not that I don't like it, so much. That particular version of my name brings back bad memories, that's all. Especially coming from you."

Leonard watched as Adrian drank from his pint, his confused gaze still peering inquisitively over the rim. Leonard decided the time had come to confront him.

"When we were at school, do you remember calling me 'Gay Lenny'? During my first week? You made the other kids around you laugh."

Adrian appeared baffled, clearly taken by surprise, his eyes darting away as he tried to search his memories. Eventually he brought his gaze back to Leonard and shook his head.

"I don't remember. That was a long time ago. Are you sure about this?"

Leonard nodded. Some things in his childhood he could never forget.

"During my first ever assembly. When the teachers were calling out names from the register. Mr Jennings called—"

"No, wait. Yes, I do remember. The first time I ever saw you. Teachers used to call the names in reverse order, yes? So instead of Leonard Day, he called you Day, Leonard. And I thought he'd called you Gay Leonard, so I frowned at him and said 'Gay Leonard'? I honestly thought he'd made a mistake. But of course, the idiots I used to hang around with thought I was cracking a joke. Jennings immediately told us to be quiet. Was that why you gave me the stink-eye every time I walked past you?"

"All those friends of yours called me Gay Lenny for the whole of the first term —"

"I don't remember —"

"Never when you were around, now I come to think of it. But even boys in my year, ones I didn't know, called me the same thing. It became a standing joke, the way kids pick up on stupid things like that."

"Oh my God, Lenny — uh, Leonard. I had no idea. If I had known, I would have told them to shut their mouths."

Instinctively, Leonard knew the truth of his words. The Adrian he had recently grown to know could never be inherently nasty or vindictive. Being so was simply not in his nature. Throughout the years, he had thought Adrian to be the culprit, the ringleader. In reality, he had simply misheard one of the teachers — an interesting lesson in how a simple misunderstanding in youth can form a lifelong perception.

"Yeah, I know you would have. And it's okay. You still get to call me Lenny. I've grown to like hearing the sound of it. And to be honest, after that first term, I used to ignore the idiots at school. Kept myself very much to myself."

"And you've been holding that in all these years? I always thought you didn't like me because of me being part West Indian."

"What?" Leonard felt genuine shock at Adrian's words. "Of course not. I'm not like that."

"That's what everyone says —"

"Ade! I'm really not. It's because you labelled me at school. Unwittingly, it seems. And honestly, I should have let it go by now, but seeing you in the pub when I returned to Drayton brought everything back."

"Well, if it's any help, I apologise for being a dick. And for not telling the other kids to shut up."

"You have nothing to apologise for. Besides, they called me out correctly on one thing."

"What do you mean?"

"I *am* gay."

Adrian pulled his glass away from his lip to stare at Leonard. After a few moments, a huge smile lit his face.

"Ah, well, mate. Joke's on me, now. Why didn't you say something earlier? When I came out to you?"

"Funnily enough, I thought about it. Especially when you struggled to explain about sharing the hotel room in your wonderfully diplomatic way. But I worried that if you knew I was gay too, sharing a room would be even more awkward and — hey, what?"

Opposite him, as Leonard had been speaking, Adrian had tipped his head back and begun laughing aloud.

"Couple of bloody idiots, the pair of us. My mother called it right. Men get worse at communicating as they get older."

Leonard grinned and shook his head. He agreed with Adrian. Throughout his life, the straight men he knew fell over themselves to avoid talking about his sexuality. Feeling as though they had grown closer through their confessions and also taking advantage of their laughter, Leonard decided to lead the conversation in a more personal direction.

"Did you ever have anyone special, Ade?"

"No," said Adrian, his humour gone, his tone flat and short. Leonard heard the hint of sadness in his voice. "Plenty of — um — encounters, especially in my twenties and thirties, but no keepers, if you know what I mean."

"I'm not just saying this to be nice — and because I need a decent and reliable builder — but honestly, Ade, I really find that really hard to believe. How old are you now?"

"Forty-nine."

"And you're still a catch. You're such a nice guy, with a warm personality and a great sense of humour. Oh, hang on a minute. Is this because of your fussiness? Because I heard your taste in music on the way down here. I mean, do you have a particular type or fetish? Must be over seven feet tall, Kenyan-Icelandic mix, Olympic stature, natural blond, ear and nose piercings, must have his own sex swing — "

"Yeah, all right, Lenny. If this is you getting your own back on me for the Gay Lenny thing then — "

"No, I'm serious. You're a good-looking bloke. I'm just stunned nobody else saw that in you, enough to want to keep you around."

At least Adrian's coy grin had returned at Leonard's words. But then, as his eyes seemed to lose their focus and he looked away, his smile slipped again.

"Mate, I had some very dark days during my late teens and early twenties. And after that, I just wanted things to be normal, to learn to like myself again before I even considered being with someone else for any length of time. And then, as time went on, I kind of got to like my own company. How about you? Did you have any relationships?"

Adrian didn't want to go into any more detail. That much was clear. Something had happened during those early years. Leonard vowed to himself that when they knew each other better, he would ask again. But right now he felt ready to talk about Kris. Adrian might be one of the few who would understand.

He explained how Kris — Krishna Goswami, both of his parents originally from New Delhi — had been an economics professor at his university in Bournemouth, twenty years his senior, and how they had clicked almost instantly. At first things had been innocent but clandestine — meetings in coffee shops to talk over study materials, but mostly to be in each other's company. Leonard had been the one to take things to the next level, pleasing Kris but also worrying him, knowing he had his position at the college to consider. They had only lived together after Leonard had graduated.

"We were together for fourteen years and lived under the same roof for ten of those. Until his death. He succumbed to pancreatic cancer at the age of only fifty-six. Everything happened so quickly. The cancer had already spread by the time he was diagnosed. His family knew nothing about us, so as soon as they did, they froze me out, didn't want anything to do with me. I honestly believe they thought I somehow gave him the cancer."

Leonard remembered the telephone conversation, watching helplessly as Kris tried to argue with his father but not having the strength. He remembered standing stunned as Kris agreed for them to come and fetch him before promising to call Leonard as soon as he managed to get himself settled. Leonard had argued with the parents and sister in their hallway, but he could tell he wasn't getting through to them.

"Apart from everything else, I think they saw me as a parasite, riding his relative prestige in academic circles, living off his money. If anyone had bothered checking, they'd have found I had my own independent wealth, through my start-up companies. But instead, they simply shut the door on me."

Despite numerous calls to the family home, and even to the hospital where Kris had initially been diagnosed, Leonard was met with stony silence. He had only met the sister and her husband one other time, four weeks later, when they'd turned up one Saturday morning to pick up Kris' clothes and personal belongings. The sister had the same stubborn streak he had seen in Kris and had told him nothing. In retrospect, he could have shut the door in their faces — would have been completely within his rights to do so — but one thing they'd had in common was an interest in Kris' well-being. When she had barged her way upstairs to rifle through Kris' things, Leonard had simply let her. The husband had stayed behind with Leonard, embarrassed, and appeared genuinely sorry for him. Poor guy, he had tried to help but had known very little, only that the family physician had begun palliative care and that they had quarantined Kris, locked him away in a room in the family home.

"I only found out a year later they had taken his cremated remains back to India, to be scattered in the Ganges River, but had commissioned a plaque in a garden of remembrance near their home in London. Fortunately, when we bought the house, Kris had insisted on using my name for legal purposes to give me sole possession, said he already owned his own and his sister's house. Maybe that was true, or perhaps he'd wanted to give me some insurance because of our age difference — it never became a topic of conversation — but whatever, that was the one thing the family couldn't take away from me when he died."

"I'm so sorry, Lenny."

"Happened so long ago. But it feels good talking. I only have a few close friends, but when we do get together, the last thing I want to do is burden them with this. Especially something that happened more than ten years ago — "

"Yeah, but some things stay with you for life."

Leonard sensed a true understanding in Adrian's sympathetic gaze. No doubt about it, he had his own story to tell.

"They do. And you never really get over things like that, they become a part of you. But since Kris, there's never been anyone serious for me."

"No seven-foot-five African-Scandinavian Olympic weightlifters take your fancy?"

Leonard chuckled along with Adrian. He took a sip of his coffee then cradled the cup in his hands.

"You know, that first year in high school, I used to come along to all the home games. I stood on the sidelines, usually hiding behind the other kids. Although I would never have told you so at the time, you were bloody incredible on the field."

By the widening of his eyes, Leonard could tell Adrian was genuinely surprised, his grin even betraying a little pleasure. All Leonard could remember was the Herculean and, frankly, sexy figure of Lamperton either wrestling another boy to the ground or standing stock-still, ready to convert a try and put the team comfortably in the lead. And all the time he'd thought this legend didn't like him, had considered Leonard as nothing more than an insignificant gay kid.

"Most of those games that season were played in the rain."

"They were," said Leonard. "I viewed most from beneath someone else's umbrella. But man, Ade, you were amazing, the way you ploughed through the opponents. All the kids in my year thought you would go on to play professionally."

Once again Adrian's smile slipped and he looked down at the rim of his beer bottle.

"Yeah, well. Some things are not meant to be," he said cryptically.

Leonard wanted to ask more but felt they had already shared enough that night.

"So, tomorrow," said Leonard, bringing things back down to earth, "depending on the weather and the traffic, we have a good five- to six-hour trip back. I suggest we head off around midday. How does that sound?"

"You're the boss."

"Not yet. But I will be next weekend, once you're on the clock. So let's head to the house tomorrow morning, take one last look around. Maybe snap some pictures on our phones. Then, you can tell me what equipment or materials you think we might need, so I can either buy or hire—"

"I think it's probably best if I do that. Then I'll invoice you later."

"Well, if you think that works better. And as long as you're not out of pocket."

"Trade discount. And let me put together a plan of work during the week. We're not going to get everything done in a weekend, but we can make a good start."

Leonard finished his coffee and paid the bill while Adrian slipped away to use the restroom. When he returned, Leonard already wore his coat, ready for the short walk back to the hotel. Adrian pulled his own from the back of the chair and slipped the garment around his shoulders.

"And if I haven't said so already, Ade, thanks for everything. For agreeing to accompany me, for your excellent observations and most importantly, for your enthusiasm. I know this is probably like any other job for you, but I've really enjoyed this weekend, really enjoyed your company."

Despite feeling a little awkward, Leonard felt the words had needed saying. If he had come to see the house on his own in the pouring rain, he would probably have had one quick look around and ended up selling the place to his aunt. Right now he felt an excited optimism about the site, and also felt as though he had made a new friend.

"Don't thank me yet," said Adrian as they stepped out into a rain-free evening and stopped on the pavement.

"Why's that?"

"You haven't heard the playlist I've picked out for the journey home yet."

Leonard stood and laughed, but then became serious when Adrian's face didn't return the humour.

"Should I be worried?" asked Leonard.

"Depends."

Adrian walked on ahead, but then stopped, spun around and folded his arms.

"How do you feel about ABBACulture Club?"

Chapter Ten

Renovation

Wednesday afternoon, Adrian lounged in his regular spot on the sofa with his bare feet up on his coffee table. For a change, the television remained switched off as it had been all week. After an early morning jog around the town followed by his indoor workout, and in between skimming a well-thumbed John Grisham thriller, he'd used his time to rough out some ideas for the renovation.

On the tabletop he had a large sketchpad with a roughly scaled design of the house in Wales and some suggested changes, based on their conversation on the way back from Disserth. Even as a kid he'd had a knack of drawing things from memory almost to scale. At his mother's insistence, he had framed three of his pictures of famous English landmarks — the Royal Pavilion in Brighton with its Indian architectural influence, the Tower of London, and the Royal Observatory in Greenwich — and hung them pride of place on his living room wall.

That morning alone he had completed designs for the bathroom in Wales to add to those for the kitchen and the bedrooms. Pleased with the results, he had snapped a copy of the draught kitchen plan on his phone and fired the preview off to Lenny that morning. Two thumbs up emojis followed by two words 'looks fantastic' had been returned. When they met up on Thursday, he was looking forward to showing Lenny the other designs .

He couldn't believe how much he had enjoyed the previous weekend and how much he anticipated heading back with Lenny on Friday. And the daily text message exchanges with Lenny to remind him of things he needed to bring or buy always ended with a humorous remark that had him smiling.

And that small change didn't escape his notice either. Just seeing Lenny's name appear on his phone sent a thrill through him. On Monday morning his waking dream had Lenny leaning against the bathroom door frame in the hotel, but this time with the bathrobe falling open to reveal his naked figure. Waking rock-hard and full of lust had led Adrian to take his erection in hand and pump out a release, spilling onto his stomach and chest. Not an unpleasant experience but one that had left him feeling a sense of guilt.

Like many areas of his life, Adrian had simplified his relationships. Men he liked but did not find attractive became friends. Those he found hot but did not particularly warm to—like Nick—became fuck buddies. And he made sure the two never met. The one or two who filled both requirements—rarer and rarer as he grew older—he would usually put on hold until they slotted naturally into one category, or avoid and eventually phase out of his life, even if they did demonstrate a mutual desire.

The cooling off period worked well for Adrian because misjudging a friendship for attraction was a mistake he would never make again.

Lenny had lived with a university professor, a respected member of the faculty. Why on earth would he want anything more than friendship? Besides, Lenny also had his own life and successful businesses to take care of back in London, so had no time for anything more.

No, Lenny fitted perfectly into the friends category.

And yet small gestures and throwaway comments had Adrian feeling confused, that something more lay beneath the surface.

On the way back from Wales they had agreed he would return on Thursday morning instead of Friday to check in with his mother and get her to sign some legal forms. At the same time, they would pick up mattresses and buy other items from the furniture store in Norwich and store them in the back of Adrian's truck, ready for their trip down on Friday morning.

Even with Lenny being busy in London—despite assurances to the contrary, he'd had a mound of work to catch up on—he still managed to check in with Adrian each day. As Adrian put the finishing touches to the third kitchen design, and as though reading his mind, his phone pinged with a message.

Lenny: Shopping tomorrow. Hope you made a list.

Adrian: And checked it twice. Gonna give your credit card a good workout. What time shall I pick you up?

Lenny: Ten too early?

Adrian: See you then. Text me your address.
Lenny: Sounds like a date.
Adrian: Well we are picking out bedding together.

The phone went quiet for a while, and Adrian worried he had gone too far, but he could see Lenny was typing. Eventually, another text pinged through.

Lenny: Always the funny guy. Thanks again for agreeing to do this, Ade. Make sure you give me invoices for everything this time around.
Adrian: Look forward to seeing you tomorrow.

Had he overstepped the mark? Maybe he should dial the chumminess down a notch or two. He didn't want to give Lenny the wrong idea and scare him away.

* * * *

"Is your mother okay?"
They had been shopping in the large department store in the centre of Norwich like an old married couple. Lenny had turned up dressed casually in a long-sleeved, old-fashioned rugby shirt in purple and yellow stripes, the style they don't seem to wear on the field anymore, and a pair of well-worn jeans and trainers that only made him look hotter. As soon as they'd set off from his mother's house, he told Adrian he had ordered the king-sized mattresses earlier in the week. They sat in the store's loading bay ready to be thrown onto the back of Adrian's truck. Both had the same idea when it came to bedding — something modest but comfortable. Four pillows — two for each bed — two king-sized quilts and covers in ivory for one

room, navy-blue for the other, together with matching sheets. Not particularly imaginative, but neutral enough so that whatever décor Lenny decided upon, they would still be useable.

"I usually don't see her more than twice a year, so it's been a bit overwhelming for her lately. And when I do turn up to get her to sign important documents, she reciprocates by handing me a list of things she needs doing. When I declined and told her I'm only here to pick you up and drive to Wales, she got a little antsy. As you saw."

"That explains the warm welcome."

"Sorry about that. If it's any consolation, my mother tends to be somewhat frosty with anyone she doesn't know. At least she offered you a cup of tea. And I have to say again, Ade, those sketches are amazing, even though I only glanced over them. Maybe you can talk me through them tonight over dinner without my mother hovering over us. To be honest, I could do with someone like you on my team, to give clients some quick, imaginative visuals of how something could look. Professional architects and even interior designers are exacting and take so damned long to produce anything, as well as being expensive. You've got a hidden talent going on there. You even managed to get a hum of approval from my mum."

Every time Lenny praised him about anything, a ripple of pleasure ran through Adrian. And Adrian had noticed, too, the way Lenny's mother had glanced at them with something bordering lukewarm interest as she'd handed him a mug of tea — even though he had asked for coffee.

"She probably gets lonely now your dad's not around."

"Yeah, I did think that. You know, when I got back to London this week I phoned her every day, like a dutiful son. On Wednesday she asked me to stop calling so often. Can you believe? But I know she sees a lot of my Aunt Marcie. She lives across the street and they seem to get on really well."

"Maybe I should introduce her to my mum?"

Lenny shook his head decisively.

"Incompatible. As soon as your mother mentioned anything about the church or religion my mother would call a cab."

Each of them pushed a shopping cart as they wandered into the electrical section, while Adrian checked his prepared list.

"But all joking aside, Lenny. If she needs anything doing like moving furniture or lifting boxes, manual kind of stuff, you could give her my number. She's met me now and I am local."

Lenny seemed to mull the idea over, and after a while smiled and nodded

"I'll let her know. That's a nice thought, Ade."

They walked on again in comfortable silence. Lenny steered them in the direction of the electrical equipment.

"So how has your week been?" asked Adrian absently.

"Pretty good. Everything seemed to run fine without me there. Mainly spent my time either proofreading contracts or meeting new clients. Isabelle had a couple of problems while I was away, but used her common sense to sort them out. Maybe not what I would have done, but everything got resolved. Sometimes I wonder if they need me there at all."

"Nah, that there's the sign of a good manager. They know you're at the end of a phone in case they need you, but they also know you're not breathing down their necks expecting them to do everything your way."

Partway down the aisle, they stopped at the lighting section while Adrian pulled out a selection of bulbs of varying wattage, including spares.

"Kettle," said Lenny. "We mustn't forget to buy a kettle."

"I've already packed mugs, tea bags, a jar of coffee, milk and sugar," said Adrian. "So, yes. An electric kettle is a necessity. I'm not sure I trust that gas stove."

After picking out a mid-priced kettle and a couple of long power extensions, they made their way to the towelling section. Adrian was determined to make sure the boiler and the shower above the bath worked, so insisted they needed to have at least a new towel each. He had even shopped for a new showerhead, a large container of shower gel, shampoo and a couple of packs of soap. Other bathroom accessories could wait until they'd finished renovating the bathroom. While Adrian picked towels out, Lenny began to fill him in on other developments.

"So I managed to get the number of the gardening company suggested by Mrs Llewellyn. That woman seems to know everyone in the area. One of their people went along to spec the place out, and they gave me a rough quote on clearing the front and back gardens and making the whole thing look more respectable. Very reasonable, actually, so one of their representatives is going to pop along and see us while we're there this weekend."

Adrian grinned then and noticed Lenny looking at him quizzically.

"What?"

"I thought I was the one fired up about this, sketching ideas of improvements, but seems like you've been doing a heap of things behind the scenes."

"Let me just clarify, Mr Lamperton. This is my house."

Adrian laughed at the mock-serious tone.

"I know, I know. But you have a hundred and one things on your plate at the moment, what with your businesses. While I'm sitting at home twiddling my thumbs, wishing for the weekend to come early."

"Yes, well. Turns out I'm truly getting into this personal project. There's something motivating and empowering about being able to do things the way I want them, instead of having to please a client. Especially when they come up with ludicrous ideas."

"I hear you there, brother."

"Right, come on," said Lenny. "Let's head for the checkout and then load the mattresses into your truck. I'm afraid I have to have dinner with my mother tonight, so I'll see you first thing in the morning. Don't be late."

"Six o'clock sharp."

* * * *

Agreeing to set off early in the morning on Friday had been an excellent plan. Beating much of the rush-hour traffic, Leonard drove his vehicle and led the way. With clear weather and lighter traffic than the weekend before, they arrived at the house just before midday, even after a brief stop for a late breakfast. This time Leonard found the home quickly. Adrian had cut away the flora covering the signage for Bryn Bach on their previous visit and had left the gate open. More conspicuously, a large metal rubbish skip sat in the lane outside the property.

As Adrian steered the truck into the driveway, he noticed Leonard had driven his SUV past the façade of the house and pulled up beneath a low-hanging tree. Apart from his red brake lights beaming, the car was almost totally hidden from view, leaving Adrian plenty of room to park right outside the front door. Turning the engine off, he smiled to himself with approval. At work he liked his site managers to be smart, proactive and practical. Lenny certainly displayed those qualities, arranging mattresses, landscaping contractors and now a rubbish skip. Adrian clambered out and strode beneath the cover of the portico just as Lenny joined him. Before Lenny fished out his door keys, they both stretched their stiff limbs.

"Now what are you smiling at?" asked Lenny, eyeing Adrian sidelong while sorting through the keyring.

"Nothing." Adrian nodded towards the front gate. "See you ordered a skip. Very organised."

"If I weren't, I wouldn't be in business." Lenny unlocked and pushed open the front door. "Come on, let's get the back of the truck unloaded."

They set to work straight away, unloading mattresses, boxes, toolkits and other items into the front corridor, ready for use.

After thoroughly cleaning the fridge and making sure the appliance still worked—which, thankfully, it did—they agreed to clean the upstairs first of all to make the bedrooms habitable. However, they decided to concentrate on renovating downstairs that weekend, ripping out kitchen units and stripping flooring and walls. Only if they made good progress would they consider tackling any of the upstairs rooms.

Adrian found himself enjoying working alongside Lenny, chatting occasionally but never slacking. Lenny seemed to be on the same wavelength. He even felt a pang of pleasure at Leonard's impressed surprise when he produced the industrial vacuum cleaner he had brought and started cleaning the floors in the front bedroom. As he worked, Leonard wiped down the bed frame and began removing the plastic packing from the first of the mattresses.

"What?" Adrian asked as he switched off the machine.

"And you call me organised."

"You pay top dollar, you get only the best."

"So I see. Here, give me a hand with this."

Adrian went over and helped Lenny haul the mattress onto the bed. Although snug, they had measured correctly and the mattress fitted nicely. Even with the stark décor — peeling beige paint, faded floral wallpaper and drab dirty-white curtains — the room had a comfortable feel and overlooked the short driveway below, even though trees blocked any view of the lane beyond.

"Do you want this room tonight?" asked Lenny. "Or the one at the back?"

"This one is fine."

"You don't want the one with the view?"

"I'll leave that to the master of the house. Come on, let's get the sheets and duvet on the bed. Then we can use the plastic sheeting from the mattress to drape over. Even with the door closed, there's bound to be dust from downstairs."

Just after they'd finally finished setting up the back bedroom and stood back to admire their handiwork, a female voice sounded from below stairs.

"Hello? Is anybody there?"

Adrian met Lenny's curious gaze. The voice had a very distinctive Welsh accent.

"Did you leave the front door open?" asked Adrian, walking over to the door to peer down the stairs.

"Why wouldn't I?"

"Well, it sounds as though you have a visitor. Word certainly gets round in these parts," said Adrian, grinning, before shouting out. "We're upstairs. Give us a minute."

"It's probably the gardening contractor. They're a little early, which in my book is always a good sign."

Adrian finished securing the plastic packing from the mattress over the bed and descended the stairs behind Lenny to see a woman standing by the front door, her face frozen in shock.

"Luke?"

"Uh, no. I'm Leonard. Leonard Day. And you are?"

Somehow, maybe hearing the timbre of Lenny's voice or seeing Adrian standing behind, but something appeared to break the spell, and the woman's face relaxed. She had a tanned complexion and ruddy cheeks, and wore her grey hair tied back severely from her face. Lending to the outdoorsy look, she sported a green Barbour jacket over an oatmeal jumper, with jeans tucked into green Wellington boots. If Adrian had to hazard a guess — he was usually hopeless at guessing the ages of women — he would place her in her early fifties.

"I am so sorry. I'm Philippa Redfern. One of the owners of Redfern Landscaping. For a moment there you reminded me of someone I used to know. Or, at least, how he would have looked now — "

"Luke Darlington?" asked Lenny.

"Yes, actually." The woman stopped again and stared at Lenny. "Thought I'd seen his ghost for a moment. You knew him?"

"I never met him, but Luke is — was — my cousin. So there might be a family resemblance," said Lenny, before stepping down into the hallway and allowing Adrian to join them. "This is my — uh — friend, Adrian."

Even though he thought of them the same way, Adrian felt a twinge of pleasure hearing Lenny refer to him as a friend. The woman, Philippa, smiled then, and shook hands with each of them before placing a hand over her heart.

"I am so sorry, but honestly, in this dim light, you looked the image of him. Older, of course, than the last time I saw him. But even the way you moved, the way you hopped down those stairs. Gave me quite the start, you did."

"In which case, I'm sorry, too. Let's go through to the living room. It's a bit of a mess, I'm afraid. Thanks for being punctual, by the way." While Lenny led the way in, Adrian pulled open three of the folding chairs around the small collapsible table he'd been wise enough to bring and they all sat down. But they didn't get straight down to business, Lenny curious to know more. "In case you were wondering, I inherited this home from my father. Hence the renovations. I thought you might have had trouble finding the place."

"Ah, well, I've been here before," said the woman. "Many times, actually."

"Really? Is that how you knew Luke?" asked Lenny.

"Yes. We were good friends. Years ago, of course. I'd have been Pippa White back then, before I married. Used to hang out with Luke and the Williams twins, Freya and Howie."

"Philippa. Yes, Mrs Llewellyn at the Manor Inn pub in Newbridge mentioned you. Thick as thieves, she said."

The woman laughed at the comment, while clutching the sizeable flat valise to her chest.

"Not much ever got past Megan or her mother. But yes, we were great friends. And please call me Pippa."

Adrian liked her; she had a nice, open laugh. But he felt uncomfortable sitting, listening as they talked about something personal to Lenny's family.

"Can I make us some tea or coffee?" he asked, standing. "Tea with milk, no sugar, Lenny?"

Lenny grinned and nodded in response. Philippa opted for the same. Adrian headed to the kitchen where he'd placed the kettle and box of refreshments. While he wiped down one of the surfaces and set about making mugs of tea and coffee, he could still overhear their conversation.

"I suppose you know all about what happened to Luke. Were you here at the time?" came Lenny's voice.

"No, I was studying at Durham University. I can't even begin to tell you the shock I felt when I heard. His sister, Mary, phoned me. Told me how Luke had accidentally slipped from a step ladder while working on a light switch in the bedroom. I know it sounds odd now, but I believed her. Luke loved doing handiwork around this place on his own. But for something like that to happen to someone so talented. Tragic. I moved heaven and earth to get to the funeral, but I could tell they were hiding something. It was only at the gathering afterwards that his father confided in me what had truly happened. Which, honestly, made even less sense. I suppose you know that Mr Darlington was the one who found Luke. He walked out on them not long afterward. I've always wondered if the suicide had something to do with that. Of course, the wife could also be difficult."

"Luke's mother?"

"Have you met her?"

"Only once, recently. At my father's funeral. She came across as quite — um — opinionated."

"You could say that. Luke wanted to study photography. In the upper sixth form he applied to the RCA in London for a degree in arts and humanities specialising in photography. Got accepted, too, and while his father didn't mind — the father was pretty chilled about everything the few times we met him — Luke's mother refused, insisted he study something more respectable like law or politics or economics. If you'd ever met Luke, you would know how much he despised those subjects. Art defined him. He could sketch proficiently, and even with his instant Polaroid camera — this was back in the eighties, remember — he took some incredible shots. Some people instinctively understand light, shade and composition and how to capture a scene. Luke was one of those."

"So he hadn't even started his studies?"

"He planned to. I don't know why he didn't. I know his mother threatened that if he did, they wouldn't pay a penny towards the fees. But I got the impression they didn't have much to contribute anyway. Luke didn't care. He hated the idea of a student loan, so he planned to defer, to spend a couple of gap years working hard and saving as much money as he could and then take the smallest loan possible, if at all. The people at the RCA were understanding and said they would keep a place open for him. I remember him telling us that he had lined up a couple of casual jobs after the summer, working weekends as an assistant to a wedding photographer and during the week as a labourer on a building site."

"And what happened?"

"That's all I know. The next thing I heard was that he'd died. If you get a chance, you should have a chat with Freya. I think she still lives around here."

"And her brother?"

"Howie?" Something about the way she said his name made Adrian feel that she had been fond of him. "Heaven knows where he is. Timbuktu, probably. Couldn't wait to get away from Newbridge. Well, from the UK. Born with wanderlust in his veins, according to his dad. For as long as I knew him, he talked about travelling the world on a shoestring."

"But Luke felt happy here?"

"He loved the area, and especially this house. Often came here earlier than the rest of the family. He'd usually entice us and others into getting the place tidy, or help get the garden looking presentable. Even did a bit of decorating in some of the rooms."

As he grabbed the three mugs to bring into the main room, Adrian grinned, realising now why the decorating seemed to have been performed with more enthusiasm than skill.

"Did you know his grandfather was going to leave the place to him, to Luke?" asked Philippa.

"No," said Lenny. "I didn't. He left it to my father."

Adrian wondered if Lenny's aunt wanted the place so badly because she knew about that promise. Maybe he would share those thoughts with Lenny later. He placed the three mugs on the table before sliding one over to Lenny and absently squeezing his shoulder.

"I imagine that's because your grandfather outlived Luke." Before taking the mug, she placed her flat case by the side of her chair. "Ah, tea, thank you, Adrian. Can I ask a personal question?"

After Adrian had moved a mug to her side of the table, he found her looking at him. The question had been meant for him.

"Of course," he answered, taking his seat.

"Hope you don't think I'm being presumptuous, but are you two a couple?" she asked, plainly, before blowing on the surface of her tea mug.

Lenny choked on his tea, while Adrian could not help but chuckle.

"No. I'm the hired help for the long weekend. Lenny needed some muscle to assist with the manual work."

"But you're friends?"

Adrian peered over at Lenny. For some strange reason, his *friend's* cheeks had flushed noticeably.

"Are we?" he asked Lenny.

"Of course we are. Used to go to the same school back in Norwich. So what proposals do you have for me, for the gardens?"

Diverting attention to the garden plans seemed to get Philippa motivated and Lenny's discomfort back under control. From her case, she pulled a two small booklet containing computer-aided plans of the gardens, front and back. Adrian flicked though one, impressed at the professionalism, the designs shown in three dimensions.

"These are your copies. I have to be honest with you," said Pippa, "the design is not that different from the original layout, but I've added easy-to-maintain shrubs to the back garden, in case you're not here that often. In my opinion, the most important thing is to make sure we don't block that amazing view. I've included replacing the patio with new material – your choice, really – but maintaining the same design. And you'll see in one I've added a small gazebo at the far end of the garden on the right. We often use a couple of reliable local gardeners who can come in for maintenance from time to time. To make sure the garden doesn't end upon in the same state again."

Once they had briefly gone over everything, Philippa left the plans with Lenny for him to mull over. He agreed to give her a call over the weekend, to get the ball rolling as soon as possible. As Adrian cleared their mugs away, Philippa stood and shook hands with Lenny.

"I'm glad you're fixing the place up," she said once they had finished. "A good friend of mine would tell you this place has amazing Feng Shui, a real sense of peace and harmony if you know anything about the Chinese practice. Were you told anything about the origins of the house?"

"No," said Lenny. "But I had wondered."

"Luke was doing some digging. I know he found out the house was originally commissioned in the 1880s. That's about all I remember."

"How did it end up in our family?"

Pippa laughed then. She had a nice, unaffected laugh.

"That's what Luke spent ages trying to find out. We're talking about the early eighties here, so you couldn't search online like you can today. Luke loved a mystery. Maybe that's why he warmed to the house so much."

"I'm beginning to know how he felt," said Lenny, and even Adrian understood. "There's something incredibly peaceful about this place. Hey, Philippa. If you're around over the weekend, why don't you pop into the Manor Inn one evening and have a drink with us? Bring your husband, if you want."

"Sounds like a nice idea. Let me check his schedule and I'll drop you a line."

Both Adrian and Lenny walked her to the front door before stopping in the hallway.

"Before you go, can I ask you something?" said Lenny. "About Luke?"

"Of course. Anything."

"Do you think—uh—do you know if Luke might have been different?"

Philippa smiled and gazed away, shaking her head very briefly before looking back at him.

"Are you asking me if Luke was gay? Because he told us in the strictest confidence. Didn't want anything to get out to his family. But the simple answer is yes, he was."

Lenny seemed happy with this answer, but Adrian had to know something else.

"And do you think that's why he killed himself?"

"No. Absolutely not. Although I didn't see him the two or three years before his death, he was adamant that studying at the RCA would be his liberation. He often mused about living in London and becoming the next Robert Mapplethorpe."

"You see," said Adrian. "That's what I don't understand. What you're telling us is he had everything to live for."

"I know. We struggled, too, afterwards. You really ought to speak to Freya, if you get a chance. She was here the whole time and probably knew him better than any of us. If anyone is going to have answers for you, it's her."

Chapter Eleven

Collaborate

Throughout the afternoon, Leonard did his best to match the strength and energy Adrian put into the work. But anyone could tell—had anyone been watching—that Adrian had years of experience on his side. At Adrian's insistence, they both wore goggles, masks and thick gloves and used mainly manual tools—crowbars, hammers and knives—and sheer brute strength to tear out most of the kitchen cabinets before breaking them down to maximise the space in the dumpster. Leonard found the exertion both energising and therapeutic. Once they had finished in the kitchen, only the sink, the fridge and the gas stove remained standing. In the process of removing the cupboards, Adrian had managed to salvage a couple of broken saucepans, a rusted tin of powdered bleach, and a large red bucket full of damp sand.

"There you go," he said to Leonard. "Shows how old this place is. These days we'd recommend appropriate fire extinguishers for kitchens. Sand must be what your family used in case of fires, although it looks as though it's never been used."

"Nice. I'd hate to clean up after using that lot. Shall I dump it in the skip?"

"No, leave it by the fireplace for now. We can get rid of the sand later, but that old bucket looks in good nick. Might come in handy."

"What do you think we should do about the pantry?"

A narrow door at the end of the kitchen opened into a large walk-in cupboard with a few steps down to the floor. Empty shelving covered all three walls and a picture frame-sized window sat high up near the ceiling.

"That's your call, Lenny. Personally, I love these period features. Notice how naturally cooler it is in there, which is why in the past that's where they'd have stored fresh goods — meat, butter, milk. But, of course, these days we have eco-friendly fridges for that kind of thing. Come on, give me hand getting this lot into the skip."

Once they finished clearing debris away, they worked separately in the living area. Adrian effortlessly tore up the linoleum from the floor then ripped off the plywood boards from one side of the fireplace. Leonard tried to keep up but was no match. Adrian worked quickly and efficiently, leaving Leonard huffing and puffing and swearing quietly to himself. But then, he told himself, this was what Adrian did for a living.

"Are you okay over there?" asked Adrian.

Leonard had been trying to lever the plywood away on the left side of the chimney stack, but the broad panel had been fixed in place securely, and trying to pull out the long nails with the hammer claw was proving tedious but also a challenge. Not only that, but there seemed to be something substantial behind the boarding, maybe loose bricks or debris. Concentrating carefully, he plugged away, attacking each side of the panel in turn, working from the top downwards.

When he glanced over, Adrian had not only cleared the whole floor — with a pile of old linoleum broken into smaller pieces and the rest taken out to the skip — but already had the other boarding at the side of the fireplace removed. Just as he had guessed, they had uncovered a small nook of age-yellowed wallpaper with pretty, faded red flowers, hiding a stack of old but sturdy planks of wood.

"You're making me look like a rank amateur over here," said Leonard. Adrian stopped what he was doing and studied the wall on Leonard's side.

"Why is the panelling bulging and tipping out like that, Lenny? Careful, it looks as though it's moving. There must be something —"

Barely had the words left his mouth when, with a series of cracking and popping sounds, the whole wooden panel began to come away from the wall. Leonard, taken by surprise, put his arms out and braced the front of his body against the flat panel to try to stop the wall falling. But whatever had been squashed in and hidden weighed a tonne.

For a moment, he found himself struggling, staggered back a step, and feared the whole weight might fall on top of him.

Suddenly Adrian stood right behind him, with his solid body pressed flush up against Leonard's, his strong arms reaching out to stop the falling wall.

They remained frozen that way for a few moments, Leonard because he was unsure what to do next. Until his mind stilled and his body began to betray him. Adrian's chest and groin pressed up hard and tight against him, his head over Leonard's left shoulder and his heavy breath brushing Leonard's ear. Not surprisingly, strange things started to flutter through Leonard's stomach, and he began to feel his cock hardening.

"Is it me, or is this a tad awkward?" he said, trying to defuse the situation and tame his body's auto-response.

Adrian's chuckle and the rumble in his chest only made matters worse for Leonard.

"I'm not saying I'm not enjoying this, but maybe we should think of a plan of action before the walls come tumbling down, so to speak."

Once again Adrian's laughter came, and this time Leonard felt sure something clicked in Adrian because he tried to pull his noticeably hardened groin away from Leonard's backside.

"Okay, listen," said Adrian, becoming serious again. "I've got this. When I say so, we push together to get the panel back up. Then I'll give you space so you can let go. While I hold everything in place, get a couple of those planks over there and hammer them across the top. That should shore this temporarily until we find a better solution."

"Can't we both just step away and let the whole thing fall?"

"We could. But I'm worried one of us might not get out of the way in time. Safety first, Lenny. It's drummed into us on every building site. Let's do the sensible thing, shall we?"

As they pushed together, Leonard felt as though he had done very little, Adrian's strength shifting the weighty structure effortlessly. Once they had the panel pushed back in place, Adrian kept his hands braced against the wall but stepped back a little to make space for Leonard to move. Instead of getting out of the way, Leonard rotated around one-eighty degrees until he had his back up against the partition, and faced Adrian.

"Well, will you look at this? I have you in my complete control right now. I could have my evil way with you and there's not a damn thing you could do—"

"Lenny!"

Leonard jumped into action. He ducked out, grabbed the nearest thick plank of wood and placed it within easy reach. Adrian had left the toolbox open nearby, so Leonard grabbed the hammer and some fresh nails. Once he had hammered in one side just above Adrian's right hand, Adrian moved his hand up to hold the board and the wall. When Leonard moved behind Adrian, his eyes could not help drifting over the muscled torso from behind—the thick-set shoulders and massive back, the muscled thighs and backside, the way his friend effortlessly supported the weight. Minutes later, he had the first plank in place, and Adrian let go.

Adrian took over then, hammering more nails into the first plank before fixing the second far more securely and professionally. Eventually they both stood and surveyed their handiwork.

"That should hold for now," said Adrian. "We're going to have to deal with it at some point, but I suggest we get some dust sheets, maybe one of those old mattresses to cover the floor beneath, so we're ready when we let the damn thing go. Don't want to damage any of these fantastic floorboards."

Before anything, they went into the hallway where they had propped both mattresses against a wall. Once they had one in place beneath the panel, Adrian began tidying up the room and vacuuming the floor.

"I wonder what the hell is behind there," said Leonard, from across the room, hands on hips, staring suspiciously at the panel.

"Could be anything. But if the bodge job is anything to go by, it's probably bricks or rubble or any other kind of rubbish they couldn't be bothered to toss out."

"Do people do that kind of thing?"

"All the time. One of my mates found an upright piano behind a wall once."

"Owner probably wasn't a music lover. I'm just hoping it's not a dead body?"

"Wouldn't be that heavy. Besides, I think we would know already if it had been a dead body. Rumour has it they give off a smell worse than your kitchen fridge when they're decaying."

"You are a mine of wonderful information, Ade. At least I'll sleep better tonight, knowing nobody got buried alive behind a wall."

"Talking of which, do you think we should call it a day?"

Leonard checked his watch. Almost five-thirty.

"Where the heck did the time go?" he asked, with shock as Adrian smirked at him. "I suppose we ought to think about dinner? We could drive into Llandrindod Wells. They've got a bigger selection of local restaurants, even a chippy, if that's what you fancy?"

"How about we go to the pub again? We know the beer's good and it's a nice evening, a bit cool, but not too cold to sit outside."

"Good plan. Shower first? Or shall we go as we are?"

"I'm already hungry, and I'm not pleasant when I get *hangry*. Let's have a quick wash and head out. I fixed the shower, by the way. Not only is your old boiler running fine, but the new shower attachment works like a dream. So let's just wash up and go as we are. If we sit outside in the garden, Mrs Llewellyn surely won't mind us wearing our work clothes."

"Done deal."

* * * *

Adrian's suggestion turned out to be a good one. In direct contrast to the previous week, the evening felt warm, and although the sun had begun to fade, enough light remained for them to sit out on a bench, enjoy a pint and hot dinner. Being Friday night, a few other people — probably locals — had decided to do the same.

Leonard had not been overstating when he'd praised Adrian on his talent for sketching. The drawings not only demonstrated a clear understanding of space and design, at least from Leonard's limited knowledge, but also showed an incredible sense of creativity. Leonard would have been happy to have any of them framed and on show in his home. As he turned again to the third of the bathroom layouts and nodded his approval, he looked up to find Adrian smiling at him. When he grinned back, another little quiver of excitement went through him, at peeling away another layer of this incredible but humble man.

"Of course, this one might need work." Adrian narrated each design to explain what he had set out to achieve. "For instance, you would need to make sure you've got exactly the right-sized appliances for the gaps between the fitted units."

Amazingly — bearing in mind Leonard could be very particular where design was concerned — they both agreed on the same layout choice for all rooms. Another small piece of a puzzle, of a picture Leonard had not quite visualised until then, fell into place.

When Leonard returned from getting them a couple more pints, ones they decided would be their last because of the quickly fading light, Leonard ventured to ask something he had been purposely avoiding.

"What happened to you that last year of school, Ade? My cousin said you disappeared off the face of the planet." Leonard leant forwards and put his hand on Adrian's forearm. "But if you don't want to talk about it, then that's fine. Tell me to mind my own business."

Adrian's gaze veered away across the village green, and Leonard saw a slight sheen of sadness fill his eyes. Eventually, still looking into the distance, he spoke.

"Honestly, Lenny, I don't tell many people because I'm not proud of that period in my life. When some people come out to the people they love, they have a rough time. Others are accepted, some unconditionally. My coming out fell into the first category. Not sure if you remember, but my best friend at the time was Stephan Harrington."

Leonard remembered him. A well-built player, charismatic, with blond hair and blue eyes. Not as good-looking as Adrian but almost as popular. Where Adrian had looked puzzled at Lenny every time they'd passed each other, to Stephan, Lenny might as well have been invisible. He and Adrian had made for an eye-catching duo among their clump of less-remarkable followers.

"So at fifteen, I was spotted by a talent scout for the Leeds rugby league club. That much everyone seems to know. I heard from them two days after we broke from school for the summer and remember being on such a high that day. No idea why, looking back, but at the same time, I came out to Stephan and told him I really liked him. You know, *liked* liked. Stupid, looking back, but I felt invincible that day. Anyway, at first he thought I was joking. After a while, though, I didn't get quite the reaction I'd expected. I remember the disgust on his face and the words 'You? You're a fucking queer boy?' coming out of his mouth. And the funny thing is that I was more shocked because, in all the time I'd known him, I'd never once heard him swear. Anyway, before I had a chance to think what to say, or to tell him to keep it to himself, he backed away and ran off, leaving me there, feeling shame, and guilt, and self-disgust. It's only looking back now I realise I'd bottled those feelings up for years. But at that moment, all I'd wanted was for the world to rewind by an hour so I could keep my mouth shut and leave those words unspoken for the rest of my life."

Adrian let out a deep sigh and took a sip of beer before continuing.

"Later, after walking around the town, I calmed down a bit, but got home to find my father waiting to confront me. Stephan's father had phoned him, told him what had happened, and how I'd tried to seduce his son. My mother stood by watching, pale and drawn, tears in her eyes, and while my dad lectured me, she didn't say a word.

"When he asked me if it was true, I suppose I should have denied everything, told them Stephan had made a mistake. Because the truth was I hadn't tried to corrupt him. But honestly, I thought they would just send me to my room, maybe make me go to confession with my mum, or ground me for a week.

"Instead my father picked up the phone and dialled a number. For a second, I thought he was calling the police. But when he put the phone down, he told me that the next morning someone would come from God's Path to pick me up and take me to a summer camp to help boys like me. Then he told me to go up to my room and pack a bag. Of course, I knew about the place. I'd overheard him talk about it when he thought I wasn't listening, heard horror stories about kids who had been sent there to be *fixed*."

"Conversion therapy?" asked Leonard.

"Yeah. I didn't know it was called that, but I knew what they did. When I tried to argue, he told me things I will never forget. Said that if I didn't get cured, I would never be accepted as a man let alone a rugby player, because I would get laughed off the pitch. Worst of all, he said I would catch AIDS and die and go straight to hell. I didn't argue back, but went upstairs to pack my rucksack and dig out all the money I'd saved and my passport. I could hear them talking downstairs. Felt like forever while I pretended to sleep in my bed in the dark until they'd gone to sleep."

"Fifteen years old, I remember standing outside that house, my home, at one in the morning, staring up at what until seconds before had been the window to my bedroom. My first impulse was to give in, head back and do as he had asked. But I stopped with my hand on the garden gate. Even back then, I knew who I was, knew that was never going to change. But now I knew how he felt about me and people like me. Some things once said can't be taken back. I slept on a park bench that night."

"Didn't you have anyone you could go to, any aunts or uncles?" asked Leonard.

"Nobody locally. At least nobody I could think of. My Uncle Pat—my mother's younger brother—lived somewhere in London. They didn't have kids, and whenever they visited, we got on well. I never met any of my dad's family. And everyone else I knew was either connected to school or the church. And honestly, I wasn't thinking straight. If it hadn't been the school holidays, I might have gone to see the school counsellor in the morning. But I was hurting, Lenny, and all I could think about was getting as far away from Drayton as I could, from everyone and everything, and never coming back."

"What did you do?"

"The next morning I caught the first train to London. Naive really, but I thought I might be able to figure out where my uncle lived. Even though I had no phone number and no address. We'd driven there a couple of times, but I'd never paid attention, had slept most of the way. As you probably guessed, I wasn't the brightest of students, because I'd pinned all my hopes on a future being a professional rugby player. All I remembered was the town they lived in had the word green in it somewhere. So the first place I went to was Green Park, in the heart of London. Of course, I didn't recognise anything."

"Christ, Ade. What happened then?"

"I ended up living on the streets. This would have been back in the early nineties. I fell in with other homeless kids. Homelessness is still an issue in this country but was huge back then. A group of us turned tricks to survive, which was dangerous but put food in our mouths. Not sure if you remember, but that was back when Colin Ireland, the serial killer, was on the loose, killing gay men he picked up from the Coleherne leather bar. Makes me shiver when I think about it, because that place was one of our haunts. They warned me some clients could get a bit rough, but I had size and muscle on my side, so nobody tried to mess with me. I didn't drink alcohol back then or take any of the drugs they offered, either, so always kept a clear head. Honestly, Lenny, I'm not proud of some of the things I did, but I had to get by somehow. Not just that, but doing what we did was illegal — the age of consent was still twenty-one — so any clients were also committing a crime."

Leonard stared horrified at Adrian, trying to imagine a scared fifteen-year-old version desperately trying to survive on the city streets. He took a mouthful of beer but the liquid tasted sour on his tongue. However futile the idea, he couldn't help wondering what might have happened if he had confronted Adrian about the name-calling at school and found out the truth. Would they have become friends? Would Adrian's life have taken a different turn?

"Eventually this old guy, Felippe, asked me to move in with him. There used to be a traditional pub called the City of Quebec behind Marble Arch — not sure if it's still there — where elderly gay men would hang out at the weekends. A friend introduced me. Somewhat unkindly, he labelled the place the elephant's graveyard. Young boys like me could make fast cash, often for very little work. For some reason, Felippe took a shine to me. The few times I went home with him, all I ever did was pour him drinks, listen to him tell stories about his life during the war — he served in the Royal Navy — sponge him down in the bath and sleep next to him for the night. Not once did we do anything remotely sexual. He lived in the heart of Marylebone, in a beautiful studio apartment. I've no idea exactly how old he was, but I guess he must have been in his early eighties. Anyway, the four or five times he invited me back, I suppose he was trying to gauge whether he could trust me. One Sunday he asked me to be his full-time houseboy — buying food, keeping the apartment tidy for him — he had an old Irish woman who came in and cooked and cleaned every other day. His eyesight wasn't good, so I'd read newspaper articles, books and sometimes letters aloud to him — he'd help me with words I didn't know, and explain what they meant, so we both benefited. I also made sure he took his medication, bathed and dried him. Sometimes he had dinner parties at home with these other old gay men — got professional cooks in for that — and I used to act as a waiter wearing only tight shorts and a tight vest. The old boys loved that. I even had a front door key, new clothes to wear and an allowance."

"How old were you?"

"When I started there? Sixteen. Seventeen, maybe. I stayed with him for about four years. One of his nieces came round from time to time to look in on him. She clearly came from money and always turned her nose up at me as though I'd dropped off the bottom of her shoe. And then I came home from the shops one day to find Felippe in his favourite leather chair by the fire.

Thought he'd fallen asleep but when I touched his hand, he was as cold as stone. I phoned the niece, who called her doctor friend, and they confirmed he'd died. Peacefully enough. After that, other people came in and took over, and I was tossed back out on the street with the black plastic rubbish sacks."

"Bloody hell, Ade."

"All in the past. And it wasn't like you, Lenny. You lost a lover. I only lost a job. A cosy one, I grant you, but that's all it really was. The problem was that by then I'd lost touch with my street mates. Began to find out many were either in hospital or had died. One West Indian friend, Tommy, got me into this gay escort agency at night as well as selling the street magazine for homeless people, *The Big Issue*. Those were some of my darkest days. I was doing exactly that on Christmas Eve, freezing my arse off outside St Martin-in-the-Fields when a man stopped across the pavement and called my name. Uncle Pat. You know, you asked me if I was religious and I told you I'd had some special moments? Well, that day, a miracle happened. Yeah, maybe you could call it coincidence, but there he was. Said he recognised me from my hair, even though I was a lot older and had lost a lot of weight by then. Told me he'd heard from my mother what happened and she'd asked him to keep an eye out, in case I'd made my way to London. We went for a coffee, and he insisted I come home with him, and stay with him and Aunt Penny for Christmas. Turns out they lived in Hither Green. Got me an apprenticeship with his building company and that's how I started in the building trade. I stayed with them until they retired, then rented my own flat locally. And that's where I remained until I got the call from Mum, to tell me Dad had been diagnosed with dementia. At first I told her to stick him in a home — I still hated the man — but my aunt talked me round. She'd been a nurse before retiring, and I remember her words to this day. She said, 'There is no cure for dementia, Adrian. I know he turned his back on you once, but you are a better man than that. In his time of need, don't be the same man as your father. Go and help your mother.' So I came back to the town I hoped never to see again, and between the two of us, my mother and I took care of him until he passed away."

Thankful for the fading light, Leonard felt warm tears welling. He always considered the way Kris' family had treated him to be unjust and unfair, but compared to Adrian's life, he had been living in a comfortable cocoon.

"Your aunt was right, Ade. You are an extraordinary man, a better man than anyone I know, and I'm not just saying that because you're helping me. I wish I'd gotten to know you at school, wish we'd been friends then, and maybe all those dreadful things might never have happened. But then I might not be sitting in front of the same Adrian."

At those words, a smile curled Adrian's lips.

"No, maybe you'd be sitting in front of an ex-England international rugby star. Begging for my autograph."

Leonard laughed aloud. Despite everything, Adrian could still crack jokes. The simple act of surviving what he had been through would have crushed most men.

"Yeah, okay. You just keep telling yourself that. Do you still see your uncle and aunt?"

"Of course. As often as I can. They've retired now and live in a bungalow in Hastings on the south coast. Honestly, Lenny, they showed me more love and understanding than my parents ever did. Uncle Pat wanted me to get back into rugby, but that ship had sailed. Wow, it's getting a bit nippy now. Do you want to go inside? Or shall we head back?"

"Do you mind if we head back?" said Leonard, pressing his fingers into a sore spot on his left shoulder. "My muscles are starting to ache. I think I'm ready for a long, hot shower and a good night's sleep. Do you mind taking the empties back while I bring the car round?"

"Of course."

Leonard studied Adrian as he headed towards the pub door, the way he moved, so carefully for such a big guy, before he disappeared inside.

All this time and he had considered Adrian a homophobic bully. Before his father's funeral, if anyone had asked him if he'd ever known Adrian Lamperton, he would probably have dismissed him as a dim-witted sports jock he went to school with, who probably ended up having everything handed to him on a plate as a professional rugby player.

How wrong could he have been?

But somehow their lives had collided, and Leonard had grown not only to admire Adrian but to feel an undeniable attraction to him. Maybe Adrian had been right about fate. Both were approaching fifty, both having resigned themselves to being alone, both having given up hope on finding anything — or anyone — lasting for the rest of their lives. Although Leonard was rarely given to such whimsical notions, he had to wonder if their various meetings — at the local pub, by his father's broken-down car — had not been chance at all. Maybe they were both being given a second chance.

His friend, businessman Kennedy Grey, had once mused to a group of friends that '*opportunities alone are merely choices that happen to fall into our laps. It's whether we have the balls to act on them, and what we decide to do with them that changes the course of our lives.*'

Leonard had not been fooled. Everyone had thought he had been talking about business, but Leonard had known full well Kennedy had meant every word about how he had managed to snag his prize husband, Kieran.

After standing and dragging out his car keys, Leonard took a bracing breath of cold air and headed for the car.

Time to take a chance.

Chapter Twelve

Together

In the front bedroom, Adrian sat on the edge of the bed, the damp towel still wrapped around his waist, feeling an odd mix of embarrassment and craving at what had just happened. At some point, as soon as Lenny had finished showering and his bedroom door had closed, Adrian would need to take care of business. From the aching in his balls to the painful erection he sported, that refused to go away, he would need to take care of business soon, to stroke his cock until all his tension had been released. He only hoped the poor old bed frame didn't complain too loudly.

At any other time they might have laughed off the incident. Having no lock on the bathroom door hadn't helped. Or the fact that Adrian had accidentally left the door ajar while under the shower. Probably hearing the water no longer running, Lenny had burst in naked while removing the towel from around his waist. Adrian had been standing there equally naked drying his hair. The shock on each other's faces might have been comical for an onlooker, but both had frozen in horror until Adrian's lustful eyes had taken over. How could he have resisted drinking in Lenny's naked body, the dark hair matted across his chest pouring down in a single line to the beautiful cock nestled in a mound of equally dark pubic hair? Buried memories of things he had learnt, of how to arouse a man's body into a finely tuned instrument, and echoes of his own shuddering climaxes, flickered to life. Mere thoughts became foreplay and Adrian had felt his obedient cock filling, readying for action. What had not helped was when he had raised his eyes to Lenny's and noticed him checking Adrian out in the same way.

The ensuing stuttered apologies, self-blaming, clumsy covering up and hurrying to get away from each other had been bordering on farcical.

Adrian scrubbed his fingers through his short hair and clamped them around the back of his thick neck. He had poured his heart out tonight outside the pub — told Lenny more than he had ever told another living soul — and Lenny had listened sympathetically to every word. What was it about the man that made him open up? He looked up when he heard the door to the bathroom open and close, and let out a deep sigh until he noticed the footsteps along the corridor getting louder.

Lenny stood in his open doorway, wash bag dangling from his hand, with only a towel wrapped around his waist, his bare chest exposed.

"Mate, I think we need to have a little chat. Don't you?"

"Look, I'm sorry, Lenny. I thought I'd shut — "

"It's not about that, Ade. Can I come in?"

"Of course."

Lenny stepped cautiously into the room but did not look directly at Adrian or approach him. First of all, he went to the window and pulled back one side of the curtains, stared out into the night sky.

"Look, Ade. I'm no good at this — out of practice, I suppose — but I'm also too old to beat around the bush. We both are." Lenny let the curtain go and turned around, perching his backside against the windowsill. "I'm into you. I mean, *really* into you. I'm sure you know because I'm pretty bloody hopeless at trying to be subtle when I'm checking you out. So I'm sure you've noticed. I just don't want to make an arse of myself, misread the situation and do something I regret that ruins our friendship."

"Oh shit, Lenny. Of course I fancy you, too." Adrian lowered his head, stared at his feet and scrubbed his hands through his hair again. While he sought for the right words, Lenny's bare feet appeared before him. "But you're not like my other casual hook-ups. You're so much more, and I didn't think someone like you could ever — "

With his eyes still lowered, his words stopped short when Lenny's wash bag and towel dropped to the floor around the man's feet. Before he had a chance to look up, Lenny's gruff voice sounded.

"So stop thinking. If you want me, Ade, I'm yours."

When his eyes rose slowly, studiously, to take in all the muscles and crevices and beautiful hairy contours of Lenny's naked body until they reached the darkened gaze, the tension in his body all but exploded. Lenny's eyes widened slightly as Adrian lurched to his feet, ripping his own towel away before wrapping his arms around Lenny's waist and almost pulling him off the floor. At first Lenny grunted with surprise, but then wrapped his legs around Adrian's waist and brought his head in to kiss him. Adrian returned a chaste peck on the lips before nipping his jawline as he clamped his hands tightly onto Lenny's smooth backside.

Turning around with Lenny still held tight, he lowered his body onto the bed. Pausing for a moment, he straightened up and eyed his prey. Lenny's face gleamed with wonder, open and vulnerable, his eyes wide. As Adrian stood there, drinking in the body below him, Lenny began to sit up. But Adrian stopped him by placing a single hand in the middle of his chest and pushing him firmly back down again. Lowering his own body on top, he grasped hold of each of Lenny's hands and held them down above his head. After brushing his lips along the skin around Lenny's throat, then kissing beneath each ear he pulled his head away and waited for Lenny to open his eyes.

"Are you sure you want this?" whispered Adrian.

Words appeared to have escaped Lenny. With his pupils dark with desire, he simply nodded.

"All of it?"

A gulp and another round of nods, more urgent this time. Adrian smiled.

"Then you do exactly as I say. And right now, I want to explore you. Shift yourself onto the bed and grab onto the bed frame above your head. Both hands. Then lie perfectly still for me until I tell you otherwise, okay?"

Without a word, Lenny nodded again and did exactly as told.

Adrian took his time. He straddled his friend's waist, his erection resting above Lenny's navel. After squeezing his thighs either side of Lenny's torso and noting the deep but slow rise and fall of his friend's chest, he began running his fingers down both arms from his hands to his shoulders, before drawing his fingertips across the furry chest, thumbing the nipples and producing a gasp. Lenny never once dropped eye contact. When Adrian ran his tongue across the gooseflesh skin around this sensitive nipple, Lenny arched his back off the bed and groaned again, and Adrian felt a hot cock tap him on his backside. When he nipped one of the hardened nubs, the erection knocked repeatedly. Adrian brought his mouth away and smiled down.

"Someone likes that."

When he shifted farther down the bed, positioning himself in between Lenny's legs, he carefully spread them apart. After drinking in the musky scent of the aroused man, he smoothed his hands down his sides to his waist, down to his outer thighs before moving in towards his shaft. Lenny's squeezed his eyes shut, his chest rising and falling rapidly now, his body seeming to react to every breath, every small touch, maybe in anticipation of Adrian's final destination. But he never once let go of the bedframe.

"Beautiful." Adrian's breath caressed Lenny's erection, making the poor thing twitch and leak precum.

Eventually, Adrian used one hand to grab the base of Lenny's cock, the other cupping his balls, rolling and squeezing gently. Lenny's eyes flew open then, and Adrian grinned up at him, his mouth an inch from the head of the erection. Wetting his lips with his tongue and not once losing eye contact, he licked the length from base to the sensitive tip, his tongue tracing every bulging vein, every inch of the man, until his hips jerked upwards, needing more. Without hesitation,

Adrian took all of him into his mouth, deep into his throat. Lessons learnt on the streets had stayed with him. And if the filthy, tortured groans leaving Lenny's mouth told him anything, Adrian had not lost his ability to give a memorable blowjob. Pushing both arms underneath Lenny's knees, he lifted his legs into the air, releasing his cock from his mouth. This time he ran his tongue along the perineum, sucked on his balls, then licked leisurely up to the top of Lenny's shaft before taking him in his mouth again. With his arms hooked around the knees, Adrian's hands reached to pinch each nipple, something Lenny seemed to enjoy, if the soft gasps and whispered expletives told him anything.

But he still wasn't done. Pushing his hips forwards, Adrian drew the length of his own cock along the crack of Lenny's backside while continuing to suck him down, a trick he had mastered. This time he felt the body beneath him tremble at the touch and smiled while still taking his length into his throat. When he eventually pulled his mouth away, Lenny's eyes bored into him, waiting to meet his gaze.

"I want you to fuck me."

Adrian felt a smile curl his lips.

"You prefer to bottom?"

Lenny frowned slightly, and appeared conflicted by the question.

"No. I mean, yes. I mean, I like both. But right now, I want you inside me. There are condoms and lube in the wash bag."

"Like I said. Well organised." Adrian knelt to the floor, opened the bag and pulled out a box of condoms and a tube of lube, both still in their plastic wrapping. Adrian snorted as he ripped the plastic covering off.

"So you were planning to get lucky with me this weekend?"

"Hoping. Quick word of warning, Ade. It's been a while, but I'm really sensitive down there. What you might call hypersensitive. Kris used to joke that sometimes our—um—lovemaking was over before it had begun because he rubbed too hard in the right place during foreplay. And that was me finished."

"Good note. So no touching the sweet spot. I'll save that for the main event."

Adrian dripped generous amounts of lube onto his fingers and, after lifting one of Lenny's legs onto his shoulder and kissing the inside of the knee, applied the cooling liquid expertly around the outside of his entrance. Already Adrian had become aroused at the very noticeable tremors emanating from Lenny's body, at the way his cock twitched whenever he touched him in certain places. While probing a finger inside, he turned and lightly bit into Lenny's calf to distract him from any discomfort. Slowly, painstakingly, one finger at a time, he opened Lenny up, making sure not to delve too far, until everything about Lenny screamed arousal—the erect nipples, the straining erection, the look of abject desperation in his wild eyes. Withdrawing his fingers, Adrian reached for the condom, quickly ripped the wrapper open with his teeth and rolled the latex onto his shaft. After smoothing more lube onto himself, he positioned the tip of his cock before hooking his arms beneath both of Lenny's knees and moving forwards, but not yet entering. He waited until Lenny opened his eyes and looked at him.

"We do this at your pace, Lenny. As slow or as fast as you want. If you feel any discomfort at all—"

"I'm ready, Adrian. Stop bloody talking, will you?"

Adrian grinned and planted a quick kiss on Lenny's lips before moving his hips forwards, breaching the entrance. Tightness and heat squeezed his shaft pleasantly, and he resisted his impulse to plough straight in. Lenny would need time to adjust to his size, so Adrian studied his eyes, squeezed shut, and his expression for any sign of pain. Each time he felt the muscles relax minutely, he moved farther forwards. Finally, he stopped.

"That's all of me."

Lenny's forehead shone with perspiration, but he looked almost beatific when his eyes opened and he smiled up at Adrian.

"Can I assume you know what to do next?" he quipped.

Adrian snorted aloud before beginning the steady push and pull, bump and grind. Every time he slid in all the way, Lenny let out a soft groan, his eyes rolling back into his head. At one point Adrian went to reach for Lenny's straining erection, but had the hand swatted away and received a gentle shake of Lenny's head. Sensory overload. Instead, they held onto each other's hands while Adrian concentrated on his own pleasure, pushing fast and slow, shallow and deep, while moving the legs up onto his shoulder to kiss Lenny's shins. Soon the old bed frame began complaining, thumping out a steady rhythm against the bedroom wall and raising powdery plaster dust.

Signs of Lenny's orgasm came in the tightness of the muscles inside him clenching and the way the pace of his breathing quickened. Accompanied by a long, blissful moan from Lenny, his cock began spraying shot after shot of cum, at first onto his hairy chest then on his stomach. All the time Adrian kept ploughing him, deeply but now erratically, his own climax stoked at the sight until he could hold no longer. Orgasming was usually the only time Adrian allowed himself to come unglued, to feel free, letting the pleasure, the release, rip through him. Knowing he was filling the condom inside Lenny heightened the ecstasy in a way he had never experienced before.

When his eyesight began to come back to him, when the dopamine haze cleared, he lowered himself on top of Lenny's body. Heat and wetness met his chest and stomach, but he didn't care and breathed heavily next to Lenny's ear. After a few moments, wondering if his weight might obstruct Lenny's breathing, he withdrew his deflated cock and rolled to one side, onto his back.

They lay together unspeaking, staring at the ceiling. Neither moved, Adrian listening to Lenny's heavy breathing and waiting for his own to normalise.

"Holy shit. Told you I was a lightweight," said Lenny, turning nervously to Adrian and chuckling.

"You were amazing. Don't move."

Adrian threaded his fingers into Lenny's and squeezed once before getting up from the bed. Without a word, he went to the bathroom. Soaking a washcloth, he wiped himself down first, before rinsing and bringing the damp cloth and a hand towel back to the bedroom. Very slowly and carefully, he cleaned Lenny's body. All the time, even though Adrian never looked directly into them, Lenny's eyes never left his. As Adrian's hand wiped across Lenny's chest, he caught Adrian's wrist and held on until their eyes met.

"Can I sleep here tonight? In bed with you?"

Adrian's breath hiked. Sex he could handle. Intimacy felt like unchartered territory. Even with his occasional hook-ups, he usually ended up sleeping the night alone in his own home. Apart from Felippe, he couldn't remember the last time he'd shared a bed for the night with another man. Perhaps Lenny spotted the dilemma playing out in his head and across his face because he came to the rescue with a get-out.

"Only if you want, Ade. No pressure."

"Um, let me just—let me take the cloth back first."

Adrian placed his hands on the cooling edge of the pink porcelain bathroom sink. He needed a few moments to himself, and while rinsing out the cloth again, he stared at his reflection in the cracked and mottled bathroom mirror. Why the hell did he feel so apprehensive? Lenny had already admitted to being a friend. But the last time he'd ever showed anything resembling feelings to anyone—Stephan Harrington, his best friend in high school—his heart had been trodden into the dirt. And even though the whole drama had played out over thirty-five years ago, Adrian still remembered every small detail with crystal clarity, of being terrified and ashamed by the disgusted reaction of his best friend. Since then, God only knew he'd enjoyed plenty of sex, and he had formed a couple of friendships—but never together with the same person.

"Are you okay, big guy?"

Lenny's tender voice from the doorway made him flinch, and his eyes jerked up to the naked reflection in the mirror. Lenny appeared equally nervous.

"Hey, Adrian, I didn't want to freak you out—"

"You didn't, it's just—I worry I might snore and keep you awake—"

"We've already had that conversation, remember? And we have shared a room before, have we not? At the pub? Look, if it makes you uncomfortable, I'll head back to my room —"

"No!" Even to Adrian, the firmness of his voice startled him. "Sorry, I mean, I want you in bed with me. It's just been a long time. But I would really like it if you slept next to me. If you would. Please."

And just like that, the smile that blossomed on Lenny's face made the small gesture worthwhile. Before Lenny turned away, Adrian spied him giving his naked body another appreciative once-over.

"Good. In which case I'm going back to snag the dry side of the bed."

Adrian laughed aloud as Lenny turned and left, purposely showing off his firm backside as he went.

Yes, he told himself, *I can do this. Lenny may be sex on legs, but he's also different. He would never trample my heart into the ground.*

He hoped he was right.

Chapter Thirteen

New Day

Leonard emerged slowly from sleep on Saturday morning, his eyes gradually becoming accustomed to the light of a strange room, dust particles dancing in the ray of sunlight from the crack in the curtains. After a deep breath, he looked around and realised he was alone.

Or maybe not.

Wafts of bacon cooking seeped through the house, igniting his sense of smell and making his stomach rumble. When he shifted onto his side, his body ached in the intimate places he vaguely remembered from his past, sweet aches and a reminder of their coupling the night before. Another session had begun not long after Adrian had finally joined him, pressed up against his back and neither of them able or willing to staunch the resurgence of desire. Did he dream it, or had they fallen out of bed at one point, caught up in wild lovemaking and crashing loudly to the bedroom floor? Even still sleep-befuddled, he wondered how Adrian had known which of his buttons to push. Because the night before had been the stuff of Leonard's most erotic fantasies. Only one small missing piece had him baffled, which was hardly noteworthy, but Leonard enjoyed kissing. All he had managed to get from Adrian last night had been an almost chaste peck on the lips. Lots of red welts from bite marks along his neck and upper chest, but no kissing. Still, after such a long dry spell, Leonard wasn't about to complain.

Pulling himself to the side of the bed, he swung his feet down and stood up naked. While stretching his body with a couple of fluid Qigong movements, he wondered if the morning might prove awkward. He hoped not, because his body felt an inner calm and warmth, despite the chill air in the bedroom.

Heading to his bedroom, he pulled on underwear, track bottoms and a sweatshirt before slipping his feet into trainers and strapping on his watch. With a snort, he noted the time. Eighty-twenty. He rarely slept past seven even at the weekend.

As he rounded the bottom of the stairs, heading first into the main living area, he witnessed first-hand the mess from something that had collapsed during the night, where the panelling had given way. Before heading to the kitchen, he went over for a closer inspection. Grey dust and rubble covered the back and sides of something that seemed to be a solid piece of furniture made of dense wood.

Adrian's voice came from the kitchen doorway.

"I think it's some kind of wardrobe."

"So that was the crash I thought I'd dreamed in the middle of the night," said Leonard, turning to grin and wink at Adrian. "And here's me thinking it was you rocking my world."

Adrian snorted, but his grin morphed into a pleased smile, and Leonard hoped his levity had dissolved any awkwardness between them. Leonard's only regret was that Adrian had already dressed in his overalls and black T-shirt, ready for the day's work. In the bright light of day, he had hoped to see more of the man's flesh.

"I'm making a spot of breakfast—eggs, bacon and fried tomatoes. Very basic and no toast, I'm afraid. Just bread and butter. No idea if this gas thing has a grill for making toast, and even if it did, I wouldn't want to chance blowing the place up. Hope that's okay? After we've eaten and washed up, maybe we can try to haul that huge monster back onto its feet. Give it a thorough clean up and then have a look at what you've got there."

"Sounds like a plan." When Leonard stepped away and headed for the kitchen, Adrian backed up and went to the gas stove. "Anything I can help with?"

"The kettle's boiled. Can you make tea and coffee?"

"I'm on it."

Leonard moved carefully around Adrian, not wanting to take anything for granted. But as he stood at the large sink, rinsing out two mugs, he sensed Adrian stop behind him. Stepping forwards, Adrian pushed his body up close, wrapped his arms around Leonard's stomach and rubbed his nose on the back of Leonard's neck—like an Eskimo kiss—before moving back to the stove. Leonard let out a breath he hadn't realised he had been holding in.

They sat either side of the foldable table, eating quietly, in companion silence. Now and again Adrian caught his eye and grinned, but otherwise maintained a calm expression throughout the meal, with no sign of awkwardness. Leonard wanted to talk about the night before, but before he could, Adrian had already started talking business.

"Now we've managed to rip out the kitchen cupboards, we'll need to start the structural changes. I'm thinking maybe I stop down here this week and get a building pal of mine to join me, knock out this wall. I've taken a few photos on my phone and fired them over. My pal, Toni, is not only a brilliant builder but a qualified electrician. That way you can get the wiring checked out, and then you'll know what needs to be done to bring everything up to code. At the same time, we can open up the kitchen for you. Have everything ready for when you come down next weekend."

"Have you checked whether this electrician friend is even free next week?" asked Leonard, hoping he didn't give away the frisson of jealousy he felt when Adrian mentioned the guy's name.

"I'll need to find out. But it shouldn't be a problem. There's not a lot of building work going on around Norwich right now. But you really want to get all the wiring work planned to coincide with the design of a new kitchen, with the fixtures and fittings, and the new bathroom. Especially before you start decorating. It'll probably take a couple of weeks to rewire the whole house. Need to make sure everything's in the right place, too. Things like light switches, plug sockets, fuse box. Don't leave that kind of thing to the last minute."

"And would you both stay here in the house?"

Adrian eyed Leonard quizzically, a slight deepening of the groove between his brows.

"Makes the most sense, don't you think? But not if you don't want us to."

"No, I—I don't have a problem."

"Don't worry. She'll be fine living on-site if that's what you're worried about. Trust me. We've both stayed in a lot worse places than this to get a job done."

Wait, thought Leonard. *She?*

"In case you ever need her skills, by the way, Toni Frankston — Toni with an 'i' — is the best builder and electrician in and around Norwich. And I've worked with a few. More importantly, I know she needs the work. Her partner, Jack, is a damned good landscape gardener, but we don't need one of those. You've already got that covered."

"I have," said Leonard, smiling down at his plate, at his stupidity. "And will Toni with an 'i' be able to give me a quote on what needs doing? Sometime next week?"

"Of course. Or do you want to meet her first?"

"No. Absolutely not. I trust you completely." Something hit Leonard hard then, in that he genuinely did trust Adrian. If only he had someone like Adrian on his preferred list of freelance builders back in London, someone who could source other experts in other fields when needed. Maybe that could be another conversation. "Which reminds me. I got a set of keys cut for you. To the house. They're upstairs in my jacket pocket."

"Perfect. So let's get these breakfast things cleaned up then get to work."

* * * *

After they had finished, they both donned their goggles, gloves and mask and hauled the fallen piece of furniture upright. Each took one side, and Leonard struggled at first, but with Adrian's strength soon had the curio back on its feet in an open space in the living room. While Adrian went to fetch a broom to sweep the floor and a damp cloth for Leonard to wipe the unit down, Leonard made a quick inspection.

What he discovered was a beautiful Welsh dresser, much grander than others he had professionally dealt with before, this one made of heavy oak. When he examined the floorboards in the newly opened alcove he noticed one of them had collapsed over time, probably from damp, which must have been what caused the dresser to lean forwards and buckle the wall panelling.

Adrian set about sweeping the rubble away and shifting the mattress they had wisely left in place. Leonard tackled the new item with care and something bordering excitement.

From the top down, the dresser had three shelves to house plates and other chinaware, three deep drawers arranged horizontally at waist height, probably for easy-to-reach cutlery and tableware, and finally two solid-looking cupboards below. Leonard tried them but found all drawers and doors to be locked. Each drawer had identical ornate bronze plates with old-fashioned keyholes, and two matching bronze handles, all age-darkened but beautifully crafted. Even the woodwork, with the gentle curves and curls running in parallel either side of the shelves, to the floral designs carved into the cupboard doors, spoke of skilled craftsmanship. In all his time in the antique business, Leonard had rarely seen such incredible workmanship.

"This is stunning, Ade. And despite being buried in the wall, it's still in excellent condition. At an auction, this would sell for a small fortune.

"Are you going to flog it, then?"

"Absolutely not," Leonard answered immediately. "The dresser belongs here, and this is where it stays."

"So I guess the question is, why would somebody stuff something as valuable as this into a wall space?"

Leonard had been so engrossed in assessing the dresser he hadn't considered Adrian's very reasonable question. He stood back and studied the piece before answering.

"From what I understand my aunt and uncle were strapped for cash. And I know this sounds a bit mean, but I wonder if they sold off the rest of the furniture. Got someone to give them cash to take a job lot— everything except the beds and the appliances in the kitchen. If I'd been Luke, I'd have wanted to keep this classic piece safe, and one way to guarantee that would have been to redecorate the place and effectively hide this beauty away from greedy eyes. Honestly, Ade, even back then this would have brought in a tidy sum of money. And remember what Pippa said, that Luke was eventually going to inherit this house?"

"Makes sense. If so, Luke was a smart guy. I wonder if there's anything of value in the drawers and cupboards? Want me to force them open?"

Leonard felt torn and stood for a moment, staring and thinking. He felt the same tug of inquisitiveness but also wanted to keep the dresser intact. Maybe this called for a little patience.

"Let's not risk damaging the woodwork. I've got a set of skeleton keys back in London for this very purpose. I'll bring them with me next time and we can investigate then. For now, can we set this against a wall somewhere and put a dust cover over?"

"How about the other bay. I've already stripped the walls and checked the plasterwork. Just need to make sure the floorboards are sound."

Thankfully, the floorboards to the other bay were undamaged, and the dresser fit the space perfectly. Adrian brought a spare sheet from his truck and covered the whole thing. Satisfied with their efforts, they began the job of removing wallpaper from the rest of the room.

During a late lunch of sandwiches and soft drinks, Leonard's phone rang. Although he didn't recognise the number he told Adrian he would take the call. Adrian suggested they take a break so he could use the opportunity to head outside and call Toni.

"Leonard Day speaking," said Leonard, perching against the window ledge.

"Hello, Leonard." He immediately recognised the soft female voice with the Welsh accent. "It's Pippa here."

Pippa from Redfern Landscaping. He had been expecting her call, to find when she would start work on the house.

"Look, you mentioned meeting up at the pub, and I wondered if you were doing anything tonight? Completely by chance last night, I bumped into Freya Williams in the car park outside the superstore in Llandrindod Wells. Told her about you renovating the house. Anyway, I said you might like a chat with her, seeing as how she knew Luke and all. So I arranged for us all to meet up in the Manor tonight, early like. Freya's not a night owl, see? She likes to be in bed by nine. So how does six-thirty sound?"

Leonard checked his watch. Two-thirty.

"Six-thirty sounds perfect. We might be in our work clothes, though."

"Oh, I'm sure Megan won't mind. She probably considers you locals by now."

"Great. And while you're on, Pippa... My friend, Adrian, is going to be staying on for the week, continuing the internal renovations while I check in with my business back in London. Just in case you were thinking of getting started on the gardens this week. Didn't want to worry you if you saw someone beavering away inside. And I'm sure he'd be happy to give your guys access to a kettle, in case they need a brew."

Just then, he noticed another incoming call—Mr Dawson, his father's solicitor.

"That's brilliant. I'm hoping we can start work next week. So thanks for the heads-up."

"Let's catch up tonight at six-thirty. Got to run. I've got another call coming through."

Pippa signed off and Leonard took the next call. Dawson did not seem his usual calm self, his voice more than a little rattled.

"I am terribly sorry for calling you at the weekend, Leonard. But we have just had formal notification from a solicitor in Bristol that your aunt and cousin are planning on challenging your father's will."

"I see."

Leonard stared out of the window to where Adrian had his phone clamped to his ear. At that moment their eyes met, and both smiled. Leonard savoured the warm feeling the simple contact gave him before dragging his gaze away and bringing his attention back to the call. What was it about the property that had ruffled his aunt's and cousin's feathers so badly? Did they really need the house so desperately? Or had his mother said something tactless to them over the phone? He wouldn't put it past her.

"Honestly, Leonard. I thought I had made it perfectly clear what a bad decision that would be. Both parties will simply end up accruing hefty solicitors' fees and, unless there are extenuating circumstances in their favour of which we are currently unaware — which I doubt because why would they not have presented them already — they will have no hope of winning. I'm calling to check whether you want me to represent you. But I have to forewarn you. Disputes are not really my area of expertise — "

"No need, Mr Dawson. I appreciate you letting me know, but I've dealt with business and property disputes throughout my career. And I have a tried and trusted legal contact who, I'm sure, will be more than happy to take this on. Do you mind if I get them to contact you directly, so you can brief them and pass over any file notes? I'll provide written authorisation."

"More than happy."

Dawson's call would mean Leonard getting in touch with Helen Wallis, someone he had used for business disputes and for one particular personal case. A hardened lawyer, someone he trusted implicitly, she had been briefed on Kris' situation following his death as a precaution, in case the Goswami family came after Leonard's house. She had been brilliant, armed to the teeth legally speaking, and had admitted to being a little disappointed when nothing transpired. Using Helen would mean Leonard driving back early on Sunday morning, and seeing her later that afternoon. Semi-retired, she only maintained a couple of clients and spent most of her time tending the abundant garden of her Richmond house. Helen had her quirks. She didn't take business calls over the weekend, but he knew her well enough to know she would be too intrigued not to pick up a text message about his dilemma. And for all her insistence on people respecting her self-imposed seclusion, he knew she would welcome hearing about the challenge over a pot of Assam tea and a plate of scones.

"Thank you again, Mr Dawson," said Leonard, as Adrian came back into the room and winked at him. Leonard pointed to his phone and carried on talking.

"Her name's Helen Wallis. She works part-time on Mondays and Thursdays, I think. I'll need to check whether she's available, but she usually moves any other work she has around for me, if I need urgent help. If everything's good, I'll give you a call from her office first thing Monday. And a quick question. We've already started renovating the property. In your opinion—and I'm not looking for legal advice here, just an opinion—do you think I should stop work completely until this complication has been resolved?"

"With the way things stand right now, Bryn Bach is legally yours, to do with whatever you wish. But once you receive any formal notification, that situation might change. When that happens, the solicitor acting on your behalf will be able to advise you better than I."

"Thank you. That's all I needed to know. I appreciate the call, Mr Dawson. Have a nice weekend."

"You too, Leonard."

Adrian stood before Leonard, intrigued, his hands on his hips. Leonard smiled at him before quickly finding Helen's contact details and composing a brief message.

"What the hell was all that about?" asked Adrian.

Leonard hit the send button and looked back up.

"What do you want first? The good news or the bad?"

"Bad. Always bad. Rip off the plaster."

Leonard explained the calls he had taken, explaining the aunt and cousin's legal action before telling him about meeting Pippa and Freya for drinks later.

"I only step out for ten minutes and look what happens. What's going on with your aunt, Lenny?"

"Heaven only knows. But one thing's for sure. I'm not about to give this place up without a fight."

"A battle cry." Adrian slapped his gloved hands together before placing each of them on Leonard's shoulder. "That's what I like to hear. In which case, you can take it for granted that you've got me in your corner."

"Good to know. But I would never take you for granted, Ade."

Adrian held Leonard's eye contact, something else going on behind his eyes. For a moment Leonard thought he might say something more, but the moment passed, and he brought his hands away from Leonard's shoulders.

"Well, more good news is that Toni's on board and she's driving down tomorrow. Apparently she's been climbing the walls at home, driving Jack crazy. They're both really grateful to get her working. She's bringing her truck with all the equipment we need to take this wall down. So you'll get to meet her."

"Probably not," said Leonard. "I'm going to need to leave early tomorrow morning if I'm going to see my solicitor back in London. I want her on the case as soon as possible."

"Oh, okay," said Adrian, his disappointment evident.

"Ade, I need to deal with this," said Leonard, squeezing Adrian's upper arm before moving past him. "And anyway, Toni's going to be here to keep you company. Not only do I need to go and show my face at work, but I need to brief my legal counsel in person."

"Sure, I understand," said Adrian, nodding. "But in the meantime, Mr Day, we've both got a lot of stripping to do."

Leonard had been on his way to the stairs, but stopped in the doorway and turned to Adrian. Leaning against the door jamb, he gave Adrian a wink.

"We do? Already? Don't you think we should get some work done first?"

"Okay, funny man. Where do you think you're going?"

"To use the john, if that's okay by you."

"Fine. But after that, you get your cute arse down here and get working. I'm on the clock, remember? And save the dirty talk for later tonight."

Leonard had been wondering if Adrian would want him again that night. As Adrian approached him, he couldn't help the smile of pleasure that lit his face.

"Yeah?"

Adrian leant past him to get the broom he had left in the hallway but brushed the back of his hand against Leonard's groin. When their eyes drew level, Adrian almost growled.

"Hell, yeah."

Chapter Fourteen

Freya

Maybe he shouldn't have voiced anything about them having sex later and certainly should not have brushed his gloved hand against Lenny's cock, because throughout the afternoon, whether purposely or not, Lenny kept breaking Adrian's concentration, kept finding ways to make him hot under the collar.

And if he planned to keep on giving Adrian that sly, sultry smile every time their eyes met—he had chosen not to wear his mask or goggles after his call—Adrian was going to have to pull him off his feet and haul him upstairs.

They finished stripping paper from the drawing room—the smaller room on the left just inside the front door—and at each end of the long living room, and now began on the wall housing the fireplace. After Adrian had agreed and marked off the area of kitchen wall to be removed—no point wasting effort doing any work there—he started circling patches where the plaster would need replacing. When clump after clump of powdered plaster came away with the wallpaper on the long wall, he gave up. They would need to replaster the whole side. Their proximity, combined with the smell of Lenny's body and the occasional, supposedly accidental touching, had Adrian's cock waking up and taking notice. To put some distance between them, Adrian suggested he start dismantling the chunky and, frankly, ugly built-in cupboard beneath the bay window. At least that way they would not be so physically close. Except, every so often, he looked up to find Lenny gazing at him with a playful bordering salacious grin.

"Seriously?" said Adrian, yanking off his mask. "You keep that up, and I'm dragging your arse upstairs."

"Promises, promises."

"I mean it, Lenny."

"But I'm filthy," said Lenny, pretending to be shocked, his hands on his hips.

"The look you keep giving me certainly is."

"What look?"

"That one! Don't play dumb. Just pack it in. Otherwise we're never going to manage to get upstairs this weekend."

"Oh, we will get upstairs at some point. That much I promise you."

Adrian couldn't help but laugh.

"Lenny!"

"Okay, okay." Lenny checked his watch while laughing, but then stopped abruptly. "But it's four-thirty already. And we've made amazing progress. We probably need to shower in an hour and get ready to go out. And I'm not going to be here tomorrow. So I just thought—"

Adrian stopped abruptly and eyed Lenny. This sexy man had truly gotten under his skin. Without another word, Lenny dropped his gloves on the floor and had already started moving towards the staircase. After a resigned sigh, Adrian followed him up the stairs and noticed him disappear into Lenny's bedroom. When he stopped in the doorway, Lenny stood by the bed, his hands on his hips, a mischievous grin on his face. Adrian removed his goggles and gloves, and stepped over the threshold, glancing at the bedspread to see supplies already lying there. Lenny had planned this. Without hesitating, he approached Lenny with only thoughts of getting his fill of the man.

"Hang on a minute, Ade," said Lenny, holding Adrian's wrists when he reached for Lenny's belt. Adrian stared back in confusion. Had Lenny changed his mind?

"No, no," said Lenny, smiling and shaking his head before bringing the hands to his mouth and kissing each of them in turn. "Of course I want to have you. But I wondered if we could do things more — uh — my way this time?"

Adrian eyed him with amusement.

"Is this about to get kinky?"

"No. Well." Lenny looked almost uncomfortable and Adrian wanted to tell him not to worry, that nothing could shock him where Lenny was concerned. "Look, I sometimes equate sex — and I know this is going to sound a bit lame — with a rocket firework going off. If you look at things in reverse, the big explosion in the sky is the orgasm, the whizz and fizz as the rocket leaves the ground is the sex leading up to the big bang and the sizzling fuse is the foreplay. Yeah, I know. Not the best analogy. But — and this is the crucial part for me—kissing is like the light, the match, the flame that sets the whole thing in motion."

"Kissing? Kissing's never really been my thing."

"And that's fair enough." Adrian couldn't help but notice Lenny's disappointment. "I was just testing the water. I would never ask you to do anything you're not comfortable with. Let's just forget—"

"No, no. Hang on a minute. I didn't say I'm exactly adverse to the idea. I just don't usually—you know—kiss."

Adrian had felt his previous ardour begin to dwindle at the turn of the conversation, even though, in all fairness, Lenny had piqued his curiosity.

"Which is fine. But let me ask you this. How often have you kissed someone? I mean, *really* kissed them. And I'm not talking about a peck on the lips or the duelling tongues you see in those ridiculous gay porn movies. Kissing for real is about sensation and connection, not a spectator sport. A passionate kiss is all about what occurs deep inside the people kissing each other."

Maybe Lenny had a point. On the streets his mates had told him not to kiss any of his johns. Some had wanted to, but he'd never agreed, so got into the habit of avoiding kissing. He had even said so upfront. Pretty much anything else they wanted, as long as they'd played safe and paid well, he would be game. One of his straight mates who'd had a girlfriend had told him that if you didn't kiss the john before you blew him or fucked him, then it didn't count, it remained just a job, a way to earn a living. And since then not kissing had become a way of life.

"God, Lenny," said Adrian, scrubbing a fist in his hair. "You're making me out to be a sexual novice here."

Lenny snorted with surprise and shook his head.

"Novice? Ade, if last night was anything to go by, then you're far more experienced than me when it comes to sex. I just thought we could try something a little more intimate before we get to the main event. Are you up for a bit of experimentation?"

Never in his life had the thought of sex with someone made him feel nervous — until that moment. What if he turned out to be crap at kissing? Would Lenny be put off? Would it ruin what they already had? Fuck, he was almost fifty and he'd never really kissed someone. How lame was that?

"Hey, buddy. Stop overthinking this. You're in very safe hands. And if you don't like it, we stop, alright?"

"Okay. I think. So what do you want me to do?"

"I need us both to strip down to our underwear."

"Now you're talking my language. I'm liking this already." Adrian began to remove his clothes, taking a moment to admire Lenny's body as he did the same.

"Good. Now I want you to get comfortable on the bed, on your back, face up."

"Shall I drop my underwear?" asked Adrian, his hands on the waistband of his briefs.

"Nope. Just — as you are."

Adrian did as asked, lying down with his head on the pillow and his arms tucked lazily behind his head. After a moment of appraisal, Lenny climbed onto the bed and straddled Adrian's waist. The combination of warmth and the hair from Lenny's thighs, and just the sight of Lenny mounted on top of him, had Adrian's pulse speeding up and his cock taking notice. When

Lenny began to lean towards him, Adrian chuckled timidly.

"Not sure if it helps," he said, his nerves rising. "But I chewed gum after lunch."

Lenny laughed affectionately then smoothed a thumb across Adrian's lips.

"You could be chewing garlic for all I care. Close your eyes."

Lenny began by pressing soft kisses to Adrian's lips. Adrian just breathed and lay still, not reacting nor feeling the urge to kiss back, but he did feel his body calming. The sensation wasn't bad, quite pleasant really—just didn't light any fires. After a couple of minutes, Lenny began to slow down, to press harder, to wet his lips and brush them along Adrian's, and once he even pulled on Adrian's bottom lip with his teeth. With the tiny action, the minuscule nip, Adrian breathed deeply, his eyelids almost fluttering open. As one of Lenny's hands caressed his hair, the other gently smoothed over the chest and down his body. A tiny quiver went through Adrian, something he had never experienced. Maybe Lenny sensed the tremor, but his tongue pushed past Adrian's lips and, almost by reflex, Adrian opened his mouth. Lenny must have been expecting this because his tongue slipped inside, connecting their tongues.

And that's the moment the unexpected happened. A regular trick once told Adrian that he had a talented tongue because he could make this guy come just by rimming him. But this was something entirely different. Moist and warm inside his mouth, their tongues wrestled and slithered and snaked around each other, one moment exploring Adrian's mouth, the next, Lenny's. Kissing Lenny lit a bonfire inside him.

Adrian would freely admit to being the one to take control in any sexual activity, but this time he'd let Lenny take the lead. Which, as it happened, had been a total turn-on. When he heard Lenny's loud and downright filthy carnal moan, he hiked in a deep breath, he brought his hand up to clamp around the back of Lenny's head. Needing more, he deepened the kiss. His pulse spiked and his cock strained to get in on the action, just as Lenny's hand brushed against his erection. Instantly, Adrian rolled them over and pulled his head away, staring hotly down at Lenny's reddened, moist lips and dilated pupils.

"You sure you've never done this before?" asked Lenny, grinning and breathing heavily.

"You are a demon," said Adrian, before diving in for another taste of Lenny's mouth. At the same time, he lined up their bulges and began to move his hips forwards, to rub them together, even though they were both constrained by the material of their briefs. No matter, the friction felt incredible, and if the noises coming from below meant anything, Lenny enjoyed the sensation, too.

Adrian braced his arms either side of Lenny's head, savouring the kiss and freeing Lenny's hands to roam. Pinching both nipples to bring them alive, Lenny rubbed his thumbs around the sensitive flesh before smoothing both hands down from his chest to his stomach. This time Adrian moaned into Lenny's mouth and began moving faster, pressing their erections harder together. When Lenny wrapped his arms around Adrian's neck and wound his legs tightly around Adrian's waist, he pulled away to take a breath. After their eyes met briefly and he dove back to graze his teeth along Adrian's neck, Adrian almost lost control. But Lenny was the one to come undone first, his body stuttering and shuddering through his orgasm, with Adrian not far behind.

Adrian flopped onto his back next to Lenny, both of them staring at the ceiling. After a few moments Adrian felt Lenny's hand thread into his own—another type of intimacy he had never allowed himself. The simple act had him as confused as the kiss, and rather than give in to the instinct to pull his hand away, he decided to lie there and savour the moment. Lenny was affecting him in a way nobody had ever done, and although he found the effect confusing, even a little worrying, he trusted Lenny.

"Okay. So. Messing my underwear wasn't quite what I had in mind," came Lenny's amused voice.

"You didn't enjoy it?"

"I *loved* it," said Lenny, squeezing Adrian's hand. "I—what we just did is a first for me. Not the kissing part. But you keep surprising me, Ade."

"Same here."

"Really? You're an amazing kisser, by the way."

"And that, believe it or not, was a first for me."

"Was it good?"

"Better than. And even though we need to go shower and change now, I'll give you whatever else you need later tonight, when we're back here. Deal?"

"Shit."

"What?"

Adrian sensed Lenny turn his way and met his gaze.

"I wish I wasn't heading off tomorrow now. Imagine what we could be doing if—"

"You're coming back next weekend, aren't you?"

"Of course."

"Then we can hold off for a week. Think of the sexual anticipation. Toni will be gone by Friday. Maybe you can check with your work folks and see if you can come down a little earlier."

"I just checked with the boss. He said it's fine."

Adrian laughed as Lenny jumped up from the bed and held out a hand.

"Come on. The sooner we see Freya, the sooner we can get back in bed."

* * * *

They parked up outside the pub just as the heavens opened. Torrential rainclouds had darkened the sky as they made their way from the house. Fortunately, Adrian had picked a spot in front of the main door and let Lenny out first before racing over to join him.

Lenny pointed out Pippa Redfern, sitting inside the pub by a bay window, overlooking the gloom of the waterlogged back garden and village green. Facing their way, she waved as they entered, and Adrian wondered if he imagined relief in her expression. The woman sitting opposite turned her head slightly but not enough to see them. She had a shock of pure white hair, worn long and wild, tamed only by thin braids tied off at the back. Both women had hardly touched their drinks, so when Lenny waved back, Adrian opted to get beers for them both.

"Now there's a sight you don't see every day," said Mrs Megan Llewellyn, pulling a pint and nodding over Adrian's shoulder to where Lenny joined the ladies.

"Freya Williams?" asked Adrian.

"She rarely leaves home these days. Once a month, maybe, she drives to get her food shopping over in the big store in Llandrindod Wells, which in itself is strange because she's known to be a bit of a recluse. Surprised she doesn't opt for home delivery. Would have thought she'd hate the crowds in that big store."

"I don't know. Sometimes you can hide a lot easier in huge, busy places."

"Fair point. One thing I know for sure, though. Last time she came in here must have been over twenty years gone when her grandmother passed. I've not seen her here since. And I'm surprised to see her with Pippa. The two fell out years ago, not long after Freya's brother went off on his travels. Is she here for your Mr Day?"

"She is, yes," said Adrian, grinning. An oddly warm feeling filled him hearing her label Lenny as *your Mr Day*. "Mrs Redfern suggested Lenny talk to her about Luke."

Megan shook her head slightly while looking down at the pint glass she filled.

"For whatever good it'll do now. But I suppose he would be interested, being family and all."

"I think that's it, in a nutshell. Pure curiosity."

Megan carefully set the second pint down in front of Adrian.

"And we all know what curiosity did to the cat, now don't we?"

Rather than listen to her elucidate, Adrian handed over the money.

"Keep the change," he said.

When Adrian brought the drinks over and took a seat, Lenny did a quick round of introductions. Adrian sat on the same side of the table as Pippa. He noticed Freya hugging a cloth carrier bag to her chest and barely looking at any of them as Lenny talked. Adrian realised then just how deft Lenny was at small talk, telling Freya how he had become the owner, about their progress on the renovations and his plans for the future of the place.

"You'll be pleased to hear that my team is set to start first thing Monday if that's okay by you?" said Pippa, and then to Freya. "Leonard has hired my company to do the landscaping."

"That's great news. Not sure I said on the phone, but I won't be around. I need to get back to London," said Lenny. "But Adrian here will be staying on all next week. He can give you access to the house if you need anything."

"Thanks. Good to know."

"I've got another contractor coming to join me," added Adrian. "We're doing some structural work. And then it's plastering and sorting out the flooring. But Lenny has some firm ideas on that."

"Used to be lovely," said Freya, surprising everyone.

"Sorry?" said Adrian.

"Freya's right. The house used to have lovely varnished floorboards," said Pippa. "Until Mrs Darlington insisted on covering everything up with that dreadful linoleum."

"Cheap. The woman was cheap," said Freya, and Adrian couldn't quite stifle a chuckle.

Having heard Freya speak, Lenny asked her a few gentle questions about what she did for a living. They found out she worked from home for an examination board helping to set the curriculum for national school examinations, as well as providing online tuition for students. She answered other questions guardedly, with few words. They discovered she lived alone, or at least with her two rescue cats. From the little she spoke, Adrian guessed Megan had been right, that she rarely left her home or mixed socially.

"Can I ask? When did you first meet Luke?" asked Lenny.

"When would that have been, Freya? Back in the seventies? I'm the oldest, and I'd have been around fourteen, so you'd all have been, what, twelve?"

"Twelve, yes. We were the same age, Luke, Howard and me," blurted Freya, turning to Lenny. "But Luke was an old twelve, if you know what I mean?"

"True," said Pippa. "A bundle of energy and fun around us, but serious otherwise. He was only usually here for three or four weeks over the school summer holidays, but we all took to him immediately."

"Have you met the brother and sister?" asked Freya.

"Only Matthew," said Lenny.

"They took after their mother," said Pippa, with a slight roll of her eyes. "Accompanying her on long walks in the countryside. Reading aloud to each other in the back garden. Church service on Sunday mornings followed by lunch in the gardens here. Then home for a simple tea in the afternoon. Like a family out of a Victorian novel."

"Doesn't sound so bad," said Adrian.

"Mrs Darlington had her rules. They only read sanctioned books—which often resulted in them defaulting to Bible passages. And nobody was allowed to speak during their walks, except to smile and say hello to any fellow ramblers they met along the way. They had a television in the house nobody was allowed to watch. She forbade them from making friends here, because she said this was a temporary home and local children would most likely be unsuitable—"

"And yet Luke found you," said Adrian.

"We found each other," said Freya, which seemed an odd thing to say.

"Luke was a bit of a rebel," said Pippa, giggling at the memory. "Just like in *Star Wars*, he used to say. The three of us—Freya, Howie and me—were sitting together on the village green the day he appeared. He wandered over to say hello while the rest of his family were finishing their lunch. Just plonked himself down, he did, cross-legged without waiting for an invitation. But he was one of those people you just gravitated towards. I remember seeing his mother get up and march over to get him, and that's when I saw the annoyance in his eyes. Before she was within earshot, he'd arranged for us to meet up the next day, same place, same time. Said he would find an excuse to get away from them. And he did."

"Did their father ever come with them?"

Pippa looked across at Freya.

"I never met him. Did you?"

"Once or twice," said Freya. "And then he only stayed a couple of days. Luke said he worked really hard."

"Strange," said Lenny, sadly. "To think the two of you know members of a family I never met."

Freya stared at him and appeared to remember something at that remark. She pulled the bag away from her chest and drew out a large brown envelope.

"I brought some old photographs. Ones I've kept over the years. Thought you might like to have a look."

She reached inside and placed the small pile into the middle of the table. While Lenny sorted through the Polaroids with Pippa, Adrian picked up the single, larger monochrome shot of the group, worn and wrinkled but still sharp and clear, taken using what must have been a quality, maybe even professional, camera.

In the photo, the young man who was obviously Luke sat cross-legged in the middle of them all, beaming happily at the camera. In the bloom of youth, he had been a beautiful boy — transitioning into a handsome young man — with similar features to young Lenny and even sporting the same messy mop of chestnut hair Adrian remembered on Lenny from school. No wonder Pippa thought she had seen Luke's ghost when she came to the house. To his left, the somewhat masculine features of a young Freya had been caught in a candid moment as she smiled adoringly at Luke, so different from the tired and faded woman sitting opposite. Pippa on Luke's right, also caught unexpectedly, had been captured as she glanced sideways up at the camera. Older than the rest, she sat almost kneeling with her legs tucked to one side, a thick textbook open on the grass in front, her fair hair worn long and falling over one side of her pretty face. In the background, a boy that had to be Howie crouched down behind Luke, his tongue poked out and his hands placed either side of his forehead to look like antlers. Even pulling the funny face, and except for wearing his dark hair short, the resemblance to Freya was unmistakable. Overtly masculine, he had the same square chin and a Roman nose, the same bright eyes beneath thick eyebrows.

"My father took that one. In their back garden at Bryn Bach," said Freya.

"I thought you said Luke's mother didn't like him having friends to the house?"

"She didn't," said Pippa. "But like I said, he used to come down at least a week earlier. To get the place ready for the family, he'd say. His dad was in sales and the head office was in Shrewsbury, so he used to drop Luke off here. And then we'd all usually help Luke out. The rest of the time, we'd just hang out together."

"His real family," added Freya.

"Can you show me the photo?" asked Pippa.

Adrian handed her the picture, and they examined the group together.

"Goodness," said Pippa, chucking softly, running her fingers over the surface. "I remember this well. I must have been twenty, in my second year at Durham, studying business management. That's my huge economics book laid out in front of me."

"How old would Luke have been?" asked Lenny.

"Eighteen," said Freya. "Same as me. But he always looked and acted older."

"Who's this?" asked Lenny, holding a Polaroid up.

In the faded photo a chubby girl with her brown hair tied back in a severe ponytail ate the remains of an ice lolly, her lips a deep raspberry colour.

"That's Mary, Matthew's twin sister," said Pippa. "She was okay. In small doses. Fancied the pants off of Howie. She'd often agree to be Luke's decoy, telling his mother they'd gone for a hike so Luke could meet up with us. He'd bribe Mary with ice creams and sweets and the promise of time with Howie so she wouldn't snitch on him. We still exchange Christmas cards each year."

"Is anyone eating?" asked Adrian, halfway through his beer.

The question appeared to stir something in Freya, and she quickly finished her drink.

"I have to go," she said, squeezing into her waterproof and pulling a closed umbrella from her bag. "My cats need feeding. And I have dinner already prepared at home."

Adrian noticed the disappointment in Lenny. He'd enjoyed looking through the old photographs.

"Well, thanks for coming and showing us these, Freya—" he began, collecting them up and placing them back into the envelope.

"No, no," she said, putting her bony hand on top of his. "I brought these for you. I thought you'd like to keep them. I have copies of the larger ones and lots of other Polaroids."

With Freya gone, they ordered food and drinks, and the atmosphere relaxed noticeably. Pippa handed an envelope to Lenny— the contract for the landscaping work—which Lenny skimmed through and signed at the table. Adrian took the opportunity to chat with Pippa.

"Freya was in love with Luke, wasn't she?"

Pippa choked on the vodka she had been drinking.

"How did you know?" she asked, eyes wide.

"The large photo," said Adrian. "It's so obvious. She was totally smitten."

"You know, she absolutely hated when Luke gave me any attention. We fell out about it a couple of times. But I think all of us were a little bit in love with him, to be honest. Even Howie. Luke was like the brother he never had."

"Yeah, I can see that," said Adrian. "Luke had a certain charisma, didn't he? So he and Howie were only ever friends, if you know what I mean?"

Pippa became pensive then.

"I was the one Luke confessed to. About him not being interested in girls. I think he sensed my attraction to him and wanted to let me down gently. But I've often wondered if there was something more between him and Howie. We spent a lot of time together, so if there was, well, let's just say they kept everything well hidden. I remember one year both Luke and Howie got chatting to an Australian guy, a good-looking casual worker on a local farm, but I think that was more about research for Howie. He wanted to know the best places to visit in Australia. And then, of course, he disappeared off on his travels come his twenty-first birthday."

"When was this?"

"Howie disappearing? The year before Luke killed himself. But honestly, I feel sure the two things aren't connected. Howie's intention to escape wasn't a secret. For four years he'd worked a bunch of part-time jobs and saved up money to do exactly that, to go travelling once he was past his teens."

"Did you ever hear from him again? After he left?" asked Lenny, looking up.

"No. Not even a postcard. But that doesn't surprise me. Luke devoured books and enjoyed writing letters and postcards. Howie read comic books and signed the occasional greetings card, but that was about it. He wanted adventures, the wilder the better. Planned to travel and work his way around the world. And as I said, he couldn't wait to get away from Hobbiton, as he called this place."

"How about Freya? He must have kept in touch with her."

"So there's another thing. They may have had some similarities in appearance, but they had very different interests and rarely got along. Which was one of the reasons my mother asked me to befriend Freya. Luke was the one who brought us all closer somehow, partly because we were all so fond of him."

"What about Freya's mother and father?"

"For the most part, they were brought up by their grandmother," said Pippa, and she appeared uncomfortable telling the story. "I don't know how to say this without sounding indelicate. Freya and Howard were born out of wedlock. Their father had just turned sixteen, and had a holiday fling with a nineteen-year-old from Manchester, down this way for their summer holidays. A year later the girl's parents turned up the doorstep and gave him an ultimatum. Either he took the babies or the girl's parents would put them up for adoption. Mrs Williams, Freya and Howie's grandmother, was a thoroughly decent woman, and agreed immediately. And with the help of her son, the father, they raised them both."

"Is the father — ?" asked Lenny.

"No, he's dead. So is the grandmother. I think Freya's grandmother's death seriously affected her. Even as a kid she was never particularly outgoing, but the loss of the steadying presence of her grandmother sent Freya further back into her shell."

Everyone fell silent for a moment, contemplating the story.

"Well, this has been a fun evening," said Adrian at last, which at least raised a chuckle from Lenny and Pippa. Right at that moment, their food order arrived. "Tell you what, Pippa. To distract us and lighten the mood, why don't you tell us what plans you have for the gardens of Bryn Bach?"

By nine-thirty, they decided to end the evening. Finally, the rain had stopped, and a full moon had even decided to turn out. Adrian offered Pippa a lift, but she only lived a short walk away in the opposite direction and chose to enjoy a stroll in the cool night air.

After bidding her goodnight, Adrian walked alongside Lenny as they dodged puddles in the lamplit car park, skirting the building and heading towards Adrian's truck. When Lenny breathed out a tired and steamy yawn into the evening air, Adrian grabbed him by the arm and pushed him up against a wall.

"Wh-at?" laughed Lenny, his eyes wide with surprise.

"Oh no, you don't," he said. "You're not sleeping on me. We've got plans tonight."

And with that, he brought their lips together and felt Lenny chuckle into the embrace, before stilling, taking the kiss deeper and groaning. After a second, he pushed his hands on Adrian's chest.

"Okay, point taken. Let's get back."

Adrian got them home on the empty roads in record time and parked the truck beneath the tree canopy. Lenny went ahead to unlock the front door, and when Adrian reached him, he had already stepped across the threshold, to flick on the hallway light. When he turned back to Adrian, a glint in his eye, he sauntered seductively backwards into the house, smiling his intention. Adrian snorted and had been about to grab at him when something caught his eye.

"Lenny. Stop moving."

Lenny must have seen the seriousness on Adrian's face because he halted and looked around.

"What, Ade? What is it?"

"The floor. Look at the floor."

A set of damp footprints still glistened and darkened the dusty floorboards, moving from the hallway to the living room then back out towards the front door.

"We've had a visitor."

Chapter Fifteen

London

On his drive back to London on Sunday, Leonard mulled over the events of the night before. After a thorough sweep of the house — and finding nobody hiding, ready to pounce out on them — he and Adrian had locked and bolted the exterior doors, front and back. Nothing had been touched. The dresser, hidden beneath a dust sheet, had not been disturbed. All the intruder appeared to have done was to stroll as far as the French windows overlooking the back garden then retrace his or her steps out the front door. No footsteps had marked the stairs.

Adrian had been fearless, prepared for any confrontation, his fists clenched in readiness. Leonard had been impressed with his quiet but determined resolve, something that must have served him well on the streets. But the fading footprints had been enough to convince Leonard. Whoever had been in the place had long since departed.

"Should we call the police?"

"And tell them what?" Leonard had asked calmly. "There are no signs of a break-in. And most of the footprints have already dried up."

"I took some pictures on my phone," said Adrian. "And there might be fingerprints. By the size of the footprints, these are clearly men's shoes, so this *has* to be your cousin Matthew."

If he was going to be honest, Leonard had thought the same thing initially. But he had read enough mystery books and seen enough television crime shows to know associating shoe size with gender would have even the most junior of police constables raising an eyebrow in disdain.

"We don't know that, Ade. Yes, the person clearly has a set of keys to the house. But my aunt could have had more cut. Wouldn't it make sense to give a set to someone locally in case of emergencies? This is my fault. I should have changed the locks the moment I got here. On any other job, I would have done. Let's not push this. Nothing's been touched or taken, and nobody's been hurt. But if you could arrange for a local locksmith to come in during the week, that would put my mind at rest."

"Bugger that," said Adrian, still rattled. "I'll do it myself. As soon as Toni gets here, I'll find a local hardware store, buy the bloody locks and fit them myself."

"Whatever you say. And once we've finished the renovations, I'm going to invest in a home security system. I have a close friend who will do me a good deal."

In the bedroom that night, Leonard thought the intrusion might have dampened Adrian's sexual ardour, but the opposite occurred. As soon as they stepped into the room Adrian grabbed hold of him, kissed and undressed him, and made love to him as though Lenny were a patient needing special care and attention.

One thing was for sure. Adrian had relaxed into their coupling, slowing down and allowing Leonard to take control sometimes, no longer fast and furious as though he was on the clock. But also, something inside Leonard had reawoken. The actual act of sleeping next to Adrian felt as intimate as their lovemaking, more so perhaps, something he realised he had missed in his life, missed with all his heart and soul.

Even with the cheerful thought of catching up with his team in London, leaving Sunday morning had been an emotional wrench, especially when Adrian had taken the lead to kiss and hug him goodbye at the front door.

* * * *

On Monday, after visiting his solicitor's office for the official call with Dawson, Leonard arrived at his London office just before midday. After doing a round of greetings, he stayed at his desk, catching up on paperwork, signing letters and looking over contracts. Although tempted by the offer to go for lunch with his team, he chose to get the backlog of work out of the way. Other things could wait.

Helen Wallis' advice had been pretty much as expected. Unlike Dawson, she did not maintain any of the old-world politeness and charm associated with her profession. Neither did she mince her words. In her early seventies, she had fought her way around a courtroom and bettered many of her male counterparts.

These days she preferred loose-fitting, comfortable clothing she could wear just as easily in the garden, her hair tied up with a scarf—and wore the same attire to her office. The handful of clients she agreed to retain were long-standing and accepted her quirks along with her sharp legal mind.

"Short of proving you're not Leonard Day, not actually Colin Day's biological son, that is, or that your father was of unsound fucking mind when he signed the will—which according to Dawson, he wasn't—then there is not a court in the land that would rule in favour of your dear Aunt Millicent. These carrot-crunching fuckwits at Hope and Masters know that, but they'll still happily take the case and empty her bank account. From what you've told me, this woman is bordering certifiable, so I strongly suggest you find somebody she will listen to and get them to bitch slap some common sense into the old bag before she pours a fuck-ton of money down the drain."

"That's essentially what Dawson said. Without the expletives. If this were to go to court, how much are we talking? An estimate?"

"All depends on the angle they take and the complexity of the case. If they insist on DNA tests and getting medical professionals involved and goodness knows what the fuck else, then I'd say she should make sure she can put aside between a hundred and fifty to two hundred thousand. Hopeless Bastards will most likely ask for a retainer. How much is this property worth?"

"I've not had it valued yet. But at a guess, I'd say around three hundred thousand."

"Seriously, Colin. Is there someone who can drum some fucking sense into this woman? Even if by some miracle she were to win, she'd only end up having to sell the property to pay off her legal fees."

"That's the problem. I don't know her that well. I might see if I can reach out to her daughter."

"Can I suggest you do that sooner rather than later?"

On the drive back to the office, Leonard had wracked his brains to figure out how to contact his cousin Mary. First he'd reluctantly considered phoning his mother, until he remembered Pippa saying she exchanged Christmas cards with Mary. Perhaps Pippa might have an email or a home address.

Back at his desk, settling into his plush chair, he was about to compose a text message to Adrian, but then decided he needed to hear his voice. After only two rings, Adrian picked up.

"Hey, sexy. How's your morning going?"

Leonard could not help the smile and warm feeling filling him at the endearment.

"Pretty good. Call between Helen and Dawson as predicted, and I've just arrived at the office. How are things going there?"

"Toni works like a demon. We've already got the equipment in place to take the wall down. And the Redfern outfit turned up first thing this morning. They're already making quick work of the front garden. We're stopping for a spot of lunch right now."

"Shit. I wish I was there to see it all come together."

"Yeah. Me too, Lenny."

Adrian's soft, subtle tone of yearning was not lost on Leonard, and he stalled for a moment, overcome by the sudden flood of emotions.

"I changed the locks front and back. Drove to the superstore yesterday and found a fairly decent hardware place," continued Adrian. "I'll let you have a set of keys when you get here Friday. Toni helped me make sure all windows are secured properly. You might want to think about setting up a motion detector light at the front and back. Oh yes, and I also sent you some more design ideas for the kitchen and bathroom this morning. Thought you may want to think about getting orders in for kitchen units, in case there's a long lead time. If you need help with that, let me know."

"You're an absolute star. I'll get onto that. And I'm thinking about furnishing the house with pieces from my antique furniture catalogue, maybe use the place as a kind of showroom. Hey, if she's there, can you ask Pippa if she has an address for my cousin Mary? She mentioned sending her a Christmas card."

"Will do. What time do you think you'll get here Friday?"

"I'll try to leave early and be with you by four. Why?"

"I'll make sure Toni's gone by then. Missing you. I'm going to make dinner or get takeaway so we don't need to go out. And you may need to bring more — um — supplies, if you know what I mean."

Leonard smiled down at the phone just as a shadow fell across his workspace. When he looked up, he saw the grinning face of Kieran, who slumped across the partition between their desks. Leonard felt his cheeks heat up and coughed involuntarily into the phone.

"Will do, Ade. Uh, I'd better go. Got someone hovering, waiting to see me. Give me a call during the week, let me know how things are going?"

"Will do. Take care, sexy."

"Um, you too."

Leonard shook his head, annoyed at being forty-seven and still feeling flustered, as though he had been caught out doing something illicit or embarrassing.

"Bit of privacy here, Kieran," he said, pointing to his phone. "This could have been confidential."

"In which case, you'd have taken the call in the fish tank. So come on, Len," said Kieran, propping his elbows on the partition and cradling his head in his hands. "What's going on? You're grinning at that phone like you've just won the lottery. Or did your father also leave you a vintage Ferrari and private airplane to complement the Welsh farmhouse?"

On a video call, he had explained to his whole team about the home his father had bequeathed him, a building that needed extensive renovations. A few soft comments of '*sweet*' and '*wow*' had come down the line, but he knew they all equated the place to just another job added to his company's long list of makeovers.

"Hello, Kieran. I've missed you, too —"

"Oh fuck," said Kieran, jumping back and placing a hand over his mouth as though Leonard had just struck him. "You got laid, didn't you? While you've been away? *That's* what's written all over your face."

Leonard's eyes flashed around the rest of the office, which was thankfully still empty.

"Keep your voice down!"

"I knew it! You finally got your end away. Wait until I tell Kennedy. Who is he?"

"Not a word, Kieran. I'm serious. It's all new and may not lead to anything."

"But look at you," said Kieran, waving a hand in a circle at Leonard. "You're so — so — unknotted."

"What? What the hell's that supposed to mean?"

"Less tense, less wound tight. Chilled. Beaming. Was it good? It was good, wasn't it? Give me details."

"I'm not giving you details, you little perv," said Leonard, chuckling. "Get back to work before I sack you."

"Yeah, that's never been much of a threat," said Kieran, his eyes brightening again. "Hey, tell you what. Bring him over Sunday for lunch. Kennedy will cook. We need to give him a thorough professional eval—"

"Oh, no. No, you don't. Like I told you, it's all new. And anyway, he lives in Norwich. Besides, I'm driving back to Wales next Friday for a—"

"Dirty weekend?"

"Site inspection. And we've still got a whole load of work to do on the place, including sanding and plastering. So, yes, there will probably be dust and— Kieran! Will you stop smirking at me like that!"

No matter how hard he tried, he could never keep a serious face with Kieran around.

"You're spending a lot of time at this place. You do remember that you have tickets for the Harrogate Classic Car Show the second weekend of May? And you're also booked in to view a couple of properties in and around Dublin the weekend after? Or do you want me to take over?"

Kieran's offer was genuine. Leonard knew him well enough to know he would step in if asked, and wouldn't even complain. And the truth was that Leonard was enjoying his weekends in Wales, spending time remodelling the house, working alongside Adrian and especially sharing a bed with him. But Kieran needed his weekends, needed to spend time with his young family, and Leonard was not about to mess with that.

"No, I'm still good for both. We're getting to a point where there's not much else I can contribute to the building work, where I need to step back and let the professionals take over. And on that note, can you have a word with your husband? I need to have a state-of-the-art security system installed once the remodelling is complete. If I give you Adrian's contact number, can you get one of Kennedy's team to call him?"

"Ah, so his name's Adrian, is it? And he's a professional builder. Very nice. You know we're going to have to meet him one day, don't you?"

"Let's see how things pan out. With the house, too."

"Ooh," said Kieran, reaching behind him onto his desk for an envelope. "And on that note, boss — I got you the original plans and history of the house from the Land Registry that you requested. Very interesting reading."

"How so?"

"Did you know the house was commissioned in 1888?"

"I do now. But that's kind of what we thought."

"Hang on, that's not the best bit. The house was commissioned by Lord Charles Hawesworth."

"Okay," said Leonard, shrugging. "Sorry, should the name ring a bell?"

"He was a lord, dummy. Don't you find that interesting? Anyway, there's more. But let me start at the beginning. Being the curious but adorable person that I am, I did some digging around and Lord Charlie's father, Lord Theophilus Hawesworth — who the hell calls their child Theophilus — owned a bunch of textile mills in the Midlands. On the research, he is listed as an industrialist, philanthropist and social reformer. Oh, yeah, and did I mention that he made his fortune exploiting the working classes in Victorian sweatshops, making quality cloth for the upper-monied classes? Philanthropist, my arse. Charlie was his youngest of three."

"Very interesting. Is there a point to all this?"

"Oh, it gets better. Lord Charlie became an architect and drew up the plans for the house, his own pet project, by the sound of things. Died of tuberculosis in 1897 at the ripe old age of forty-seven, poor sod. And guess who he left the place to?"

"Queen Victoria?"

"Ha ha. No, he left the place to one Harold Hampton Day. Your great, great grandfather."

This piece of news caught Leonard's attention.

"Why?"

"How the hell should I know? Give him a ring and ask him. After that, the property remained in your family."

"Give me that," said Leonard, snatching the envelope from Kieran.

"And that, Mr Day, is why you pay me the big bucks. So are you at least going to show me a photo of this hottie of yours?"

The question stalled Leonard. For the first time, he realised he had no photos of Adrian.

"Actually I don't have one. But I tell you what. I'll snap one next weekend, and show you next time I'm back."

"The hell you will. You know how to add a photo to a text message. I know you do, I showed you. So send me a copy as soon as you snap one."

"You're a pushy little so-and-so, aren't you? How does Kennedy stand it?"

"He'd be lost without me. So would you."

Leonard would, too, but said nothing. If Kieran was as much of a fireball in the bedroom as he was in the office, then Kennedy was one lucky — if perennially tired — husband.

* * * *

Friday couldn't come soon enough.

Even with the hectic distraction of the office, Leonard had gone back alone to his empty house each night. Never before had doing so been an issue. He had resigned himself to the idea of living out his final days alone in the house he'd once shared with Kris.

Something fundamental had shifted.

A couple of times that week he had found himself in the office whistling or humming tunelessly along to a song on someone's playlist, something he had never done before and much to the annoyance of those around him.

On Monday, Pippa had texted Leonard the home address for Mary Whitby, his cousin. She had no telephone number or email address, so Kennedy used some of his company letter-headed paper and sent her a note asking if she could call or email him

Every evening, Adrian called — they spoke more than texting now. On Thursday he could not suppress his excitement when he updated Lenny about the progress on the house.

"Damn good choice with Redfern, Lenny. Pippa's crew will be pretty much done by tomorrow. Honestly, the back garden looks amazing and the front is almost finished. Not only can you see the incredible view at the back now, you can actually tell there's a house here. I was going to send you photos, but I think you should see for yourself in person. They're going to wait for you to decide whether you want to replace the patio tiles before adding the finishing touches. We can discuss that at the weekend. Toni's helped me remove the kitchen wall and open up the back for the new patio doors. And, as instructed, on Monday I ordered them on your account along with the windows you requested, the wooden-framed ones that match the original style. Ten-day turnaround, they say. So they're being fitted on Friday of next week. I thought getting things sorted out here in the sticks would be far more difficult. Pippa gave me the name of a local guttering expert, someone who can check, then match replacements or patch what you already have. They'll be here Tuesday. Toni started checking the electrics this morning. They're not in a bad state of repair but are going to need updating. She reckons she'll have downstairs done by next Thursday — so we can start plastering the following weekend — and the rest by the Friday after that. I suggest you get those kitchen units ordered A-SAP. Did you get a chance to look at my rough sketches?"

"Wow, slow down a bit. Rough sketches?" Leonard snorted. He had one open on his desktop monitor. "Swear to God, Adrian, these are better than professional architectural blueprints. They're all to scale too, aren't they?"

"As near as."

"Love the idea of steel-grey and white units. Monochrome, but there will be enough natural light from the rear doors, and the lighting design above for the evenings to compensate. They'll also blend with the original dark pine flooring. In fact, I love it all. And I agree with you on the Aga front. They may look fancy and they're great if you know what you're doing — but I don't. I'm going to opt for a simple but large conventional cooker with a double oven. I'll also go with a double-door fridge freezer. How many bar stools can we fit one side of the kitchen island?"

"Comfortably? Four, with one either end. But I imagine you'll put a family dining table in the space by the patio doors."

"I've already picked one out and reserved a list of other pieces from my antique site. Got a couple of amazing burnished brown leather Chesterfield sofas and side chairs for the living room. And the table and chairs will complement the Welsh dresser."

"On that note. Don't forget the skeleton keys. So we can unlock those drawers. Toni needed the dresser moved away from the wall — to check out the wiring — and had to have a nose around beneath the dust covers. She was really impressed, asked me if you'd consider selling the piece if she gave you a good price. I said she didn't have a hope in hell."

Lenny laughed. Adrian already knew him well.

"You're right. If Luke wanted it in the house, then so do I."

"Good. One last thing. A slight change of plan tomorrow evening."

"Sounds ominous."

"The handbrake on my truck has been playing up for a while and seems to be getting worse. Nothing too serious, but I'm getting it looked at Saturday morning. The thing is, the mechanic's from a place called Newton — half an hour's drive away — but doesn't know the area well. Rather than him getting lost trying to find Bryn Bach, I asked Megan if I could leave the truck in their car park and the keys behind the bar. The Manor Inn's a pretty easy-to-find landmark. So I thought I'd drive there tomorrow after finishing here and park the truck overnight. But that means I'll need to meet you at the pub tomorrow, rather than at the house. Is that okay?"

"So you're not cooking for me?"

"I could still do that. You'd need to pick me up from the pub first."

"No, it'll be too rushed. Let's eat and drink there again."

"I'm really sorry, Lenny. I had it all planned, a nice cooked dinner. But I don't want to chance anything when it comes to the brakes, especially on a long drive back to Norwich."

"Totally agree. I want you in one piece. It's no problem, Ade."

"I can still cook for us on Saturday night. I'm buying the food fresh tomorrow. That old fridge of yours is running fine, by the way. A bit noisy but working. I've even used the stove a couple of times this week."

"And haven't burnt the house down?"

Adrian chuckled. Leonard sensed he had been disappointed about changing their plans, but they would still have the night together.

"House is still standing."

"See you tomorrow night then. Looking forward to it."

"Yeah, me too, Lenny. Me too."

When Leonard ended the call, he smiled to himself, pleased he had no nosy marketing manager looking over his shoulder. Tossing the phone on to his sofa, he looked about the house he had lived in for twenty years, at the familiar but largely empty walls, at the simple, but now tired and uninspiring furnishings.

Since Kris' death, he had used none of his creativity or enthusiasm to breathe life into his real home, to try and turn the place into somewhere he wanted to inhabit. Instead he treated the space like a mausoleum. All his recent attention and newfound enthusiasm had been focused on Wales.

Maybe in the future, with Adrian's help, that was something he would remedy.

Chapter Sixteen

Familiar

Adrian arrived at the now-familiar bar of the Manor Inn at six-thirty, lucky to find a small round table still available. He straddled the knee-high stool facing the front door as soon as he'd bought drinks, anticipation filling his chest. The place had almost become as familiar as the Red Lion back in Drayton and, if pushed, he could probably recite the bar menu word-for-word. He'd introduced Toni to the place on Monday — almost empty, as usual — when she'd met Megan and the daughter, whose name turned out to be Maggie.

Friday night and the place was bursting at the seams, with all the larger tables already occupied. Tonight Megan was assisted by a man around the same age — her husband probably — and her daughter, all helping to serve the crowds. He noticed the man at one end of the bar now, during a lull in service, chatting and laughing with a group of men around the same age. Even being busy, both Megan and her daughter found time to come over and say hello, to collect the truck keys from him and ask after Leonard and the renovations on the house. No doubt they had become a popular topic of gossip in the quiet town.

"You're a proper regular now, aren't you?" said the daughter, Maggie, as her mother returned to the bar with empties. Adrian recognised the flirty look well, had spent a lifetime reading the signs.

"Feels that way," laughed Adrian. "Who are all these people, anyway. And why is the place so busy?"

"Are you serious? It's the May bank holiday weekend, isn't it? Where have you been?" Adrian had been holed up in the house all week, with just Toni's smartphone playlist and Bluetooth speaker to keep them company. "Most of them's holidaymakers. Dad's pleased, of course, 'cause all our rooms are booked up and we'll probably be rushed off our feet next week."

"Is that your dad behind the bar?"

"Yeah, lazy sod. Usually lets us run the place when it's quiet. Had to get off his backside tonight. Those old blokes are all his local buddies. You should go say hello."

"I'm good, thanks," he said, winking at her, which made her laugh and put some colour in her cheeks.

When she left, Adrian rechecked his phone. Almost seven. Leonard had texted him from Swindon and said he'd be arriving around sixty-forty-five, traffic willing. Why the hell did he feel such nervous excitement just looking at the message? Maybe because he wanted Leonard to relish the way the house was shaping up as much as he did. Or more likely because he knew he would have someone sharing his bed tonight.

During the week, Toni had insisted they venture out farther during a couple of the evenings, to find different places to visit and more varied food to eat. Adrian had come to realise just how provincial the area actually was— probably the way Howie had felt about Newbridge and the surrounding area. Drayton in Norwich, where Adrian lived, was hardly a metropolis, but at least the town had a regular bus service, its own train station and more shopping choices. Then again, maybe that was the charm of somewhere like Newbridge, that the town remained far enough away from the noise and trappings of modern life.

"What are you smiling at?" came the warm, all-too-familiar voice.

Adrian's head shot up, followed by his body, which almost knocked the table over.

"Lenny," he said, wanting to hug the man, but quickly coming to terms with his surroundings. Instead, he thrust a hand out in welcome.

"Whoa, careful there," said Lenny, his own hand coming down to steady the table. Without caring what people thought, Lenny ignored the outstretched hand and stepped around the side of the table. Without hesitation, he grabbed hold of Adrian and pulled his body into his own. Adrian allowed himself to be encompassed by the man, let the warmth and strength of his arms hold him as though they were long-lost friends.

"Are you sniffing me?" muttered Adrian after a second, chuckling while squeezing Lenny back.

"What if I am?" said Lenny, letting him go and taking a seat. "I've missed you."

Adrian waited until they both sat down, for Lenny to remove his coat and settle, continuing to stare intently at him until their eyes met.

"I missed you, too," he said, winking. "What was the hold up?"

"In case you hadn't noticed, there's a gale whipping up out there. Don't think there'll be rain, but it's going to be a wild night." Lenny winked back at Adrian. "If I play my cards right."

Lenny's grin widened into a full, unabashed smile, and railroaded Adrian's usually ever-present appetite for food. He wanted them both to drink up so he could take Lenny back to the house.

Unfortunately, Lenny had other ideas.

"Before that, however," he said, placing his phone and car keys next to the pint glass, "I really need this pint. And I'm famished. Haven't eaten since breakfast. What are the specials tonight?"

While Lenny chugged on his beer, Adrian rattled off the three specials, none of which had particularly caught his imagination. They both settled on the beef and ale pie with onion mash, on the basis that it would probably be quicker to prepare and finish up.

When Adrian returned from the bar, Lenny was on his phone. Adrian stood by his stool and mouthed to Leonard whether the call was private, Lenny shook his head and pulled the phone to his chest.

"It's my cousin, Mary. Just give me a second."

Adrian nodded and tried to concentrate on his pint of ale but kept catching Lenny's eye.

"It's okay," said Lenny into the phone, meeting Adrian's eyes and winking. "Your mother explained that to me at the funeral. I hope everything's okay?"

Adrian grinned and looked away. He noticed the man he'd pegged as Mr Llewellyn, chatting with his daughter and peering over at them.

"I see. So listen, the reason I wanted you to contact me is because my father left the family's Welsh holiday home to me. That's right, Bryn Bach. Well, it seems your mother is none too pleased about the outcome—"

Even Adrian could hear the voice at the end of the phone becoming loud. Lenny looked at Adrian and pulled a face, which had Adrian chuckling.

"The point is, she's threatening me with solicitors to challenge the will and, from everything I've been told, she doesn't have a hope in hell of winning. She'll basically end up throwing a lot of money away based on—"

Lenny stopped again to listen and nodded slowly while taking a sip of his beer.

"That would be really helpful, Mary. Let me know how you get on. I don't really want us to go down that route, but I've had to deal with disputes all my life, so I have my own legal adviser ready to go."

Once again Lenny waited for her to finish talking.

"Perfect, thanks, Mary. And I didn't say, but I'm in the process of renovating Bryn Bach, giving the place a new lease of life, so to speak. Once we're done, and only if you're happy about it, I would love for you and your husband to come for a house-warming."

Lenny smiled into the phone.

"Absolutely. Just let me know. But it would be great to finally meet you. And one last thing before I go. Do you know if your brother still has keys to Bryn Bach? Or if somebody locally might have a set? I'm only asking because I think someone's been keeping an eye on the place. Is that right? Okay, I see. Well, I'll let you go and thanks for your help."

When he put the phone back down, and after gulping beer, he filled in the gaps for Adrian.

"She said she's not surprised. Her mother is a chronic obsessive. Once she gets her mind set on something, she never lets go. Just hope you never meet her, Ade."

"I don't know. I'd like to see her go a few rounds with my mother," said Adrian, grinning. "Does Mary still see her? Your aunt?"

"That's the weird part. They're no longer on speaking terms. She sees her father still, but refuses to talk to her mother. Never said why, though. Funny how Aunt Millicent never mentioned that little nugget at the funeral. Anyway, she said that although her mother won't speak to her, she knows somebody who might talk some sense into her. She's going to try, then get back to me next week."

"That's good. Mary sounds like a grown up. And what was that about Matthew?"

"She called him hopeless, said if he kept the keys at home he'd never remember where he put them. Apparently he used to leave them down here somewhere, but she has no idea where or who with. And another thing. She said that, to her knowledge, he hasn't been down here for years. Which is not what he intimated at the solicitors' office."

"Interesting. So our intruder could be a local?"

"Let's not think about it. Come on. How's progress going? I can't wait to see the place."

Adrian brought Lenny up to speed with the few things that had happened since their call the night before. Adrian had managed to call the local guttering specialist, who also provided roofing services. So he had asked them to check both and make any necessary repairs when they came on Tuesday. Even over the phone he had been able to tell the man knew his stuff, referencing the photos Adrian had sent him and explaining about the local materials used. Towards the end of his short update, Maggie appeared at their table and crouched down to their eye level.

"Sorry to interrupt. I was in the kitchen putting your order in when chef says we got a delivery today. Fresh steaks," said Maggie, her voice lowered. "Wagyu rib-eye. Not on the menu 'cause he's only bought a few, see? Thinking about adding them to the menu. And as you two are as good as regulars, he thought you might like first pickings. Don't get me wrong, the pies are fine, too, but he thought you might like something different. For sides, he's got French fries or Lyonnaise potatoes, with fried onions, grilled tomatoes and mushrooms. Only if you're interested."

"Now you're spoiling us," said Lenny. "And I would love the steak. Cooked medium, with the Lyonnaise. Ade, how about you?"

"Same. French mustard, too, if you have any."

"Same," said Lenny.

"You two make me laugh," said Maggie, chucking genuinely. "You're like bookends, always ordering the same. I'll let Chef know. There's a bit of a lull in the kitchen right now, so it shouldn't be too long. If any of the nosy buggers comes over and asks, tell them you ordered them through the chef who got them in specially for you."

"The friend I had with me asked your chef if he would ever consider serving up steaks," said Adrian. "On Monday. Is that why—?"

Maggie said nothing, simply smiled conspiratorially before patting her forefinger against her nose a couple of times, and leaving them both laughing.

"We're officially locals," said Lenny.

"Feels good, doesn't it? But promise me something."

"What's that?"

"No matter how hungry you are, we skip dessert. I need to get you back to the house."

"To show me the progress you've made. Yes, I know."

"Yeah," said Adrian, smirking. "That, too."

* * * *

Lenny parked his SUV in the usual spot, hidden beneath the low-hanging tree. By the light of the headlamps, Adrian had begun to explain the changes to the front garden as they drove past the full skip sitting in the lane—now covered with a tarp sheet in case of overnight rain—through the open gate and down the driveway. But the blustery wind buffeting the newly pruned trees and bushes, viewed in the headlight's glow, did not do the work justice. Eventually he decided Lenny should wait until morning, for the weather to calm and for the clear light of day, to see the transformation for himself.

As soon as Lenny moved past the threshold with his holdall and closed the front door behind them, Adrian had him pressed up against the wall. Lenny's bag hit the floor when Adrian brought their mouths together. How had he managed to go his whole life without discovering the magical power of lip-on-lip action? Lenny still tasted of beer and steak, but Adrian focused his mind on the brush of their tongues.

"Whoa, hold up, Ade," said Lenny, chuckling but gently urging them apart, scanning something behind Lenny's head. "What's the rush? We've got all weekend."

"You've been away for a week. A whole bloody *week*. And I'm fifty later this year," said Adrian, trying to pull Lenny's shirt over his head. "Before long I won't even be able to get it up. So I'm taking what I need, while I still can."

Lenny burst into muffled laughter when Adrian pulled the shirt over his face.

"Don't be ridiculous," said Lenny, giving in and helping Adrian remove his shirt. "You've got more energy and stamina and appetite than someone half your age, so quit with the sob story. I haven't even showered yet—"

"I don't care. Don't make me carry you up the stairs."

"Okay, okay. But can I have a quick look at the living room first?"

"Quickly, then."

Adrian reached past him and flicked on the lights to the living area. Still smiling, Lenny strode past Adrian and stood in the middle of the completely opened-up space, turning a full three-sixty. Adrian watched him with mounting pleasure, Lenny's eyes marking out what had been done during the week—the complete removal of one wall that used to section off the corridor and the kitchen, the plastic sheeting along the back of the house, filling the hole where the sliding patio doors would fit, the sanded-down floorboards and woodwork.

"Security-wise, are we going to be okay with plastic sheeting on the back of the house?" asked Lenny.

"Security-wise," said Adrian, matching Lenny's business-like tone, "there's absolutely nothing to steal in the house—apart from that dresser, and I'd like to see anyone try—so they'd be wasting their time. And even if they did get past the plastic, they'll be confronted by me. Or worse still, Toni. So I pity any poor bugger who does try to break in. And remember, by next Friday the new doors and windows will be installed and the place will be completely secure."

Lenny turned and grinned at Adrian.

"Is that your way of telling me to stop worrying?"

"That's my way, Mr Day," said Adrian, stepping closer and grabbing Lenny by the arm, pulling him towards the stairs, "of telling you to stop talking and to get your damn clothes off."

By the time they reached the top of the stairs, both men were down to briefs, each holding clothes in their arms, Lenny still clutching his large carryall. Adrian led Lenny purposely to the back bedroom, where a light burned, because he wanted him to sleep there and view the remodelled back garden by the morning light.

But first things first.

Adrian had never experienced anyone like Lenny, the complete trust he gave, the way he actively sought to reciprocate sexually. All his past encounters had been one way — even those he hadn't gotten paid for — and his objective had always been to make sure the other person left satisfied in as short a time as possible. Some habits had become ingrained. Lenny, by contrast, insisted they take their time. And what had initially seemed exasperating had become a revelation and a total turn-on, exploring, experimenting and memorising the other's body, remembering touches, and kisses, and ways to elicit gasped reactions.

Adrian had been with men of all ages, young and old and in between — but nobody like Lenny. Everything about him aroused Adrian — the man's natural woody scent, how nothing appeared to faze him in the bedroom, and more than anything, the way he pushed Adrian's boundaries of intimacy and left him ravenous for more.

Before they slept, Lenny insisted on taking a shower then laid out his clothes for the morning. Once again, he had brought the bare minimum. Track bottoms and trainers, socks and underwear, a couple of sweatshirts and tees. In bed with Adrian, he wore nothing, not even briefs. And Adrian did the same. As they settled back in the bed and lay next to each other, Lenny threaded his hand into Adrian's, another cosy quirk that had begun to mean the world to Adrian.

As they lay there in silence, both not quite ready to sleep, Adrian filled in the silence.

"Hope you don't mind, but I showed Toni the Polaroids Freya gave you. Told her the story of Luke. Only fair really, as she agreed to sleep under this roof. Some people might have freaked out."

"And? Was she fine?"

"Yeah. Nothing fazes Toni. Strong as they come. But she was visibly upset about Luke."

Lenny went quiet beside him. Maybe he shouldn't have brought up Luke, especially after the fantastic sex they'd enjoyed. Perhaps he should just let Lenny savour the house and the present. But Toni had suggested things neither of them had considered, something Adrian wanted to discuss with Lenny in person.

"Do you think Luke was in love?" he asked.

Lenny turned his head on the pillow and scrunched his eyebrows up at Adrian.

"That's a strange question. Why do you ask?"

"It's something Toni said when I showed her the snapshots. She says that in the later ones, when he's probably in his mid to late teens, he has that smitten look about him. And when I studied them again, I noticed she was right. He has this knowing smile and bright, laughing eyes when he stares into the camera lens. She thinks he was in love."

"With Howie?"

"I asked her that. She says it might have been, but she doesn't think so. Said in all the shots they're together, they don't seem anything more than just friends. She said she thinks it's a secret love."

"Secret love, huh? Romantic much, this Toni?"

"Yeah," chuckled Adrian. "But it would be nice to think Luke had someone to love, before he took his life."

"Or maybe that's why. Maybe the love wasn't returned."

"Unrequited love. Sounds very Shakespearean. But yeah, I never thought of that. And I guess it's not something we'll ever know."

* * * *

That night, Adrian's dream felt real. He sat in an open field of tall grass, knowing beyond any doubt that Lenny was with him, but never quite in his line of sight. Under a hot summer sun, a fantastic picnic had been set out with selections of cold meats, cheeses, Scotch eggs, pork pies, sausage rolls, pickles, with a basket of fresh fruit and loaves of fresh bread. Luke sat cross-legged opposite Adrian on a red and green tartan picnic blanket, with a young Freya and Pippa each side of him like bookends. He laughed at something Adrian had said while ripping a bread roll into smaller pieces. Pippa unscrewed a bottle of soda, a tube of paper cups in front of her, while Freya laid out the food, arranging the fare artfully onto a wooden cheese board with slices of green apple and dried apricots. Now and again Luke's smile would blossom, at the rumble of a diesel engine running in a distant field, his eyes drawn to something or somebody over Adrian's left shoulder. Still, whenever Adrian turned to look, he could not make out the image, the person or thing continually lost from view every time he tried.

Despite the sense of fun and innocence, Adrian felt an undercurrent of something evil, a danger lurking just out of sight of the long grass. Once again, he turned to try and find Lenny, but his lover was nowhere to be seen. When he turned back, Luke's eyes had become serious, concerned, his gaze on the clouds. And in that moment, the skies darkened unnaturally and someone—Lenny?—was urging them to get up and run, forcibly shaking his shoulder, bringing him out of his reverie.

"Adrian, wake up. Wake up!"

Adrian wanted to protest, insisting the storm would pass, but the voice was unrelenting, the hand continuing to jostle him roughly. Something acrid and toxic assaulted sense of smell. Had somebody set light to the field?

"Ade. Seriously. Get up."

Adrian surfaced blearily at Leonard's urgent tone, and noticed him already up, hopping into his track bottoms and track shoes.

"Get some clothes on. I think the house is on fire."

Chapter Seventeen

Woken

After sleeping soundly at first, Leonard had woken in the small hours. Rogue gusts of wind rustled trees in the back garden and battered the side of the house, making ghostly howling sounds down the chimney and rattling a loose windowpane. Intermittent moonlight, occasionally appearing past what he assumed to be racing clouds, shone through a crack in the curtains, projecting a silver sword across their bedcover. Adrian slept soundly lying on his side facing him, his chest rising and falling, the sound of his breathing even and oddly comforting.

Breathing life back into the old Welsh house had warmed Leonard, in the same way getting to know Adrian first as a friend and now as a lover had felt like a rebirth, a resuscitation even. After meeting a client, followed by the long day of driving and an unexpectedly enjoyable steak dinner, he had been ready to fall soundly into slumber. But Adrian had a way of waking his body, which in turn stimulated his mind better than a problem waiting to be solved. Now he lay there, awake and alert, thinking about the strange sequence of events since his father's funeral.

A sudden rush of wind hitting the side of the house dwarfed the faint sound of breaking glass, agitating the trees again and making the whole window frame shudder. Maybe he had imagined the glass shattering, but something nagged him about the sound. When ghostly moans and wails came down the chimneystack and echoed from the fireplace, he lifted his head from the pillow.

He strained his ears to listen when the wind subsided, but a strange calm had filled the room. Until something else nudged at his senses. Leonard had been around enough building sites to know the distinctive smell of burning.

"Adrian, wake up. Wake up!"

By the time Adrian had woken, Leonard was ready to head down the stairs but Adrian, pulling on his sweatshirt and boots and only a fraction behind, insisted they go down together.

From the top of the stairs the orange flicker of fire already lit the stairwell. As they rounded the bottom of the stairs, tall flames burnt fiercely amid broken glass by the front window. Contained in one spot, the blaze already reached as tall as Leonard, feeding on a dust sheet discarded on the floor.

"This is not good. I'm sure that's petrol I can smell," said Adrian, who looked tired still, but had rallied from sleep remarkably. "Go outside and call the fire services. Let me handle this in here."

"Sod that, Ade. I'm going to stay and help."

"Fine, but please call emergency services first. In case this gets out of control."

Leonard dialled the emergency number and gave details. He noticed Adrian's eyes flicker around the room before he headed towards the kitchen area. As soon as Leonard ended the call, he went over to the fireplace and picked up the red bucket of sand. Unfortunately, over time, the sand granules had clogged together, and he had to tip the bucket upside down and thump the base to unstick the contents. By the time he had dislodged the sand and scooped some onto the fire with little effect, Adrian had returned carrying a large fire extinguisher and immediately started dowsing the flames with white powder.

Leonard stood back, amazed at how quickly the flames receded. Before long Adrian had extinguished the fire completely, and the room returned to its darkened state. Both of them stood unmoving, Leonard still stunned at what had happened. Moonlight shone in through the plastic sheeting at the back of the house.

"Do you think it's safe to turn the lights on?" he asked eventually.

While he had been talking, Adrian must have moved over to the light switch, because the room was suddenly flooded with light. By the starkness of the naked bulbs, they could see the extent of the damage. Not too much, from what Leonard could tell. Fortunately, they hadn't started decorating yet, so whatever smoke damage had happened could be disguised with fresh plaster and paint. He noticed Adrian studying the front window, pointing to the jagged hole in a large pane of glass.

"This was no accident, Lenny. I'll bet odds this was a petrol bomb. You want me to see if I can catch whoever did this? They can't be long gone. I will, if you say the word."

"Christ, no. Absolutely not, Ade. If they're capable of this, then what else are they capable of? I don't want to put you in any more danger."

"Fine, but this time we get the police involved, yeah?" said Adrian, heading towards the front door, and turning in the doorway to address Leonard. "This is why we always shift all fixtures from the property as soon as possible when we're renovating. Imagine if we'd piled all those old wooden kitchen units up by the window. This place would have gone up like a tinderbox. Hold up, I think I can hear them approaching. Let me go out to the lane and let them know it's been contained."

When Leonard listened, he could hear the faint sound of a siren in the distance. Adrian wanted to be of help, so Lenny let him go. Instinctively, he checked the time on his phone — 4:55 a.m. Alone with his thoughts, he looked around the room. Last night he'd barely had the chance to view the renovations, but now he acknowledged the great job they'd done, his enthusiasm tempered in the aftermath of the fire. All walls had been plastered and levelled, all floorboards either sanded down or replaced, ready for a coat of varnish, even the power sockets and light switches Leonard had chosen were installed downstairs. Adrian and Toni had worked hard and the place, when finished, would look amazing. And now somebody seemed intent on undoing everything they had done.

Why on earth would somebody want to burn the place to the ground? Did this have something to do with Luke's dysfunctional family? Adrian was right, though. Maybe Leonard did not see the need to tell the police about the intruder, but this little stunt could not — *would* not — go unreported. Tomorrow he would call the home security company he used — Kennedy's outfit, Grey Steel Global — and get them to install the best they had, front and back. No expense spared and no more pussyfooting around. What if this had happened with Adrian and Toni alone in the house? Had they been injured or worse, he would never have forgiven himself.

Within twenty minutes the room filled with firefighters and a couple of police officers. As best he could, Leonard stayed out of the way and let Adrian do the talking, while he made hot drinks for everyone. Fortunately, somebody — Toni, maybe — had brought a large pack of paper cups, so all Leonard needed to do was boil water and spoon coffee or dunk in tea bags. No doubt, at some point, one of the policemen would want to speak to him, but for now he enjoyed seeing Adrian in action. Both police and firefighters had singled him out because he had been in the house for the whole week and also because he'd had the foresight and good sense to have a class two, dry powder fire extinguisher on-site with him. One of the firemen also pointed out the plastic sheeting on the floor, which was coated with a flame retardant.

As expected, one of the policemen, the younger one, came over to take down Leonard's contact information and other details. Leonard thought he might ask questions about the incident. Eventually the older of the two, who had been busy looking over the grounds and the rest of the house, moved over to talk to Leonard and allowed the younger man to continue his work. Sensibly, they had divided up their tasks. Much older than his counterpart, this policeman reminded Leonard of the jovial-looking village policeman depicted in early British films.

"You're the new owner, Mr Day. Is that right?"

"Correct."

"I'm PC Morgan. Charlie Morgan. I saw you in the pub only last night. I was having a pint with Dave Llewellyn, landlord of the Manor Inn, and our friends. Megan says you're the late Colin Day's son."

"You knew my father?"

"No, son," said PC Morgan, chuckling. "I'm only fifty-eight. But some of our older residents remember him coming to Disserth, and I've known some of your other family members. Why don't you give me your account of what happened here tonight."

Leonard pulled out a couple of the folded chairs and invited him to sit. PC Charlie Morgan turned out to be a good listener, nodding and asking pertinent questions. In between, he talked about himself over his cup of tea, as though they were old friends.

"Fifty-eight and still with the Dyfed–Powys Police. Should have got pensioned off years ago, what with all the cuts in forcing, but they managed to keep me hanging on. Not sure if I'm pleased or pissed about that."

Partway through being interviewed, the firefighters, the other policeman and Adrian came to join them in the very basic, very empty kitchen. Everything appeared to have been wrapped up and they decided to enjoy a bit of respite together. Someone even brought over the yard broom they'd used to clean up the debris. Leonard happily dished out more teas and coffees, found a packet of digestive biscuits in a plastic tub, and placed everything on the small square table. Amused, he realised this would constitute the first gathering he had ever had in the house.

"So what do you think happened here?" asked Leonard as they made appreciative noises about the beverages. Behind their heads, outside the plastic sheeting, Leonard noticed the sky becoming paler.

"From what we can tell," said the older of the firemen, "the fire was started by a very crude Molly— Molotov cocktail—a petrol bomb. They used a clear glass bottle with a plastic stopper, filled with petrol and traces of engine oil. The bottle smashed on impact but the stopper and bottle top are still intact. Good job you don't have curtains or furniture in the house, otherwise there could have been more serious damage."

"I only ever employ the best builders," said Leonard, winking at Adrian, who smiled back. "Who assure me that a clean site is a safe site."

"Quite right too," said the fireman, then to Adrian, "I hope he's paying you well."

"He's very generous," said Adrian, winking at Leonard.

"Well, we're done here," said the man clearly in charge. "Charlie, we'll have a proper report on your desk by Monday, if that's okay. You coming with us?"

"No, you go on, lads. I've got a couple more questions for Mr Day and Mr Lamperton. Bobby, go and move the car, will you? Give the lads room to back the fire engine out of the lane."

Eventually, the firemen and the younger policeman filed out of the house and closed the front door behind them. Once they had gone, Adrian unfolded a collapsible wooden chair and joined them.

"Very nice brew this, Mr Day."

"Leonard. Please call me Leonard. And this is Adrian."

"Leonard and Adrian, it is. So you and Adrian know each other professionally?"

Leonard caught Adrian's anxious gaze.

"We do. But we're also old friends."

"Old friends who shared the same bed last night?"

Adrian coughed and Leonard felt his cheeks getting hot.

"Don't mind me," said PC Morgan, grinning. "I'm not judging. I had a peek around upstairs and couldn't help but notice only one bed had been slept in. But I'm also just trying to figure out motives, and why somebody would want to try to burn the house down in the middle of the night with the two of you still inside. Of course, that's assuming anyone knew you were inside. Your car is completely concealed by the tree outside and there'd otherwise have been no signs of life. Do you keep any lights on inside the house?"

"None. I'm a bit of an energy freak about lights, about leaving them on."

"Fair enough. Although sometimes a couple of lights in a house can be a good deterrent. But what I'm getting at is that somebody could have assumed the place was empty. Of course, that still doesn't excuse them or explain why they would want to burn the place to the ground."

Leonard volunteered how his late father had left him the property and how his aunt had decided to challenge the will. Leonard also told him about the intruder.

"And you didn't think to report this?"

"With hindsight, I should have done. Adrian thought I should, but no harm was done. And to my knowledge, the only other person with a set of keys is my cousin. So we got the locks changed and assumed that would be that."

PC Morgan jotted down a few notes on his notepad as Leonard gave him the details.

"I see. And the full names of your aunt and cousin?"

"Millicent and Matthew Darlington," said Leonard as PC Morgan stopped writing and looked up from his pad. "I don't know if they have other names."

"Millicent Darlington? Now there's a name I didn't think I'd ever hear again."

"You know her?"

"I know *of* her. Let's just say I've been here before. In this house. Long time ago, mind. Suicide. Dreadful affair."

"Luke Darlington?"

PC Morgan had been looking about the room as he spoke but brought his gaze back to scrutinise Leonard.

"She told you about him, did she?"

"Not her. My mother told me. Luke was my cousin."

"Was he now? First suicide I'd ever dealt with. Terrible affair. I think it pretty much broke his father."

"So I heard."

"Three years after I first joined the force. Twenty-five, I was. Still really doing my apprenticeship with my old gaffer, PC Rhys Schofield. He passed on some ten years back. But I remember the day well."

"You found him?"

"His father found him. Story is he'd gone missing and been reported locally to the Clifton police. Mike, his father, sent the younger son, Matthew, to look in all Luke's regular haunts around Clifton, while he drove here. We got the call at lunchtime, from the Manor Inn. They didn't have a landline in the house back then. Was in a proper state, was poor Mr Darlington. He'd had the sense not to touch anything. Something I've learnt in my career is that in emotional cases like that, people often touch things at the scene, try to cut down the body, and in doing so ruin what could be decent evidence. When we arrived here, the lad was still hanging there, the ladder tipped over on the floor."

"Anything suspicious?" asked Adrian. Leonard could almost have predicted the question from him.

PC Morgan laughed at that.

"My old gaffer was scrupulous. Wanted everything checked and double-checked. He treated someone taking their own life on his patch as a personal affront. But Luke had written a suicide note, penned by his own hand, neither forced nor forged. Only Luke's prints were in the room. Everything had been carefully arranged by him. No doubt about it, he took his own life. Mrs Darlington was the only one who didn't come down, but she insisted we record the fatality as accidental death, fairly screamed at my old gaffer down the phone, she did, when he refused. Seemed more upset about that than the actual death of her son. But there was no mistaking. He'd taken his own life."

"What was the motive?" said Adrian. "From what we've heard, he had everything to live for."

"I'm afraid that's something he took with him. Although I have my suspicions."

"And what were they? Just out of interest?"

"From what I could tell, Luke got on with his dad, but his mother wore the trousers in the family. Luke fought against the current but I reckon he got to a point where he couldn't take any more of her. My gaffer thought he may have also had certain inclinations and proclivities—and I'm sure you of all people know exactly what I'm alluding to here—that went against the mother's strict religious ideology."

"Pippa Redfern, an old friend of his, seems to agree with you. I like to think we live in more enlightened times." Leonard purposely smiled at Adrian then. "So what happened? After Luke was found?"

"Another story altogether. The fallout from the incident was almost as bad. After that, the Darlingtons stopped coming to the area. Don't think they were welcome anymore, not by most. Locals gossip, naturally, and the whole incident fairly shook up the townsfolk. You see, crime round here was, and still is, committed largely by outsiders over the holidays. Mostly petty stuff, you know? Drunks disturbing the peace, drink driving, the rare case of domestic abuse, kids shoplifting, that kind of thing. We used to have four or five caravan sites dotted around the area back then. Farmers made extra income renting out fields. We rarely saw serious crime. Most deaths aren't suspicious. They're mostly from natural causes and on occasion from accidents on farms usually involving casual labourers doing stupid things."

As PC Morgan spoke, Leonard looked up with disbelief when Morgan's counterpart stepped in through the plastic sheeting at the back of the house. The realisation hit him hard that anybody could get into the house if they wanted, despite Adrian's reassurance. He made a mental note to chase the window company, to see if they could deliver and install earlier, and if not, to provide more substantial security at the back of the house. Oblivious, Adrian pulled out a chair for the young policeman and handed him a cup of tea.

"I remember we had three accidents the year I joined. Unheard of in these parts. All preventable, but made worse by the heavy rains over the summer. One local guy, Max Williams, lost his footing while repairing a fence on the steep side of a duck pond. Down on the Hughes' farm, it was. Tragic. Nobody knew the poor bugger couldn't swim. By the time Hughes' son went to check on him it was too late. Then we had this popular Australian bloke, Hunter somebody, helping on the farm out by Franksbridge. Loved driving the tractor, he did, but went up a wet slope far too steep. Bloody thing came down on top of him. Didn't stand a chance. Locals would have known better. Last was an English lad, not much younger than me back then, slipped and fell off the roof of a farmhouse in Nantmel and landed on some machinery, cleaning leaves from the guttering of all things. Sort of thing you ought to leave to the professionals, in my book."

"Max Williams?" asked Leonard. "Freya's father?"

"You're becoming a proper local, aren't you? Fairly common name around these parts, Williams. But, yes, that's him. Nice bloke, he was. Took after his mum. Thirty-six, he would have been when it happened. Used to do odd jobs around the town, anything he could get to provide extra cash for his mum and his kids. But also volunteered helping out with local causes. Folk really liked him."

Leonard nodded. Perhaps he was beginning to understand how Freya had come to be a recluse, losing her father at such a young age, her brother going on his travels the following year, and then Luke taking his own life the year after that. Her grandmother passing away must have been the final straw.

"Charlie, do you think we could get back?" said the younger policeman. "Only, we've got to write up this report and, well, I wouldn't mind getting back to the missus before the kids wake up."

"Yes, of course, Bobby. Don't mind me. You know how I like to gab when I get the opportunity. Okay, gents. I'll leave you be. Make sure you get that window boarded up."

"We will. And just to let you know," said Leonard, "I'm putting in CCTV at the front and back of the house, and also installing security lighting. Early next week, if the installers can fit me in. So if anyone else tries anything, I'll be able to provide you with solid video evidence."

"That sounds like a sensible precaution. In the meantime, I'm going to check into Matthew Darlington's whereabouts and Bobby here's going to examine local footage on road cameras to see if anyone was in the area last night. Unfortunately, I know for a fact that we have very few in this area, but we'll do our best. We've got your contact details, so we'll be in touch."

Leonard stood with Adrian at the front door, watching the men in uniform stroll back down the driveway by the early morning light, chatting together. Once they were out of sight, Leonard closed the door, sighed, and thumped his back against the wooden door panels.

"Do you think it was your cousin Matthew?" asked Adrian. "Who started the fire?"

Once again, Adrian had been reading Leonard's mind. The more he thought about what Mary had said, the more he agreed that Matthew was too ineffectual to bother going to such extreme lengths. But if I wasn't him, who was it? And the more burning question — for want of a better expression — was why?

"I've no idea. Let Morgan do his job and check him out. One thing's for sure. I'm making a call later, once the world's woken up, and calling in a favour from my friend Kennedy. I want this place safe for you to work and stay in next week. God, Adrian. Have I done the right thing? Refurbishing this place? The last thing I want to do is put you and Toni in any danger. I'm wondering if it's all really worth the effort — "

"Stop right there," said Adrian, abruptly, before taking Leonard by the arm. "And come with me."

Leonard let Adrian lead him across the living room towards the plastic sheeting. Sunlight had begun to glow through the opaque, translucent material. Reaching out with his free hand, Adrian found a parting in the sheet and scooped a handful aside before pulling Leonard through, into the morning light.

As soon as Leonard stood still and took a lungful of fresh morning air, he realised what Adrian was doing. From the vantage point of the raised patio, the garden had been transformed. Lush, manicured lawn stretched down to the outer edges, where evergreen bushes marked out the boundary. As promised, Pippa's company had erected a pretty gazebo in the far right corner, with a small bench inside looking back to the house. All around the edges of the lawn, bushes of differing heights and varieties had been planted, with some original flora — the apple tree behind the brand-new garden shed, the three firs along the right boundary. But it was the panorama beyond that caught Leonard's breath, the sun rising over a blanket of various shades of verdant patchwork marking out the farmlands of Wales, with dark waterways meandering through, all beneath a sky of pure blue optimism.

"Now tell me it isn't worth the effort," said Adrian, lacing his fingers into Leonard's.

"Okay. Point taken. Next time I start to complain, bring me out here. This is truly amazing."

Everywhere Leonard looked, he picked out more details. A small bird box had been installed in the apple tree, while all around the patio, Pippa's company had provided long garden boxes of what he assumed to be herbs and colourful but easy-to-maintain garden flowers.

"What time is it?" asked Adrian.

"Coming up to six-thirty," said Leonard, checking his phone. "What do you want to do? Go back to bed?"

"After all that drama, there's no way I could sleep."

"Who said anything about sleeping?" said Leonard, squeezing his hand.

Adrian snorted, released their hands and folded his arms.

"As much as I like the idea, I think I ought to board up that window first, while you go and tidy up the kitchen. You'll be done before me, so I suggest you go up and shower first, I'll follow. And then, because I need to be fed, we head to the Manor Inn for breakfast. I don't fancy doing anything around here this morning. Is that okay?"

"Agreed on the breakfast front. But I thought maybe this morning I could put my skeleton keys to good use and find out if there's anything locked away in the drawers of that dresser."

"I forgot about that," said Adrian, brightening. "Good plan."

"No idea why, but I've got a feeling we might find some answers today."

Chapter Eighteen

Discovery

As a rule, the Manor Inn only provided breakfast for in-house guests renting rooms, the actual pub closed for business until ten-thirty. But Megan, who was on duty that morning and usually pretty strict with her house rules, welcomed them like family. Only once they had been seated did they realise why.

"First off, the car mechanic from Newton came by at six on the dot this morning and drove your truck away," she said, her eyes on Adrian. "But more to the point, what in the name of all that is good happened last night? Fire engine siren blaring past here in the early hours, waking the dead. We'd only gotten to bed at one, what with all the weekend revellers. My Dave said it sounded like they was heading out your way. Phoned the fire station in Llandrindod Wells to find out. They wouldn't tell him much but I assume you must have had a spot of trouble. Am I right?"

Adrian looked to Lenny. He didn't know how much he wanted to divulge. Fortunately, Lenny answered for them.

"We had a fire in the house. Nothing serious and Adrian here managed to get everything under control before the fire crew arrived. But we called them out just to be on the safe side."

"Oh," said Megan, a slight hint of disappointment, pulling a small pad and pencil from her apron pocket, ready to take their order. "Well, of course you're right. Better to be safe than sorry."

"I've been on building sites all my working life," said Adrian. "So I know to keep a decent fire extinguisher handy. But of course, once the firefighters had been called out, they needed to do a full inspection."

None of what they said was untrue. No doubt, though, at some point—if PC Charlie Morgan were close friends with Dave Llewellyn—they would know the real cause. Adrian wondered if they ought to confide in Megan. After all, she had eyes and ears everywhere. Once again, Lenny was way ahead of him.

"Megan, can I tell you something in confidence?" asked Lenny. "You'll probably hear about this sooner or later anyway."

Adrian almost grinned at the instant change in Megan Llewellyn's expression, morphing from the relaxed, friendly but somewhat bored landlady, to being completely engaged and focused.

"You can tell me anything, dear," she said, her voice low, as she pulled out a seat.

Lenny explained not only about the petrol bomb thrown through the window, but also about having an intruder letting themselves into the house. Adrian watched as Megan's mouth dropped open in shock. As Lenny described them getting the fire under control before the firefighters and PC Morgan arrived, Megan simply nodded and tutted a few times, but did not once interrupt.

"The thing is, Megan, to my knowledge, the only other person who knows where the place is and has a set of keys is Matthew Darlington—"

"And Freya Williams."

"Sorry?"

"The Williams family used to have a set of keys. Didn't Freya tell you? From what I understood, one of their family kept an eye on the house all the year round, and used to go in to clean, dust and air everything before they arrived. Well, the Darlingtons didn't use the place from one year to the next. So once the Williams' got notice, they'd clean up and also put some basics in the fridge. They'd also go in and clean after the Darlingtons left. You didn't know?"

"No, I didn't," said Lenny, catching Adrian's eye.

"You should check with Freya. I think Mr Darlington paid them a little something for their trouble. But after everything that happened, they may have taken the keys back."

"Just out of interest, though," continued Lenny. "When was the last time you saw Matthew? It's probably nothing, but I'm just trying to rule him out."

She sat back in her seat then and scratched the pencil into her scalp.

"December just gone," she said, eventually. "Would have been a Friday. But he didn't stop over. He'd been to check the pipes in the house on that death-trap of his. Came in here for his lunch on his way back to Bristol. Never one for chatting much, is Matthew. You don't honestly think he was behind it?"

"Probably not," said Lenny. "As I say, I'm just trying to rule people out."

"Death-trap?" asked Adrian. "What do you mean?"

"His motorcycle. Dave knows the make. Noisy old thing should have been put out of its misery years ago."

Adrian turned to Lenny, who appeared to know instinctively what Adrian was thinking and shook his head. Lenny had been the one awake and had not heard the sound of a motorbike last night. Although, in fairness, the winds could have muffled any engine sounds.

"But I'm guessing you never heard a motorcycle engine last night," said Megan, catching on too. "Because, believe me, if he'd been on that noisy thing, you'd have known. Sounds like a machine gun, it does."

"Point taken." Lenny laughed, relaxing. "And no, we didn't hear anything."

When the conversation lulled, Adrian piped up.

"Can we get two of your fantastic fry-ups with all the works?"

"Of course you can, dear," said Megan, who appeared a lot brighter now. "First, let me fetch you some tea and coffee the way you like it."

Once they had finished, at around seven-thirty, Adrian asked Lenny to drive him to the food superstore in Llandrindod Wells.

"Are you sure you want to cook?" asked Lenny as they pulled out of the pub car park.

"Absolutely. I was going to make dinner last night, remember? Least I can do is cook for you tonight."

"And as much as I appreciate the gesture, that's not part of your contract."

"Neither is sharing your bed. But I'm still keen to do that, too. And anyway, more to the point, what contract?"

Lenny tipped his head back and laughed.

"Good point. I never did get you to sign anything, did I?"

"Your word is good enough for me."

The comment had been made lightly, but Lenny became quiet. After driving along an empty lane for a few moments, he reached a hand across and squeezed Adrian's thigh. Adrian placed his hand on top and laced their fingers together.

"How did I ever find you?" asked Lenny.

"I think we found each other."

* * * *

With the food shopping done, they arrived back at the house at ten o'clock. As Adrian collected the food bags from the back seat, Lenny opened the glove compartment and pulled out a small wooden box. Intrigued, Adrian stood and watched him, and Lenny lifted the lid to display a keyring with over thirty ornate-looking keys of all shapes and sizes.

"For the dresser," he explained to Adrian, before heading for the front door.

"I thought when you mentioned a skeleton key, there'd be one master key that opened everything. Like they use in every television crime drama series I've ever seen."

"For some modern locks there is. But with antiques, the carpenter could have used any number of styles of lock, which means the keys will also vary. But I've pretty much got them all covered here, so it's just a case of trial and error until we find the right one. To be honest, I could probably pick the lock—I've got a small tool that I've used before for that—but this way, we get to see what key has been used and I can get replacements made."

"I've got no patience for that kind of thing," admitted Adrian. "Let me put the food away, and while you do that, I'll carry on with the list of outstanding jobs Toni left me."

"Sounds like a bossy so-and-so, this Toni."

"She's the best in the business. Thorough and professional. Think yourself lucky she was free."

"I do. I'm only kidding. I think myself lucky to have both of you. I'll give you a shout if I manage to get any of the drawers open."

Adrian set about his mini-tasks — sanding down the wall in the kitchen, readying for Toni to complete the wiring and plastering, checking floorboards downstairs and marking with chalk any mismatched or damaged ones and replacing the broken floorboard in the alcove where they'd found the dresser.

With Lenny huffing over at the dresser by the front window, he began prising up the floorboard. Tony had cut out plywood and covered the area to ensure nobody stepped onto the faulty board. Within minutes, Adrian had the old board pulled up and found a replacement from the spares they had removed from the kitchen. Lenny had decided to lay flagstones in dark-grey limestone to delineate the kitchen from the main living area. Cutting the board into place, Adrian heard Lenny again, cussing softly, keys jingling on the keyring. As he passed Lenny, he leant in and pecked him on the cheek.

Almost by accident, when Adrian went to check the area for the new floorboard, he peered into the floor space and spotted something in a small dusty sack with a drawstring around the top. Using his gloved hand, he lifted out the item. When he pulled the drawstring open and tipped the bag up, three bronze keys clattered into the palm of his other glove. Unable to stop the burst of laughter, Lenny looked over.

"Look what I found buried in the floor," said Adrian, holding them out. "Any idea what they might be used for?"

"You're kidding me? They've been there all this time? Bring them over here and let's give them a try."

Adrian handed them to Lenny and stood by, curious to see if they had found anything.

"These look right. I'm guessing the smaller key opens the three drawers and the larger ones are for each of the cupboards. Do you want to do the honours?"

"No, Lenny. This is your property and your family. You go ahead."

A mood of anticipation surrounded them as Lenny unlocked the first drawer. Surprisingly, the drawer opened smoothly, but all they found inside was an old newspaper lining the bottom. The other two drawers proved stiff and more difficult to open, but neither revealed anything of interest — a button in one, a couple of rusty screws and drawing pins in another.

When Lenny tried the first of the cupboards, the one on the left-hand side, they struck lucky. Wedged inside he found a cardboard box of Polaroids. Most of them were of Pippa, Freya and Howie, but they were far more interesting, far more candid and unposed than the ones Freya had shown them. Some were of Luke, wearing headphones, a Walkman in his hands. Occasionally the shots included Luke's sister, Mary, and sometimes, an older man, probably in his thirties and usually in the background, who Adrian assumed to be Freya and Howie's father. Included in the collection they found less candid pictures — these ones posed and formal — of Matthew and his sister, sitting on the lawn in the back garden of Bryn Bach, reading or drawing. At the same time, a much younger, recognisably severe-looking Aunt Millicent looked on from her deckchair on the raised patio. But even those told a story.

Towards the bottom of the box, Lenny pulled out a brown envelope containing shots of random older men, the collection only slightly faded with time but still sharp and surprisingly homoerotic. All of the men looked to be in their twenties, one handsome guy with freckles and red wavy hair, bare-chested and smiling unsurely at the camera. Another shot, taken in what looked to be the garden of the Manor Inn, showed two men with drinks at a wooden table, straddling the bench so that they sat facing each other, and grinning broadly at a shared secret. Multiple snaps of a bronzed and muscled farmhand stood out, a blond-haired guy wearing a thin white vest, almost obscenely short blue shorts with thick thighs and long legs descending into Wellington boots, who looked to be fixing the massive wheel of a tractor. Unlike the others, this man smiled and laughed openly, enjoying the attention, posing almost seductively for some pictures, but in others comfortable in his work and seemingly ignorant of the camera. The photos had been taken at different times because in one he was wearing a rugby shirt and chatting with Pippa and Howie. One thing was for sure. The cameraman had been captivated by his subject.

"We ought to find out who that is," said Adrian.

"He's good-looking, isn't he?"

The pang of jealousy Adrian felt caught him entirely by surprise.

"Is he your type?"

"When I say he's good-looking, I'm speaking objectively. He does nothing for me in that way. Too young, too clean cut, too innocent. Turns out you're my type."

Even if he had wanted to, Adrian could not have stopped the smile that rose from deep within him.

"Yeah?"

Lenny leant in and kissed him on the lips.

"Oh, yeah."

"So maybe we should show some of these to Pippa," said Adrian, putting one snapshot to one side. "She's in this one with him, so she might remember who he is. What's that at the bottom of the box?"

"Postcards," said Lenny, reaching for them and flipping one over to read. "Sent from Bristol. Addressed to Howie and Freya from Luke to let them know the dates he would be coming to Bryn Bach."

"Try the other cupboard."

The second one turned out to hold even more interesting items. From inside, on the top of a pile, Lenny pulled out an old camera in its original packing.

"This is an Olympus OM1," said Lenny, turning the box in his hands. "They were all the rage when they first came out. I wonder if Luke had hidden this to use later for his photography course."

In the cupboard, they also discovered a collapsible camera tripod with six unopened boxes of Kodak 35mm film, and an old cassette recorder. While Lenny sorted through them, Adrian pulled out a pile of old books. One had pages of photographs by the famous portrait photographer, David Bailey, another showed the Polaroids of Andy Warhol, while the third entitled *The Americans* was by a photographer called Robert

Frank. Apart from that there was a pile of well-thumbed paperbacks, including the first *Tales of the City* by Armistead Maupin, *The Collected Poems of Wilfred Owen*, *Maurice* by E. M. Forster, and a small, tattered, *Berlitz Travel Guide to Italy*. Adrian had read them all except the travel guide. Armistead Maupin's *Tales of the City* series had been his go-to books in London during many a dark day when he had been feeling low, something to lighten his spirit and make him feel the world was an okay place to live in, no matter who you were, or how you chose to live your life. He took the book from Lenny and smelled the musty pages. He was moved knowing he and Luke had cherished the same book, had read the same words.

Adrian flicked through the pages and noticed a couple turned over in the corner. He used to do the same thing, not as a bookmark, but to highlight passages or sections he enjoyed reading over again.

"Oh my goodness. Look at this," said Lenny, handing Adrian a couple of larger photographs. In another envelope, he had discovered a sheet of folded paper and some very old pictures, in what Felippe had once referred to as sepia tones — dark brown and cream colours. Adrian smiled, seeing the image of Bryn Bach during its construction. In another, six workmen of varying ages in shirt sleeves, flat caps, baggy trousers and work boots had been arranged rather stiffly and uncomfortably around a man in a smart black suit with a waistcoat, a high collar and black tie. Obviously from the upper classes, this besuited man sported long sideburns and peered haughtily at the camera.

"Lord Charles, I'm guessing. But have a look at this."

In the last photograph, Lord Charles had his arm around the shoulders of one of the younger construction workers, one who bore a passing family resemblance to Lenny.

"Looks like Lord Charlie took a shine to your great, great grandfather."

"I think you may be right. And look at this. It's our family tree."

Adrian peered over Lenny's shoulder at the beautiful calligraphy mapping out the family's bloodline.

"No doubt our ancestral tree began before this, but Luke must have been intrigued to know about Lord Charles Hawesworth, the man who left the house to Harold Hampton Day, our great, great grandfather. According to this, Harold married at twenty-one and had four children, the oldest being Denham Charles Day."

Adrian followed Lenny's finger down the page, where someone had pencilled in Bryn Bach against individual names. All through their family history, the house had been left to the oldest son in the family.

"Why would your grandfather decide to break with tradition and leave the property to Luke? Surely your father should have been the rightful owner after him."

"Maybe he knew how much Luke loved the place. Maybe he discovered how oppressed Luke was by his mother and wanted to provide a safety net. I met Grandpa George a number of times. My father always referred to him as frighteningly perceptive. I remember my grandpa saying to my parents once, in front of me, that I was never going to waste my life in academia, but destined for commerce or other things more business orientated. I'm betting he told my father of his intentions to leave Bryn Bach to Luke and probably explained why."

"You think he knew Luke was gay?"

"No idea. But as I said, the old fox could be perceptive. And my father would have understood. He clearly had no interest in the house, otherwise we'd have visited."

"But it still ended up his and yours," said Adrian.

"Ironically, it did."

"So," said Adrian, "I guess the crucial question remains. What does all this tell us?"

"What it doesn't tell us is why Luke would take his own life. Putting personal items aside is the kind of action someone takes if they're thinking about their future."

"We definitely need to talk to Freya and Pippa again. Show them what we've found."

"I agree. And maybe we can find out if Freya has a set of keys to the house."

* * * *

Adrian found the simplicity of the old cooker's controls soothing. No digital timers or confusing LED controls, no convoluted fan-assisted or conventional cooking options, just one large white dial for the oven's temperature. Sometimes he agreed with his mother that modern societies had overcomplicated their lives with fancy gimmicks and gadgets they didn't really need with features they spent hours trying to master – and didn't need either.

Adrian showered before Lenny then set about food preparations. With everything cooking, he set the small table with a red and white paper tablecloth and matching napkins, items he had bought at the superstore. Even though he'd brought plates and cutlery from home, they had no wineglasses, so the bottle of chilled Chablis with the meal would be enjoyed out of glass tumblers, continental style.

With only the old fridge, the cooker and the sink in the kitchen, the space seemed ridiculously vast, but at least the smells coming from the oven made up for the lack of decoration. One downside to the old-fashioned stove was the solid metal door design, not glass like modern ovens, which prevented him from checking progress without opening the door and losing valuable heat. But he had cooked the recipe often enough to know when the food would be cooked.

They had shared many meals, but for some reason, this one felt special. Maybe because just the two of them would be sitting in the room, or perhaps because this would be their last for a few weeks.

"Okay, Chef, how's it all coming together?" came Lenny's voice as he rounded the corner. "Smells amazing."

"Pretty good, all things considered."

"That old oven must have been built in the seventies," said Lenny as Adrian stood at the cooker, checking the potatoes in the saucepan. Lenny pressed his body up against him, put his chin on Adrian's shoulder and kissed his neck. "I'm surprised it's still working."

"Us old things were built to last." Adrian pushed his backside gently into Lenny's groin. "Make yourself useful and pour me a glass of wine."

Lenny moved away to the old fridge and pulled out the bottle.

"Next time I'm here, we'll have a modern kitchen with fitted units, a long kitchen island, a huge oven and an even bigger fridge."

Three weeks. Lenny had told him he'd be gone for three weeks because he had a motor show in Yorkshire and some Irish properties to view over the next couple of weekends. He had tried hard not to show his disappointment when Lenny told him. On the plus side, he could knuckle down and get the place finished without any distractions. Apart from a few odd jobs and unlocking the dresser, they had done very little this visit.

Except sex.

They'd had plenty of sex.

"Just so we're clear. We're going ahead with the downstairs shower room and the full upstairs bathroom, with a separate bath and shower cubicle."

"Correct. All units and fixtures should have been ordered. If you think of anything else, let me know and I'll give you a quick decision. I've got Toni's and your invoices, so I'll get those paid within the next couple of weeks."

"You know, most of the clients I work for have at least a sixty-day payment clause. Fourteen days is unheard of in my profession."

"Yes, well. You're doing me a favour. And I'd like to think I'm more than a client."

As Lenny poured the white wine into glasses, he caught Adrian's eye and winked.

"And what do you think about Toni's suggestion?" asked Adrian. A waft of heat blasted his face when he opened the oven door and checked on the food. "Solar panelling? You've definitely got enough roof space. And I can help her install them for you. It'll save you a heap on electricity bills, even if it won't mean getting off the grid completely. I just think it makes sense, if you're not living here all year round."

"I think it's a brilliant idea. Sorry, I thought I'd already said so. I'm going to have to meet Toni. She's done amazing work in the house. You both have. When I'm down next time, could we all have dinner together?"

"I'll let her know. Maybe I can invite her partner, Jack, to join us," said Adrian. Using a dessert spoon, he dished up the salmon and vegetables onto plates, ready to serve. "Can't believe that next time you're here, we'll have pretty much everything finished. And then I'll be out of your hair."

Only after placing both plates of food on the small table did he meet Lenny's eyes. While handing Adrian a tumbler of wine, and clinking glasses, Lenny asked, "And what if I like having you in my hair? What then, Ade?"

Adrian couldn't help smiling at Lenny. He had been thinking along the same lines. They lived so far apart, but the last thing he wanted was for this intense connection to end.

"We'll cross that bridge when the time comes."

Somehow they would need to find a way.

Chapter Nineteen

Summons

Leonard hadn't seen Adrian for three weeks.

Three whole weeks since he had shared a bed with his lover, and, of course, since someone had tried to burn the house down. Which is why he had been relieved to hear Adrian enthuse about the comprehensive security system, one the installers had shown Adrian how to control using his mobile phone. Adrian had talked Leonard through installing the application and they had set a secure password together, so Leonard could now view all around the house externally, and also inside the downstairs living areas.

And in those three weeks, while Leonard had been running around England and Ireland on business, Adrian and Toni had made incredible progress. Adrian had kept him in the loop, naturally, with photos showing the transformation.

Leonard had felt a personal pride in finally getting the old family home restored. Moreover, if he was going to be perfectly honest, he had also enjoyed letting go and trusting Adrian to work his magic without Leonard being there. He knew Adrian would work to Leonard's same exacting standards.

With the new windows, window boxes, external painting, garden, guttering and roof repairs completed, they had turned their attention to completing the final tasks. The house now had a new open kitchen and bathroom suites, fully compliant electrics, plastering, painting and tiling, treated and polished floorboards and staircase. On his instruction, Pippa's team had even replaced the garden patio and low surrounding wall, matching the original design they'd seen in Freya's snapshots as well as adding boxes with flowers and herbs around the patio. All he needed now was to fit in the pieces of furniture he had chosen with Adrian.

But in Leonard's mind, all of their hard work would have proven pointless without one final arrangement. To fill the house with friends, family, fun and laughter. And with that thought in mind, he had already contacted his friends and colleagues to tell them to reserve a date for a house-warming at the end of June. All he needed to do now was to talk to the locals he knew around the area.

Early in the week, Adrian confirmed that Toni and her partner would stay over on Friday night, in part to help them put the furniture in place but also to be his first official guests for dinner. Once they left on Saturday morning, he would have Adrian all to himself.

Everything seemed to be going exactly to plan.

Until Wednesday morning when Mary had sent him a cryptic text message to tell him her mother, Aunt Millicent, had asked to discuss something urgently with him and could he drop in to see her. At first he'd hesitated, wondering why they couldn't simply speak over the phone or why his aunt couldn't meet him halfway. Mary had explained how her mother rarely left her flat, and what she wanted to discuss needed to be done face-to-face. Leonard had finally capitulated and arranged to see her at midday on his way to Wales.

"It's not a worry, Lenny," said Adrian, placating him again on Friday morning, as Leonard sat in his car readying to leave. "The important thing is that you're going to be here later today."

"We could have been having lunch together if the woman would deign to use a phone. Anyway, depending on what she has to say, I should be with you by four, at the latest."

"Then chill. But remember it's Friday, and traffic will be manic."

"Listen out for the furniture truck. You'll need to check everything and sign off for me. I doubt they'll be able to get down the drive, but you can try. If not, you may have to help them unload."

"If you're not here when it arrives, do you mind if I get Toni and Jack to help me arrange the furniture in place? I already know where you want everything."

During their weekends together, Adrian had helped Leonard choose the furniture and decide what would look best in which part of the house. They had agreed on most things, and the few they had disagreed about, Adrian usually had a better, more practical reason for the placement.

"As long as you guys don't mind. Will be great to see the place finished. But I'm not being much help, am I?"

"I'll think of a few ways you can pay me back when you're here."

Leonard laughed aloud and felt instantly better. He'd missed Adrian. With everything finished, he would need to sit Adrian down and figure out how they were going to move forwards. One thing was for sure—he wanted Adrian in his life.

Before setting off, he checked the address and postcode given to him by Mary and tapped the details into his GPS. From previous conversations, he seemed to remember people saying they lived in Clifton in the Bristol area, but the address of the flat was for somewhere called Broadmead. Not knowing the city, he assumed the latter to be a neighbourhood of Clifton.

Even with the GPS, he still managed to get muddled and stopped to ask a passer-by for directions. Just as well, too, because the old chap he spoke to recommended he park up at a nearby municipal car park then walk the five or ten minutes to the council flats. If he chanced parking outside in that part of town, his 'nice-looking motor' would either get towed or stolen or stripped bare. Those were usually the three options in that area, he was told.

So he chose to walk and arrived at an uninspiring low-rise apartment block, nothing out of the ordinary, just before midday. Despite an apparent attempt to spruce up the external façade of the building, the interior felt old and tired and worn.

His aunt's flat stood on the second floor at the end of a long walkway. The peeling purple door had a once shiny stainless-steel letterbox cum knocker, now mottled by opaque blotches. Unable to find a doorbell, he knocked and waited. A few minutes later, someone unlatched the door.

"Ah, Leonard," said his aunt, smiling thinly. "How nice. Please come in. Go through to the parlour."

Although she still had the same pinched and guarded expression, the same dark, suspicious eyes, she seemed older somehow than when Leonard had seen her at the funeral. Grey strands of hair, those that had escaped the brutal restraint of her black headband, fell to the sides of her face. Over a drab but straightforward stone-grey dress, she wore a baggy black cardigan with a hole in the left arm, the pale flesh of her forearm showing through and a dried mustard-coloured stain near the neckline. Only the pink woollen fluffy slippers seemed at odds with the rest of the sombre ensemble.

She opened the door wide, and he entered into the corridor of the duplex, the stairs to his left. As he approached the back room, he noticed a large crucifix fixed above the entrance.

The room seemed comfortable enough if a little spartan. A two-seater sofa and single armchair in faded green corduroy faced an ancient box-like television, the view from the windows obscured by bleached-white net curtains.

"Take a seat while I fetch us some tea. Then we can talk."

With his aunt gone, Leonard scanned the living room. A worn pair of leather slippers, men's style, sat next to the room's old electric heater. Most of the titles on the bookshelf meant nothing to Leonard, except for the Bible. But the collection had theological themes or made direct reference to faith and Christianity. To one side of the shelves, only one photograph stood pride of place, of Aunt Millicent in the middle, with Matthew on one side, probably in his teens, with a girl he assumed to be Mary on the other. Apart from her shoulder-length hair, they looked almost identical.

Even though they dressed in summer wear, only Mary smiled at the camera.

Five minutes later she returned and lowered the tray onto the glass coffee table before perching on the edge of her seat, back stiffly upright. Barely bending forwards, she poured tea from the white teapot into each mug, one plain purple, the other with the red and grey crest of a football team.

"With or without?" she asked, holding up the carton.

"With, please."

After pouring a splash of milk into the chipped football team mug, she stirred the tea with a white plastic spoon before handing the drink to Leonard.

"How is your mother?" she asked, handing him the mug.

"Thank you. She seems to be coping well. I've been checking in with her regularly, maybe a little too much. She's always been fiercely independent."

"Everyone grieves in their own way. Some of us prefer solitude, time alone with the Lord, when dealing with our losses."

Knowing his mother's stance on religion, the words of solace would have meant nothing. She had been far from alone spending much of her free time in the company of his Aunt Marcie. But then his aunt appeared to be alluding to her own mechanism for coping with loss. Was she referring to the death of her son? After taking a sip of her tea, she appeared to get straight down to business and Leonard steeled himself.

"Can I assume you're planning on keeping Bryn Bach, Leonard? Seeing as you're already in the throes of restoring the old place. And that you're not planning to sell?"

How she knew about the renovations, he had no idea. He had told Mary, but Mary said they didn't talk to each other. Maybe Mary still communicated through Matthew.

"Yes, I'm keeping the house. Surely that's not why you asked me here?"

"In part," she said, before plucking a crisp white letter from her lap and handing the single page to him. "The main reason for inviting you here was to tell you I've formally dropped any legal action concerning the will. This is the acknowledgement letter from my solicitor. Matthew convinced me to see reason, to respect the legal process and my brother's wishes and to realise that keeping the house in the family is what's important. We've enjoyed the home for many years and I'm grateful nobody else, outside the family, is going to become the new owner."

Leonard studied the concise letter from Hope and Masters briefly before handing it back. So Matthew had eventually persuaded his mother to back down. Maybe his cousin had some influence and common sense after all, although Leonard had a feeling that somewhere in the background, his cousin Mary may have played a part.

"No, I am going to keep the house. But just so we're clear, because I don't think you have a true measure of who I am as a person yet, I was fully prepared to drag you through the courts, if that's what it took. And even if it had taken years, and thousands in legal costs, I would not have lost. Do we understand each other?"

His aunt sat studying him impassively for a few moments.

"We do," she said, her lips pouting. "Yes, I recognise certain traits of my brother now. The same single-minded stubbornness."

"I'll take that as a compliment."

"Whatever you wish," she said, before reaching into her pocket for another envelope, this one old and well-worn, and removing an aged piece of paper. "But just so you understand my original concerns around the property, this is a letter I received from my father many years ago."

Leonard took the crumpled letter and read. The words, written in his grandfather's cursive handwriting, confirmed what Leonard already knew. In a clear and steady hand, the crux of the message stated—

Traditionally, ownership would have passed to the eldest surviving male member of the family, which in this case is your brother, Colin. However, I have decided to break with tradition and leave the house to your eldest. I have arranged for my solicitor to amend my will accordingly. Your brother knows of my intention and is fully supportive of my decision.

"With the property being transferred to my side of the family, Leonard, I hope you can see that it was only natural for me to expect the house to revert to me."

"Don't be absurd," he said, handing the letter back. "After your eldest died, and long before my grandfather's death, he amended the will again to leave the house to my father."

"Without my knowledge."

"I seriously doubt that," he said, not caring if he rattled her. "My grandfather had no reason to hide anything from you. If you're so adamant, why don't you check with his solicitors, if they're still around. In any case, you would have known at the reading of your father's will, an occasion I can't imagine you would have missed. Not that any of this matters to me. In changing his mind and his will, he did nothing illegal."

"Unless he was coerced into doing so by my brother."

"Good luck trying to prove that."

Whatever ridiculous point she was trying to make, Leonard knew better than to listen. He had somewhere to be. Leonard's father had inherited his integrity and common sense from his own father. Aunt Millicent seemed to sense Leonard's hardened resolve because her face softened a fraction.

"Have you written up a will of your own, Leonard? And have you considered who would inherit Bryn Bach if anything were to happen to you?"

"I have a will. But I haven't thought about Bryn Bach specifically. Not yet."

"And do you have any expectation to marry?"

"That's nobody's business but my own."

She nodded, whatever thoughts going on behind her frosty exterior hidden from him. As though reaching an internal decision, she smiled at him.

"I must admit to being pleasantly surprised to hear you are restoring the old house."

Leonard folded his arms and relaxed back in his chair. If she wanted, he could play nice. Not difficult when he thought back to the progress they had made.

"In my line of work, I deal with period homes all the time. Bryn Bach is a simple, but solidly constructed house, which lends itself beautifully to the surrounding countryside. What came as a pleasant surprise was learning the history of the house, and getting to know the local area, as well as finding traces of our family, especially Luke—"

"No!" she snapped, thumping her mug down, her eyebrows drawing together. "We do not mention that name in this house."

Leonard frowned, startled by the whiplash change in his aunt's mood and tone. Her face had now tightened around the mouth and eyes. After a few moments, he regained his composure.

"I don't understand. He was your son—"

"You will *not* mention that name. Do I make myself clear?"

As far as overreactions went, Aunt Millicent's seemed absurd. Moreover, how could any mother refuse to recognise the existence of her child, even if he had taken his own life? Leonard's mother was hardly the most maternal in the world, but at least she acknowledged and supported her son. If his aunt were intent on making him feel uncomfortable in her home, he would abandon any politeness.

"Well, while we're on the subject of the house, can I ask what happened to the furniture? My furniture? I understand my grandfather had some nice pieces, because I've seen the photographs of when your family used to stay. And the will stated quite clearly that I was to be left the house and all chattels, which in my experience means the contents of the house."

His aunt sat up even straighter and stiffer in her chair, exuding an air of defiance.

"I had the furniture sold. Many years ago. Your grandfather approved. This was long before your father took the house from us. I had children to put through schooling and my late husband was, among other things, an incompetent provider."

Late husband? On their call, Mary had said she still kept in touch with him, and from what he could tell, she hadn't meant through a spiritual medium. Did his aunt tell people her husband had died to save her the embarrassment of telling them he had walked out on her? Whatever. Leonard was not about to be fobbed off.

"You had my grandfather's written consent for the sale, I assume?"

Not once did she blink when she replied.

"Consent was granted verbally. What does it matter? The furniture was old and needed replacing anyway."

Based on the Polaroids Leonard had seen, the furnishings looked far from worthless. But without being able to corroborate her story with his grandfather, he could nothing realistically about the missing furniture.

"I see. I suppose I should be grateful for the cast-iron bed frames and the dresser—"

"Dresser? What dresser?"

"The Welsh dresser. Boarded up in the wall," said Leonard, enjoying the moment. "You didn't know?"

Once again, Leonard discerned a moment of surprise followed quickly by annoyance cross her face.

"I wasn't aware. My son, Matthew, negotiated a lump sum for the furniture clearance many years ago. That particular piece must have escaped his notice."

"Or maybe hidden by the person who should rightfully have inherited the house. There were some interesting old photographs and other items inside the dresser's cupboards."

She studied him coldly now, clearly curious and waiting for Leonard to elaborate. She could wait. If she wanted to play games, then so could he. Instead, he decided to move the conversation in another direction.

"Not sure if you were aware, but one of my online businesses deals in antiques. And I'm told that particular dresser is a classic piece, in almost mint condition. Would fetch a tidy sum at auction. Not that I intend to sell. A beauty like that needs to be returned to its rightful place in the living room, now the rest of the house has been restored. I'm on my way to complete the final checks as soon as I leave here."

She sipped from her mug of tea and glowered at him over the rim.

"That's nice. And how have the renovations gone?"

"For the most part, very good. Although over the May bank holiday, while we were asleep in the house, someone threw a petrol bomb through the front window into the living room and started a fire."

Aunt Millicent's tea mug froze on its way back to the tray.

"While you were —?"

"Asleep. I was asleep in the upstairs back bedroom, the one overlooking the back garden. Fortunately I'm a light sleeper. We managed to get the fire under control before any permanent damage could be done. But of course the police and fire services had to be called, and the incident officially reported."

Seeing his aunt's ashen cheeks, Leonard felt sure this piece of information came as news. What he was not about to tell her was that since then, he had arranged for security lighting and a comprehensive camera surveillance system to be installed both front and back. If anyone tried anything similar again, he would catch them. Of course, since the incident, nothing more had happened.

"The bank holiday, you say? Probably hooligans on holiday from the Midlands. That part of Wales always did have a problem with petty crime over the holidays. Caused by heathen youths, no doubt. I blame the parenting. Discipline seems to be a thing of the past."

Leonard said nothing. He cringed inside to think of his aunt's views on discipline.

"I've gotten to know a number of people in the area since I started the work. Some you might know. Megan Llewellyn at the Manor Inn, Pippa Redfern, Freya Williams." Leonard took a sip of the milky tea before continuing. "Had a good chat with PC Morgan, too, when he came to investigate the fire. He remembers you well."

"Does he?" asked his aunt, her stare unwavering.

"Sounds to me as though you had some lovely holidays in the area. As a child, with my father, and also with your own family."

His aunt put her mug down on the table and composed herself, a thin smile on her face.

"We did, Leonard. Which is why families need to stick together and help each other —"

"By threatening to take them to court?"

"And on the subject of helping each other," she said, ignoring his question, "I hope you don't mind me offering you some advice."

Leonard hesitated. What advice could his aunt possibly have that he would want to hear?

"I was informed you have a Mr Lamperton working for you at the house. A freelance builder. Is that correct?"

Leonard met her gaze, staunching the temper rising in him.

"Informed by who?"

"Whom, dear. It's informed by —"

"Who told you?"

"Does it really matter? The point is, how well do you know this man?"

"Well enough."

"Look, I may seem like a humble woman—"

Leonard had to stop himself from snorting out a laugh. Aunt Millicent could be called a lot of things, but humble was not one of them.

"But I do have connections," she continued. "And one of those who has links to the police force did a—what does one call it?—background check on this Lamperton person as a favour to me. You need to be careful, Leonard. Were you aware this man has a past as a known deviant and a sex worker with a number of criminal convictions including soliciting and assault—"

"Stop right there. I know who Mr Lamperton is, and he is completely trustworthy. We went to school together. And, moreover, he has explained everything to me. Due to a cold, heartless, uncaring family, who thought more about their faith than their own son, he had a tough time finding his way early on in life. What kind of monster does that to their child? Anyway, he is a good person, a better man than me."

Aunt Millicent put a hand up in defence.

"Fair enough. If you already know, then that's fine. I just wanted to make sure you understood the kind of person you're employing, the kind of lifestyle he chooses, and ensure you're taking all necessary precautions, especially if he's doing manual labour. Make sure you're not in a situation where you might be tainted by this man's blood."

Hoping to give nothing away, Leonard met her frosty stare. Was she implying what he thought she was implying, that Adrian was HIV positive? Or was this merely the wild speculation of a nasty woman? Despite his best efforts to ignore her words, the insinuation wormed a hole into the pit of his stomach. Whatever she intimated, he would not give her the satisfaction of reacting.

"I trust Mr Lamperton—Adrian— unreservedly. And if by 'the kind of person he is', you mean the fact that he's gay, then you should know that we are the same kind of person, Adrian and myself. I trust you are not too obtuse to understand my meaning, Aunt."

Her posture straightened again, her face draining of blood and her pencil-thin eyebrows drawing together in anger. She understood. Not that Leonard cared. He had heard enough. Even though he wanted to know who was updating his aunt about him, he wished to be gone from this woman's toxic presence.

"Thank you for the tea," he said, feeling nauseous, but standing and making his intention to leave plain. "And once again, just so we're on the same page, am I right in saying you're no longer planning to challenge the will?"

"That's correct. As you've seen, I've informed Hope and Masters. Have they not contacted that ill-mannered and foul-mouthed woman who represents you? Maybe they're trying to find the courage to pick up the phone."

Finally, Leonard had cause to bark out a laugh. Helen Wallis would be professional, of course, but she would also have given them a piece of her mind for taking on his aunt's case in the first place.

"In all the years I've used that ill-mannered woman, she has never lost me a case."

"That's nice. Will you let yourself out?"

"It would be my absolute pleasure."

* * * *

On the drive to Wales, his mind kept being drawn back to his aunt's comment about Adrian. Had she really found out something about him in a police report? Or had she just heard rumours from her source in Wales and decided to get on her a homophobic bigoted high horse? He leant more towards the latter. If Mary saw her father still—a man very much alive—then Aunt Millicent clearly had no problem telling bare-faced lies.

He didn't want to believe a word she said, but then how much did Leonard really know about his new lover? Not that he cared if Adrian turned out to be HIV positive—well, he did care, of course, but only about the man and whether he was healthy, taking care of himself and on the right medication.

But if that was the case, he wanted Adrian to trust him enough to tell him. They'd had sex repeatedly now, safe sex every time, and Adrian seemed like the kind of man who would be open and honest about that kind of thing. One thing was for sure. He would not let the hurtful words of a woman he had come to despise affect what was blossoming between him and Adrian.

However awkward or uncomfortable the conversation might be, they needed to talk.

Chapter Twenty

Toni

Adrian held the sketch up to the light and rechecked the living room layout. He knew he had been fussing with the arrangement for the past twenty minutes, but he wanted to get everything looking perfect. Two Chesterfield sofas and two matching armchairs in burnished brown leather sat around a Persian rug and a teak Thai coffee table, facing the newly restored open log fireplace, effectively partitioning the front of the room from the back.

"It's faultless, buddy," said Toni, her hands on her hips.

As usual, Toni had her blonde hair tied up with a red polka-dot silk scarf and wore a pair of denim dungarees over a white tee, looking like a second world war poster for female manual workers. Even peppered in grime and dirt, she managed to look sexy. Jack certainly thought so, because she kept telling him '*lay off*' every time he snuck up behind and wrapped his tanned, muscled arms around her after they had finished helping him shift another piece of furniture into place.

"Lenny is very exacting. And I don't want him to have to move anything around again when he gets here."

"Aww, that's so sweet," said Toni.

"I'm looking forward to meeting this guy who has you all hot and bothered," said Jack.

In only a black singlet and denims, Jack looked like a lean model off the front cover of *Men's Health*. An intricate tattoo sleeve covered his muscled right arm from shoulder to wrist, and the head of what appeared to be a lion sat between his firm pecs and poked its head above the cut of his vest. Even following an afternoon of moving furniture, his black, slicked-back hair and long stubble looked perfect and defined his tanned masculine sexiness. Right now, Jack pulled Toni onto his lap in a corner of one of the leather sofas. Adrian wanted to tell them not to get dirt on the leather, but they had been apart all week and he knew how that felt.

"Not as much as me," said Adrian.

Toni laughed, jumped up and pulled the sketch out of Adrian's hands.

"Ade, the only things lacking in this room are chinaware for the dresser shelves, cushions for the settees and artwork. Those walls are far too bare."

"That's Lenny's call. I wasn't sure what his choices would be."

"You should be framing these and putting them up," she said, waving the sketch at him. "They're fantastic. If he doesn't want them, I do."

"Is it beer time, yet?" asked Jack, heading for the fridge.

Adrian and Toni had stocked up on supplies during the week, now the house had a working kitchen. And Jack had bought food with him, according to Toni. But they still had the basic kitchenware Adrian had brought from home. At some point, Lenny would need to decide on pots, pans, plates and cutlery. Adrian checked his phone for the time, four-fifteen, just as a message popped up on his display.

Lenny: Five minutes away.

"Okay then. I think we all deserve some downtime. Lenny's almost here. Let's sit around the dining table until he arrives. Have you thought about where you want to go for dinner tonight?"

"I'm cooking," said Jack.

This was news to Adrian. He took a seat at the table opposite Toni and peered at her quizzically.

"He insisted," she said, with a shrug. "And believe me, you won't be disappointed. Jack is almost as good in the kitchen as he is in the bedroom."

"Okay. TMI. Are you two going to try to keep the noise down tonight?"

"Funny," said Toni. "I was going to ask you the same thing."

Jack barked out a laugh and brought a fistful of beer bottles to the table. With a flourish, he twisted off the tops in turn and thumped them down on the tabletop.

"And I am christening your oven tonight. Toni tells me neither of you are vegetarian, so I'm cooking us my own signature beef bourguignon served with new potatoes—"

"You can't. We don't have a casserole dish," said Adrian.

"Way ahead of you," said Jack, taking a seat next to Toni. "I brought everything with me. Toni warned me. Everything's already prepped, sitting in the fridge and ready to go. And the oven's already preheating. Just needs popping in for three hours. I've even brought plates and cutlery from home. All you have to do is sit and eat."

"Fetching us beers and now cooking," said Adrian to Toni. "He's a proper little housewife, isn't he?"

"Been there, done that," smirked Jack, making Adrian laugh. "Even have the T-shirt as proof."

Jack was the first trans man Adrian had ever met. Or at least the first he had known about. Toni had tried to explain the kind of shit he'd had to suffer — hormone replacement therapy, sex reassignment surgery and so much more — to get his body looking the way he'd always wanted. Toni had stood by him every step of the way. Adrian had seen pictures of Jack when he had been Jacqueline — a lifetime ago — and wondered if the decision had put a strain on their relationship as two frankly beautiful and totally-in-love lesbians. Seeing them together now, he realised he didn't need to ask.

"Shit, I really envy you, Jack. Well, both of you."

"Envy?" asked Jack, peering over at him in puzzlement. "Seriously?"

"Okay," said Adrian, holding his hands up in defence. "I know you've been through a whole lot of shit, but when I look at you now, hell, when most men look at you, whether gay or straight, I reckon they're all a little envious. Gay men because they want to sleep with you, straight men because they want to be you, especially seeing you with this beautiful woman on your arm. As a couple you look perfect, and you get to go anywhere you want hand in hand, to touch and kiss in public, and nobody blinks an eye. And if they do, it's only because you're a hot couple and they're jealous."

Toni and Jack turned to each other, chuckled and pecked each other on the lips.

"It does have its perks," said Toni, sadly. "But it wasn't always this easy, Ade. And neither of Jack's parents speaks to him anymore."

"Well, if it's any consolation, I know how that feels. Or did. My mum talks to me again, when she can find the time. But I just wanted you to know how proud I am of you, and how much I love you both."

Jack turned to Toni then and pulled a face.

"You never told me Adrian was such a big sap."

"He's in love. What do you expect?"

"I am not—"

But Adrian could not finish the sentence, because the truth hit him like a bulldozer. He had never really felt anything similar since Stephan, the friend who had trodden his heart into the mud. But he really missed Lenny.

"Uh-huh," said Toni. "Hey, have you thought anything more about what I said? Chatting with that friend of mine, Tom Bradford? I told him about you, and I know he's desperate for good, reliable builders. And more importantly, you would fit in so well. Unlike Norwich, they have a shitload of work on right now with new-build homes, and they're struggling to get experienced builders. And I also know for a fact that he pays top dollar."

"I live in Drayton, Toni. His outfit is based in Greater London, isn't it?"

"Yes, and you have a truck. Two and half hours and you're in the heart of the capital."

"But you know these kinds of jobs aren't for a day here and a day there, they go on for weeks. And I don't relish doing that drive every day."

"Then don't. Isn't there someone you could stay with in London? Look, you don't have to call Tom if you don't want to, I just thought it might be nice to move on from this dry spell. I like Pete Ross, I really do, but he's let us both down so many times recently with the promise of work."

"Let me think on it. Maybe another beer might help, Jack."

"Bloody cheek," said Jack, rolling his eyes, but still jumped up from the table and headed to the fridge.

"And can you get one for me, too?" came a voice from the front doorway. They all turned to see Lenny standing there, a bag in hand, his eyes scanning the room, a huge grin on his face. Nobody had heard him enter. "Wow. Will you look at this place. Amazing."

Adrian scraped his chair away from the table and strode over to Lenny. After dropping his bag, Lenny pulled Adrian into a really fierce hug that lasted longer than usual. Had they missed each other equally?

"Like what you see?" asked Adrian, pulling away. Maybe it was his imagination, but Adrian thought he sensed some hesitation in Lenny, a slight nervousness or apprehension.

"Yes," said Lenny, looking around again before bringing his gaze back to Adrian. "The house looks great, too."

Adrian grinned then, his insecurities melting away.

"Come and meet the gang."

Within the hour, after introductions and a couple more beers had been consumed, they sat laughing together like old friends. Jack got up partway through to put in the casserole, and before long delicious aromas began to fill the living room space. Adrian sat back and smiled, listening to Toni explain to Lenny about the changes to the electrics and the lighting plan he had agreed for each room. Already the house had begun to feel like a home. When she asked Lenny about the dresser, he explained how he had come prepared.

"I've got a car boot full of things I picked up at our warehouse. Staffordshire plates and platters to go on the dresser shelves, beautifully designed with matching floral patterns. Cutlery sets and assorted cushions for the sofas. The only thing I haven't shopped for is modern kitchen appliances — toaster, blender, coffee maker, other things that might come in handy. I thought we might do that this weekend, Ade."

"How about paintings for the walls?" asked Toni

"Tough one, that. I'm going to leave that until last. But I do have a few ideas up my sleeve that I'm going to run by Adrian first."

"And the burning question," said Jack, from behind the kitchen island, "is what are you going to do with the place, now that it's almost finished?"

Adrian looked to Lenny, who smiled knowingly and appeared calm. Adrian had no idea what Lenny planned to do, they hadn't discussed that far in advance. Everything they'd done so far leant towards him renting Bryn Bach out, or selling the house to somebody, which felt so wrong.

"Well, the first thing I'm going to do is to throw a big house-warming party on the twenty-eighth of this month, so make sure you're free because I've already put the front bedroom aside so you two can stay. After that I'm going to keep the place for weekends away from the big smoke and let her out to friends and family, people I know and trust to keep the place tidy. And yes, before you ask, you are on the A list."

"In which case," said Jack, grinning at Toni, "we're going to open the special bottle of Chateau Margaux we've been saving, to share with you at dinner and to christen the house, because you've said all the right things."

"We don't have—" began Adrian.

Jack held up a hand, cutting him off.

"And I also brought red wineglasses with me for this very occasion. A box of four as a house-warming gift."

Toni giggled over the top of her beer bottle before clinking glasses with Adrian and Lenny.

An hour before Jack served up dinner, they all showered and changed. Having the downstairs shower room made things so much easier, and when Adrian had changed and joined them downstairs, he found Jack and Toni busy laying the table, while Lenny had opened up the balcony doors and allowed the garden fragrance and the last of the daylight to flood into the living room.

"Look at that view," said Lenny, putting his arm around Adrian. "Might get a bit nippy later, so we should enjoy the remains of the day. Come on, let's get out of their way. Bring your beer and sit with me on the stone steps where we can savour the view and chat."

Adrian hummed his approval before following Lenny to the top step. Adrian's heart swelled at the simple act of sitting beside him, their warm sides touching. Both sat watching in silence as the sun slowly descended, bathing the back of the house in warm yellow light, the view over the countryside spectacular in its beauty, simplicity and tranquillity.

"Lenny, I need to talk to you about something."

"Good," said Lenny. "Because I need to talk to you, too."

Lenny had seemed anxious from the moment he'd arrived, and Adrian wondered if he had been thinking along the same lines, about the upcoming deadline for the completion of work on the property and what would happen next between them. He considered being patient and allowing Lenny to start, but knew he needed to say his piece while he still had the courage.

"Okay, but let me go first," said Adrian. "I'm normally hopeless with words, but I need to get this off my chest while I've mustered the courage. These last three weeks have been tough without having you here. I mean *really* tough. But it's made me realise that I don't want anything casual anymore, the thought doesn't even appeal. I only want you, to have a future with you. But to do that, I need to be really honest, I need us both to be honest with each other. Do you understand?"

Lenny had gone very quiet, but he managed to answer with a single nod.

"So before I ask and make a complete arse of myself, I need to know. Do you see me in your future, or is this simply a Chapter — ?"

Lenny swung his head around quickly.

"I want you in my life, Ade. Fuck, I *need* you in my life, in my future. I want to grow old with you."

A gasp of relief burst from Adrian, a breath he hadn't even realised he'd been holding

"Is that it? Is that what you wanted to ask me?" said Lenny, aghast. "You wondered if I wanted to be with you?"

"Yes. Well, no. Well, partly."

"Okay. Well I'm glad we've cleared that up…"

They both laughed at the same time, and Adrian decided to take the next step.

"I know I'm in Drayton and you're in London, but I'm prepared to drive to you whenever I can. Or you can come and stay with me, rather than staying with your mother. But I imagine there's a lot more for us to do where you live. What I also wanted to know, and only if we were both agreed on being together, is how you might feel about ditching the condoms."

Next to him, Lenny's mouth dropped open in shock, which was not the reaction he had been hoping for, but maybe he needed to clarify.

"Only if you want to. And only after we've both been tested, of course. I've stayed clean all these years, but I wouldn't expect you to agree to this without us both getting tested together. Hey, what's the matter?"

Lenny had dropped his head forwards, pushed his hands into his eyes and shook his head slowly from side to side. Seeing this, Adrian put his arm across his shoulders and pulled one of Lenny's hands away.

"Hey, buddy, are you okay? We don't need to —"

"No, I'm fine," said Lenny, taking Adrian's hand and squeezing. "In fact, I'm more than fine, I'm fantastic. I haven't felt this alive — this optimistic — in years the way I have these past few months or so since meeting you. So yes, whatever you want, I'm prepared to give you. And more."

"This does mean you'll probably have to meet my mother."

"Fair enough. You've already had the pleasure of meeting mine. But I promise you this, you will never, ever have to meet my aunt."

"Oh, yes. I didn't ask you how that went. Should I bother?"

"She's dropping her claim to the house. Sounds like Cousin Matthew might have managed to talk her around. But family or not, she will never change, Ade. You should have seen the look on her face when I told her I was gay. I know your mother's religious, but from what you tell me, she tries to do good things for other people in the community, socialising and getting you to go around and help out if anyone's having trouble with their house. Yes, I know she didn't fight for you when you really needed her support, but I sense that was more because she feared going against your father's wishes."

"I don't blame her, Lenny. Not anymore. She told me she argued with him about me the morning after I left and did her best to try to find me. But they had no idea where I'd gone because I dropped all contact. Finally she did what she could, contacting her brother and asking him to keep an eye out for me."

"But what I'm trying to say," continued Lenny, "is that good people use their belief to promote kindness in the world, they see loving each other as the most important message for the living. My aunt is not like that. Her belief is her armour, makes her feel superior and protected, locked away from the realities of life. Can you believe she forbade me from using Luke's name in her presence? The woman is damaged. She refuses to show any kind of remorse, or humanity, or kindness, or courtesy. And, family or not, I don't need that negativity in my life."

"Sounds like you've had a rough day. But if you no longer need to worry about going to court, that must be a relief. And you end up keeping this beautiful home."

"And this beautiful boyfriend."

Adrian's smile turned into a small grimace.

"Ooh, boyfriend, huh? At my age? Maybe we can think of something else."

"Partner sounds like we're in business together. How about fella?"

"How about not. And I'm not keen on better half, either."

Lenny chuckled.

"Let's agree to a work-in-progress. I'm thinking we have a few things to talk about this weekend. But all that matters to me right now is that you're going to be a part of my life. How did I get so lucky?"

Adrian put his hands either side of Lenny's head turned him around and kissed him full on the mouth, enjoying the sensation for a long moment, before finally pulling apart.

"I love you, Lenny Day."

Lenny's eyes had been lingering on Adrian's lips, but with the words spoken, darted up to meet Adrian's gaze. Instantly, a smile blossomed on his face.

"Yeah, me too. I love you, Adrian Lamperton."

"Okay, lovebirds," came Toni's voice from behind them. "Dinner's about ready. Or do you want to carry on making out on the terrace."

Adrian began to stand, but Lenny held him down, and got out his phone.

"Toni, I promised a persistent work colleague I'd get a photo of us together. Can you take a couple while we still have that amazing sunset in the background?"

"My pleasure."

Adrian and Lenny sat with their arms around each other until Toni was satisfied. After that, she handed the phone back to Lenny.

"Come and eat. And remember to have a think about what I said, Ade. Maybe see what Lenny thinks. I know you need the work, and Tom's always on the lookout for good builders."

"Who's Tom?" asked Lenny.

"Ah," said Adrian, as they headed in and sat next to each other at the table. "So how would you feel about having a house guest if I were to get some work in London?"

Chapter Twenty-One

Domestic

The next morning the four of them enjoyed a simple breakfast sitting around the kitchen island, of sliced fresh fruit, and warmed croissants with butter and jam, washed down with tea and coffee. Leonard listened in to the conversation while making a list of the appliances they needed.

Something in the air told him that today was going to be a magical day. All the signs were there. Adrian had spoken about the potential for work in London and needing somewhere to crash, leaving Leonard grinning uncontrollably. Even if he thought himself an atheist like his parents, he could almost believe in some higher power bringing them together, bringing him everything he had ever wanted.

"How did you sleep?" Adrian asked Jack.

"Best night's sleep in as long as I can remember," said Jack, who had already showered and looked freshly groomed, as though ready for a photo shoot. "Man, it's so quiet here. I feel like I've slept for a couple of days."

"Peaceful as a sanctuary," said Toni, in a loose-fitting burgundy tracksuit for the drive home.

"When people aren't throwing petrol bombs through the window," Leonard chimed in.

"Yeah, what was that all about? Have you heard anything more?" asked Toni.

"I forgot to mention, Lenny. PC Lewis called me last Monday. Said they'd found nothing unusual on the traffic cams. But kids were reported in the area, from out of town, causing trouble that holiday weekend. I told him we'd had the alarm system installed, so if anything else happens at night we'll have the culprit on video."

His Aunt Millicent had come to the same conclusion. Leonard still couldn't shake the feeling that someone had explicitly targeted his house.

"What are your plans for today?" asked Toni. "You're all finished now, aren't you?"

"Not quite," said Leonard. "Got a few more things to shop for. Then I want to do some finishing touches. Make the place feel more like a home."

"Already does, if you ask me," said Adrian. "I can still smell beef bourguignon from last night. The place finally feels lived in, don't you think?"

"Once we've had a house-warming," said Leonard. "Then it will."

"Booked in our calendars. We'll be here front and centre," said Jack. "Let us know if you need anything bringing. And on that note, we'd best make a move. Beat the traffic. Long drive back to Norwich."

Once they had driven off and the breakfast dishes had been tidied, Leonard suggested a road trip into one of Wales' more substantial cities, Newport, where the shopping promised to be more varied.

Right now he pushed the trolley down an aisle of a homeware superstore while Adrian picked out electrical items. They were already on their second trolley after Lenny spotted a couple of rectangular ottoman-style storage units for the bedrooms. Adrian's insistence on bringing his truck instead of Lenny's car had turned out to be a good one. Not only that, but his taste in appliances matched Leonard's. Only the complicated-looking coffee machine had been Adrian's choice, not something Leonard — being a hardened tea drinker — would have considered. But just hearing Adrian enthuse over the branded contraption had won Leonard over.

"If we're going to be spending more time together, you need to know that decent coffee first thing in the morning is non-negotiable, especially if you want me in a good mood. And this baby with reusable pods will be a huge hit whenever you decide to hold dinner parties at the house. Trust me."

"I do trust you. Personally, I'm more stoked about the four-slice toaster."

"Coffee brewing and bread toasting. It's what makes weekend mornings special."

Leonard thought back to the weekends in his London home. The only thing that had made them special was not being there to wallow in his loneliness. Weekends in Bryn Bach had been another matter altogether, sharing his house and bed with Adrian.

"I'll take your word for that," said Leonard, checking his watch. "Hey, once we've paid and loaded this into the truck, would you be up for having a spot of lunch in town?"

Adrian grinned and tilted his head to one side.

No words needed.

* * * *

They found a small bistro off the main high street and settled at a table. Once they had ordered their food, Leonard went to use the bathroom. When he returned, he found Adrian ending a phone call and looking pleased with himself.

"That was Tom Bradford. Toni doesn't hang about, does she? Anyway, he wants to meet me in person next week. They have a big project coming up during July and August in somewhere called Herne Hill in London. Do you know where that is?"

"Are you serious? Herne Hill's pretty much around the corner from me, a fifteen-minute drive."

"Convenient, then?"

"Very," said Leonard, unable to help his smile. "So that means you'll definitely need somewhere to stay. This day keeps getting better."

Adrian winked and nodded, and once again, Leonard couldn't help the feeling of light optimism filling him, of things finally coming together in his life.

* * * *

When they got back at two-thirty, they unloaded the ottomans and kitchen equipment into the house. Adrian unpacked the gadgets while Leonard took his time to arrange and test the new items on the work surfaces. Once they had finished, Adrian put himself to use doing manual tasks like unloading the dishwasher, cleaning, vacuuming floors and changing bedclothes — the kind of things Leonard assumed he did for himself at home.

Everything felt domestic between them, the way they went from one task to the next without speaking, the way they carefully worked around each other. Now and again, neither of them could resist pulling the other in for a kiss or a hug, or purposely brushing up against the other as they squeezed past. By four, most of the significant chores had been completed, and Leonard could sense Adrian's restlessness.

"I know it's a bit early, but what do you want to do for dinner tonight?" asked Adrian.

"Well, for a start, I don't fancy cooking," said Leonard, arranging cutlery in one of the kitchen drawers. "Not that we've got anything here to cook, anyway. Do you want to go out and eat? Feels as though we've done the Manor Inn to death."

"How about a takeaway on the terrace and then an early night? I can drive into Llandrindod Wells and pick something up. I can also pop into the superstore and stock up on wines and beers. Any preference for food?"

"I honestly don't mind."

"How about Chinese takeaway. What dishes do you fancy?"

"Okay, you should know I'm pretty boring when it comes to Chinese takeout," said Leonard. "If I was on my own, I'd probably order my staples of crispy spring rolls, sweet and sour chicken balls in batter and special fried rice. It's what I call my comfort-food coma. So get whatever else you fancy."

"You're kidding me, right?"

"Too boring?" asked Leonard.

"No," said Adrian, shaking his head. "Not at all. It's just, that's my usual order."

"Better double up then, knowing what your appetite's like."

"Hey, I need the energy," said Adrian, digging out the keys to his truck. "I know it's only four, but if I go now, we can heat up the food when we're ready to eat. Do you want to come along for the ride?"

Leonard chuckled at Adrian. He sensed the remaining menial jobs, like deciding where to store placemats and tablecloths and cookware, as well as polishing furniture, did not appeal to him. Although he would gladly help with the more fussy house chores, Leonard could tell he was happier ripping up floors and knocking down walls.

"No, you go on. Give you something to do. I'm going to finish up in the kitchen and then give the dinner table and dresser a good polishing before sorting out the chinaware I've brought. Once that's done, apart from buying some pictures and hanging them, that will finish the living area off nicely."

As he readied to leave, Leonard dragged him into a hug and a kiss that lasted far too long. Eventually Adrian pushed him away with a chuckle, Leonard feeling his lover's arousal matching his own.

"Good call," said Leonard, standing in the doorway. "Otherwise you'd never leave."

"Won't be long. Call me if you think of anything else we need."

Leonard closed the front door and heard the engine start up and move away. With his back to the door, he sighed and smiled to himself. They worked well together. Adrian would not have been happy polishing furniture and wiping plates. Leonard, on the other hand, found those kinds of tasks therapeutic, not just cleaning but arranging and adding the finishing touches to a room.

He had only just applied a coat of wax to the top shelf of the dresser when his phone rang. He dropped the rag onto the table and saw Adrian's name on the screen display.

"Lenny, are my house keys there?" came Adrian's voice before Leonard had a chance to speak. When he looked over to the kitchen island, he saw the keys lying there. "I picked up my phone and car keys, but I think I left—"

"Don't panic, they're here. On the kitchen island. Is this something I need to be aware of going forward, your forgetfulness?"

"Hey, I'm normally pretty good, but I must have been distracted by something as I was leaving. Can't think what! I lent them to Jack when he popped out yesterday and forgot to put them back on my keyring this morning. I'll call you as soon as I'm on my way back. How are things going there?"

"Give me a chance. I've only just started. I'm starting on the dresser, giving the piece a final spruce-up before arranging the plates and platters on the shelves. And then the table. I think it's going to look amazing. In case I'm tied up, I'll leave the front door open for you. Then you can let yourself in."

"No. Let's not tempt fate. I'll come around the back."

After ending the call, Leonard lost all sense of time. Applying his preferred brand of beeswax polish to the dresser from top to bottom, the furniture eventually sparkled and smelled amazing. Kneeling on the floor, he viewed the showpiece in a new light with its starkly empty shelves. In his enthusiasm to start, he had forgotten about the boxes of plates and other items in his car boot. Three trips later, and boxes of plates and platters and other items covered the surface of the dining room table.

Having already removed the old newspaper and cleaned the insides of each drawer, he filled the first with placemats. Once loaded, the compartment slid comfortably shut. The second drawer, stacked with assorted tablecloths and silk table napkins, proved a little more problematic, needing more effort to close and, even then, moving stiffly. The final one, now containing table decorations of candles and candle holders, napkin rings and wine openers, moved with the same ease as the first.

Something nagged at Leonard. The middle drawer kept sticking slightly and didn't sit right, not like the others. At first, he dismissed this as either wear and tear or careless workmanship. Except, bearing in mind the precision and attention to detail of the whole piece, the theory went against all logic.

Exasperated, he pulled open the middle drawer again and placed all the linen back on the table, then tried closing the drawer again. But he still met with the same resistance. Eventually, frustrated, he pulled the drawer out, lifting the compartment to remove it from the main body of the dresser. After checking the sides and the back, he turned the drawer over – and there lay the culprit.

Something had been taped to the bottom. Wrapped in thick plastic – almost like the plastic sheeting they had used at the back of the house – he could not make out the contents. The whole thing had been taped securely in place with thick brown packing tape. Somebody had wanted this to remain hidden.

Leonard's curiosity ramped up a notch.

To cut away the tape he would need a sharp tool and remembered he had a small toolbox in his car boot. When he returned with a box cutter, he noticed a missed call on his phone from Mary.

She would have to wait. He'd call her back as soon as he had finished. Sitting down at the table, his face towards the dresser, the drawer in front of him, he went to work methodically. Slicing carefully, he eventually unwrapped the plastic cover and very delicately unfolded the contents onto the table.

Taking up most of the space was a large brown envelope, the type with a cardboard backing used to send photographs and stop them from bending in the post. In fact, in the bottom left-hand corner, the words 'Please Do Not Bend' had been printed in red. On top of the large envelope there were two regular-sized envelopes; one sealed with the phrase 'To Whom It May Concern'. The other, and the one that caught Leonard's eye, had already been opened. Using what he assumed to be official stationery, the envelope had the words 'Holy Trinity Church, Newbridge', along the top, and had been addressed to Luke Darlington, typed up using a plain white, official-looking label.

Inside he discovered a flyer for a church summer fair and, tucked inside that, a letter on what seemed like tracing paper – very thin, almost translucent. Carefully unfolding the delicate paper, he read the words.

My Beloved Luke,

I received your letter, and I know you told me not to reply, but how could I not, no matter how risky? Which is why I am using this envelope and a typed label, so your family will hopefully suspect nothing.

Leonard held his breath, reading the words, realising Toni had been right. There had been a secret someone in Luke's life.

My love, I share your pain, of course I do. We live in an age of contradictions, where we can drive a car, marry a girl and start a family. An era where we can fight and kill, or be killed for our country, and even get drunk every night of the week – but one where we are not allowed to be together, not in the way we wish to be.

Know only this, that I love you deeply and unashamedly, that I am content to wait the three more years until you reach the age of consent. Even then, things won't be easy, our families and friends may not understand, may be hurt and confused, may even turn against us, but we will weather that storm because we will have each other and will stand firm together.

As far as the furniture is concerned, you cannot hope to salvage everything, my love. So I suggest you board up your favourite cupboard behind the wall when you decorate and before your family can take that away from you. From what I know of them, they will never know anything's missing. Come a little earlier this summer, and I promise to help. I have some beautiful photographs of us to show you.

Most importantly, don't lose hope. One day, we will do all the things we've talked about. We'll tour Italy, visiting Venice and riding in a gondola together, we'll climb the Spanish steps in Rome, cycle through Tuscany and watch the sunset in Florence. We'll even visit the old war memorials of northern France, if that's what you really want. And I promise to stand beside you while you photograph every precious moment.

But for now, my love, be patient and keep the faith, our faith.

Forever yours,
XXX

Leonard sat at the dining room table, reverently refolding and placing the letter back into the envelope. After a pause, a moment of reflection, he opened the larger pack, the old-fashioned type with the cardboard backing.

Very gingerly, he slid out a collection of beautifully maintained photographs, six vivid eleven-by-fourteen-inch black and white portraits. But he did not need to study them all, because when he saw the one on the top, the one that met his eyes, of Luke being held by another man, both smiling at each other, everything fell into place. On the back, in the same careful handwriting as the letter, a short message was penned —

One day we will be able to hang this photograph for everyone to see. One day, when we have a home of our own, when we are both free from commitments, we will live together and nobody can touch us, nobody will be able to come between us and our love.

And right then, right on cue, he heard the sliding door at the back of the house swoosh open.

Adrian had returned.

"Ade, come over here. You need to see this."

Footsteps entered the room but came to a stop a few paces away. When Leonard looked up from the table, the person standing there, the person pointing a sawn-off shotgun at his head, was not Adrian.

"You couldn't leave well alone, could you?" came the voice. "You had to pry. You had to keep digging."

Chapter Twenty-Two

Intuition

All the way along the route to the superstore, Adrian had been smiling to himself. If anyone were to ask any of his workmates about his annoying habits, they would mention his obsessiveness about keys and locks and security in general. The fact that he had left them on the table spoke volumes about how much of a distraction Lenny Day had become, and how much he had let his usual unwavering guard down.

He found a spot in the retail park near the front of the superstore. To optimise his time, he decided to walk across the main road to the Chinese restaurant and place his order. Then, while the kitchen prepared his food, he would head back to the superstore and stock up with drinks and breakfast items. If the weather stayed clear and sunny for the whole weekend, he would treat Lenny to breakfast in the morning, served on his new terrace.

Fortunately, probably due to the early hour, the Chinese restaurant was empty, and after placing his order and paying, he strode across to the superstore. He stocked up with breakfast items, then headed for the alcohol aisle, preparing to pick out beers and wine for their meal. Rounding a corner, he almost bumped into another shopper carrying a basket. Without looking up, the woman moved to one side and began to pass by Adrian, until he realised he knew the person.

"Freya. How are you?"

Startled at being addressed, Freya recovered quickly and managed a smile. She wore rather unflattering baggy tracksuit bottoms in grey cotton, with a large woollen sweater in oatmeal, the sleeve cuffs pulled down over her hands as though trying to keep them warm.

"As good as can be expected. Where's Leonard?"

"He's back home, putting finishing touches to the house."

"On his own?" asked Freya, her eyes widening for a moment.

"Yes," said Adrian, smirking. "Don't worry, he's a big boy. I volunteered to come out and do the shopping. We're having a takeaway tonight from the shop across the road."

"That's nice," she replied, about to turn away. "Anyway, I'd better —"

"We found some of Luke's personal belongings, by the way. Hidden away in an old dresser concealed in the wall."

"Did you?" she asked, turning back, suddenly interested. "And?"

"Nothing out of the ordinary. An old camera and tripod stand, some books and old Polaroids." Freya looked away and smiled, nodding. "Nice, actually. Lots with your friends when you were younger. One included a good-looking, blond-haired guy. Standing by a tractor wheel. I don't suppose you remember who that was?"

From Freya's expression, Adrian could tell she was not impressed.

"Tim something. Can't remember his last name. Danish. He hung around us sometimes that year. Thought he was God's gift. Too loud, too brash for my liking. But he got on really well with the boys. And Pippa, of course. Well, she pretty much threw herself at anyone back then. Tim worked for Megan's mum and dad behind the bar over the summer. He went off to London after that."

"Wasn't that the same year your dad passed away?"

"Yes." She sighed, a wistfulness filling her eyes. "I try not to think about it."

"I talked to PC Morgan. He said your dad drowned. An accident. I'm really sorry."

Freya seemed to deflate.

"All so senseless, so preventable. Fixing a fence on the steep side of the duck pond. Nobody knew Dad couldn't swim. How ridiculous is that? Not that the pond was usually deep. Water rarely came up to the waist, according to Geraint Hughes, the farmer, but we'd had heavy rains that year. Still find it difficult to conceive. They had the pond drained and filled in after that. Never forgave himself, Hughes, God rest his soul."

"And then Howard disappeared the year after."

Freya appeared confused.

"Sorry? Disappeared? Howie left, he didn't disappear. He'd always planned to go travelling after he turned twenty-one. We all knew that, Gran as well as Dad."

"But people said he just upped and vanished."

This comment got a reaction — a sharp shake of the head followed by a loud huff of disapproval.

"Which people?"

"Everyone. Pippa, Mrs Llewellyn — "

"Heavens. What's the expression? Small towns, small minds? Just because he didn't throw a big going-away party — which would hardly have been appropriate a year after burying Dad — doesn't mean he disappeared. You should have asked me. I am his sister, after all. Yes, he left Newbridge. But he kept in touch, still does. He's living just outside Jakarta in Indonesia right now with his wife and three kids. Keeps writing to ask when I'm going to visit. But I'm not one for travel. Now his oldest is at university, he may visit with his wife one day. He's always threatened to show her the dung heap he grew up in."

Adrian smiled and shook his head. He needed to head back and let Lenny know. At least that was one mystery solved.

"Look," said Freya, looking about herself. "I really need to rush — "

"Before you go, Freya. Lenny's going to throw a house-warming party on the twenty-eighth of this month, Saturday afternoon. He's probably going to invite you formally anyway, but please say you'll come?"

"I'm not sure. I'm not good with crowds — "

"But you ought to come along and see how beautiful the finished house looks. Lenny's put so much effort into restoring the place and I know he would love to have you there. Pippa will be there, too."

"Let me think about it."

"Please do. And one other thing before you go. Sorry to keep harping back to this, but the year Luke took his own life, did you see him? Pippa said he used to come down early, before the rest of the family."

"No. Everything happened at Easter. We only saw the Darlingtons during the summer. Nobody knew he was here. Usually he'd send a card to let us know and we'd get the place ready for them. But then, Gran and I were the only ones here. Howie had already left and Pippa was at university."

"I see," said Adrian, recognising her eagerness to go. "Well, have a nice evening. And don't forget what I said."

"I won't," she said, heading off. He watched her go and noticed her discard her basket containing the few goods she'd picked on a pile of boxes by the checkout before rushing out to the car park, to an old black Ford Fiesta. She was an odd little thing, Freya, living a life of solitude, and Adrian almost felt sorry for her. Except that he had lived a similar life before meeting Lenny.

Back to business, Adrian stood at one end of the long wine aisle and scratched his head. He had no clue about wine. Beers he could handle. Felippe had talked about various types of grape and wine, which one suited which food, how to properly decant a bottle of red. But Adrian had paid little attention apart from learning the names, so he made sure to fetch the right bottle. Did people drink a specific wine with Chinese food?

"Having a spot of trouble over there?" asked a cheerful older man who had stopped next to him, confidently picking out wines and putting them in his cart.

"I am, actually. I know this is going to sound like a stupid question, but what wine would you recommend to go with Chinese food?"

"Actually, that's not stupid at all. In the past we'd never have used those words in the same sentence, wine and Chinese food. But honestly, these days, everyone has their own preference. And, of course, it'll depend on the dishes you're serving. People forget that China is a huge country with lots of regional varieties of cuisine. But my rule of thumb is that for your basic stir-fry or deep-fried dishes I go with something acidic like a Riesling or a Pinot Gris. If you prefer red wine, then you can't go wrong with a Pinot Noir. Here's a nice, reasonably priced Pinot Noir from Napa Valley, and the Rieslings and other white wines are at the end."

"Thanks for your help. I'll get a bottle of each."

"Sounds like a good plan. Enjoy your meal and have a nice evening."

"You too."

Adrian watched the old guy move off. People tended to be much friendlier and more helpful in the smaller towns, which Adrian took to be a universal truth. He'd had similar experiences in Drayton. In London, people had been more inclined to keep themselves to themselves.

Satisfied with his purchases, he finished up at the checkout and dropped his shopping in the truck cabin before heading back to the Chinese restaurant. With his bags of hot food, he returned to the truck again, passing by a police car parked up in the retail park. He had been about to text Lenny when he spotted PC Morgan sitting in the driving seat with the window wound down, his elbow poking out.

"Trouble?" asked Adrian as he drew level and caught PC Morgan's gaze.

PC Morgan laughed.

"There will be, son, if they've run out of chocolate digestive biscuits. Bobby — PC Lewis — is getting them for the boys back at the station. Here he comes now. And he's smiling, so that's usually a good sign."

"Quiet day?"

"You could say that."

"What you got there?" asked PC Lewis, grinning at Adrian before resting his backside on the bonnet of the car. Adrian hadn't appraised the younger PC Lewis before, but he seemed far more relaxed and friendlier than the policemen Adrian had dealt with in London.

"Chinese takeaway. And before you ask, there's only enough for two."

PC Lewis laughed good-naturedly.

"And how's the house coming along?" asked PC Morgan.

"Pretty much finished," said Adrian, with a smirk, before jiggling the phone in his hand. "Lenny had the home security specialists around. Motion detector lights front and back, with a top-of-the-range home security system. Constant surveillance and infrared motion sensors like something out of a *Mission Impossible* film. I can even see everything from my phone — front and back of the property *and* throughout the downstairs interior. The security company should have registered the address and landline with you at the station, in case there's any more trouble."

"Be good to come and have a look at some point," said PC Morgan.

"You'd be more than welcome."

"Anything else since the last incident?" asked PC Lewis.

"If there was, you'd have been the first to know. But no, there's been nothing."

"Bobby checked the road cameras along the surrounding A roads for that night, but there was no unusual traffic, nobody speeding away from your area."

"I called Mr Lamperton and told him already, boss. Either they knew to avoid the cameras, or they were on foot or maybe on pushbikes," said PC Lewis.

"Out of interest, Mr Lamperton, can I take a look? At the camera security system on your phone?" asked PC Morgan.

Adrian didn't want to hang around chit-chatting. He wanted to get back to the comfort of Bryn Bach and Lenny, but he obliged the older police constable. After all, they would probably be the ones called out if an alarm went off. At some point over the weekend, he needed to talk Lenny through the system operation. Obliging PC Morgan, he opened the app and tapped in the password, displaying a full-screen colour feed of the front driveway. After a glance at the crystal-clear view of the front gate of the house, he passed the phone over to PC Morgan and watched amused as the policeman poked his finger at the screen.

"We've had no eyewitnesses to the incident," continued a playfully grinning PC Lewis, who had clearly seen the humour in his old boss navigating the telephone app. "But honestly, in that secluded part of town I'm not surprised. Bryn Bach's the only house for about two miles in any direction. I told you we had some reports of vandalism over the holiday weekend — kids, they think — but yours was the only one involving a petrol bomb. If anyone does come forwards, we'll let you know."

"Look at that," said PC Morgan, showing the phone display to his colleague. "Clear as summer's day."

"Yes, boss," said PC Lewis, rolling his eyes at Adrian. "I've seen similar set-ups. Much better quality than our traffic cameras."

"Difficult not to be," said PC Morgan, chuckling at the screen and swiping awkwardly with his finger.

"Anyway, gents," said Adrian, wanting to wrap up and get away, "I should be heading back before the food gets cold."

"Just came from down from your way," said PC Lewis, standing straight and about to move around to the passenger side of the car. "Almost tempted to pull over a motorcyclist heading for Newbridge. That wasn't your Mr Day, was it? If so, you should tell him to keep an eye on his speed. Lucky for him we don't have the new integrated digital speedometer fitted yet. I bet if we'd clocked him, he'd have been over the legal limit."

"Lenny drives an SUV—"

"And there's your Mr Day now, talking to his guest," said PC Morgan, squinting his eyes at the phone as he talked over Adrian.

"Guest?" said Adrian, puzzled. "We don't have a guest. At least we didn't when I left the house about an hour ago. Our two friends left this morning."

"Hang on, let's look from the other end of the room. Yes, there you go. See if you can recognise—" PC Morgan expression morphed into a frown. After pushing his forefinger on the screen a couple of times, he turned the phone to PC Lewis then to Adrian. "Son, I think we've got a problem. Do you recognise this person?"

There on the screen stood a figure carrying what looked to be a shortened shotgun pointed directly at Lenny. Wearing a grey tracksuit with a grey hoodie covering the head and the upper part of the face, the heavy-set figure was impossible to identify. Maybe that had been their intention.

"Shit," said Adrian, his pulse speeding up, cold dread running down his spine. "I've never met the guy but, from how Lenny described him, I think that might be his cousin, Matthew. And he has a motorcycle, so maybe that's who you passed. Although honestly, the two things might be unrelated, and that person could be anyone. Why the hell would they be pointing a shotgun at Lenny? I have to get back. He needs my help."

"Hold on, son," said PC Morgan, placing a hand on Adrian's arm. Like a switch being flicked, both his and PC Lewis' comportment changed, both straightening up and becoming serious, their professional training kicking in. "You're not doing anything. This is our problem now. Does this security system of his record sound?"

"I have no idea," said Adrian, frowning impatiently. "I think so. Is that really important right now? We need to get to Lenny. He's in danger."

"And we will," said PC Morgan, getting out of the car. "Bobby, take the squad car and call this in. Tell them the intruder's armed and we're gonna need AFOs just in case things gets nasty. Head straight to the front entrance and park up. Use your lights, but no siren. Mr Lamperton and I will take his vehicle. I'll keep an eye on things with the security feed, and I may use the back way to the property. But I'll need you at the front."

"Right you are, Charlie."

Back way? Adrian had thought the house had only one access point.

"We'll monitor what's going on from the car. From here to there's no longer than ten minutes. Whatever you do, don't spook the intruder. As I say, I'll keep you posted on what we're seeing on the security camera."

"Copy that, boss."

"Mr Lamperton. Let's head to your truck."

Adrian moved quickly, feeling idiotic with the bag of Chinese food still dangling from his hand. As soon as they reached the truck, he unlocked the driver's side and dumped the bags in the back.

"Do you want me to drive?" asked PC Morgan.

"No," said Adrian, climbing into the driver's seat. Adrenaline filled his veins, but he managed a thin smile and a shake of the head. "But, don't worry, I'm fine to drive. And I know how this truck handles better than anyone. Do you want me to head the same way I came? The Newbridge road?"

"Yes," said PC Morgan, jumping into the passenger seat, slamming the door and clipping the police-issued mobile phone onto his yellow jacket. "That's the quickest route back. And as long as you drive safely, you'll be okay to push the speed limit, son."

Once they'd both belted up, Adrian put the car into gear and headed for the car park exit. Keeping his calm, he took them smoothly out onto the main street.

"What's an AFO?" he asked, without taking his eyes from the road. "You told PC Lewis you needed AFOs?"

"Authorised firearms officers. Look, I don't want you to worry, son. As police officers in this country we're trained to deal with these situations, even though we don't carry firearms. But in cases where a person is armed, we need to call in AFOs just in case the situation turns ugly. I'm sure it won't come to that, but we have to follow procedures."

Adrian loved hearing people say they didn't want him to worry because that was precisely what he ended up doing. While he concentrated on driving, PC Morgan kept close tabs on the video movement on Adrian's phone. With the mobile device on his lapel, he stayed in constant communication with PC Lewis.

"Bobby. Looks as though they're moving outside. Out onto the back patio. The external camera only covers the lawn down to the end of the garden."

Adrian's pulse hammered in his neck. His heart cried out to be there with Leonard, even though his head reasoned that having the police with him right now was the best he could hope for. If anything happened to Lenny, and the person was still standing, Adrian wasn't sure what he would do to them.

"No, Bobby. Stick to the plan. Come in from the front of the premises. See if the intruder used any mode of transport. If anything happens, they'll have to come back out that way. Hang on."

Adrian glanced over at the phone in PC Morgan's hand.

"Mr Lamperton, would you or Mr Day have left the front door open?"

"No. After the intruder, Lenny knows to keep the door shut."

"Good to hear. But is there an access path around the side of the house?"

"There is. To the right of the front door."

"Did you catch that, Bobby?" said PC Morgan, then to Adrian, "Looks like they're leading your friend to the end of the garden. They'll be out of camera range in a moment. Good job I know this area well. Take the next right up ahead."

"What?" said Adrian, his head snapping round to look at PC Morgan. "But that's not the road to — "

"Do as I say. I'm fairly sure I know where they're heading. There's a pathway from the back of your place that leads directly to the Hughes farm."

Adrian slowed the truck and took a hard right, before bumping and bouncing down a small lane. A few minutes farther along, through the gaps in hedgerows, Adrian glimpsed a dark-coloured vehicle parked just beyond a turnstile. Only as they drove closer and PC Morgan told him to stop did he realise the make and model.

An old black Ford Fiesta.

Chapter Twenty-Three

Sins

Leonard had not seen his cousin since the funeral. Back then, Matthew had dressed in a black suit and tie, with dark glasses. Today he wore a dark-grey hoodie covering his head, matching grey track bottoms more befitting a teenager and black motorcycle boots. Without the sunglasses to hide them, his dark, wild eyes darted around the room, checking each corner, before settling to glower at Leonard.

When Leonard met his gaze, Matthew levelled the gun directly at his chest. More from a primal instinct than anything, Leonard sensed by his cousin's shifty body language that he was unbalanced.

"You couldn't leave things alone, could you?" came the nasally voice, which might have sounded amusing under any other circumstances. "You had to pry, didn't you? Had to keep digging? You couldn't just leave things alone."

"Matthew. What are you doing here?"

"Is that it? Is that what you found?" said Matthew, his head turning to the Welsh dresser, the barrel of the gun flicking in the same direction. "Where did he hide it? There was nothing here last time I came."

"Boarded up behind that wall," said Leonard, pointing to the side of the chimney breast. When Matthew turned in that direction, Leonard used the heel of his left palm to push the envelope beneath the drawer on the table.

"Don't lie to me," said Matthew, returning his glare. "That alcove was empty when I came here last."

So Matthew had been the intruder.

"In which case, we'd moved it to the other side. Covered by a dust sheet. Is that what you want? Is that what this is all about, the dresser?"

"Shut your mouth. What did he hide in there? What lies did my sick excuse of a brother leave behind for you? Did he blab about what happened here that summer?"

"I don't know what you're talking about. There are some Polaroids of your family and his friends, a camera and film and books, nothing more. You can check if you like. They're still in the cupboards."

"Liar."

"Why would I lie? See for yourself."

Matthew stood stock-still. His mind appeared to be working, his hands and the barrel of the gun shaking slightly. Once again his eyes flicked to the dresser. Leonard realised then that Matthew had not thought everything through, something he might be able to use to his advantage.

"Did you kill him?" asked Leonard.

Asking such a direct question might run the risk of provoking Matthew, but he reasoned that if he could keep Matthew talking, maybe Adrian would return and notice something amiss. Did Matthew bring his motorcycle with him, and if so, would he have left the machine visible in the lane? Leonard hadn't heard anything. And the last thing he wanted was Adrian walking in unaware and stepping into the firing line. Perhaps he could distract Matthew somehow and then try to alert Adrian.

"Did you kill Luke?"

"Don't be ridiculous. Luke took his own life. He hanged himself. Another of his sins, the sin of *desperatio*, the rejection of God's mercy, because when he choked himself he would have been unable to ask for repentance. Not that a heathen like you would understand."

"But why, Matthew? Why did he hang himself? Surely not because he was gay?"

"Homosexuality is also a sin. My brother was an abomination, a sinner and a pervert. Just like you. Yes, my mother told me. And just like him, you will be going straight to hell." Matthew thrust his chin out with pride. "I was the one who caught him, you know? Caught them both. That dirty, evil paedophile who molested my brother."

"Max Williams?"

Now hidden beneath the drawer, the beautiful monochrome photograph Leonard had uncovered showed a clearly besotted Luke being cradled in the arms of Max Williams.

"In our house, in our bedroom, lying there with my brother, kissing and touching each other. Disgusting. Not only was it a sin, it was against the law. He tried to deny everything when I confronted him. But I took an instant photo of them without either of them knowing."

"And Luke denied it?"

"Not Luke. *Him*. I went to see Williams. On the farm. Told him I would go to the police if he didn't do what I asked. Get him thrown into prison. And I would have, too. But then he got all crazy and tried to grab me, take the photo from me, and I screamed back at him, told him not to touch me with his filthy, corrupting hands. I didn't mean to push him so hard, but he slipped in the mud and fell into the water."

"You pushed Max Williams into the pond?"

"I didn't — it was *his* fault. I never meant him to fall. I wouldn't have even told anyone, as long as he'd agreed to give me the money I asked for. But when he tried to grab me, to *touch* me with those *disgusting* hands, I had to fight back. After that I ran back to the house to tell Mother. She told me not to worry, that it was God's retribution."

"Your mother knew and did nothing? Did Mary know?"

"What do you care?" said Matthew, frowning, but then an eerie, calm expression settled on his face. And then he smiled. "No, just me and Mother. And, of course, we had to tell my brother. That's how she finally got him to agree to enlist, to become a real man and exorcise the sickness from him. Except he managed to weasel out of that by taking his life."

Poor Luke. From what Leonard could tell, he had only just carved out a life for himself, a happy ever after, only to have everything ripped away from him by his family. Being coerced into join the army must have been the final straw.

"You tried to blackmail Max Williams?"

"I needed money. I still need money. Some of us have — debts — to pay. And then you go and steal this house from me, this house that should rightfully be mine. I'm the oldest male member of the family, not you."

Right at that moment, Leonard's phone rang. When he looked down, the name Mary appeared on the display. Leonard leant forward, began to move his hand towards the device.

"Don't!" shouted Matthew.

Leonard turned at the sudden movement of Matthew striding forward, ramming the handle of the shotgun into Leonard's head. Knocked out of his seat and sent sprawling across the floor, agony flooded his temple. Black spots swam before him, dotting his vision. After a second or two, the ebb of warm liquid began to pool in his hair, with each heartbeat, each agonising throb of pain. He touched the spot gingerly with his hand and pulled away to find his palm covered with blood.

When he looked up, Matthew had cradled the shotgun in the crook of this arm, and had picked up the device to silence the call. After that, he put the phone into his pocket. Returning his attention to Leonard, he pointed the gun at him again and stood back a couple of steps.

"I warned you."

"Whatever it is you're thinking," began Leonard, cold dread filling him, "you don't need to — "

"Shut up!" he said, waving the gun in the direction of the garden. "You have left me only one way. Get up. Go out through the glass door. Walk to the end of the garden. Slowly. Left-hand side. There's a door in the back fence. Go through and follow the path. And don't try anything, because I'll be right behind you and I will not hesitate to shoot you in the back."

Leonard did as asked, climbing slowly and awkwardly to his feet, a wave of nausea hitting him when he stood upright. All the time Matthew observed him carefully, obsessively, the gun pointed at his body. Leonard stopped at the door, placed a hand on the cold glass to steady himself. After a moment, Matthew prodded him forward with the barrel of the gun. Outside in the garden the cooler air filled his lungs and steadied him, sharpened his consciousness. Very slowly and a little unsteadily he walked ahead, but could hear Matthew's footfalls behind. He had never checked the back fence of the garden, so had no idea what to expect. But just as Matthew had said, a gate of slatted wood stood behind one of the larger fir trees, already open. He stepped through, leaving the doorway open.

"Where are we going?" he asked.

"I told you to shut up," came Matthew's voice, followed by the sound of the gate scraping closed behind them.

Leonard noticed brown earth marking out a path between the tall grass and bushes growing wild either side. When he trod forwards onto the route, he heard Matthew's heavy breathing right behind him.

"Why are you doing this, Matthew?"

"You know why I'm doing this. Because with you gone, the house will pass to me."

"I have no idea what kind of delusion you're under, but if anything happens to me, everything passes to my mother."

"And from what I saw at the will reading, she cares as much about Bryn Bach as your father. With you out of the way, she'll give me what is rightfully mine."

"Not if she finds out you've killed me."

"She won't. Nobody ever will."

Leonard's skin began to prickle. Had Matthew planned to get rid of him all along? Surely Adrian would think to come and look for him. He tried desperately to come up with ways to stall Matthew, but all he could think about was trying to stay alive.

"I don't get it. If you wanted the house so much, why did you try to burn it down?"

"Because I wasn't thinking straight. I worried that my brother had left behind lies about me, worried you might discover something incriminating. And I decided if I couldn't have the house, then nobody would. I had no idea you were staying there that night. When I heard and found out you'd been lucky enough to survive, how a tragedy had been averted because what would have happened if you'd gone up in flames along with the house — well, let's just say, the solution suddenly presented itself. There was a much better way to get what I deserved, what I needed, staring me in the face. My mother always told me that everything comes to those who wait. Well, now I've had the patience to wait for you to rebuild and redecorate, I'll get a far bigger sum when I sell."

"My friend is expecting to find me home. Any minute now. He's driving back from Llandrindod Wells."

"If I have to, I'll deal with him, too."

If Leonard needed any incentive to stay alert and alive, Matthew had just handed him one. He only hoped Adrian would notice the bloody handprint he had purposely left on the sliding door and realise the danger.

"You don't have a clue about this area, do you?" said Matthew. "I bet you've never even ventured outside the house. If we keep to this path, we'll end up at the Hughes farm. How about a history lesson to bide the time? A couple of centuries ago there used to be lead mining around this region, but the mines were abandoned long before Bryn Bach was built. Nobody's even sure where the entrance used to be and only a few of us know there's a sinkhole just off this path. We used to come here as kids. Goes down some sixty feet, by my reckoning. A sheer drop into darkness. Might even be full of water this time of year. How do you fancy a dip?"

Dismay washed over Leonard. His cousin had already thought this through.

Five minutes later and they had reached a curve in the path, surrounded and secluded by tall bushes, where the ground on the left of the path sloped gently down.

"Step off the path here, to your left, and keep going."

Leonard staggered into the long grass where no path marked the way and, for another few minutes, kept moving down the incline. Eventually he reached a clearing with a much steeper slope. Almost immediately he spotted the edges of the dark hole in the ground, at least two metres in diameter. Somebody had tried to erect a knee-high wire fence around the perimeter, but time and the weather had knocked over most of the posts on one side. When Leonard stopped, Matthew moved to the left, around the rim of the slope, to where a cluster of evergreen bushes grew.

"Go to the edge of the hole and turn around to face me," called Matthew, pulling Leonard's phone from his pocket. "Good, stop just there. Now you're going to put your password in this phone and unlock it. Then throw it straight back to me. And if you try anything stupid, I *will* shoot you."

The phone landed on the grass by Leonard's feet. He picked up the device and did as asked. What else could he do? On the display he noticed more missed calls from Mary but nothing from Adrian. Was this how everything would end? Just as his life had begun again? Once he had the phone unlocked, he lobbed the device back to Matthew. With one hand cradling the shotgun, and while constantly glaring up at Leonard, Matthew tapped a message into Leonard's phone.

"There. Done," he said with a grim smile. "Now as far as your friend's concerned, you've decided to stretch your legs and get some fresh air, gone for a stroll to investigate the field behind the property. According to your message, you'll be back soon. But, of course, you won't. And one day they'll find poor Leonard left the path and, tragically, fell into this long-forgotten sinkhole. Or, then again, maybe they never will."

"You're insane."

"In debt, maybe. But I am most definitely not insane."

A soft rustle of wind in the trees caught Leonard's attention. Was his imagination playing tricks on him or did something dark move in the bushes behind Matthew?

"Put the gun down, son," came a familiar calm but assertive voice, from a completely different direction.

Leonard turned his head towards the sound. PC Morgan stood there in full view with Adrian behind, appearing on the far side of the sinkhole. How had they known where to find them? Leonard had difficulty interpreting Adrian's attention which was fixed on Leonard, and seemed to carry a mix of fear, despair and anger. In the meantime, Matthew had swung the shotgun around to point in the policeman's direction.

"Come closer and I will shoot."

"And if you do, you will go to prison for a very long time, son. Is that what you want?"

"I want what's mine. The house should be mine."

"He thinks that with me gone, Bryn Bach will be his," said Leonard.

"It will. Even if I go to prison, my mother will sell the house on my behalf."

"And keep the money for herself," said Leonard.

"Shut your fucking mouth!"

"Drop the gun," came another voice, from the same direction he and Matthew had come. PC Lewis stood there now and Matthew backed up a step against a bush, swinging the gun wildly in all directions.

"Don't come any closer. Or I will kill all of you."

"That's a double-barrelled shotgun, son," said PC Morgan. "Even if you're a sharpshooter, you'll only get off two shots before you need to reload. There are four of us and, if you listen, a lot more on the way."

In the distance Leonard could hear the faint sound of multiple police car sirens approaching, probably arriving at the front of the house. Matthew heard too, because his eyes started to dart around the clearing.

"Shut up. Shut up all of you. Or I will at least kill *him*."

Matthew appeared crazy now, turning in a half circle, aiming the gun at each of them before levelling both barrels at Leonard.

"He told me, Adrian," said Leonard, stepping to one side of the hole. Feeling more emboldened, he reasoned that if Matthew chose to shoot him now, at least Adrian was safe and there would be multiple witnesses to his action. "He confessed to me how he tried to blackmail Max Williams and then killed him."

"Shut the fuck up! I didn't kill him. He tried to grab hold of me. So I pushed him away and he fell. I didn't—"

"You didn't try to save him, though, did you? You could have jumped in to help, but you didn't. You let a drowning man die."

"Why shouldn't I? He was a paedophile, a bastard-fathering pervert, as well as the worst kind of sinner — just like my brother. He deserved to drown like the pathetic rabid dog that he was—"

But Leonard's cousin didn't get a chance to finish the sentence.

Hidden within a thick evergreen bush where Matthew had been standing, a figure stepped forwards and swung what looked like a cricket bat at his head. The blow was not only fierce and powerful, but done with frightening accuracy, striking him on the side of the head. Matthew stumbled sideways, falling to his knees, dropping the gun and rolling slightly into the slope. All at once, seeing their opportunity, both officers began to move quickly forwards to try to reach him. Leonard took the opportunity to hurry away from the sinkhole. But the officers were too far away and Matthew, conscious still and desperate, scrambled to raise himself from the ground while reaching a hand out for his gun. This time, behind him, his attacker strode fully into view.

Freya Williams.

Matthew managed to fire off a random single shot before Freya, without fear or hesitation, connected another blow directly to the back of his head. This time he fell forwards, his body rolling down the rest of the steep slope and dropping into the crevice before anyone could reach him. Almost instantly, a splash could be heard. After a quick glance at the fierce, triumphant and frankly frightening face of Freya, Leonard joined PC Lewis, who had dashed to the edge of the sinkhole and grabbed the cricket bat from Freya. Behind them Leonard could hear PC Morgan barking orders into his phone.

"Dispatch. We need emergency services with a ladder. And get some medics here, pronto. We have one man fallen into a sinkhole, another with a head injury and one shot in the chest."

With a loud crackling of tramped grass, other police officers, these in stark-black uniforms with black helmets and carrying guns, began appearing from each direction. Instantly, PC Morgan ordered them to stand down their weapons. Leonard wondered who had been shot, until he turned to see PC Morgan leaning over the figure of Adrian, laid out on the ground.

"No." Leonard mouthed the word but no sound came, and began to rise. One of the black-uniformed officers moved over and pushed Leonard firmly back down, telling him not to move. But he could still turn his head.

Adrian lay unmoving on the ground, his eyes closed. Blood oozed from the left side of his chest.

"Please, no," he finally choked out.

Chapter Twenty-Four

Casa di Luca

Adrian arrived at Bryn Bach with a special house-warming gift for Lenny the day before the house-warming party. Apart from wanting to be with him earlier and help out in whatever way he could — injury willing — he also felt nervous about this particular present.

Friends knew he always went the extra mile in seeking out meaningful gifts for people, but he didn't know Lenny well enough to guess how he might react.

Having his left arm in a sling still meant him being restricted, and even though he felt a twinge of pain now and then, he had pretty much mended. Being unable to drive with one hand, Lenny had wanted to pick him up from Drayton, but his man had been crazy with work and then needed to rush to Wales to sign off on final items of work on the house.

Instead, Adrian had cadged a lift with Toni and Jack who had both volunteered to help Lenny with the arrangements. Just as well, because Toni wanted to hear all about Adrian's meeting in Cambridge on the way down.

Apart from recuperating in Drayton, Adrian had found a day to meet up with his new boss, Tom Bradford, in nearby Cambridge and, after some negotiations, had confirmed he would be starting work for him in London the following Monday. Lenny had breathed a sigh of relief when Adrian had called with the news. Lenny wanted him in his London home as much as he ached to be there.

Adrian directed Jack to park up in the lane rather than outside the house. He wanted to inspect the fruits of their labour on the walk to the front door. With his good arm braced on the top of the door frame of the cab, he climbed out of Jack's pickup, then turned around and retrieved his bag and wrapped gift from the back seat. While he waited for Jack and Toni to collect their holdalls, he surveyed the driveway.

Lenny had left the entrance open, probably expecting them to drive up to the house. A fresh coat of white paint made the gate sparkle, set against the backdrop of professionally groomed hedgerows and manicured trees and bushes, so different from the overgrown mess that had originally met them all those months back.

They scrunched their way in companionable silence down the gravel driveway to the house, each of them remarking when the newly spruced up façade came into view.

Since his last visit, the original flint work all around the lower level of the house had been thoroughly cleaned, the speckled rock cladding now vibrant and authentic and offset by the brick upper level which had been given a fresh coat of white paint. Only those looking for modernisations would spot the new sash windows of dark wood — probably oak — and the new guttering along the front of the roof, both items sympathetically chosen to match the originals. Even the portico and front door had been given a makeover. As Adrian approached he felt sure he could feel the house smiling.

Lenny had not heard them arrive and the sheer delight on his face at opening the front door and seeing them on the doorstep filled Adrian with a fondness he had only experienced since meeting Lenny, and one he had come to treasure.

After hugs and kisses, with Lenny ushering Toni and Jack into the house and telling them to drop their bags in their room, Adrian took his turn in his lover's arms but then held Lenny back. After taking a deep breath, he held out his present.

"I hope you don't mind, but I commissioned these for the house. A friend of mine in Norwich runs her own pottery studio and I asked her to create a couple of identical house signs in ceramic, a replacement for the one at the front gate and one to display here above the front door."

Lenny unwrapped the ceramic tiles in front of Adrian. In bold letters, they announced the name of the house, which in Welsh meant 'small hill', and, in a curvy script beneath, he had added three simple words in Italian, because in Max's letter to Luke he had written about Luke's dream for them to travel across Italy together.

B r y n B a c h
- Casa di Luca –

Luke's home.

Leonard stood staring down, frozen to the spot. Adrian was about to ask if he liked the artwork but then noticed Lenny's hands shake slightly, saw him swallow a couple of times and a tear form in the corner of his right eye.

"Oh, shit, Lenny. I didn't mean to — "

"No, no. They're beautiful, Ade. Perfect. I love them," said Lenny, squeezing the bridge of his nose between thumb and forefinger before reaching out and pulling Adrian into a gentle hug, careful not to touch his left arm. "We are so much on the same wavelength. I feel the same way. This is Luke's house. Always was and always will be. Let's fix them up today ready for the party tomorrow so everyone can see them. But before that, I've got something I need to show *you*."

He led Adrian to the living room, to what was once the bare wall in the alcove to the right of the fireplace, where a small cabinet now stood. Six large-framed photographs hung there now, two in the old sepia tones of the construction of Bryn Bach and Lord Charles with his arm around a young Harold Day. Two were of Luke and Max together. But the last two Adrian had not seen before, of Lenny and himself. One had them laughing at a joke together in the shell of the living room, in overalls and covered in plaster dust, while the other was them sitting on the top step of the terrace, with the sunset behind. All around the larger pictures, long white rectangular frames had been mounted — some positioned vertically, some horizontally — that held the small Polaroids of Luke's friends at play.

"Toni took the ones of us. Brilliant resolution on her phone camera. Kieran got them all framed for me. What do you think?"

Adrian had to take a moment before responding. Of course, he appreciated the photographs of Luke and Max and the construction of Bryn Bach. But the ones of Lenny and himself, of their burgeoning relationship, touched a place deep inside him.

"Amazing. And speaks to the history of the house."

"Exactly. A Bryn Bach history wall."

When Adrian turned to look at Lenny, his eyes deflected to a large oil painting over the fireplace. He took a moment to realise what he was seeing. Someone had replicated the photograph of Luke, Pippa, Howie and Freya playing in the garden together as teenagers. The whole ensemble with the dance of light behind them felt like life, and youth and joy personified. Whoever had painted Luke, had captured his features wonderfully, the eyes with the same longing they'd had in the original photograph.

"See what I mean when I say we're on the same wavelength? I asked for the actual photo to be enlarged, but Kieran's contact told him the print had too many wrinkles and creases, and that he couldn't do the picture justice without losing some of the resolution. I'm not sure I actually believe him now, because almost straight away, Isabelle, who I work with, piped up and asked if a friend of hers could make an oil painting based on the photo. And as you can see, her friend has a rare talent. For most people this is simply a happy portrait of youth. But for those of us in the know, this is a special moment in time captured and enjoyed in this house."

"Oh my goodness, Lenny. It's absolutely brilliant. Has anyone else seen this wall?"

"Apart from me? No, you're the first. And I think I can hear Toni and Jack coming down the stairs, so they'll be next," said Lenny. "And from tomorrow? Everyone who comes to the house."

* * * *

The official kick-off for the party was one o'clock.

To keep in good favour with the locals, Lenny had asked Megan Llewellyn and her team to cater the party. They'd even hired Maggie Llewellyn — her daughter — and two of her young friends to don white shirts and black skirts or trousers and offer guests drinks and finger food on silver platters in the house and garden. Maggie, her friends, and the burly Manor Inn chef — they never had figured out his name — arrived at eleven to set up tables and chairs in the garden and a bar to one side, and to begin preparing and laying out the finger food in the kitchen. Both Lenny and Adrian stayed well out of the way, seeing the hive of activity, and giving them room to work their magic.

Mary texted Lenny to say she would be arriving early, because she had to pick up another guest, and also because she wanted to park in the driveway, her husband having mobility issues. Lenny said he had offered Mary and her husband the downstairs room, but Mary had declined, saying she wanted to get them back home the same day.

She arrived at twelve-thirty, and Adrian joined Lenny at the front door. Her resemblance to Matthew should have been frightening, except her features seemed softer in some way and her personality was open and friendly. After whispering to the man in the wheelchair, and him nodding in return, she came up, and without a single word of introduction, threw her arms around Leonard.

"Leonard. I am so sorry. I feel partly responsible."

"How could you be responsible?" asked Lenny, returning the hug then letting her go.

"Not sure how much the police told you, but Matthew called me the day he decided to come here. Said he was going to have it out with you once and for all. My brother is nothing but bluster most of the time, full of hot air, and when I called Freya, she assured me you had a friend staying who looked as though he could handle any trouble." Mary looked over at Adrian and smiled. "I had no idea Matthew would be carrying a gun, otherwise I'd have called the police myself. Honestly, that's not like him at all. But then, I had no idea he was in such dire financial straits. He'd borrow money from me every once in a while—more of a handout, really—usually citing the fact that Mum wasn't working. And I knew he liked a flutter here and there, but never realised things had gotten so serious. The police told me that he's involved with some pretty nasty and ruthless loan sharks."

Adrian refused to feel sorry for Matthew. On the streets he had witnessed the results of addiction first-hand—drink, drugs and gambling, sometimes a combination of all three—and had experienced far worse hardship in his own life than owing money. With the right support, by talking to the right people like Citizen's Advice or even Gamblers Anonymous, Matthew could have gotten legitimate help without resorting to crime.

"It's all water under the bridge, Mary," said Lenny, as magnanimous as ever. "I'm just pleased you and your husband agreed to come."

Mary introduced her husband, George, in the wheelchair—also a lawyer—and pointed to an older gentleman with a walking stick, currently leaning into the back of their car.

"And that's my father."

Aha, thought Adrian, Mr Darlington was very much alive and well. So much for what Lenny's aunt had told Lenny. Once their introductions had been made, Adrian took the gift of wine from the older man and led them through the house towards the outdoor furniture overlooking the back garden. Maggie and her crew enjoyed a well-earned rest at one of the garden tables before the bulk of the guests started arriving. While Lenny chatted to his guests, Adrian went to fetch everyone drinks.

"Yes, I still kept in touch with Matthew," said Mary, wheeling her husband to one side of the table. When Adrian looked back in the house, he noticed Mr Darlington had stopped to look at the photos in the alcove. "Largely, I suppose, because I felt a little guilty after college, leaving him alone with our mother."

"I thought Matthew married?"

"He did. They lived with her. Can you imagine? The marriage lasted all of three months before the poor wife moved back in with her parents. But I've kept in touch with Freya and Pippa over the years. More so with Freya. Will be great to see them later. I just hope Freya's still talking to me, now she knows what really happened to her father. But Freya's how I knew about your progress on the house, which is absolutely lovely, by the way. Already brings back so many good memories."

"She's coming. I asked her to arrive early, too. For a chat before the pandemonium begins."

When Adrian took the glass of red wine over to Mr Darlington, Lenny and Mary came to join them, leaving

Mary's husband on the terrace. As he approached the alcove, Adrian could see the older man's resemblance to Mary as plain as day, whereas Luke looked more like Lenny's side of the family. When Mr Darlington accepted the wine, he dabbed at his eyes with one knuckle.

"You know, I can't help thinking a large part of this is my fault," he said, shaking his head. "Mary knows all this, but my marriage was over long before I walked out. Even when we were together I provided financial support as best I could, bought and paid for the flat my ex-wife is still living in, but spent as little time there as possible. Mainly because when the twins were growing up, Millicent changed, became intolerable with her preaching and nagging and lecturing. But what happened to my eldest brought things to a head. Most summers, when they came here, I either spent time working far too hard in a sales job that was frankly going nowhere, or with the woman who later became my second wife. I'm not without blame here and I can't help thinking I failed Luke."

"You did your best, Dad," said Mary, squeezing his arm. "You supported his dream to go to art college."

"Not financially. Because I simply didn't have the money—"

"He knew that," she added. Mary's fondness for her father became evident. "Which is why he planned to take a few years out, to work before starting college."

"And I had no idea Millicent had pressured him into joining the armed forces," said Mr Darlington. "My son, the pacifist. She didn't consult me and, worst of all, Luke said nothing."

"Nobody knew. That was the year after Mr Williams died. Luke shut down, talked to nobody, not even me.

I sensed something wasn't right, when she outright refused to let any of us attend Mr William's funeral, after everything he'd done for us. We didn't come here the summer of that year, just stayed at home. What a lot of people didn't know about Luke was when he was in high spirits, he was the life of the party, so much fun to be around. But when the lows took hold, he sank to rock bottom. He would close himself off completely from everyone. I only found out much later from Matthew about our mother pressuring him and getting him to agree to enlist. I imagine he would have agreed to anything by then."

"I should have been there," said Mr Darlington, shaking his head. "I should have done more—"

"We all should have," said Mary, putting her arm around him while looking at the photo of Max and Luke. "But none of us knew the whole story. Not until now."

Everyone fell silent. Adrian knew only too well about parents failing their children.

"From what I've heard, from people in the area who remember him," said Lenny, talking directly to Mr Darlington. "Luke seemed to be at his happiest here in this house. I only wish I'd known him. I bet we'd have been good friends."

At this Mr Darlington smiled sadly but appeared to relax. At the same moment, Adrian heard the newly fitted front doorbell ring. As he went to see who had arrived, he overheard Mr Darlington's words.

"I'm sure you would have been. And I can't thank you enough for what you've done here. Not sure if people might think it morbid to see photographs of my dead son on the walls, but for me, it's an absolute joy."

When Adrian opened the front door Freya stood there, a cloth shopping bag drooping from her arm, her hair newly styled, looking fresh-faced and happy. Before Adrian had a chance to say anything, she hugged him tightly around the waist, which surprised a breath out of him.

"I'm so glad you answered the door, Adrian. While I've got you here, I owe you an explanation. Pippa and her husband gave me a lift. They're just parking up the car right now, so I'll be quick," she said before letting the embrace go. "I'm sure Mary will have told you by now, but just before I saw you at the supermarket, she'd called me up and told me her concerns. I told her not to worry, that you two were perfectly capable of looking after each other. But as soon as you told me Leonard was alone, well, I felt responsible, so headed over here. I didn't want to panic you, so I didn't say anything. Matthew has always been all bark and no bite. Then on my way to your place, I saw his motorcycle turn into the side road for the Hughes farm. Anyway, I hung back a while and then followed. I know the fields around the Hughes place like the rooms in my home. And there was his motorcycle, parked up next to the turnstile to the back path we used to get to Bryn Bach. I got Howie's junior cricket bat from the back of my car and followed the path to the back of the house. And then, when I saw Matthew leading Leonard in my direction, I knew exactly where he was taking him, so I got there first and hid in a bush. But admittedly, when I overheard Matthew claiming responsibility for my father's death and the vile things he said about him, well, I just saw red. I'm so sorry you had to see that and if I scared you or Leonard."

"Don't apologise, Freya. Honestly, we were glad to have you there. You seem a lot more cheerful today."

As Adrian stood there, Pippa appeared along the driveway, arm in arm with a man he assumed to be her husband. She waved happily at Adrian and Freya.

"I finally agreed to visit Howie in Jakarta. Life's too short, don't you think? I also baked you a loaf of my favourite sourdough bread, fresh this morning. And you may not use this today, but I make my own apricot jam and marmalade. So I've brought jars of both."

"You're a woman of many talents. Let's go and meet the others."

* * * *

Adrian stood between the kitchen and the terrace, leaning against the sliding door, watching the revelry of a house-warming party in full swing. Around the verdant lawn, each of the trestle tables had been decorated with a simple white tablecloth and a small posy of colourful flowers picked from the garden. Guests sat around chatting with one another, people who either knew Lenny or Adrian or both, and now got along like old friends. How on earth Lenny had managed to drum up almost fifty people had been nothing short of a miracle, but not only was the driveway currently packed with cars, many had parked along the lane leading to Bryn Bach.

Luckily PC Morgan had made an appearance in the morning and given them the okay to park along one side, as long as they left space for others to enter and exit.

Finally meeting Lenny's employees had been a hoot, hearing stories about his work life, little idiosyncrasies about the man. Everything was said light-heartedly, the people who worked for Lenny clearly adoring him. Lenny's cousin Eric and his wife had brought Lenny's mother and his Aunt Marcie from Drayton. They had also given Adrian's mother a ride and, by some miracle, had all arrived not only intact but the best of friends.

Right now, the serving staff negotiated the back garden with fresh platters of food, while artfully dodging Kieran and Kennedy's two kids and their ball of ginger lightning that passed for a dog, snapping at their heels. Megan and her husband Dave had been invited as guests and enjoyed the fun, although Megan couldn't stop herself from helping out in the kitchen now and then, or pointing out things that needed to be done — much to the annoyance of her daughter.

Had the house ever known such merriment?

Adrian hoped so. If not, it would have been a tragedy, because Adrian could not help smiling and chuckling just hearing the walls echo with lively chatter and laughter, the squeals of children giggling coming from the garden, the occasional jangle of a wind chime on the balcony and the yapping of the pooch. Mid-June and they couldn't have picked a more glorious day, sunshine streaming in through the open patio doors, the smell of gardenias and jasmine from the balcony boxes wrestling with the aroma of sausage rolls and quiches baking in the oven.

If a house could breathe a sigh of contentment, he thought as he looked on, then that's precisely what Bryn Bach would be doing right now.

But at one point, two weeks before, everything had hung in the balance.

Thank goodness for PC Morgan's experience and quick thinking, because within half an hour Adrian had been temporarily patched up by one of the emergency services professionals and carried off to a waiting ambulance with an ashen-faced Lenny glued to his side. Another hour later — and with pain medication dulling his senses — Adrian had been wheeled into the accident and emergency ward of a nearby public hospital.

Fortunately he had been standing some way off when Darlington fired the shot, and the shell had hit the left side of his chest, knocking him over. As he'd fallen, he'd hit his head on an errant log, knocking him unconscious. Despite losing blood and having pellets lodged in his shoulder, he had not been seriously injured. More concerned about him having a concussion, the doctors had kept him in a hospital bed for two nights for observation.

Matthew Darlington had landed in chest-high water but being unconscious had almost drowned — which under the circumstances might have been poetic justice. In fact, the chill water had brought him back to consciousness, before the police had descended into the hole and hauled him out. Apart from a mild concussion — no fracture or more severe injury — he had been kept in hospital for a couple of days. Right now he was being held in custody on charges of carrying an unlicensed firearm, threatening behaviour, threat to kill and a whole list of other misdemeanours, including a potential charge of manslaughter.

Lenny's new state-of-the-art security system did indeed record both image and sound, much to everyone's relief.

Both police constables wrote up Freya's actions officially as self-defence, and privately as an act of bravery. And Adrian and Lenny concurred while also vowing never to get on her wrong side.

"What's the average sentence for manslaughter?" Lenny asked PC Morgan. Although both had been on duty, he and PC Lewis had popped along that morning for a quick glass of orange juice and to wish them well.

"Depends on the severity of the offence. In Darlington's case with Max Williams, nothing was premeditated, everything done in the heat of the moment, so it's really hard to say. Sometimes a judge will take a more lenient approach to first offenders, but your cousin has a string of previous minor misdemeanours. Already having a record together with subsequently threatening your life and admitting to trying to torch your premises isn't exactly going to work in his favour. At a guess, I reckon he's looking at three to five years, maybe more."

"And what about Lenny's dear Auntie Malevolent?" asked Adrian, making Lenny chuckle.

"Not sure what will happen there, son," said MC Morgan. "She's bound to get called to testify, but a lot will depend on the son's confession. They could charge her with failure to act on her son's crime on the grounds of omission. But I doubt that will stick."

Adrian knew Lenny didn't care. As far as he was concerned, she had already built a prison around herself. They had chatted a little more about the day in question, with PC Morgan telling them some of the things they didn't know, like how Freya had punctured both tyres on Matthew's motorcycle before coming to find Leonard, and how incredibly clear the security footage—both audio and video—in the house had been.

"I would normally ask people throwing a party to keep an eye on the noise," said PC Morgan as they had both readied to leave. "But the beauty of this location is there's nobody to hear you for miles around."

"Not always a good thing," said Lenny, raising an eyebrow.

"Point taken, son. Luckily for you, on that particular day we were already on the pathway when we heard Darlington mouthing off. Otherwise we'd have carried on down to the Hughes farm."

"Freya knew," said Lenny. "Not sure how things might have turned out if you hadn't been there as a distraction. Matthew thought he was being clever, taking me to the secret spot. But apparently they all knew about the sinkhole."

"Is she coming?" asked PC Morgan.

"She said she would. I'm glad, because I want her to see the house."

"I must say," said PC Lewis, at the front door, "you've done amazing work on the place since we were last here. Even the little touches, like the pictures and the new nameplate above the front door."

* * * *

Throughout the afternoon, as people came into the house and wandered around, nosing around the bedrooms and bathrooms, Adrian felt pride that he had been part of the team to put the house back together again. A couple of times he even acted as a tour guide, showing the nice, minimalist bedrooms with the antique wardrobes and chest of drawers. He enjoyed pointing out the lack of radiators because of the underfloor heating Lenny had agreed to install and the huge family bathroom with a free-standing cast-iron tub and separate shower stall, all done with modern fixtures and fittings.

Megan Llewellyn even sidled up to Adrian during the afternoon to ask if Lenny might consider selling. Adrian already knew the answer without having to consult Lenny. The house would be staying in the Day family for now.

While most of the guests were polite to one another, Lenny's mother was, perhaps not unexpectedly, the exception to the rule.

"Mum. This is Mary, your niece. Mary, this is my mother."

"Lovely to meet you, Aunt Geraldine. My own mother won't be coming," said Mary, shaking Mrs Day's hand.

"I should hope she wasn't invited," said Mrs Day.

"Mum," said Lenny, with a gentle reprimand.

"What, Leonard?" said Mrs Day, more than a little hostile. "The woman deserves to be locked up and the key thrown away. Trying to get my son killed. If your cousin Matthew were here with her right now, I'd make them both a nice pot of tea with some of your father's more exotic mushrooms. They'd never know what hit them."

"I'm sorry, Mary," Lenny began.

"Please don't be. I would happily help you pour the brew into their cups, Aunt Geraldine," said Mary.

After that, the two of them chatted like old friends.

"Oh, my goodness," said Lenny to Adrian, looking mortified as they moved away. "Apparently homicidal tendencies run in the family. Are you sure you want to associate with me, Mr Lamperton?"

Adrian pulled him around and kissed him full on the lips.

"I'll take my chances."

* * * *

At one point later in the afternoon, Lenny managed to steal Mary, Freya and Pippa away. He sat them down in the front of the room on the leather settees, talking about the oil painting and handing around some small Polaroids Luke had taken, the ones that hadn't made the walls. Between them, the three ladies talked happily about the times they'd spent together. Mary had fewer recollections, having spent most of her time with her mother and Matthew. When Lenny passed around the letter from Max to Luke and the extra photos that hadn't made the walls, Pippa read the letter first but then Mary and Freya read together, both teary by the time they refolded the paper and handed the letter back. Eventually Lenny told them the whole story of him and Adrian finding the dresser behind the wall, of the day Matthew arrived at the house with the shotgun, and how he had only just found the photos and read the letter from Max when Matthew had appeared. The police had told them each very little during their interviews.

"Now things make more sense," said Mary. "The last summer we ever came here was the year Mr Williams drowned. Luke had done some decorations around the house, including painting the walls and covering those alcoves. Honestly, I didn't even notice the dresser had gone. My mother had arranged with Matthew to have the house furniture sold off earlier in the year, and they would have collected everything after we'd left."

"That's right," said Freya. "After Dad's funeral. I let the clearance men in, before my grandmother and I came in and gave the place a good clean. And then you didn't come back the next summer."

Everyone fell silent again, processing this information.

"You said there were two letters," said Mary. "What was in the remaining one?"

"Kind of a goodbye note," said Lenny, going over to the dresser and pulling open the top drawer. "Meant for whoever found the dresser. In case Luke never could retrieve the furniture himself."

Lenny settled himself back down and began to read aloud.

To Whom It May Concern. If for any reason I am prevented from following my dream, if I am unable to restore this beautiful piece of furniture to its rightful place in this beautiful house and this letter remains unopened, then I am lost. I have been kept from living out my life as I want with my love (and I know there's a member of my family who will try to stop this from happening). If that is the case, then I bid you all Ty Adar, *which in Welsh means farewell. Luke.*

Everyone except Freya fell silent.

"That's not right," said Freya, surprising them all. "*Ty Adar* doesn't mean farewell. And Luke would never get something like that wrong. *Ty Adar* means birdhouse or aviary in Welsh. Don't you have a bird box in the garden?"

"Yes, you do," said Adrian. "In the apple tree. But I don't know if it's the original or if it was replaced with a new one. Any idea, Pippa? It certainly looks old enough."

"It's the original. We only cleaned the thing up a little."

"Let me go have a look," said Adrian.

Adrian went out to the apple tree at the end of the garden. A couple of the guests smiled as he went past but soon went back to their conversations. The old bird box sat towards the back fence, within easy reach, fixed by wire from a thick branch of the tree. Made entirely out of sheets of beech, the bird house had a couple of large holes drilled into the front and a single perch installed inside. At the back, Adrian found a panel which could be lifted up and used to clear the mess from the interior.

He found nothing out of the ordinary but then thought about how Luke had hidden the photographs and letters in the dresser. Using his fingers, he reached into the box—which was thankfully relatively clean—pressed the floor inside and pulled, which also slid open a panel. Inside he found a tiny pack wrapped in thick plastic. After a second, he replaced the other parts of the bird box and returned to the room.

Everyone fell silent as he unwrapped the package. Inside he found a single TDK cassette tape with nothing written on the label, just left blank. He handed the item to Lenny.

"How will we know what's on there? Does anyone even have a cassette player these days?" asked Pippa.

"We have one," answered Lenny, standing. "At least, Luke left one in the cupboard. I didn't throw it away, but then I'm not sure if it actually works."

"Only one way to find out," said Adrian.

They brought out the old machine and placed it in the middle of the coffee table. Adrian found a mains socket and plugged in the device. On the display, a small green light illuminated, so he pressed a button to flip open the lid while Lenny slipped in the cassette tape and snapped the top down.

Everyone around took a breath and glanced nervously at one another.

"Are we ready?" asked Lenny.

Rather than reply, everyone gave a simple nod, and Adrian pressed the play button.

"Hello. This is Luke Darlington."

The recording sounded loud and tinny, Luke's voice too young, too vulnerable. Adrian adjusted the volume, and when he looked across at Pippa and Freya, he noticed their eyes had watered up.

"If anyone ever hears this, you have found my grandfather's beautiful dresser and the photographs I hid there, and I hope they make sense to you. You also need to know that what I am doing, I am doing of my own free will. I know some of you who remember me will be sad, although my mother will likely call it a sin, but I cannot think of any other way out. I don't really want to go on living, not without the one person who made everything make sense, who made everything feel good and right. I am finally of an age where I can be who I want to be, but the love I have been waiting for has been taken from me, and I cannot imagine — do not want to imagine — a future without him. Everything was bearable knowing he was out there, and especially when we were together. I was going to use this recording to name people who wronged us, but all I feel right now is a calmness I have not felt in over a year, so I am going to let things go and forgive anyone who did not have our best intentions at heart. I just hope this house that was supposed to be mine ends up with good people, who find as much joy here as I found during my short life. And who knows? Maybe we will meet one day, in another life, under different circumstances. Until then, I bid you farewell, and urge you to stay true to yourself — and keep the faith."

This time a moment of silence was shared by all.

"I can't believe he had nobody he could talk to," said Pippa. "Maybe not family, but a helpline. Or why didn't he pick up the phone and call one of us. I don't understand."

Adrian sighed. He had lived through the same time, although under very different circumstances.

"I think I understand. I've been that low once or twice when I was younger. And you know, sometimes it takes no more than a kind word or a sympathetic listener to bring you back from the edge. But you have to remember, this was back in the mid-eighties. AIDS had ravaged the gay community and homophobia was rampant. Lenny knows that I would have been around seventeen and living on the streets of London. And there were only a few gay support groups back then, the LGBT Foundation being one of them, and certainly no helplines that I knew of specifically aimed at gay men and women. Stonewall wasn't established until the end of the eighties. And even though we've still got a long way to go, many people are more socially aware today, especially with the emergence of global movements like It Gets Better, The Trevor Project and LGBTQ+ Lifeline. Today we can be openly gay and aspire to become an athlete, or a film star or even a prime minster of a country. We can get married and have kids. We even have gay characters appearing in daily soap operas and gay-themed films where the gay men or women actually have a happy ending. Back then, as a gay young man, if you had described the world we live in today, I would probably have laughed at you. I hope that if there are any Lukes out there today, they know they are not alone and only have to pick up the phone to get not only a kind word and a sympathetic listener but someone to provide practical help."

"Hear, hear," said Lenny, nodding and smiling proudly at Adrian.

* * * *

By six o'clock a few of the guests had started to leave. Adrian found Toni helping to load up the dishwasher in the kitchen while Jack had decided to help Maggie's friends collect up glasses and plates from around the garden. He noticed Lenny in the garden, laughing with his work colleagues, a silver tray in his hands, and felt a fresh wave of love fill him. Just as he turned away to check on the living area, someone tapped him on the shoulder.

"Adrian," said the man Lenny had introduced as Kennedy, a close friend of his. Adrian had instantly warmed to him and his husband, as well as their two somewhat exuberant boys. "Can I have a word?"

"Of course," said Adrian.

"In private?" asked Kennedy. "Maybe in the study?"

"Lead the way," said Adrian, as much wary as intrigued.

As they opened the door and entered the large room, he realised Lenny had already made the double sofa bed to allow Kieran and Kennedy to stay the night.

Their boys would be sleeping on an inflatable mattress on the floor with their dog. But Adrian hadn't noticed what else Lenny had done with the room. Apart from a desk and the bookcases filled with Luke's books and others Lenny had brought with him, there were also figurines and a framed collage of photographs showing the complete renovation of Bryn Bach to its current state, which hung in pride of place above the mantelpiece. More of Toni's smartphone photography handiwork.

"Don't worry," said Kennedy. "It's nothing serious. I just wanted to say thank you."

"For what?"

"For giving my friend a new lease on life. He doesn't stop talking about you."

"Honestly, I think you've got that the wrong way around. Lenny's done so much for me."

"Well, I just wanted to say thank you. Kieran will tell you that I've always had a soft spot for Leonard, so I'm overjoyed to see him happy finally. You know — and I shouldn't be telling you this, because he won't thank me — but a friend of ours, Pete, nicknamed Leonard 'Any Day'. When someone asked why, he replied, 'Because any day is better than Lenny Day.' Then went on to call him a walking misery. Of course, I stepped in and gave the friend a piece of my mind. But looking back, Leonard had become pretty sullen. He's a different person today and I can't help but think that's because of you. So if you ever fancy a weekend up in Scotland, I've acquired a lodge on the banks of Loch Arkaig that overlooks Ben Nevis. You can either have the place to yourself, or join us for Christmas. We have a gathering each year and the two of you would fit in perfectly with our other friends."

"Have you run the idea past Lenny?"

Kennedy laughed.

"What?"

"I can't believe he allows you to call him Lenny. And the answer is, no, I thought I'd leave the idea with you. And only if you can spare the time."

"Let me talk to him. But that's really kind of you."

"And now you're in his life, you have to come to Sunday lunch at ours. We don't live far away. And Lenny tells me you've got some work through a friend of ours."

"You know Tom Bradford?"

"We know his husband better. Marcus Vine? He's a celebrity chef. He catered our wedding."

Adrian shrugged. He didn't follow the tabloids.

"That's nice. And maybe you can come and have lunch at Lenny's place while I'm staying there."

Kennedy laughed, not unkindly, but there was definitely a dubious quality to the laugh.

"That would certainly be a first," he said eventually.

"What do you mean?"

"I don't think anyone's seen the inside of Leonard's house. Kieran has a conspiracy theory that he lives in a hotel. In all the years I've known him, he's never had a dinner party at home, let alone a full-blown party like this."

"Something else that's going to change," said Adrian.

Before he could fully process what Kennedy was saying about Lenny, one of Kennedy's boys burst into the room, looking as though some tragedy had befallen him, as only young children can.

"Dad! There you are! Link's lying across the seat cushion, being selfish, taking up all the space in the begonia. He won't let me sit down next to him."

"In the what?" asked Adrian, puzzled.

"He means the pagoda," said Kieran, breathless, catching up with his son, placing a hand on either shoulder and looking apologetically at Kennedy. "Sorry, Kennedy. It's a pagoda, Clinton. A begonia is a flower. And why can't you play nicely?"

"Dad!" said the youngster, shaking out of Kieran's grasp and blatantly ignoring him.

"Clinton James!" said Kennedy in a voice that had even Adrian standing straight and taking notice. "Don't you ever let me hear you being rude to your papa again. Do I make myself clear?"

Yes," said Clint, his bottom lip plopping out. "But Link—"

"Remember what we said, Clint?" said Kennedy sternly. "What we all agreed?"

"Yes," said Clint, quieter now, folding his arms and looking down at the floor.

"Then tell me and your papa. What did we agree?"

"That we would always be kind to other people and look out for one another, no matter what, especially our family."

As he had been speaking, behind him an almost identical version of Clint had appeared at the door, followed by their cheeky ginger Cockapoo, who poked his head from between the new arrival's legs.

"And?"

"And brothers should be friends."

"Good."

"I'm sorry, Clint," said the newcomer Adrian assumed to be Link. "Come back and play. Uncle Len's got a tray he's saved specially for us. Mini sausage rolls, sliders, cheesy puffs, marshmallows, chocolate ice cream and, your favourite, stringy French fries with cheese. Health food for kids, he says."

"Yaaaaay!" said the two of them, racing away with their yapping dog, all animosity evaporated.

"Let's go back into the main room, too," said Kennedy, leading them back through, putting his hand on Kieran's shoulder. "I was just saying to Adrian here how grateful we are to see Leonard so happy. You have no idea what a world of difference you've made. I wanted to say thank you. He means a lot to us."

"He gave me a job when nobody else would hire me," said Kieran.

"Okay," said Adrian, raising an eyebrow. "That's not quite the way Lenny tells it."

"Out of interest—I mean, you two click so well—what is it you see in him?" asked Kieran.

Nobody had ever asked that question before, and Adrian had to think it through. How on earth did he even begin to talk about all of Lenny's outstanding traits?

"I suppose, for me, it's simple," said Adrian, before smiling and peering across the room to where the pair's twin boys clambered around a laughing Lenny, who lowered a tray piled with food onto the coffee table.

As Lenny met his gaze and winked, a sudden thought came to him. Were they too old to be thinking about starting a family? Or maybe adopting a child?

"And?" prompted Kieran.

"You said it's simple for you," said Kennedy, nudging Adrian's arm.

"It's the exact opposite of what your friend on the cruise said. Any day I get to share with Lenny makes me realise how lucky I am."

Chapter Twenty-Five

Lockdown, two years on

Maybe everything was fated.

After all, Leonard knew Adrian was not a fan of surprises. And COVID-19 social-distancing measures across the UK had effectively scuppered all plans for Leonard's huge second-anniversary surprise party, two years after they had finally gotten it together in Wales. He had wanted to invite all their friends and family to his — to *their* — newly refurbished semi in Balham.

Instead they would be having an intimate dinner party at home with Toni and Jack.

And, of course, Tommy.

"Can I at least get out the Christmas lights? Hang them up above the table?" asked Tommy, hand on hip, head tilted to one side. Late afternoon and he'd already showered and donned his makeup, and now dressed as a New Romantic wannabe, like a member of Duran Duran in their heyday. Not that fourteen-year-old Tommy would get the pop reference.

"It's almost June, Tom," said Leonard, trying to find his mobile phone.

"They're just lights, Len. Your squad'll love 'em. Haziq at school says his mum uses them all through Ramadan. Praveen has them at their temple all year long. And I know for a fact Patrick has tons strung up in the Barbie boudoir he calls a bedroom. They're just lights."

Leonard finally found his phone beneath Tommy's discarded schoolbook, left open on the kitchen counter despite Leonard's request for him to take his study-from-home video call classes into their actual study. After placing a bookmark inside, he closed and set the book onto a sideboard, clearing the work surface. They would need space for Jack.

"Patrick's *boudoir*, huh? And how exactly do you know all this?"

Leonard noticed a message from Jack to say they were almost there and would arrive around five-thirty. As usual, the man had everything prepped and ready to go, but also left instructions about getting pots and pans and cooking oil prepared for his arrival.

"Oh, come on. I'm not the only gayster who's been invited into the travesty that is Princess Paddy's Plastic Palace. Talk about environmentally unfriendly tackarama."

Leonard couldn't help chuckling. Tommy had not always been so open and relaxed. He had been in numerous foster homes during the five years before Leonard and Adrian had lucked upon him. Tommy's mother had died from pneumonia when Tommy was seven. His father had put him straight into care, essentially washing his hands of the boy, before returning to his native Poland. Even now Adrian got angry every time he raked over the injustice of Tommy's past.

But these days straight-faced Tommy had a habit of making everyone laugh, even when Leonard wanted to have a serious chat with him. He had been their first ever attempt at long-term foster care, eighteen months ago, and had transformed their lives. Twelve back then, he would be theirs until he turned eighteen, or for as long as he was happy living with them. The choice was down to him and the social workers who regularly came to check up on him. Being unashamedly gay had meant him being subdued in the past, often placed in homes with other kids who either ridiculed or shunned him, ones that stifled his more creative side. Not so with Leonard and Adrian. When the opportunity to foster him had arisen, they had jumped at the chance.

"Are you being serious?"

"No cap, Len."

Adrian was better at Gen-Z speak than Leonard, but he knew the words 'your squad' and 'no cap' meant something like 'your friends' and 'I'm totally serious' respectively.

"Fish them out, then. The lights. And be careful putting them up. The last thing I need is you falling off the table or electrocuting yourself tonight before we've even eaten a thing."

Leonard peered over to see Tommy already rummaging through the cupboard on one side of the table just as the phone rang in his hand. Adrian's name popped up on the display.

"Hey, babe. What's your ETA?" asked Leonard.

Throughout the pandemic, Adrian had been trying to limit the amount of work on-site, and his boss, Tom, had been fully supportive. But this latest venture had been for an LGBTQ+ housing project—a couple of charities coming together to provide secure housing for gay kids thrown out of their homes or already on the streets. Tom had mentioned the cause to them, and Adrian had jumped at the chance to help. Ever since their house-warming in Wales, they had both agreed to devote more time to various gay charities.

"Around seven. Sorry, love, we're running behind finishing up tiling the roof while there's still daylight. And what with tomorrow being Saturday, we don't want to chance bad weather over the weekend and end up having to mop up a whole lot of mess on Monday morning."

"Totally understood. Any preference for dinner tonight?"

Dinner was already arranged but he needed to keep up the pretence.

"Have you checked with the flexitarian?"

Tommy's diet included fish but also occasionally chicken. In his case, this usually meant once a week at the most. Fortunately, tonight's three-course meal ticked all his boxes.

"How about Thai? Something for everyone?"

"Perfect. You know me. I'll eat whatever you're ordering as long as you order lots. Got to go."

Great, thought Leonard, because Jack would be cooking his delicious Thai food tonight. Tom Kha Het, vegetarian coconut soup with mushroom for starters, with his fabulous prawn cakes, while the main would be his version of Panang chicken curry with deep-fried vegetable spring rolls, Thai mixed vegetables and jasmine lemon steamed rice. Adrian and Tommy adored Jack's variations, but those got the largest number of likes in the Day-Lamperton-Piotrowski household. Dessert would be a simple store-bought cheesecake with summer berries and ice cream, followed by a special anniversary cupcake served with coffee.

"Is that the smacks we're having tonight, Len? Takeout? Why all the fuss?"

"I told you. It's our unofficial anniversary," said Leonard, realising Jack would shortly be there. He'd told Tommy about the secret anniversary dinner, but he'd managed to keep the surprise about Jack cooking to himself all afternoon. "And Jack's on his way right now. He's tonight's chef."

"Jack?" said Tommy, appearing wide-eyed from where he had been rummaging around in a lower cupboard, the lights in his hand. "*Shut! Up!* Tell me he's not cooking me his savage Thai."

"Just a quick FYI. This is our show tonight. Not everything's about you, Tommy."

"You didn't answer my question, Leonardo."

Once again Leonard had to snort out a laugh. If any of the social workers ever tried to take Tommy away from them, they would have a serious fight on their hands. The blockade at their front door would put any production of *Les Misérables* to shame.

"Yes, Tomasz," said Leonard, pronouncing Tommy's name in its original Polish form, which always had Tommy cringing and pulling a face. "Jack is cooking his special Thai dishes. For *all* of us."

"Fuuu—" Jack stopped, slapped a hand over his mouth before throwing a panicky glance at Leonard. "Funtastic news."

Although they never punished Tommy for the occasional expletive—apparently some families had— they didn't encourage him either. But Tommy had sometimes been overcareful around them, not wanting to spoil a good thing. He knew only too well that foster parents could give up on kids they felt they couldn't handle. Leonard shuddered at the idea of such a lovely kid being passed from pillar to post.

"Fucking fantastic news, you mean," said Leonard, which managed to get a grin and an eye-roll from Tommy. "And I bought the salted caramel cheesecake, the one you like, from your favourite cake shop. Now, let's get these lights up, and then I want you to lay the table for five while I chop vegetables with Jack."

"My choice of —?"

"Everything, including place settings and centrepiece. Make the table shine."

"Seriously?" asked Tommy, a glint in his eye.

"Shine, Tommy. Shine and sparkle, but no glitter, please. Makes too much of a mess."

"Gucci."

* * * *

Half an hour later, as Leonard opened the front door to Jack and Toni, the table already looked spectacular. Christmas lights faded in and out around red and white feather boas that Tommy had somehow magicked up, the table laid with matching red and white table decorations and cream-coloured candles.

"You, young man," said Toni, emerging from their downstairs bathroom and stepping over the large holdall she had dropped in their hall. She stopped before Tommy, kissing him on each cheek. "Are a natural. Your nails are too perfect for the building trade, but if you need a few connections in the interior design world when you leave college, just let me know."

"Fashion, Toni," said Leonard. "He's thinking about fashion."

"He," said Tommy, giving Leonard one of his looks, "is standing right here. And he is not thinking much further than passing his exams next year. If they work out okay, then I'll consider the next step."

"He's being modest," said Leonard.

"He's being realistic," said Jack, clunking bags of shopping down on the kitchen counter, then ripping off his reusable mask and stuffing it into his pocket.

"Thank you, Jack. Finally someone who lives on the same planet," said Tommy, standing back from the table. "So. D'you think Ade will approve?"

Leonard took another look at the table. As soon as he walked in the door, Adrian would know something was up. For starters, he would smell the food cooking, but when he saw the dining room table, he would ask about the occasion. Leonard had said nothing that morning but had wondered if Adrian remembered. Not that it mattered. Leonard had everything he could ever want in his life. Meeting Adrian had been like a door opening, and he cherished every day they spent together. Now, with Tommy around, the world had ramped up a couple of notches.

"Ade will love it, Tommy," said Jack, washing his hands at the sink. "Now, any chance of a beer before I roll up my sleeves and start creating magic?"

"You don't want to freshen up first?" asked Leonard. "You're in the front bedroom, as usual, by the way."

"No, we're good," said Jack. "Only going to get more sweaty with all the cooking. But a beer would certainly help loosen things up."

"I'll get them," said Toni, heading to the fridge. "What about you, Len?"

"Bit early for me," said Leonard. "But then it is Friday night."

"Count me in, too," said Tommy, a mischievous grin on his face. "As it's a special occasion."

"He'll have a cream soda," said Leonard to Toni, who had opened the fridge door. "Don't push your luck. If I'm still feeling magnanimous later, and only if you're good and if Adrian agrees, we might let you sample a glass of the Dom Perignon champagne we've got chilling in the fridge."

"Seriously?" asked Tommy, his smile widening. "Cream soda's fine, then. Ice and a slice, please."

Toni opened the fridge door and tossed a can to Tommy.

"Yeah. That's not going to happen. Asahi okay, chaps?"

Leonard loved having people over. Before Adrian had moved in, he'd never entertained. Now they cooked indoors all the time and, whenever restrictions lightened up, they even invited people over. Adrian had become the master of the barbecue and, because of him, Leonard had finally gotten to know his neighbours.

By the time the front door opened, announcing Adrian's arrival, the house was full of food odours and chatter and laughter. After tossing his mask and washing his hands, Adrian went over to Tommy first and gave him a hug and a kiss on the top of the head, then stood appraising the table. Leonard's gaze sought out Adrian's gold wedding ring, which sat in pride of place on his left hand. Just seeing the band gave him a sense of joy, of belonging — filling a void that had been missing for too long. Adrian always lavished his attention on their foster kid first of all, something Leonard fully supported. Tommy loved having Adrian's approval. Leonard seemed to have adopted the role of the grown up in their relationship, while Ade's bond with Tommy resembled that of an older brother. A much older brother.

Leonard could tell Adrian must have expected something because he grinned and winked at Leonard and, after a quick hug hello for Jack and Toni, walked into Leonard's waiting arms.

"You knew, didn't you?" whispered Leonard into his right ear.

"I'd planned to book a table at the steak place you like. Around the corner. Just the three of us. I asked our wayward child to do the booking and was advised, in no uncertain terms, to back off."

They both looked around to see Tommy looking nervously at them, biting on the cuticle of his forefinger.

"I never told him anything," said Tommy, the guilt written on his face. "Honest. Not about all this, anyway."

"Come here, young man," said Leonard, with mock seriousness. Poor Tommy appeared genuinely nervous until Leonard pulled him into their family hug. He managed to stay there for all of ten seconds before pulling away.

"Ugh, Ade! You smell of tarmac and brick dust and roadkill. You better not have splodged my new shirt."

"Don't worry, Prince Charming," said Adrian, tousling his hair. "You and your ruffles still look fabulous. Now I'm going up to shower and change. See you in a bit."

* * * *

After the meal, they sat in the living room sharing the bottle of champagne and cupcakes while Tommy put on some of his favourite *jams* — music. As promised, he also got his first taste of the expensive wine, and Leonard watched him savour every bubble. After that Adrian sorted out coffees using a new coffee machine that still eluded Leonard, to make drinks for Toni and Jack.

"Before anyone says anything," said Toni, sitting up and raising her glass, "I want to just say again what a great couple you make and, although this is not your official anniversary, now that you're married — "

"Shortest ceremony in the history of weddings..." said Jack.

Instead of heading to Scotland for a holiday two Christmases ago — at the invite of Kennedy — Leonard and Adrian had decided to get married. The registry office ceremony had been short and simple, only a few friends, including Toni and Jack, in attendance. For them both the important thing had been to be an official couple when they welcomed Tommy into their lives. The following Christmas they had wanted to spend time together with Tommy in Wales. By way of recompense, they had agreed to throw a big party in celebration during the summer months — until the events that rocked the rest of the world had put paid to that.

"We're glad to have been with you for most of the journey. Happy anniversary. And here's to many more."

Still sitting, they all toasted together. Tommy had taken his usual spot on the sofa, cross-legged in between Adrian and Leonard. Ever since he had been with them, he had always wanted them to sit together, as though he didn't want to let them out of his sight. But this time, as they finished toasting and everyone put their glass down, Tommy jumped up from the sofa and they heard his footsteps thumping up the stairs.

A few minutes later, as the rest of them chatted happily, Tommy returned with wrapped presents for Adrian and Leonard. They hadn't expected gifts from anyone and both men gave each other quizzical looks.

"Tommy, you didn't need to do this," said Adrian, accepting his gift and smiling anyway.

"It's not much," said Tommy, looking uncharacteristically nervous and excited. "I hope you like them. Sonia at school helped me find the material and we made them during our free periods. I based the sizes on ones you already have in your wardrobe."

"You made these yourself?" asked Toni as Leonard unwrapped his long-sleeved, button-down shirt. Although the material was white cotton, the whole garment had tiny characters all over, small leaves of a tea plant in green. Even the collar and cuffs had been carefully planned, with a green and white paisley design to complement the pattern.

Adrian unwrapped his shirt, which was a burgundy colour and had small coffee beans all over. His also had a similar design of paisley on the collar and cuffs, but this time in dark brown and wine red.

"Tommy!" said Adrian, standing up and putting the shirt on. "I bloody love it."

Leonard thought he looked damn good in it, too, worn over the top of his black T-shirt. Leonard had to remove his short-sleeved shirt first, revealing his naked upper torso, which put a grin on Adrian's face, but he managed to slip into the shirt easily. After buttoning up, he went over and stood next to Adrian, the two of them posing for Toni's phone camera.

"Absolutely love them, Tommy. You are a true talent."

"You're fam," said Tommy, clearly pleased with himself, his cheeks reddened, and, Leonard suspected, not just from the champagne. "And I wanted to do something nice. Suits you two. Coffee and tea. You know one of the teachers at school refers to you both as Mr Lemonade."

"Huh?" said Jack. "I don't get it. Why lemonade?"

"My bad," said Tommy. "I keep talking about my two guardians, Len and Ade. They must have misheard."

Adrian laughed along with them all, then pecked Leonard on the lips and was about to go and sit back down, but Leonard pulled his arm back and whispered in his ear. Adrian smiled and nodded.

"We have something, too. For all of us, actually. So I need Tommy up here with us."

While Adrian waited for Tommy, Leonard went over to the sideboard where he had left his work case. He pulled out the large brown envelope he had collected that day.

"I had to pop in to see my solicitor today. Usual work stuff. But she's been in touch with the foster care authorities and looking into the possibility of us actually adopting you, Tommy. But only if you want to. We can submit the forms now, but we need to wait another six months until you've been with us for two years. The long and the short of it is, both Adrian and I would like to make you officially and legally a part of the family. I know your real father is still out there, so you may need to take some time to think—"

"Yes. No. I don't need—" The words faded into a high-pitched sob, and before Leonard had a chance to finish, Tommy buried his head in Adrian's chest, his arms around him, his shoulders shaking along with the snuffles coming from him. Leonard placed a hand in the middle of Tommy's back and rubbed circles. Tommy's reaction drew the same tearful response from Toni and Jack.

"I hate you both," said Tommy eventually, pouting and snatching a tissue from the box on the table. "Neither of you know how much time and effort goes into putting on mascara. Now I look like an extra from *Twilight.*"

"So you're okay with the idea?" asked Leonard after they had sat back down on the sofa. But something in Tommy had softened, and he couldn't help the smile pulling at the corner of his mouth.

"Of course I'm okay with the idea," said Tommy, with the 'duh' expression he loved to lavish on his guardians. "Will I have to keep my family name?"

"That's your choice."

"Can I have yours, Len? It's so much easier to pronounce."

"Of course you can, but let's not get ahead of ourselves. Let's wait until everything's agreed before we make those kinds of decisions. This will mean you having to keep up your school grades, Tommy. If the social workers see any drop in your grades, they might take that as a sign that we're not practicing responsible parenting."

"I know, I know," said Tommy, looking flustered even though Leonard had been half-joking. "I'm doing my best. But you might have to ask Grandma if she can help me with biology again. Without her help, I'd never have made it through the half-term exam."

Grandma. Leonard had asked his mother to look through Tommy's science schoolwork, and they'd had several two-hour sessions over video chat during the holidays. He'd managed a respectable B+ in the exam, which he was ecstatic about, but his mother had phoned Leonard after one lesson and asked him if he'd instructed Tommy to call her Grandma. He hadn't— nobody forced Tommy to do anything—but much to Leonard's surprise, she loved the endearment.

"Why don't you text her? You can also tell our news."

* * * *

In bed that night, he let Adrian read over the terms of the adoption. Leonard could tell he only skimmed most of the pages because he trusted Leonard's solicitor, Helen. She had probably deferred the paperwork to someone she knew who had more relevant experience. But if Helen trusted them, then so did Leonard.

"We're going to have a son," said Adrian.

"We already do," said Leonard. "But it'll be official. And I'm going to give him Bryn Bach for his twenty-first. That way it stays in the family. Don't say anything to him yet, though. We'll let it be a surprise."

"While I think that's a wonderful idea, you might not want to keep this particular present a surprise."

"What do you mean?"

"I never mentioned this before, because there seemed no point. You were dead set on keeping the house. But Tommy asked me once if you'd ever considered donating the place to a suitable charity, maybe to be used as a refuge for teens with emotional problems, a place for them to get away from the city and heal."

"He said that?"

"He did. I told him about the legacy, the long family history, and he understands."

"But I think that's a beautiful idea, Ade. Do you want to say something to him?"

"No, love," said Adrian, grinning at Leonard. "That's a conversation between the two of you, don't you think?"

For all his bravado, their son — yes, their *son* — had a heart of pure gold. Adrian had shifted onto his side, a hand cradling the back of his head, his gaze softening as he took in Leonard.

"When things get better," said Leonard, "do you think we could all go on a road trip and meet your aunt and uncle? In Hastings?"

"Oh, hell, Lenny. You've got to stop doing this," said Adrian, rubbing a hand across his eyes. "Enough emotion for one night. And yes. Yes, of course. I would absolutely love that."

After a moment, their eyes met again.

"Why me, Lenny?"

"What do you mean?"

"You're amazing — successful, charismatic. Everyone I've ever met likes you. And yet you chose me. I suppose I just wondered why."

"Are you fishing for compliments?"

"No, I'm serious. Even that friend of yours, Kennedy, said he had a thing for you once. I just wondered what you see in me."

"Ade," said Leonard, after leaning in a kissing him softly. "I love everything about you. You're brave, braver than anyone I've ever known. Not only did you survive the streets, but you came through intact with not a bad bone in your body. I love those cute freckles you still have after all these years, and the way your eyes crinkle and only half of your mouth lifts when you find something amusing. And I love that when you laugh it's never *at* people, but *with* them. I could happily drown in the look you give me when we're both blissed out from kissing and having sex. I love that your heart is so big and yet so fragile, and despite all of the suffering you've been through, you still think nothing of selflessly helping others. When I watch you sleep peacefully, looking like a little boy, my heart breaks thinking about you being homeless, fearing for your life every night. And I want to wrap you in my arms and never let you go. But most of all — and this might sound a little selfish — I love that I'm the one who understands all this about you, that I'm the person who's won the prize of knowing your story, and spending the rest of my life with you."

Leonard could see Adrian processing everything he had said, breathing deeply. When their eyes met again, he smiled and reached a finger out to touch Leonard's lips.

"Well, I don't have your way with words, but maybe I can show you exactly how much you mean to me. Will that be enough?"

"More than enough," said Leonard, as Adrian pulled their bodies together.

Note to the Reader

While *Any Day* is about misunderstandings and second chances, about older men finding love and about forbidden love, the story also touches on mature subjects including gay teen suicide. If you, or anyone you know, are experiencing difficulties and in need of support, please seek help immediately. Below is a non-exhaustive list of current organisations providing suicide prevention services to the LGBTQ+ community.

International
The Trevor Project:
https://www.thetrevorproject.org

UK
Queer Futures Helpline:
http://www.queerfutures.co.uk/help/
LGBTQ+ Lifeline:
https://suicidepreventionlifeline.org/help-yourself/lgbtq/
Switchboard LGBT+ Helpline:
https://switchboard.lgbt

USA
PFLAG Hotlines: https://pflag.org/hotlines
LGBTQIA Resource Center:
https://lgbtqia.ucdavis.edu/support/hotlines

These links were current at the time of publishing. There are many more support resources available. If you cannot find what you need from the list above, do a browser search to locate others.

Want to see more from this author? Here's a taster for you to enjoy!

Companion Required
Brian Lancaster

Excerpt

Kennedy
London, England, August 2016

Two triple-shot espressos down and Kennedy Grey massaged his fingers into his temples. Dull throbbing had begun to resemble a migraine. Not because of the coffee—his lifeblood most days—but because the previous candidate had tried his patience to the limit. *'Is the food safe to eat? Isn't Singapore in China? Aren't gays banned in China? And will there be any fringe benefits?'* Questions about food safety he could accept, especially if a candidate had allergies. He could even appreciate them not being familiar with the geography of the travel destination. For that very reason, he had brought along a one-page map of Asia highlighting Singapore. But asking if there would be any fringe benefits had tipped him over the edge. The advert had been straightforward enough on the subject of remuneration.

Not for the first time that afternoon, Kennedy considered throwing in the towel and abandoning the whole precious idea. Maybe this was the year he made a change. After all, the signs of madness were everywhere, what with a game show host being chosen as the official Republican candidate to run for the US presidency and the people of Britain filing for divorce from Europe.

As a penniless young man straight out of university, he would have trampled heads for a heaven-sent dream of a job like this. On the laptop, he scrolled down to the UK Gay Society billboard and reread the contents of the advert.

Gay Holiday Companion Required

Based in or around London. Must have full ten-year passport with at least seven months remaining and be freely available to travel overseas for the whole month of September 2016. Candidate should ideally be between 21 and 25, non-smoking, social drinker, drug free, and must be able to pull off the role of dutiful boyfriend in front of male sponsor's close-knit circle of friends. Acting experience a distinct advantage. Any ethnicity considered.

Successful candidate will receive an all-expenses-paid holiday to Southeast Asia, starting with round-trip flights from London Heathrow to Singapore's Changi Airport, a three-night stay in Singapore, followed by a 14-night gay cruise to Hong Kong. After a two-night stay in Hong Kong, the holiday will culminate in a flight to Bali, Indonesia and eight nights staying at the sponsor's private luxury villa.

Candidate will receive a guaranteed five thousand pounds in cash for services rendered, and a discretionary bonus, should the candidate's performance exceed expectations.

If you are interested, please respond to gayvaccom@mooddle.com with a recent photo (headshots only, thank you) and CV, to arrange a mutually agreeable time for an interview.

So what if the advert bordered on politically incorrect? Marketing staff at UKGS had assured him that he had breached no advertising codes or legal regulations. Besides, the 'exceed expectations' line had only been tacked on this year, a suggestion from his best friend, Steph — a safe enough addendum, since for the past three years no one ever had.

Moreover, the advertised list of requirements told only half a story. He peered up and scanned the coffee shop. Even a couple of the young men sitting at various tables could have made the grade. In his head, Kennedy had an unspoken list of other requirements, undocumentable, such as the companion being a toned, blond twink, pretty as a royal wedding, but with a relatively low IQ. They should be no more than five feet six, and definitely shorter than his five-ten. Most importantly, they needed to be totally and utterly compliant to Kennedy's whims and wishes. And finally, once they had been paid off and returned to dear old mother England, he never wanted to see or hear from them again.

Since his split with Patrick, his partner of nine years, he'd made a point of continuing to join his friends' annual sojourn to different parts of the globe — his one break each year from the office and the boardroom — but now with a beautiful young acquaintance. Yes, perhaps bringing along a twink companion smacked of vanity, or desperation even, especially for someone in his early forties whose dark hair had begun to display grey streaks at the temples. But the simple truth was that while Kennedy found meeting and conversing with people for business purposes effortless, he found socialising awkward, especially on his own, and had always relied on Patrick to be the catalyst when meeting friends, old and new. Hence, for the past four years, he had paid for a companion to join him.

Palm Springs gay festivals, Hawaiian island hopping, gay tour of Barcelona and Sitges, cruising around the Greek islands with a week in Mykonos.

Pure culture? Maybe not. But a welcome respite from a punishing work life.

Ollie, his first post-Patrick choice, had turned out to be perfect. Previously an intern at Kennedy's corporate security company, the blond Adonis had flirted shamelessly with Kennedy and all other male staff, whether straight or gay. And even though Kennedy had been flattered and tempted, he had never succumbed. After the placement had ended, however, he'd made a point of keeping in touch. Once Patrick had decided to walk, Ollie had been his natural choice as lab rat companion. Perfect, as things had turned out, because Ollie had recently lost his job, so Kennedy had sweetened the deal by offering a sum of money to accompany him. Which was how the arrangement had first begun.

That first year the holiday had gone so well, Kennedy had not only stayed in touch but had invited Ollie along for a second helping. A huge mistake, as things transpired, because Ollie had incorrectly translated the gesture to mean that not only were they equals, but that they were going steady. And Kennedy no longer did 'steady' with anyone.

If his friends suspected anything, they said nothing. Only Steph knew the truth. And he made a point of telling any candidate the arrangement would be strictly nonsexual, unless they wanted more — which was how the idea of the playing card had come into being. But more than anything, he wanted a companion, not an escort. If the rationalisation might have meant anything to any of them, he would have cited Forster's novel *A Room With A View* and the chaperone arrangement between the two main female characters. But after he'd mentioned the reference to Ollie, and had then been lectured about that *'old James Bond movie they keep showing on Netflix'*, he'd stopped bothering to explain altogether.

For the first time since Patrick had walked out, he had been in two minds whether to ditch the charade, to simply bite the bullet and turn up alone. Only five friends had signed up for this year's sojourn — after last year's debacle — and one of those was Leonard Day. Kennedy not only had feelings for him but respected his business acumen. Maybe this year he would finally make his feelings known. If only Leonard didn't come with baggage of his own.

But Kennedy accompanying a plaything had become something of a tradition, a joke among his friends, and he wouldn't want to let them down.

"S'cuse me. You Kennedy Grey?"

Kennedy peered up from his thoughts to find an extremely blond, extremely buff young man standing over him. Steroid buff, Steph would have labelled him.

"I am, yes. And who might you be?"

"Who might I what?"

"Who… What is your name?"

"Francis."

Kennedy glanced down at his notes. Francis Slade, twenty-five years old, three o'clock appointment. Ten minutes ahead of schedule. One point in his favour. Kennedy swore by punctuality.

"Ah yes, Francis. Please sit down. So do you prefer Francis, Frank or Frankie?"

"Francis."

"Great. You've read the advert?"

"Yep."

"Good. So let me go into a bit more detail, give you a few minutes to relax. Then I'll ask you a few questions and finally let you ask any questions you may have. I've got other candidates to see, but I'll let you know whether you've been successful or not by Friday. How does that sound?"

"S'all okay."

Taking the response as his cue, Kennedy went into further detail about the holiday, explaining that in Singapore they would be staying in Kennedy's parents' house. However, the person would be introduced as a friend and would have their own bedroom. Whenever he delved into specifics — especially the rawer aspects — he always studied the candidate's face carefully to see if any of the information caused a reaction. Francis' flat face appeared incapable of showing any kind of emotion.

Whenever Kennedy got onto the subject of the cruise and his friends, he found himself becoming defensive. Yes, they could be a bitchy bunch, and a couple of companions had found them bordering on rude, but they were his long-time friends.

Bali, at the end of the holiday, was not only the cherry on the cake, but the icing, marzipan and ornate decoration. If the companion managed to survive until then, they would be able to enjoy the delights of that magical Indonesian island. By then Kennedy would usually be ready to get back to work, so would spend most of the last week either on his laptop, mobile phone, or writing up proposals.

"So far, so good?"

"Yep," said Francis, yawning and stretching his hands above his head. When his tee pulled tight, Kennedy spotted the outline of nipple rings beneath the material. Tick. Another point in the boy's favour.

"How tall are you?"

"Five-seven."

"Nice," said Kennedy, reaching next to his laptop for the supplementary document. "So here's a list of other requirements. You'll need to take a medical examination before you travel."

"Why?"

"A precaution. To make sure you're in good shape, physically."

"I'm negative, if that's what you're asking."

"That's not..." Kennedy huffed out a sigh. "Look, the year before last, my travel companion came down with acute appendicitis three days into the trip. And due to severe rupturing—which was touch and go for a while—he had to spend six days in a private hospital in Florida after which, quite naturally, he wanted to fly straight home to be with his family. If he had taken a medical examination before the trip, it's likely the appendicitis would have been diagnosed early, avoiding his suffering and my equally ruptured bank account."

"Ain't got an appendix. Got it removed when I was eleven."

"That's not the point—" Kennedy ran a hand through his hair. "I need to make sure the person accompanying me is fit and healthy in all respects. And that condition is non-negotiable. So if it's a problem for you, then you need to let me know right away."

Francis stared down at the paper for so long that for a moment Kennedy thought he'd changed his mind.

"You'll pay?"

"Sorry?"

"For the medical?"

"Of course."

"'S'okay, then."

"Great. Any other questions for me?"

"How old are you?"

"Forty-two."

Francis grinned then. At least, that was what it appeared to be to Kennedy. Either that or the lad had wind.

"You like 'em young, then?"

Kennedy had to stop himself from answering that more than anything, he liked them compliant. And most younger guys tended to be less free-willed, more willing to please, mainly because they needed the money.

"Is that a problem?"

"Nope. I'm into Daddies."

Oh, heck, thought Kennedy, *Steph is going to have a field day if Francis becomes this year's chosen one.*

"So I've got your number. I'll be in touch Friday."

When Francis stood, whether purposely or not, he yawned again and stretched his arms above his head so that the bottom of his tee rode up slightly to reveal a ripped stomach and a dark-blond trail of curly hair running down and disappearing beneath the waistband.

Kennedy almost handed him the job right there and then.

About the Author

Brian Lancaster is an author of gay romantic fiction in multiple genres, including contemporary romance, paranormal, fantasy, crime, mystery, and anything else that tickles his muse's fancy. Born in the sleepy South of England where most of his stories are set, he moved to Southeast Asia in 1998, where he now shares a home with his husband and two of the laziest cats on the planet.

Brian loves to hear from readers. You can find his contact information, website details and author profile page at https://www.pride-publishing.com

PUBLISHING

Sign up for our newsletter and find out about all our
romance book releases, eBook sales and promotions,
sneak peeks and FREE romance books!